# UNASSIGNED TERRITORY

"If you're up for a cast of characters out of a Nathanael West novel set in the High Desert, you'll love *Unassigned Territory*."
—Carolyn See, Author of *Golden Days* and *Rhine Maidens*

"God bless Kem Nunn, one of a rare breed, a novelist who isn't afraid to plot and tell a story."
—Elmore Leonard

"*Unassigned Territory* is part mystery, part science fiction, part men-on-the-edge realism. . . . Kem Nunn has the mystery writer's knack for keeping readers glued to the page. And he writes with silky-smooth elegance. . . . [He] is another one of those sons of Hemingway whose fiction is set in the American West and Midwest: Thomas McGuane, Jim Harrison, and Richard Ford, among others. Macho on the outside—writing of men hunting, drinking, fighting, pursuing women with abandon—they are really pussycats of prose, with a soft spot for the beautifully turned sentence. And their heroes' enemies are not so much other people as the phantoms within."
—*Newsday*

"The action is by turns rollicking and sidesplitting, serious and heart-rending. Like all good comedy it begins in disorder and ends in apparent order. . . . Nunn's satire, like all good satire, extends beyond the lunacies of the moment to embrace the idiotic aspects of life in general."
—*The Washington Post Book World*

"Out there among the desert's crazies and con men, its saviors and idiot savants, its holy men and homicidal maniacs—out there is where Nunn spins his darkening tale in this richly convoluted, deeply disturbing and, at times, eerily amusing book."
—*Orange County Register*

"Strongly atmospheric. . . . Delusion, spiked with the possibility of grace, is a theme here."
—*The New York Times Book Review*

# UNASSIGNED TERRITORY
## KEM NUNN

LAUREL

*For Kathryn*

I would like to thank Kimberly Kellington and Wayne Wilson, whose lyrics have managed to find their way into this text, and, especially, Robert Frizz Fuller, certainly, as Kerouac once said of Cassidy: an expert in subjects not yet identified, and without whose music the world would clearly be poorer.

# I

When I was driving through El Paso
That's when my car ran out of gaso
        Robert Frizz Fuller/R.F.F.
        *Texas Tango*

Obadiah Wheeler returned the receiver to its cradle and exhaled. He took one half of the small yellow tablet Bug House had dissected for him from the coffee table and popped it into his mouth, washed it down with a shot of Old Quaker, and followed that with a long pull from a can of Colt 45. Something to steady the nerves.

"So what now?" Bug House wanted to know.

"We wait."

"They asked you enough questions."

"Tell me. I think they're checking your card."

Bug House retrieved his credit card and driver's license from the floor near Obadiah's foot. "They think I'm you," he said.

Obadiah nodded. Bug House seemed to find this amusing. Obadiah took another swallow of the Quaker and closed his eyes against the burn. "You think that was enough?" he asked, nodding toward the remainder of the tablet.

Bug House nodded. "You don't want to sleep through it all, do you?" Obadiah thought this over; the prospect was not unattractive. He watched Bug House remove his glasses, pull a handkerchief from his pants, and wipe his brow. The flesh of Bug House's face looked pink and damp. Bug House was not a well man.

When the phone rang it was much louder than Obadiah had expected and he jumped at the sound of it. He took one more swallow of the malt liquor and picked up the receiver. It was a woman this time. The woman was certainly less businesslike than the man he had spoken to earlier. "Hello, Richard," the woman said. "Hello," Obadiah answered, hoping to sound cool. The woman's voice was soft and warm, like a wind out of the desert—the kind of voice he had expected in the beginning, he supposed. She made him repeat some of what he'd said to the man so that he guessed she was checking his story, but somehow the quality of her voice made it so he didn't mind. "You're a veteran?" she asked.

"Yes."

"Disabled?"

"A back injury." It was what Bug House had told him to say. "It's better that way," he had said. "Women don't like it if you tell them you're a lunatic."

"And what kind of girl would you like, Richard?" There were young girls, older girls, black girls, and white girls, and oriental girls. Obadiah placed an order for something in white, young but not too young. Faced with such a decision he felt that he should be more specific in some exotic way—black and nothing short of six feet. But his imagination seemed to fail and he found himself sweating in the heat of the room, his own hopelessly square voice reverberating in his ears. A twelve-year-old oriental, perhaps, but he was too late and the woman was talking to him once again. "Well, I'm sure that you will be pleased, Richard," and something in her voice made him feel that he had been right after all. "All our girls are very loving and warm," the woman added. "They wear high heels and nylons." Obadiah, not sure about how to respond, said nothing. "A girl will call you shortly, for directions. Good night, Richard."

Obadiah said good night and gave the thumbs-up sign to Bug House, who had begun to fluff cushions on the small sofa, cushions Obadiah was certain had not been fluffed in many years. The room filled with dust. Obadiah stood up, swaying slightly, and walked to the window. He stared into the dead end of Thomas Street below him, watching an Olympia sign flicker in the window of Heart's lounge. He looked north, through the red and white hoops of the neon billiard balls above Kempner's, toward that place where an emaciated neon greyhound ran in the night, electric-blue legs stretched out before the blackness of invisible mountains, and a familiar loneliness tore at his heart.

Somewhere in the darkness behind him the phone was ringing once more. When he answered, there was another woman on the line. But the magic was gone. It was clearly a voice in which the breath of the desert did not live. "Where you at?" the voice wanted to know. Obadiah was some time in replying. The room seemed to be melting slowly around him—yellow icing running in the night. "The Pomona Hotel?" His words came back to him in the form of a question, followed by silence and a faint mechanical hum. "Ten minutes," the voice said.

Once again Obadiah replaced the receiver, gave it another one, two, with the Quaker and Colt 45. Bug House stood sweating before him, dressed in a filthy pair of tan cords, a yellow and white baseball shirt. The shirt did not fit well and allowed Bug House's stomach to hang out above his beltline. Obadiah himself was dressed in a pair of gray slacks, a pale blue dress shirt, and dark blazer. His mother had picked the clothes out for him at a fairly expensive men's store. He'd worn a tie as well, a wide blue-and-burgundy affair that was now mashed into the side pocket of the blazer. He was dressed this way because he had just come from conducting a class in public speaking. The class lasted an hour. Each week there were five speakers and each speaker presented a talk on a biblical subject. It was Obadiah's job to assign the subjects, then to critique the presentations. There were about a hundred people enrolled—what amounted to most of the congregation. The younger children often needed help in preparing their assignments, as did a few of the black brothers who did not read well. On this particular night, Obadiah had actually prepared all five of the presentations himself. He tilted his head back on the couch and fingered the tie in his pocket—a nervous gesture Bug House apparently seized upon as a subtle hint directed toward his own appearance, for he turned abruptly to regard himself in a small rectangular mirror hung at an absurd angle from one wall. "Guess I could change," he said, moving away and speaking in a voice which seemed louder than necessary.

Obadiah, his eyes closed, could hear him a moment later at the closet, banging doors and rattling hangers. Bug House had names for all of his outfits. "What will it be?" he asked. "Doc Potty? G.I. Joe?" He settled on the Pomona Kimono—a silken black affair with large red flowers. "The casual look," he said, standing near the foot of the bed and pulling the foul thing over his head. "But what the hell? She's a whore, right?"

Obadiah was suddenly finding it difficult to speak. He had been pouring malt liquor on top of bourbon at a frightening pace. And somewhere in there was Bug House's pill—perhaps accounting for the strange numbness now entering his face. He pulled himself to his feet and returned to the window. It occurred to him that he was at least as insane as Bug House—government-certified or not. Had this really been his idea? It was Bug House's birthday; he could remember that much. Bug House's birthday. Bug House's card. Bug House's name. He had been Bug House. But it had been his idea—there was no escaping it. Bug House had said that if Obadiah called he would foot the bill; they would put it on his card. But Bug House had not wanted to call himself—bugged lines, CIA involvement, unforeseeable complications resulting perhaps in case reviews, disability reductions—who knows? In short, Bug House had been afraid. Now Obadiah found that he was afraid as well. He did not know why, or of what, only that fear was sweeping over him in hot waves. "Guess they wouldn't like it if they knew you were whoring around," he heard his friend say. "What would they do? Kick you out? Take away your 4-D?" He could hear Bug House chortling to himself in a wicked fashion after each question and was forced to consider the answers against a background of laughter faintly demonic.

A 4-D was the classification given by the government to full-time ministers. Obadiah was the owner of one. In order to maintain the status it was necessary to commit one hundred hours a month to the execution of ministerial duties. Twelve hundred hours a year. The class Obadiah had just come from counted as one of his duties. The month, however, was two-thirds gone and he was behind in his time. Failure to make the required number of hours for several months in a row could result in a loss of ministerial status. He looked into the blackness beyond the glass, at his own ghostlike reflection hung there above a dark street. The glass was old and rippled with time, giving back an indistinct reflection from which his features seemed to have fled, much, he suspected, like rats from a ship. He considered what was left—the bright patch of yellow hair, the brilliant sliver of an attempted mustache. He did not suppose ministerial activities could be stretched to include whoremongering. He found the prospect of losing the deferment a terrifying one and when he thought of it now, ugly alternatives seemed to rise before him like black, mutant shapes. Canada. Prison. One could, of course, go in. Bug House had gone in. He had left as Richard and come home as Bug House, home to full disability and a seedy room in the Pomona Hotel.

It was the fear of just such alternatives which had inspired Obadiah to agree to spend the next several days in unassigned territory —a last-ditch effort to salvage the month. The fact that the trip— an excursion into the desert with a group from his congregation— was to begin within the next twelve hours did, however, manage to lend a certain urgency to the insanity of the moment.

"Can't lose that 4-D," Bug House piped from what passed as a kitchen—a soiled bit of linoleum flooring at the far end of the room. "Christ no. There's guys that would kill for one of those things."

Bug House had by now moved to the edge of the carpet where he stood brandishing a pair of ridiculous-looking candle holders. The devices were shaped like the heads of Tiki gods commonly associated with the South Seas. These particular gods were made of plastic. One was red, one brown. Lighted candles sprouted from holes in the tops of their heads. "Atmosphere," Bug House said. He tripped the room's single overhead light with his elbow and the candlelight leaped to take its place.

"Minister claims pussy among duties," Obadiah said. It sometimes pleased him to think of himself as the subject of headlines, particularly when drunk. He wondered why he was such a wiseass. Perhaps he was only confused.

Bug House had come close enough for Obadiah to take note of the rather intense scowl knotting his friend's brow, of a look which might have passed for terror in his small, cubelike eyes. "I'm gonna make her sit on my face," Bug House said. "I want a whore to sit on my face."

"Sick," Obadiah said. "The man's sick."

Bug House was still holding the candles and the shadows cast by their flickering light combined with the black silk and red flowers of the Pomona Kimono to produce what Obadiah found a most unpleasant effect—as if Bug House were a kind of priest in the middle of something you didn't really want to know about. When he laughed the candles jiggled, lighting his face from the underside in a hideous fashion. Obadiah looked away. The laughter had a hollow machinelike ring to it and reminded Obadiah of the mechanical fat woman's laughter he had once heard at a county fair. It was odd, he thought, that things had worked out as they had. In a world less twisted it might have been Obadiah's place to point the way for poor Bug House, show him the light, as it were. As it was, he felt himself a partner in sickness, a sharer of darkness. He believed you were responsible for what you saw. It had come to him one afternoon while conducting a Bible study, discussing chapter nine of a book entitled *The Way of Truth*. The chapter was entitled "Why Does God Permit Wickedness?" and it had occurred to him that if this insight applied to God as well, the world was somehow a more difficult place to make sense of. He had kept the idea from his student, a tiny, humpbacked old man he was attempting to rescue from the Church of Christ, and continued as if nothing had happened.

Still, he had not begun cynically and it had not always been something like the fear of a lost deferment which had moved his faith to works. It was, after all, a path to which he had been bred. It had begun years ago on a clear winter day when a young housewife answered a knock on the door. She met a pair of attractive young women, not unlike herself. They talked about the last days and life on a paradise earth. The housewife had always, in a vague sort of way, expected to go to heaven—this when she thought of it at all. The women told her that wasn't how it worked. They left literature. Later they returned to offer a free home Bible study. The woman accepted. Much to her husband's chagrin. Who soon took to spending a great deal of his time at the local library. Though not a scholar, he intended to prove the Bible students full of shit. The plan backfired when he began to discover things he had not counted on—that Christ had in fact died upon a stake, that the origin of the cross as a religious symbol could be traced back to the god Tammuz and the ancient city of Babylon. He explored the intricacies of what this meant in the symbolic terms of the Revelation. He saw a great world empire of false religion, a shared collection of doctrine and symbol linked by a common origin. He came to understand that these bogus institutions claiming to represent God had, in fact, entered into adulterous relationships with the Kings of the earth, that though they made many prayers, it was like the man had said, their hands were full of blood. He was much impressed by Paul's argument that it was, in his day, still possible to enter into the day of God's rest—the suggestion being that the seventh day upon which God rested was still in progress, which in turn suggested that one need not consider the six days of creation as literal days but rather as creative cycles of indeterminate length. To make a long story short, the man and his wife were baptized. When their only son was born they gave him the name of a Hebrew prophet and all the answers a man could hope for.

What Obadiah's parents had joined was a much maligned, highly visible group of Bible students who, though known to outsiders since their beginnings at the turn of the century by a variety of names, remained known to one another as, simply, The Friends. The Friends did not speak of joining organizations. They spoke of entering The Way. You were in The Way or out of The Way. There was not much in between. And if their beliefs were controversial, it was perhaps that they had gotten a better handle than many on the words of the Man himself: "Do not think I came to put peace upon the earth; I came to put not peace, but a sword."

Obadiah made public his own declaration for the faith when, on the morning of his fourteenth birthday, he was baptized by immersion in water. The event had taken place in a large concrete pond belonging to one of the local brothers. The builder, a mason by trade, had also produced a large concrete globe, complete with continents and seas, which he had placed atop a brick pillar at one end of the pond. The Friends jokingly referred to the globe as the New World. At the moment of his immersion, Obadiah had opened his eyes just long enough to glimpse the New World suspended above him upon a field of cloud-streaked blue and had imagined for a moment that the thing was about to fall. Christ had received the dove. Obadiah was to be crushed by a stone. He might have guessed then that something was amiss. The moment, however, had fled, the illusion with it. He had stepped shivering into the cool autumn light, the embrace of loved ones.

The Friends were not big on ritual; they proceeded by putting things together. Obadiah had begun by learning to debate grade school teachers on the reliability of carbon-dating methods. You began by understanding that for every house there was a builder, that God had a plan. Obadiah had for many years considered himself fortunate to have been let in on this—a kind of privilege to which he had been titled by birth. And so, in 1966, when Obadiah graduated from high school and saw that a choice was going to be demanded of him immediately, he opted for the organization's offer of a ministerial deferment. It really wasn't that much of a choice. Not only was it expected of him by the people he loved, it was what he had been prepared for. The single ritualistic act of his life had pointed the way.

That decision was now four years old and Obadiah Wheeler was still home free, still carrying the small white card with the 4-D stamped in one corner, the card Bug House had said some would kill for. And yet somewhere, something had gone wrong. The man he was meant to be was becoming something else and there was more to it than just that revelation which had come to him during the course of a Bible study—the recognition of what looked like a fundamental absurdity in his position. There was something else going on and he would be damned if he could say what it was, only that deep inside, in a core no one saw, tiny gears were failing to mesh, miniature wheels had broken from their stems and run afoul of the wiring. There were times when he felt himself no less a casualty than Bug House. It just that in his case he was not exactly sure what he was a casualty of. There were, he supposed, comparisons. Each had done what was expected. For each it had ended badly. His only real certainty, however, remained the desperate intensity with which he longed for the healing touch. He thought of a woman he had never seen driving toward him through the night and he touched the cool glass before him with his fingertips. The coldness seemed to enter his arm and rush to his chest, its movement cut short by a tapping at the door. When he turned to meet it, however, the room seemed to spin violently around him, allowing the floor to slip from beneath his feet.

As the tapping continued it became clear to him that Bug House would have to fend for himself. He remembered a certain horror story—Bug House talking about the VA hospital, how when it was bad there and he was freaking they would shoot him full of Thorazine and put him to bed, but the bad things would not go away and it would be the way it is in dreams, when something evil is upon you and you want to run but can't. But then Bug House was a notorious liar, also an unscrupulous bastard for parting with his medication. A sinister plot began to unravel before Obadiah's leaded eyes. He watched from the floor, head propped now against the sofa, as Bug House crossed the room. He listened to the soft swish of the Pomona Kimono upon a carpet long gone thin and black with dirt. He heard the muted scraping of old wood and the sharp plastic click of high heels upon linoleum. He was aware of the golden light cast by a single naked bulb as it burned in an empty hall.


The whore was a large young woman, or so it seemed to Obadiah, certainly as tall as Bug House, who was not small and now scampered after her. She went straight for the phone and began dialing. "Yes," she said after a moment. "This is Mary. Yes. Well." She paused and looked around as if taking inventory. "There's two of them here. I thought it was just one." Another pause. "Yeah, well, I guess it will be okay." She looked up and spoke into the room. "I need a driver's license," she said. Bug House fumbled with a wallet. "You're Richard?" she asked. Bug House nodded. Mary read some numbers into the phone and then hung up. She smiled for the first time and crossed her legs.

Obadiah Wheeler made an attempt at righting himself but quickly saw that this was not possible, that to risk movement would be to risk everything. 'Twas a tangled web young Bug House had spun. "We would both like to get laid," he heard Bug House say. He was aware of Mary smiling at him, wide rather bovine eyes amid a sea of pale cream-colored skin, and there was something in her laughter which filled him with regret.

The regret had not gone anywhere when, roughly seven hours later, Obadiah found himself at the edge of a nearly empty parking lot on the north side of town, one of a small, waiting flock. The morning was bright, smoggy, unpleasantly warm. A brother in his mid-forties, a man by the name of Neil Davis, was trying to hold Obadiah's attention. He held a map of the western half of the United States open across the fender of his car and he wanted Obadiah to look at it—a task which, given the sunlight, the glare, and the magnitude of his hangover, Obadiah was finding nearly impossible.

It had been some time now since he last puked on the street in front of the Pomona Hotel, but the burn of it was still in his throat, and the regret, far from having dissipated, had instead swollen to obnoxious proportions—a kind of two-headed monster and the source of considerable anxiety. On the one hand he was desperately afraid he had missed out on something. On the other, he was just as desperately afraid he had not.

He was reasonably certain it was the former he had to fear. And yet there was this unsettling fragment of memory—cream-colored Mary treading softly on bare feet, a towel around her middle. He seemed to remember her bending over him. Was she fumbling with his belt? Like shrapnel, the image lay embedded in his brain. When he tried for more, however, there was only a dull pain together with a certain emptiness. It was a difficult problem. Had he sinned in the flesh, or only in the heart? From a sin in the flesh it would be difficult to go on. He was not without conscience. The honorable thing would be to go to the elders. A letter to his draft board would follow. No more deferments for young Wheeler. Some, of course, would no doubt say that young Wheeler had gone quite far enough as it was—that this quibbling over what was of the flesh and what of the heart was, in the light of everything else, a moot point. A year ago Obadiah might have agreed. At the moment, however, by the blinding light of a newborn day, he was more inclined to see the distinction. To sin in the flesh—that was the thing. The act itself. And yet he was just not certain. It was a ridiculous situation. Before him the reflected sunlight of midmorning snaked along the windshield of Neil's Buick, across the great expanse of smoothly curving glass. Obadiah's eyes burned and teared and he blinked to clear them. He squeezed the bridge of his nose between thumb and forefinger and tried once more to look at the map.

Route 15 wound like a thin gray worm across the wide-open whiteness of the Mojave Desert. People there, Obadiah supposed, who knew nothing of The Way. Virgin territory. Actually it was territory not yet assigned to any congregation because there were not yet enough friends within its boundaries to make one up. They kept track of things like that in New York; they kept a file of unassigned territories and any congregation so inclined could check one out and work it. Pomona Central had checked out Nye County, Nevada.

The territories were worked by groups from the more populous areas; they would pile into a few cars and then spend several days knocking on doors. They would stay in motels or sometimes camp out—making more of a party out of it. It could be fun. Obadiah had found it so when he was younger, sharing a campsite with his parents and a collection of other families. Once they had camped on the banks of the Kern River, shooting rapids on inner tubes in the first light, building fires at night. Somehow, though, this morning in the warm glare of the lot it seemed to him that the spirit of the thing had changed. There were no family groups. There had, in fact, not really been that much interest, so that now, sharing the lot with him, there were only six others—six, that is, from his congregation. Six not counting the morning's big surprise, Visiting Elder Harlan Low.

The Friends prided themselves on the fact that within their ranks there was no clergy/laity distinction. All were ministers. The headquarters in New York did, however, support a number of full-time traveling representatives. The men were referred to simply as visiting elders, or, occasionally, as circuit riders, this latter phrase coming from the early days of the organization when some still did their traveling on horseback. By the 1960s most did their traveling in heavyweight American automobiles with aluminum house trailers connected to the rear bumpers. Still, the old title did have a certain flair and it was what Obadiah had in mind as he contemplated Elder Low. They had not yet been introduced and at the moment the man was standing with his back to Obadiah, his shoulders straining the seams of what appeared to be a gold metal-flake sharkskin sport coat. The material flashed as Harlan's shoulders rolled beneath it, reflected sunlight ricocheting about the lot in a hideous fashion. Obadiah, blinded, turned away. At his side Neil Davis's voice had assumed a low, machine-like hum—something about gas mileage and coolants, things Obadiah knew nothing of. He massaged the back of his neck and looked at the rest of the small group.

Three of the sisters, Panama Allen, a black middle-aged housewife; Shirley Washington, of whom one might say the same; and Ruth Bishop, the mother of Ben Bishop, Pomona Central's other Special Service boy, had arranged themselves in a half circle around Elder Low. It appeared to Obadiah as if the Elder were dispensing wisdom, for the three sisters had assumed almost identical expressions of rapt attention.

Beyond the sisters, on the far side of a two-tone Plymouth station wagon, the son of Ruth Bishop, Obadiah's partner in crime, stood examining the nails of his left hand. He was a tall, pear-shaped youth, balding at twenty-three. The hand which he examined was held at arm's length, fingers extended. Boys, Obadiah had been told, look at their nails with the fingers curled, palm toward the face. Girls turn the palm down and extend the fingers. Girls and faggots. Obadiah experienced an instant of contempt coupled with wild elation. It was only necessary to direct the attention of an appropriate person in the direction of the Plymouth . . . The instant evaporated in the heat, however, and Ben Bishop, his cover intact, took to squinting toward a brown horizon while Obadiah rested his eyes upon the fourth sister, and the morning's other surprise, Bianca Allen.

Bianca was Panama's sixteen-year-old daughter. She rarely made meetings and Obadiah had not expected to see her on the trip. He could, however, see her quite well at the moment. She was a solidly built girl of medium height—solid in a muscular, athletic sort of way. She was sitting in the backseat of Ben's station wagon, the door open, one leg in, one out, a summer dress hiked back just far enough to show, should Obadiah care to look, the white slash of panties between ebony thighs. Her extended leg caught the morning sun and shone like polished stone. Obadiah was not unmoved by the sight and soon found himself thinking of cream-colored Mary, watching as her smiling face bent toward his own from a concrete sky. He swayed slightly in the heat, blinked to clear his vision, and watched Bianca pop her gum. Bianca, at any rate, was a surprise he could live with. Harlan Low was another matter.

Low was not just any traveling representative. He was, within the organization, something of a celebrity, having served recently as a missionary in Liberia, a country in which The Friends had, of late, come under extreme persecution. Harlan's own mission had ended badly when a meeting at which he was presiding was broken up by soldiers, those in attendance arrested. The brothers and sisters, Harlan included, had then been taken to a makeshift compound and kept there, without adequate food, water, or shelter, for several days, during which time they had, at regular intervals, been made to stand before the national flag and ordered to salute it. Some had. Harlan Low had not. And the soldiers had been hardest on him. Obadiah had read about the incident in the pages of the *Kingdom Progress Bulletin.* He'd read about the beatings, the heat and cold, the bad water Harlan had, alone, been forced to carry up from the river in large wooden buckets. The man had been forced to drink the water as well. But even sunburned and beaten, sick from the water, he had remained a source of spiritual strength to the others until, at the end of the better part of a week, he had been freed and deported.

Obadiah had been proud of the man. He'd been proud to be part of a group whose leaders were able to exhibit this kind of grace under fire, to stand for something—even when it was their own ass on the line. He'd heard that Harlan had come back to the Los Angeles area. He had hoped, at some point, to hear him speak. He had not expected to meet him. He had certainly, given the events of the preceding evening, not expected to meet him this morning, and he recalled now the acute sinking sensation with which he had received the news over the phone before leaving the house. It seems the elder had heard about the congregation checking out some unassigned territory and had, for reasons Obadiah did not want to think too hard about, elected to go along for the ride.

What Obadiah feared was that he himself constituted at least part of the reason. The organization had, of late, begun to take a particular interest in recipients of ministerial classifications. With the war on, the organization had its credibility to think of, and it was not interested in supporting draft dodgers. There were some, it was felt, already among the ranks, who should be weeded out. And if Obadiah was sure of anything, he was sure of this—that Elder Harlan Low was a man capable of some serious weeding. The thought produced a certain weakness back of the knees, something he sought to alleviate by returning to the more pleasant sight of Bianca Allen's ebony thighs. This time she caught him looking and grinned at him around her gum. Obadiah, disoriented, might have grinned back but was prevented by an urgent signal from his stomach. There was little doubt as to the organ's intent and Obadiah made quickly for the shelter of the building— Neil Davis still somewhere in mid-sentence behind him.

The home of the Pomona Central unit was a rectangular stucco building with a rock and gravel roof. Its finest feature was its slate entryway. The congregation had gone after the slate itself and Obadiah could remember riding with his father in an old flatbed Dodge, a six-pack between them, the Harbs, Eugenes Sr. and Jr., holding to the running boards as the truck careened along a dirt road, slipping and sliding out of the mountains, everyone laughing and tired, half looped on the beer and sun. Definitely a better day than the present. Obadiah crossed the slate and stood once more at the edge of the lot in the scant shade of a beaten palm.

He dabbed at his lips with a moist paper towel he'd brought from the bathroom and wondered if his breath smelled of barf. He tested it, breathing into a cupped hand, and then looked up at the sound of approaching footsteps, horrified to discover Elder Harlan Low heading straight toward him. Rolling toward him might have been a better way to describe it. The man was built like a beer keg —something just under six feet, was Obadiah's guess, and probably somewhere in the neighborhood of two hundred and sixty pounds. His shoulders had a thick, sloping look about them and the neck which squeezed from the collar of a white dress shirt looked to be about as big around as one of Obadiah's thighs. The man had a big red farmboy's face and a crop of thick, dark brown hair which he wore combed straight back. His hair had a wet, shiny look about it which, when combined with the glare Obadiah was picking up off the sharkskin sport coat, the big black-rimmed sunglasses, conspired to create for Obadiah the impression that he was about to be bowled over by some sort of machine—the organization's brand-new Special Service boy weeder. God have mercy. Obadiah swallowed and wiped the moisture from his upper lip.

The man removed his glasses and extended a large red hand. "Obadiah Wheeler, isn't it?"

Obadiah admitted that it was.

"So, are we off to pronounce judgment on the Edomites?"

Obadiah mustered what felt to be a thin smile and clung to the large dry hand—his own felt quite frail and damp by comparison. When Obadiah said nothing further, Elder Low turned to Panama Allen, who was just now walking past them. "The lay of the land's not dissimilar, you know. The Edomites were a desert people." He smiled and looked back at Obadiah. "Shortest book in the Hebrew scriptures," he said. "Yet every word fulfilled."

Panama nodded, appearing to turn this piece of information over in her head as she moved past them toward the door. Obadiah could think of nothing to say. He was still clinging to Harlan Low's hand.

At last Low released him. "Harlan," he said as their hands dropped. "Not as biblical as your own, of course, though I imagine you've had your fill of teasing over it."

Obadiah shrugged. "My parents were new," he said, feeling that, for some reason, an explanation was necessary. "They wanted a name from the Bible, but something different."

"Well, it is that," Harlan said. His voice, which had begun rather loud—reminding Obadiah of a used-car salesman—had since dropped in volume to a more conversational tone. He looked for a moment as if he would continue, but then paused, appeared almost to falter, and gazed instead upward, into the fronds of the stunted palm. Obadiah watched him. Elder Low's face was broad and fleshy. Around one eye Obadiah was able to detect a thin white scar. The scar followed the outline of the bone around the eye and then lost itself upon the cheek. There were several other smaller scars near the temple. Harlan Low, Obadiah recalled, had, according to the *Kingdom Progress Bulletin*, been struck repeatedly in the face with a rifle butt by an African guard. Harlan slipped a hand inside his jacket and produced a white handkerchief with which he wiped his brow. "Warming up," he said.

Obadiah nodded. He noticed the large *HL* embroidered on Harlan's handkerchief. He was not, he felt, holding up his end of the conversation.

"Well," Harlan went on, his voice now taking on a more serious, just-between-you-and-me tone. "I'm certainly looking forward to this trip—get away for a few days, out of the smog, knock on some different doors. People are different out there, you know, more relaxed, willing to open up and talk. And I hope we'll have time to talk, too." He leaned just a bit forward and placed a large square hand on Obadiah's arm. "The presiding overseer has spoken to me about you," Harlan said, and then paused. The skin around Harlan's eyes was slightly puffy, dotted with tiny beads of sweat. The eyes themselves were brown, flecked with bits of gold. "He feels that you've been an asset to the congregation here, but he has begun to worry a bit about the quality of your work. I believe he is concerned about you." Harlan paused once more and then went on. "I would like for you to feel free to talk to me about anything that might be troubling you, anything at all."

Obadiah could feel the day's heat creeping along the back of his neck. He nodded in what he hoped would appear an appreciative way. He had a good idea of what Harlan wanted to talk to him about. He had been talked to already and had proven unresponsive. Pomona Central had a certain regular assignment from headquarters in New York—a portion of the surrounding vicinity which they were to work on a regular basis. This was accomplished by dividing the large territory into smaller ones that could be worked in a weekend. The idea was to work a different territory each weekend on a rotating basis. Obadiah, however, had taken to spending more and more of his time in one small portion of the downtown area—that section surrounding Thrifty's Drug Store and the old Pomona Hotel, an area inhabited for the most part by winos and drifters.

The whole issue had come to a kind of head recently when the presiding overseer had asked Obadiah to take him along on some of his calls. Obadiah had taken him on a Bible study he conducted with a pair of alcoholics named Bob and Lucille Hubbard, residents of the Pomona Hotel. Bob and Lucille were in their mid-fifties. Lucille's health was quite poor and Bob's mind had begun to show wear after years of chemical abuse.

It was a warm, stuffy day, and a good deal warmer and stuffier inside the building. As the study progressed Lucille appeared to doze. Obadiah, reluctant to wake her, allowed Bob to read the Scriptures on his own. Some time passed before Obadiah noticed that Lucille had stopped breathing, that an odd blueness had begun to creep about her thin neck. The presiding overseer had sat with her while Obadiah ran to the street for a phone. The paramedics failed to revive her. Bob tried to kick one of them and had to be sedated. The whole incident had left the overseer somewhat shaken. Obadiah had been somewhat shaken himself. For several nights in a row he had dreamed of Lucille's thin, leathery neck, of the saliva which had collected at the corners of her mouth. And he found himself wondering now if Harlan Low would have been shaken by the incident as well, or if, perhaps, he would have known what to say, would have been able to avoid the mute stupidity with which Obadiah himself had faced the situation, or the rather trite clichés uttered by the overseer as they'd both stood sweating in the afternoon sun at the foot of the weathered stairs.

"Well," Harlan said when it had become clear that Obadiah was going to offer no further comment, "perhaps we should go in." He nodded toward the building. Obadiah agreed. They were halfway there when Harlan spoke again, his voice getting back a bit of its earlier cheerfulness. "Guess it must have given you some good opportunities, though."

Obadiah felt slightly disoriented, as if he'd missed some transition. "I'm sorry," he said. "What was that?"

"Your name," Elder Low said. "Must have given you some good opportunities for incidental witnessing."

"Yes," Obadiah said. "It has."

"I thought so." Harlan Low nodded and together they entered the small, cool building where Harlan Low was to lead them in a discussion of the daily text.

Obadiah seated himself near the front of the room and noticed for the first time that morning the hand-painted cardboard poster someone had tacked to the east wall. The poster, which had already begun to buckle, was a picture of the state of Nevada—Nye County outlined in red, with a huge sheep standing in the middle. It was a rather odd-looking sheep, Obadiah thought, short of leg and large headed—the artwork, he suspected, of Neil Davis. At the bottom of the poster were the words, also in red, NYE NEEDS YOU!

The day's text came from Jeremiah 17:9: "The heart is more treacherous than anything else and is desperate. Who can know it?"

Elder Low led them in a discussion of the text, then in prayer. And it must have been that Obadiah's were answered, because when the small group had once again returned to the lot, Elder Low elected to begin the journey with Ben Bishop in the Plymouth station wagon. It was decided that Ben, his mother, Elder

Low, and Sister Washington would ride in the Plymouth; Obadiah, Neil Davis, and the sisters Allen, in Neil's LeSabre.

Neil led the way, up San Bernardino Avenue, then east on the San Bernardino Freeway, bound for virgin territory and a still-rising sun. Obadiah rested on the passenger side of the front seat, his shoulder pressed against the door, an air-conditioning jet aimed at his chest. He watched the great sea of tract homes spreading themselves beneath him—a stucco labyrinth of sun-bleached pastels and brown shingled roofs. He imagined it divided neatly into territories; he imagined the kind of people you would meet there—dull and inarticulate, clinging fiercely to beliefs they did not understand—groundhogs afraid of their own miserable shadows. There were, of course, exceptions, but those were few and far between. It was the utter blandness of it all which had driven him to places like the Pomona Hotel. You could get more interesting conversation around the Pomona Hotel in a day than you could get in a month in the tracts below him. He had discovered something among people like Bob and Lucille Hubbard. Perhaps it was nothing more than the residue of raw experience, but it was something. He watched as the houses slipped by him with the monotonous regularity of tombstones.

The tracts. The Pomona Hotel. North of Pomona lay the town of Claremont with its associated colleges. The landscape was a little less bleak in that direction. There was more stained glass in the windows, more books on the shelves, but somehow the householders were not that different, a bit smugger perhaps, but fear was in the air there, too, just too many people with their little piece of the shit pile, and not about to blow their cover for anything that didn't smell like money in the bank.

North of the colleges there was even a prestigious school of theology and people that talked of God—or at least of someone who went by the name. He was, as near as Obadiah could tell, a slippery sort, not given to the use of burning bushes, probably not much in a real scrap either and consequently difficult to get very worked up over. Still, Obadiah had spent some time there, had even struck up a kind of friendship with one of the professors, a young man at work in the graduate school at Claremont on a Ph.D. in New Testament theology where he studied under a man who in turn had studied under Bultmann. Obadiah could accordingly spend one afternoon trying to get a handle on faith as eschatological existence and the next talking to Tex Hudnel, the inventor of Projection Prayer, a man who regularly conversed with God Himself in the closet of his room at the Pomona Hotel.

The Elders considered both a waste of time. Obadiah was without a clue. He imagined that he was after something. He thought often of Paul's words concerning the prophets.

> They were stoned, they were tried, they were sawn asunder, they died by slaughter with the sword, they went about in sheepskins, in goatskins, while they were in want and in tribulation. They wandered about in the deserts and mountains and dens and caves of the earth. And the world was not worthy of them.

It was, he thought, an attractive text, suggesting as it did a certain vitality, an aura of mysticism and commitment. He wondered where such pilgrims might be found. Not, he suspected, sporting tweeds and pipes, growing pale and pompous amid a morass of obscure texts. Nor was Projection Prayer the answer—depending as it did on certain chemical stimulants, the necessarily close proximity of closets and Thrifty Drug Stores. He once thought to find them among his brothers and sisters, but of late he had seen the fear in their eyes as well—a stone-cold paranoia connected to anything not immediately perceived to fit the system, making it look as if too many had copped out somewhere in that difficult terrain where the magnitude of the investment becomes too much and a fear of blowing it begins to override whatever critical faculties got you there in the first place. And yet many were his friends and he hated to shortchange them. At least most were not afraid to appear ridiculous, go out and pound on a few doors. And there were those like Harlan Low who, with it all on the line, had walked it like they talked it. You couldn't take that away from them and beside it talk had a way of looking cheap.

And really, when you got down to it, talk was about as far as Obadiah Wheeler had gotten; and he said one thing to some people and another to others, and still something else to himself, acting out a role to preserve a deferment, save his skinny ass from laying any real cards on the table. The situation had reduced him of late to crying jags, to indulgence in strong drink, to ordering whores in the middle of the night from the rooms of cheap motels —the mere memory of which was nearly enough to have him signaling Neil Davis for a pit stop. But he hung on, clinging to the armrest of Neil's Buick until at last he had managed the transition from serious anxiety attack to troubled sleep, wondering as he did so to just what lengths he would be willing to go to avoid that little heart-to-heart Elder Low had promised and wondering, too, at the same time, if his fear was anything like the fear he had glimpsed in the eyes of a thousand spineless householders. It was a miserable fucking thing to contemplate and it was what he slept on.

By midmorning the small caravan had stopped for coffee somewhere on the eastern edge of San Bernardino and Obadiah was again awake, rubbing his eyes in the glare of one more asphalt parking lot while the towering orange and blue-green sign of a Howard Johnson's restaurant revolved slowly in a dull brown sky far above him. Farther east, the edges of San Gorgonio were visible through the smog with the sky fading to a pale turquoise above them—a promise of more pristine vistas to come.

Obadiah's return to consciousness was marked by a painfully stiff neck and a throbbing headache. He managed to bum a pair of aspirins from Panama Allen and washed them down with black coffee as he sat with the others in a large semicircular booth.

His companions seemed in high spirits. Even Ben Bishop, normally a somber lad who, as near as Obadiah could tell, spent most of his time trying to kick self-abuse, was engaged in a rather animated discussion with Neil Davis and Harlan Low. The conversation had something to do with fuel additives and gas mileage. Obadiah sat quietly with the sisters. He managed to put down a greasy patty melt and had to admit to feeling somewhat better by the time they left—felt good enough, in fact, that when Neil asked if he would care to drive, he accepted. Harlan was now driving the Plymouth and in possession of Neil's map. "Just follow him," Neil said to Obadiah. "He knows the way." It sounded simple enough. Obadiah slipped the Buick into Drive and followed Elder Low skyward along a sparkling concrete ramp.

It was hard to say, later, just how the two cars became separated. It apparently happened somewhere around a confusing interchange east of the city. There were a number of contributing factors: Obadiah's newfound energy proved short-lived. His hangover returned with a vengeance, complicated by a greasy patty melt now riding high against his sternum. Then there was Elder Low's surprisingly heavy foot, and Neil Davis had elected to doze. The interchange loomed suddenly on the horizon—blue-gray concrete bridges rising like the delicate arcs of some mutant lawn bird, green signs everywhere, their silver letters shimmering in the desert light. Obadiah looked at the display of signs. Somehow the number twelve seemed to stick in his mind but there was a sixteen-wheeler hard on his ass and little time for decision. He bore to the right, toward bluer skies and cleaner air. Temples banging and stomach churning, he clung to the wheel with sweat-damp hands and drove on.

The interchange slipped from view. The road grew straight and long, an asphalt jewel in the brilliant light. The pounding in his temples began to subside. His stomach relaxed. At his side, Neil Davis continued to sleep. The sisters Allen rode silently behind him. It was almost as though he were alone with the landscape, and a strange euphoric feeling seemed to settle over him. A small white sign said Route 12 near a sandy shoulder and the euphoric feeling deepened. Somewhere in the distance, beyond the heat waves, he imagined Elder Low in a two-tone Plymouth eating up the highway. Panama's aspirins were beginning to take hold. He eased his foot down and felt the Buick surge beneath him. He drove until Neil Davis jerked away at his side and screamed. At first, Obadiah thought the man was having a nightmare. Before he could pull over, however, the car began to make an odd sound.

Obadiah could not be sure if Neil Davis was more upset about finding himself on the wrong highway, or at the loss of his air-conditioning. The brother stood on a sandy shoulder, beneath a blistering sun, the hood raised, a small red toolbox open at his feet. He was bent at the waist, leaning over the fender of the car. Obadiah stood on the shoulder as well, with Bianca and Panama Allen. The elder Allen looked hopefully toward Neil Davis's ass as it strained the seams of his navy blue slacks. Bianca, Obadiah noticed, was not staring at Neil but instead stood looking rather wistfully back down the empty highway in the direction from which they had come.

"I thought you understood," Neil said, his head still in the open jaws of the LeSabre. "Route Twenty-eight."

"I don't know where I got twelve," Obadiah said. "I guess I thought that was the one you were pointing at in the lot." It was, of course, a lame thing to say. He recalled the sight of a thin gray line streaking through white space.

Neil pulled his head out from under the hood. There was grease on his cheek. "Twenty-eight," he said. "Twenty-eight." Obadiah could see that he was working at remaining calm. Neil was by nature an energetic man, one given, Obadiah suspected, to occasional fits of violence. The man was a bachelor of medium height and build. His most distinguishing feature was his nose—a large,

fleshy member that seemed to dominate his face and give it, somehow, a rather gopherlike look. His head was tilted back at the
moment, nose pointed slightly skyward in the direction of Obadiah. "Twenty-eight," he said once more. "And we've lost our air."
He stepped away from the car and chucked a wrench into the
small red box.

Obadiah took a step forward and peered into the mass of metal
and wire beneath the hood. He had no idea of what he was looking
for but felt somehow that it was expected of him. He could not
shake the feeling that Neil was blaming him for the mechanical
failure as well as the wrong turn. Perhaps he had done something
wrong. "Sorry," he said.

Neil shrugged and closed the red box. "Can't be helped now,"
he said. "We may as well head back. They'll be far ahead and it's
going to be a hot ride."

"How hot?" Bianca asked. Neil and Obadiah both looked at her.
It was the first time that day that she had spoken.

"Hot," Neil said. "I'll drive."

It was definitely hot. The sun was once more coming through
the windshield. Obadiah loosened his collar and rolled his sleeves,
put his elbow out the window, and watched the tiny blond hairs on
his forearm bend like a miniature field of wheat in the hot wind.

They rode, for the most part, in silence. Obadiah could not say
how far he had driven in the wrong direction—apparently, much
farther than he had guessed. At last they stopped at a small gas
station and Obadiah joined Neil in standing to one side of it,
squinting at a narrow back road that ran away from them and lost
itself in a distant line of red-and-yellow hills. "Fellow here says this
road connects with Twenty-eight," Neil said. "And I seem to remember something like it from the map." He placed his hands on
his hips. "It would sure save us some time," he said. "What do you
think?"

Obadiah stared at the road. Above them the sun had moved into
the western half of the sky. "The guy's sure it goes through?"

"Says so. And he seems like a nice enough fella. I talked to him
while you were in the head. Even left a *Bulletin* with him." Obadiah looked from the road to the station and back again. He hated
to put a damper on Neil's enthusiasm. This had been the first really
friendly exchange since the breakdown. "Why not?" Obadiah
asked. Neil, apparently motivated by some sense of adventure,

nodded and rubbed his hands together. "I'll inform the sisters
Allen," he said, "of our decision."


Neil Davis entered the desert whistling a tune. By sundown,
with the sky the color of a bad bruise above them and the interstate nowhere in sight, the tune had given way to a tortured
silence.

"Shit," Bianca Allen said, speaking from the darkness of the
backseat, "we really lost now." Her words had been the first in
some time and when no one answered she went on. "We could die
out here," she said, "middle of nothin'."

"Nonsense," Neil Davis said.

Obadiah was not so sure. He gazed toward a distant line of
jagged rock, black against a darkening sky. He thought of what
Harlan Low had said, about how things were different out here.
They had certainly been different so far—one had to admit. He
looked once more into the road before them, as scarred and pitted
as the surface of the moon. The headlights seemed to swing from
side to side, a dance of light and shadow, and he was reminded of
his whereabouts some twenty-four hours earlier—the flickering
light of Bug House's candles, the shining plastic heads of the Tiki
gods, the priestly Bug House in black robes, and it seemed suddenly quite fitting and proper to him that he in fact should die
here. Perhaps his situation was analogous to that of Jonas, perhaps
if he pitched himself from the car now, into the blackness of night,
the others would be saved, and he imagined that the lines of an old
bluegrass song had begun to ring in his ears: "Just before the lamps
were lighted / just before the children came / while the room was
very quiet / I heard someone call my name."

S eated on a barstool at the Cock & Bull, head tilted to facilitate the act of pouring beer into his throat—a position which also enabled him to increase the volume he could comfortably handle—Rex Hummer saw the moon as it came to rest directly above a crack in the roof. Its light was white and brilliant and he thought of the hour. It was, he imagined, somewhere between Saturday night and Sunday morning—a lost and dangerous sort of time, given over as it so often is to blurred vision and impaired judgment and Rex had seen more than one atrocity carried out beneath its spell.

It was approaching closing time and the Bull's regulars were staring sadly into corners or lurching across an ancient black and white linoleum floor, willing at this point to, as the line in a certain obscure song had it, take a chance on a woman who looks like Karl Malden. Rex considered it a sad and tiresome sight, one, however, to which he was no stranger, of which his own desperate longings had so often been a part.

This night, though, was better than most. For one thing it was a Saturday. Saturdays are talent showcase nights at the junction, and on this particular Saturday, Rex Hummer had taken first place. He had won a free pitcher and a T-shirt. The T-shirt had a picture of a cock and a bull on the front (the cock standing on the bull's head, the bull's eyes rolled toward it in an expression of cross-eyed anger). On the back of the shirt were the words I'M A WINNER AT THE COCK & BULL.

Minor as the triumph might be, it was wrested from stubborn soil and Rex would take it. The occasion had, after all, marked the first public appearance of the Hum-A-Phone, a musical instrument of Rex's own invention, and he saw in this a certain historical significance. The sad part was, there was no one to share the moment with him. Sarge might have been willing but he was dead. His half sister, Delandra, was out for the evening, possibly in Kleco, fucking the fire department. And that left Floyd, Rex's uncle. But Floyd had little interest in such things and had only sneered when he'd caught sight of the device and whispered something to one of his buddies which Rex had been unable to catch.

Rex wiped the foam from his upper lip and rocked back on his stool, eyeing the machine, which still rested upon the small stage. He had seen it many times, of course, but always in the trailer, or workshed, and he was admiring now the way in which the various parts shone beneath the hot yellow spotlights of the bar, or how they seemed to attract the pale, dusty colors cast by the jukebox near an open front door. He blinked as a tiny series of contractions snaked through his guts. The sight of the instrument always seemed to stir in him the same series of feelings. At first there was satisfaction at what he had wrought, a sense of awe even, but this unfortunately was short-lived and followed quickly by a certain restlessness in which he realized that the instrument's sound was not yet, precisely, the sound he was after. The restlessness was often followed by a kind of panic. Rex swallowed more beer. He was hoping, in light of the evening's achievement, to prolong the satisfaction—possibly avoiding the panic altogether—when a peculiar wind rose up out of nowhere and came rushing through the cool clapboard night like an empty freight across the desert floor.

The Cock & Bull regulars, Rex Hummer among them, stood in silence beside an empty road and stared into the darkness covering the Mojave. At their backs an Olympia sign cut yellow patterns from the night. The jukebox was silent. They had gotten outside just in time to see Bob Holt's Aljo lose its new canvas awning and for several uneasy moments it had appeared as if a real blow was in the works. And then nothing.

Rex remained outside after the others had followed Floyd back into the bar. He could not recall a wind having risen so suddenly only to end so abruptly. But there was something else, too. Or at least he had imagined that there was something else—a moment in which the void of silence left by the wind had not yet been filled by the electric whine of the jukebox at his back, a sliver of emptiness in which a certain tone had lingered—not even what you could rightly call a sound, something lone and discordant. A fragment. He strained to hear it now, or to feel it. But the sound, if indeed there had been such a thing, was gone and Rex was alone on the porch. Still, he believed he had heard something. His sense of hearing, he felt, was a good deal more sensitive than most, trained as it was by his months of work on the Hum-A-Phone.

From where Rex stood he could see most of the junction, the gas station and market, the dozen or so house trailers climbing the slow rise above the Cock & Bull, their aluminum bodies catching moonlight so that they seemed to hang there against the blackness of the hill like so many strange aircraft descending upon the town. Looking toward the highway he could make out that spot where the old version of the interstate joined a little-used back road—wide sweep of sand and gravel—white in the light that spilled from the Chevron, and just beyond that the dark, rambling shape of his father's Desert Museum—locked and boarded now, alone with its single exhibit. And past the museum, at just about that point where his vision began to fail against the darkness, he could make out the black rectangular shape of one of his father's home-made billboards.

There'd been a whole series of billboards once, littering the highway for miles in both directions. Giant red letters on a field of white, one phrase to a board, they'd stood like mutant Burma-Shave ads at the side of the road: SEE THE THING!  MYSTERY OF THE MOJAVE!  MISSING LINK?  ALIEN BEING?  MYSTERY OF MODERN SCIENCE! And then in smaller letters on the final sign—the one Rex could just now make out: SEE THE THING! SARGE HUMMER'S DESERT MUSEUM  LAST CHANCE GAS, COLD BEER.

The signs were in various states of disrepair now, many of the red letters faded or lost completely—their vacant white backgrounds blinding in the glare of high noon. A few, however, were still legible and occasionally, at the peak of the season when people still used the old road to escape traffic on the interstate, Rex would notice some car loaded down with family—a station wagon perhaps, greasy kid faces pressed to the glass, slow as it rolled into the junction, passing the Desert Museum, its occupants having been hooked some miles out by one of Sarge's signs and eager for a glimpse of the Mystery of the Mojave. Rex Hummer had, of course, seen all of the mysteries—first to last—and he often imagined that it had done something to him, that whatever it had done was in some way connected to his current plight. He had spent a childhood in the sunlight, passing tools to Sarge, watering down Delandra as she lay red-faced and crying in the cab of the truck as sign after sign rose up in their wake, halfway to Los Angeles it had seemed then, with country music and Dodger games spilling from the radio, the wicked crack of Sarge's hammer like a gunshot against the blue expanse of sky. All things considered, it had not been a bad time.

Rex had carried a mug of beer with him from the bar. He felt the weight of it now, sweating in his hand, and he threw back his head to pour it down—cold burn warming the night. The sensation was pleasant enough but there was a certain sadness, he found, gnawing at the edges of his mood, and it occurred to him that he'd best not pursue his memories much further, that he was, after all, at just this moment, still a winner at the Cock & Bull. He looked once more across the wide sweep of land above which the stars filled the sky. He studied the great pale curve of the Milky Way. He looked toward the ruins of Bob Holt's awning in time to see the small dark shape of some desert animal crawl from beneath the canvas and scurry into the night.

Everyone had pretty much gotten back to battle stations by the time Rex returned to the bar. A couple of people clapped him on the back as he passed and said, "Nice job." Rex nodded. He had just taken up his stool and seen the last of the pitcher into his glass when he heard someone yell from across the room. "Holy shit," the voice said. A dozen metal folding chairs scraped the linoleum as the regulars, still a bit spooked from the wind, Rex supposed, headed for the windows. Floyd looked up from behind the bar and asked what the fuck was going on. "Carload a niggers," someone yelled back. "Holy shit."

This was a bit out of the ordinary. There were, of course, black people who stopped from time to time at the Chevron, but they were only strangers off the highway. There were, as far as Rex knew, none living anywhere near the junction and he was quite certain none had ever come looking for a good time at the Cock & Bull. The place was obviously a redneck bar—always a few dusty pickups out in front, and Floyd's Confederate flag decals on the front windows beneath the beer signs, and, if that wasn't enough, you could generally hear the country music spilling out the front door. Rex thought of all this as he waited on his stool. He imagined that once they got a good look at the place they would just keep going. He would keep going, he thought, if he were them.

"Jesus H. Christ," someone said. "They're gettin' out."

This, Rex believed, was serious, or at least potentially serious and he glanced at his uncle to see how the asshole was taking the news. He found Floyd staring toward the door with a kind of dull wonder written on his large, square face. When he caught Rex looking at him he winked. "What da ya say, Pork Rind?" his uncle inquired. "Looks like head-knockin' time to me."

Rex turned away. Head-knockin' was not his strong suit. For one thing he was blind in one eye and it did funny things to his depth perception. For another he was rather thick and slow. He was not good with his hands and prone to nosebleeds.

Back of the bar Floyd had begun to hum the "Niggers' Night Out," a little opus of his own devising, something he had brought with him from Texas when he'd come out to take over the Chevron franchise after Sarge's death. Rex studied the block-size head, the small features above which Floyd had managed to engineer his blue-black hair into a greasy flattop with fenders. Fights could go bad in a bar like the Bull. The law was a good thirty minutes away and none of that would mean a thing to Floyd Hummer.

Rex threw back his head and put the last of the beer into his throat. He peered with a single eye through a light fog of pale blue cigarette smoke toward that crack in the roof from which the moon had fled and he heard the front door swing on its hinges. It swung back hard enough to bang against the cigarette machine, which was backed against the front wall between the door and window, and suddenly everything got real quiet in the Cock & Bull, like it had out on the street, after the wind. Rex Hummer lowered his glass and turned on his stool. Framed in an open doorway was possibly the biggest man he had ever seen—six foot seven or eight, maybe, and close to three hundred pounds. Chest like a refrigerator, thighs like water heaters, and all dressed to kill in a dark three-piece pinstriped suit of gigantic proportions. The only thing small about the man was his head and that looked to Rex to be about the size of a small honeydew melon. The man stood for a moment on the porch, surveying the room from behind a pair of black-rimmed wraparound shades. He had to duck to get through the door, and when he straightened up it appeared for a moment as if the room would be too small to hold him.

There were three of them altogether and they formed just about as bizarre a collection of humanity as Rex had seen on the streets of the junction in some time. The second man through the door was also black. He was not as tall as the first and not as heavy, but when Rex looked at him he was reminded of something Sarge used to say: skinny as a snake and just as mean. The man had a long, bony look to him and though he, too, was decked out in a three-piece, double-breasted pin-striped, the suit did not fit properly, fit in such a way in fact as to lead Rex to the conclusion that no article of clothing ever had hung correctly from that cadaverous frame.

Bony wrists and white cuffs shot from the end of either sleeve and hung there at weird angles—ruby-red cuff links and gold rings flashing in the smoky gloom of the bar. He wore shades like the big man's and an odd-looking gray felt hat with a dark band and even the hat looked to be the wrong size—riding too low above a face that was all right angles and shining in the yellow light like it had been hacked from polished black stone.

The third man was an Indian. He was short and heavyset. He wore dark slacks and black western boots, a blue work shirt with a yellow string tie and a black leather thigh-length jacket of western cut. His hat was the kind of tall, black hat Rex had seen on the Indians from the reservation near Needles. The hat had a beaded band around it and two small feathers on one side. The Indian looked to be the oldest of the three. His face was so deeply lined Rex could see the creases from across the room. It was a face with the desert in it, he thought, not something you would ever want to fuck with. And when the Indian walked and his coat swung back Rex could see there was a bone-handled bowie knife damn near as long as the Indian's thigh strapped to his leg in a leather sheath.

The men crossed the room and seated themselves at a table. It was a quarter till closing time. Someone coughed and Rex could hear a couple of chairs against the linoleum. No one said anything. Most of the regulars were watching Floyd, and Rex could not say that he was unmoved by his uncle's predicament. It was not, after all, your run-of-the-mill carload of niggers and probably, Rex thought, a certain malign sense of satisfaction stirring somewhere back of his breastbone, a good deal more than the local crop had bargained for.

"Looks like Hollywood come to the desert," Floyd said at last. But his voice seemed to have gone hoarse—as if he were nursing a cold. "I'll be dipped in shit," he added, after another moment, but the new, weird voice was the same.

A couple of drunks at the bar managed to laugh. "Fuckin' A," someone said. Someone else muttered to Floyd that they would back his play, but judging by the way the guy was slurring his words, Rex did not imagine it was anything Floyd could take great comfort in.

Floyd stood for a moment longer behind the bar, the leading edge of his flattop glistening like a row of freshly oiled iron filings poised in the grip of some magnetic attraction. "Yeah," he said once more, "Hollywood come to the desert." It seemed about all he could come up with. You had, Rex thought, to feel a little bit sorry for the jackass.

"Fuckin' A," the same moron chimed in once more. Someone else made a crack about faggots and Rex began to get nervous once again. Splitting, however, seemed quite out of the question and so he stayed where he was, hunkered behind the white cotton shirt, the sweating pitcher—the spoils of victory for God's sake—nailed to his stool as surely as if some fifth leg had been run from the floor right into his puckered asshole. It was a position he retained as Floyd crossed the room to inquire if perhaps the big boy would not care to arm wrestle him for a round of beers. It was a ploy for which Floyd was justly famous and when the big boy was beaten he would be asked to leave—at least that was the way the scenario had worked in the past.

There was a mirror in back of the bar—wood-framed with gold letters that said OLD BUSHMILLS on it—which Floyd had picked up from some guy who was selling them alongside the road, and it was by way of this invention that Rex observed the scene taking place behind him. To his great horror the smaller of the two black men had lit a pair of cigarettes and arranged them in such a way that whoever lost would have to put one out with the back of his hand.

Rex put the last of his pitcher into his mug and chugged it. Before he could put the glass back down, however, he heard two things. He heard one of the locals say: "Make it plain," and he heard someone's hand hit the table, hard. When he looked he was in time to see Floyd Hummer grinding out a butt real good with the back of his hand. Fuckin' A.

The blacks were outnumbered three to one but not an ass left a chair. It was kind of sad, really. Floyd Hummer went back to the bar and started washing glasses and when one of the regulars got up to play the jukebox he shouted at the guy to leave the mother-fucking thing alone. It was closing time, for Christ's sake. And so it was. And before long what was left of the locals began slinking out the door, into the cold, black hours of a brand-new day.

Rex Hummer was about to leave himself when suddenly all three men rose and started toward the bar. "Say, look here, Jim." It was the bony black man who spoke. "We Vegas bound man, but we've been checkin' out these signs. See the Thing. We come to check out its crib man."

Floyd was some time in replying. He was drying a pitcher. At last he held it to the light and ran a towel around the rim. "Wouldn't know about any of that shit," he said. "You want to know about that, you talk to the sausage here." He nodded in the direction of Rex Hummer.

The black man poked at the brim of his hat with a long finger. Three freakish heads swiveled toward him and Rex suddenly found his own crazy face among them, reflected in the twin sets of Foster Grant wraparounds. It was a suffocating experience. The Indian leaned one hand against the bar and the lights caught a large silver and gold belt buckle at his waist, what looked to be some kind of hand in a circle of mother-of-pearl. "Yo," Rex said at last. What else could he say? He did own it. It was his museum and his land and if anyone owned what was left there, lying inside of it, he owned that, too.

"Well," the man asked him. "What about it?"

"Yo," Rex said once more. He was waiting for the correct words. Like Moses before the Pharaoh. Beads of sweat popped from his forehead. His mind felt like a dark and empty room. And yet somewhere his pride was like the flame of a tiny candle, refusing to go out. "Well," he began again, clearing his throat. "You can't see anything in there now. There's no lights and it would be dangerous." He stared into the dark, faintly pockmarked face of the man who had arranged the cigarettes upon the table.

The man looked at his companions, then back at Rex. There was, Rex noticed, something beneath the shades which might have been a smile. It wasn't the sort of thing you wanted to look at for long.

"What you mean by dangerous?" the man asked.

"He mean the Thing, home boy." It was the big man who spoke. "He mean the Thing don't like niggers."

"Maybe he means the Thing does like niggers," the Indian said. "He likes dark meat."

The black men seemed to find this amusing. It sounded to Rex like something he ought to leave alone. "Snakes," he said. It seemed to be the best he could do on short notice.

"Say what?" the big man asked.

"Rattlers," Rex said. "The place isn't used. Wouldn't want to step on a rattler."

The big man seemed impressed. "Dig it," he said. "Me and snakes don't get along."

The Indian laughed but said nothing. The thin man appeared to give the matter some thought. "Simple," he said. "We catch Vegas on the P.M., we catch the Thing on the A.M."

Rex Hummer received the suggestion with a quickening of an already palpitating heart. "And that's mine, too," he imagined himself saying. He was looking over the one guy's shoulder at the Hum-A-Phone glittering on the stage. "And if you want to see the Mystery, you'll have to hear the sound." And for a moment he almost thought he had said it, but then he knew he hadn't.

They were running on empty when a patch of light appeared in the distance. Bianca noticed them first. "Lights," she said, and leaned forward so that Obadiah could feel her breath against the back of his neck. Neil responded with a grunt and picked up speed.

What lay before them was neither a town nor a gas station. It appeared at first glance to be some sort of government compound. There was an American flag at the top of a pole with a light on it and at the base of the flag there were half a dozen aluminum trailers. The trailers, arranged in a square, were surrounded by a chain-link fence. There were a handful of spotlights on the fence, and between the fence and the flagpole there was enough light to cast a pale white mist on the night sky. Neil pulled up close to the chain link and killed the motor. The silence of the desert filled the car. "Maybe they will have some gas," Neil said. His voice sounded much too loud and was followed by a moment of strained silence— nothing like a government compound to make a carload of The Friends nervous. They were, after all, among the most persecuted religious groups on the planet. They had died by the hundreds in Nazi death camps. They died today behind the Iron Curtain. Obadiah knew of one brother who had died in the L.A. County jail waiting transfer to Stafford, Arizona, for refusing induction. And someday soon the apocalyptic shit was bound to hit the fan. Even Obadiah Wheeler believed in the fire next time and he was a man of little faith. He stared into the gloomy yard of the compound as Neil eased himself from the car, and thought about persecution.

When he was young, Obadiah used to lie awake nights thinking of persecution. He had stood sweating in the musty aisles of the Pomona Public Library with a copy of Fox's *Book of Martyrs* propped open before him on more occasions than he cared to remember. The book had come to have a certain hold on him, drawing him toward it whenever he entered the building. Surviving torture seemed unimaginable to him. What would you do, brother, when they put the blowtorch to your balls? He had always expected to crack immediately. When the brothers in Liberia had cracked they had become instant objects of derision among their tormentors—often faring more grimly than those who had stood firm. Watching Neil Davis pass through a gate, he found himself thinking of Harlan Low. Beatings and bad water. Days without sleep. His contemplation of Elder Low, however, was interrupted by Bianca Allen, who was leaning forward once more, her arms folded across the back of his seat, her elbow pressing against his shoulder blade.

He watched as Neil crossed the yard and approached a trailer. The door was opened by a blond woman in a maroon bathrobe. The woman looked once in the direction of the car then quickly ushered Neil inside.

"Friendly," Panama said.

Bianca made a peculiar snorting sound and Obadiah began to reflect upon what it might mean that the roofs of the trailers were skirted by a thin bead of red neon.

Within five minutes brother Davis was back in the car, having learned firsthand what the red lights were all about. "So the guy at the station has had his little joke," he said. He paused to punch the steering wheel with the butt of his hand. The wheel vibrated in the silence. "It's a house of prostitution," he said. "We've crossed the state line. This is Nevada. The nearest gas station is that way." He jerked a thumb toward the desert in what appeared to be no direction in particular. "But the woman here says the road is bad and that we should wait until morning. There's a workshed that way"—he jerked his other thumb in the opposite direction, toward the end of the trailers—"in which there may be a couple of gas cans." He paused for a moment. "She says we're welcome to it. She says that this place is pretty well known but that most people don't drive in. They fly. There's a strip over there on the other side of the trailers." Neil stopped talking and, in the silence that followed, the drone of a distant engine grew out of the night. Neil seemed to find some small satisfaction in the sound. "See," he said, "there is one."

They listened as the sound of the engine grew and a small plane did, in fact, set down somewhere on the other side of the trailers, after which they could hear the laughter of men.

"Well," Panama Allen asked, "how do you do?" Her words were followed by a burst of high-pitched, unpleasant laughter. "So where do we sleep?" Bianca wanted to know.

"I guess we'll have to sleep right here," Neil Davis said. "We certainly can't sleep in there." He gestured toward the trailer. "I believe there are some blankets in the trunk." The night had turned surprisingly chilly after the heat of the day. "I'll get them."

They could hear him at the rear of the car, shifting weight, banging things around. At last he returned and sat down behind the wheel once more. "Damn," he said. "Excuse my language, but I guess I took them out to make room for the literature."

Bianca jabbed at the back of Obadiah's seat. "I don't know about you all," she said, "but I'll sleep in there if they'll let me."

Obadiah had no choice but to open the door and let her out. As he was doing so Neil spoke up at his side. "I don't know if that's such a good idea, sister." Bianca was by now, however, standing in the lot near the door. She leaned forward, almost touching Obadiah and spoke to Neil across the front seat. "My butt's cold right now, honey. You can have the car, and this trip, too, as far as that goes." With that she turned and walked off toward the gate. "That child," Panama said, and followed the exclamation with one more burst of high-pitched laughter.

Obadiah looked toward the trailers. The red neon drew a narrow vibrating line at the edge of the sky and above the neon a piece of the moon had risen like a chip of melting ice, bathing the desert in a snowy light.

It was, alongside every other night he could think of, the longest Obadiah could recall. It dragged on interminably, charged with half dreams and bizarre levels of consciousness, the buzzing of lonely planes, and when at last he stood, along with Neil Davis, in the workshed at the far end of the trailers, checking for gas cans by the first gray light, he felt that they had been there, at the side of that narrow road, for at least several days.

There was gas—perhaps two gallons' worth, enough, the woman who had first met Neil at the door surmised, to get them to a Chevron station somewhere down the road. Neil gave the woman some money and, in a surprising offer of reconciliation, suggested that Obadiah drive. Perhaps he assumed that even Obadiah could not lose them on a road without turns. Perhaps he wished to save himself for the more important driving which lay ahead. Obadiah accepted the offer. He listened to advice on the avoidance of potholes and started down the road. For a time, he could see the woman from the trailers in the rearview mirror. She was standing at the edge of the chain-link fence in the maroon bathrobe, one hand raised to shield her eyes, one at her side. There was something in the pose, he thought, which suggested the wife of Lot, turned to statuary at the edge of Sodom. He looked at her several times and then at last she was gone and they were alone with the morning and it was, he had to admit, in spite of everything, quite beautiful. The distant hills which at sunset had turned purple appeared once more as jagged stripes of red and yellow on a field of crystal blue. The air was fresh—so fresh you could taste it, dry and clean, yet shot through with the scents of greasewood and sage. Obadiah wished he could feel more in tune with it, less a spectator. As it was, he clung to the wheel of Neil's LeSabre like a ghost while the morning slipped past him, following a narrow dirt road as it crawled through a forest of Joshua trees.

At last the car peaked a small rise and began a bumpy descent. In the distance a handful of buildings became visible—scattered across a corrugated hillside. The road curved and the buildings slipped from view.

"There it is," Neil said, "a Chevron sign, just ahead."

It seemed to Obadiah that he had seen something too—red letters on a field of white. He squinted into the dust, the twisted limbs of the Joshuas, the heat waves just now beginning to swarm at the edges of the land.

When the sign appeared again Neil groaned and slapped at the dashboard with the palm of his hand. It was not a Chevron sign at all, but rather some kind of homemade billboard.

Sunbeaten and buckled, it swung toward them from a turquoise sky. There were large letters on the sign. Once, Obadiah supposed, they had been red. Now they were the color of dried blood, flecked with white where the paint had fallen away, scarred with buckshot. Obadiah dragged a hand through his hair. "What is it?" Bianca asked from the backseat. As if in answer the dusty LeSabre made an odd kind of whirring sound and emitted a cloud of pale smoke. SEE THE THING! the billboard said. Sarge Hummer's Desert Museum. LAST CHANCE GAS, COLD BEER.

Slow Hound, Pluto, Pluggard, Stinkhorn, Link, even a Ruth: Rex and Delandra Hummer had named all of their father's creations—no matter how pathetic. And many were painfully so—some bit of chicken wire left to protrude from a twisted limb, the curled end of a sheet of fiber glass not completely covered with resin left to rise from beneath a formidable jaw. More than once, standing in the gloom of Sarge Hummer's Desert Museum, surrounded by a handful of schoolmates come to inspect the latest installment of the Mystery of the Mojave, Rex Hummer had been embarrassed by his father's reckless craftsmanship.

Rex thought about them now—the whole sorry line of homemade monsters—as he lay in the back of a twenty-five-foot Terry trailer and waited for the dawn. It was true that Sarge had honed his skills. What began as a scam had ended as an obsession. Sarge had given up on everything else, the gas station, the bar; toward the end there had only been his work—long hours in the shed back of the museum, discarding creatures almost as fast as he could turn them out, littering the desert with severed mannikin parts and fiber glass castings, turning that whole area, from the back of the building to the crest of the first hill, into a veritable junkyard of discarded Things. Sarge had known by that time that he was dying, and he had simply pared it down—Rex could see it now. The man had channeled his energies—everything else could go to hell, and had.

There were a lot of things about his father that Rex had never known—never would know, now. He had resigned himself to that, to dealing with what little he had. Once Sarge had been a Marine. He'd started out in the peacetime Corps. He had been in the Philippines in the beginning and he had been there again, at the end, when the Corps came back. He had seen some shit. He was not patriotic about it. Once to Rex's mother's great horror, Sarge had apparently started a fistfight at a Fourth of July day parade by refusing to stand for the national anthem. Rex had heard the story, more than once. Sarge had been a car salesman, a roofer, a carpet layer. He invested a small inheritance in a raceway. The venture failed. Then Sarge passed a few bad checks and wound up in the California Correctional Institution for Men at Chino. When he got out his wife was gone. She'd left with one of his partners from the raceway. Sarge's drinking increased. He wrecked a car and nearly died, receiving for his efforts an odd heart-shaped scar across his forehead. It was not long after the wreck that Sarge moved himself and Rex to the desert. Rex was five.

When Rex was eight, Sarge met another woman, a fat, sloppy woman, in Rex's opinion. The union produced a child—Delandra —a fat, dark-haired baby that looked almost Mexican. Sarge never married the woman and when she left, she left the kid, too, just as Rex's mother had left hers, and Sarge was the father of two.

It was then that Sarge hit on the idea of the Desert Museum and the Mystery of the Mojave. He'd seen similar scams and he was, after all, in the right place for it. "People will believe in things out here," he had said. "It's the space and the emptiness. And no one gives a fuck." Rex could still remember him driving into town and coming back with an armload of monster magazines and comic books, could still remember him hunched over a failing card table to produce the first childlike drawings of the Creature—they had seemed childlike to Rex even then and he was scarcely ten years old himself.

What Sarge might have lacked in talent, however, he made up for in drive. He was a thick, powerful man—a good deal shorter than his brother Floyd, but nearly as strong, with a full head of coal-black hair which he wore slicked back wet above a tanned head and the raised flesh of the curving scar, and soon enough he'd been at work on the museum, hammering and sawing, building mostly with scraps he picked up at other building sites, until at last, there at the edge of Route 15 where it wound through the Mojave Desert, on the California side of the state line, there really did spring up the low, ramshackle collection of clapboard and scrap, and there really were big red-and-white signs to attract the curious, and there really was, at one end of the odd building, in a room built especially to house it, asleep on a bed of red dirt, beneath a dusty glass case, the first crude version of Sarge Hummer's Mystery of the Mojave. It lay twisted in the musty gloom like the victim of some terrible accident, arms and legs akimbo, sand carefully arranged to cover the mistakes, dead gearshift eyes staring blindly into the raised wooden roof where thin shafts of sunlight pierced the cracks and filled the room with an eerie, almost cathedral-like light.

For the next fifteen years you could say that Rex Hummer grew up with the Thing, one Thing or another. His first real job was sneaking around in the dust attaching bumper stickers to cars which read: I SAW THE THING! The work paid a dollar an hour. It was dangerous. Most people don't want a bumper sticker admitting to such an act—particularly the kind which adheres to the chrome in such a way that removal is both messy and time-consuming, occasionally impossible. You can get the kind that ties on and Rex always wished that they would but Sarge couldn't see it.

Later, when Delandra was old enough, she would help and Rex came to understand that there was something about a girl, a pretty one: Delandra could get caught and not get yelled at.

Or maybe it was just that she was younger, for as she grew older and fatter—more like her mother in Rex's eye—people yelled at her too. But by then both she and Rex had grown more hardened to the reproof; they had also gotten better at it and were caught less. By this time, too, they had learned to make more of a game of it and Rex still had fond memories of sitting beside Delandra in the front seat of Sarge's Chevy truck watching the *turistas* spill back into the lot, blinking their eyes against the mighty sun, some shaking their heads, some chuckling, or maybe explaining to some kid too young or too stupid to know better that it was all a joke, that some guy had just made it himself. And sometimes a few would stumble out laughing because Delandra had snuck in that night and replaced Sarge's usual bit of drivel (the part about how he had found the Thing in the desert and how it had been examined by scientists, and so on—which information he kept on a small card at the foot of the glass case) with something clever of her own. Delandra's cards usually said things like "Beat me. Fuck me. Call me Ruth."

The smiles, however, tended to fade when their owners saw what had been done to the rear bumpers of their cars—that bright yellow sticker with the black squiggly letters, like they'd come from some horror movie poster: I saw the *Thing*! Sometimes they'd go back and bitch at Sarge about it but usually it came to nothing. There was always something about Sarge, his big square head and hands, his thick sloping shoulders, those quick black eyes that had seen all the shit. Most people just drove off complaining and it was Rex and Delandra's turn to smile. I saw the Thing, sucker.

The really crazy part, though—Rex thought later, when it had all ended—was that none of them, none of those families on their way to Death Valley, none of the Vegas-bound high rollers, fifty-dollar haircuts, white belts, and double knits ablaze beneath a desert sun, none of those husband-and-wife Harley-Davidson teams in color-coordinated leathers, none of the conventioneers—the endless parade of UFO watchers, 4-H'ers, cowboys, and truckers—not one of the whole miserable crowd, ever did get to see the last and final version of the Thing—the one without a name because just to look at it had been enough to send both Rex and Delandra running for the door and the night beyond it, the one that was so very smooth without a hint of chicken wire or fiber glass or resin, the one whose strange and cavernous skull held eyes that were somehow still alive and could roll right with you, smoke you sucker, on the very spot, and Rex had to admit that it would have been worth something to have stood there just one time with the Sarge, to have watched just one batch of tourists spill out of that clapboard gloom and make for their cars—real fast, the way Rex liked to imagine it, tripping over their own goddamn feet, fumbling for keys and yelling at their squalling brats—driving like madmen back out into those terrible miles of nothing, knowing at the bottoms of their stingy souls that somehow things were just a little weirder than they had originally thought, that the Mystery of the Mojave was for real, Jim, you'd better fucking believe it.

**B**ut of course it never happened that way and Rex Hummer was able to treasure no such memories. Vindication had been a long time coming. That it would one day arrive was the stuff of Rex Hummer's dreams and he thought often of his own first glimpse of Sarge Hummer's revenge. It had come on a cool and moonless night. Rex and Delandra had known by then of Sarge's illness and when he failed to present himself for dinner on a second consecutive evening they had gotten worried.

The museum that night was without light—Sarge having recently blown some fuses which he had failed to replace. Rex had carried a flashlight and together he and his sister had followed its weak beam through the familiar rooms. As they approached the resting place of the Mystery of the Mojave, however—which room it was also necessary to cross to get to the shed—it appeared that another kind of light was seeping from beneath the closed door to meet their own. The light had an odd greenish color about it, together with an unpleasant odor—something distasteful and acrid, something like the odor of burning batteries, something that had made him want to turn away—and he had stood there for a moment, hesitating, turning to Delandra, their faces close enough so that even now he could remember the scents of tobacco and Juicy Fruit on her breath, the greenish light reflected in her black Mexican eyes. At last he had pushed open the door. The odor grew stronger, as did the greenish light which was clearly coming from the glass case containing Sarge Hummer's latest installment of the Mystery of the Mojave—a version neither Rex nor Delandra had yet seen. Rex approached the box slowly and what he saw there he had never, even after all this time, arrived at a satisfactory way of describing. Sometimes it seemed to him as if the Thing was an animal, and sometimes it seemed to be a machine. The body was big and there were whole areas covered by what he could only describe as matted fur, or possibly feathers. In other places there was no fur at all and things that might have been bones swelled out bare and smooth, shining softly in the dim light. Still other parts had a hard, armorlike quality about them and gave off a faint iridescent sheen. The green light seemed to come from the Creature itself—if indeed it was a creature—to seep from peculiar cavernous openings in what Rex supposed was the Thing's skull. And beneath two of these openings were what appeared to be a pair of smoldering eyes. The eyes were the worst, or most magnificent—or at least the most memorable—part of all. They seemed capable of movement and on the evening in question had for some indeterminate period of time effectively reduced Rex Hummer's spine to jelly and his tongue to wax while somewhere high above his head a peculiar wind—or at least he had first imagined it to be a wind—had begun to sing among the wooden rafters, and something like tumbleweeds had begun to scrape the parched clapboard walls.

It was hard to say now just how long he and his sister had stood

there, struck dumb by what their father had wrought, but at last
their legs had begun to work and they had run back breathless into
the night and the desert where Sarge himself was to die just
twenty-four hours later—not hard and ugly like the doctors had
said: he just stopped and died and that was it. They'd found him
facedown in the rust-colored sand, by the butane tanks in back of
the Chevron.

For Rex Hummer, that night in the museum had come to mark a
turning point, a bisecting of his life in which the cluttered slate of
what had gone before was wiped clean and nothing that came
after it could ever be quite the same. Sarge Hummer had passed
from a figure of ridicule to one of immense mystery. Thomas had
touched the side of Jesus, his fingers in the open wound. Rex
Hummer had seen the Thing. He pasted one of his own bumper
stickers to the rear of his trailer and prided himself on its secret
meaning. And yet it was a full year before he returned to the
resting place of the Mystery of the Mojave.

It was during that year that Floyd moved out from Texas to take
over the station and Delandra moved into town. And Rex had
been left alone with Sarge's land, the trailers, and the Desert
Museum. He grew used to the loneliness. The land was all owned
free and clear and Floyd was willing to pay for odd jobs around the
station and bar. There were times he thought of leaving. But
where would he go? And how could he leave what Sarge had left?
It was like some secret knowledge passed on from one generation
to the next. It was what made him different. And what gave him
power—or could be made, he knew somewhere in his heart, to
give him power. It was a puzzle he reflected on at great length and
at last he began to visit the museum once again.

He had to. By the end of a year he was afraid that perhaps his
memory was playing him for a fool. He discovered to both his
relief and his astonishment that it was not, though it seemed to
him that with the passing of time the greenish light and peculiar
odor had faded—almost, as if the Thing were cooling down. And
soon he was returning on a regular basis, though always by night.
And he took to wearing certain clothes, to the practice in fact of
certain repeated gestures and thoughts before entering the room
itself. And finally an only half-articulated idea had begun to form
and the lights had once again begun to flicker in Sarge Hummer's
old shed. And while the regulars around the junction sat pickling
their brains at the Cock & Bull, chasing the few unattractive

women the climate had to offer, occasionally punching one another out and in general squandering and debauching their sorry lives in the pursuit of trivial pleasures, Rex Hummer took his first faltering steps down that path least traveled, storing for himself something no thief could steal, nor moth and rust consume. He began work on the Hum-A-Phone and an odd music had begun to play in his head.


He began with the horns he found in the rusting carcasses of cars he came upon back among the hills. He particularly liked the horns from the older cars—curved and rusted like the bodies he had taken them from, touched by the desert. The desert, he discovered, was always there, in the parts he liked best. He found it in the scraps of corrugated tin he took from empty mining shacks, in the pieces of broken glass and in the small smooth stones.

He attached rubber balls to the horns and mounted them on racks so he could squeeze several at once. He cut the tin into thin strips of varying length and suspended them on wires from a metal rod. He filled small coarse sacks with rocks and put the pieces of broken glass in the bottom of a pail. He made pedals for his feet and connected them to mallets with which he could bang the glass in the pails or hit the strips of metal. He made a rack with hollow sticks on it and when he blew into the sticks they produced a high, strange whistling sound. He added the keyboard from a child's xylophone he found in a charred ruin. But whatever he added, it always seemed to him that something was still missing. The Hum-A-Phone grew to a ridiculous size and when he had shown it to Delandra on her return to the junction—the used-car dealer dead, a warrant hanging over her head, looking as tired and burned-out as he'd ever seen her—she had only shaken her head as if the sight of it made her feel even older than she looked and told him he was as bad as Sarge Hummer and something had moved inside of him as she said it, as if hearing just those words spoken out loud had triggered a series of recognitions capable of delivering both joy and unbearable sadness. He understood for the first time that he could add to the machine forever, that there would always be one piece missing, one element of a sound which played almost continually now in his head, that was not just as he wanted it, and that what really he had set out to reproduce was what he had heard that first night in the museum, what he had taken for the whine of wind in the rafters, the dried thorns of dead weeds upon clapboard walls, and yet a sound that was somehow more than the sum of those parts—something like the last plaintive cry of a wounded gull circling an endless winter sky—the voice, in fact, of the Thing itself, and when he understood that he sat down and cried. He walked barefoot in the desert and cut his feet on rocks and he felt for the first time what he guessed Sarge must have felt in his workshed—why he was always there, always discarding the last version in favor of the new, never satisfied—until perhaps at the very end when at last he had made the connection and, having made it, lay down to rest. And so Rex understood something else as well—the meaning of Sarge Hummer's legacy, the mark he had been left to match. He was at once proud and brokenhearted. A lifetime of yearning unwound before him like some lost and endless highway, humming in a voice he could not name.

A cold sweat had collected on Rex's brow by the time the first lines of color had begun to gnaw at the edges of a cool and inhospitable day. It had been a sleepless few hours and he could not recall a night having fled so quickly. He stood now on the cold flooring of the Terry trailer in his bare feet and considered his predicament.

He had often imagined a reopening of the Desert Museum. Strobe lights. Stereophonic sound. Rex Hummer in white buckskin at the controls of the Hum-A-Phone. The unimaginable creature paired with the unimaginable sound. Enough to turn any citizen's spine to piss. For months he had worked toward such a goal and he had waited for a sign.

He had often tried to imagine what form the sign might take. The possibility of pimps in a dust-covered de Ville had in particular eluded him. And that he should be bullied into an advance tour before he was ready seemed a mockery of all that he had done; yet there seemed no alternative to meeting them as he had said he would back on the street in front of the Cock & Bull. It would be better to be there himself than to let them nose around without him. And these were clearly men who did what they damn well pleased—some throwback to the wildmen that had once roamed these plains and Rex did not for more than a second or so imagine he was the man to call their hand, or draw against the drop on the main street of the junction.

He thought of the brutes now as he studied his reflection in the small square mirror above the plastic sink—the broad, fleshy face, the thick, sloping shoulders. He was indeed Sarge Hummer's son, and he could not help wondering how Sarge would have handled the situation. There was a rifle under the bed in the trailer—

something else Sarge had left him—but Rex had never fired the thing and was more than willing to leave it there now. He would meet them he supposed with nothing more than a few shots of bourbon in his guts to ease the pain.

He went to the kitchen and took a pint bottle of Jim Beam from the cupboard beneath the refrigerator. He knew what people thought of him. They thought he was weird. They'd thought Sarge was a little weird, too, but they had respected him. In Rex's case they just thought he was weird. They were, of course, moronic assholes and he was bound one day to set their heads on straight. He took a couple of pulls on the bottle and chased it with some water from the sink. He recapped the bottle and stuck it back under the fridge. Fuck yes. It was something he liked to think about—setting heads straight. Vindication would cast her shadow among these barren hills yet and if she was a long time coming it was at least good to know that upon arrival she would swing a heavy boot.

Fifteen minutes later, the Jim Beam still burning his empty stomach, dressed in T-shirt, jeans, and broken-down cowboy boots, he made his way down a steep trail toward the main drag of the junction.

He paused at the bottom of the grade, long enough to drag a hand over a three-day beard and then back, through his hair, which felt thicker than it should have with grease and dirt.

Up on one hill he could see the ruins of Bob Holt's canvas awning. He noticed, too, Delandra's dirty green Dart parked near the Chevron. He stood for a moment eyeing the car. It was badly dented from all the things she had run into. Some of the dents were new, others had gone dark with rust. There were two yellow-and-black stickers on either side of the rear bumper. I SAW THE THING! And indeed she had. Though all she'd ever said about it was that it was no big deal, that he should have gotten good at it— it being all he had done—and had then gone on to note that the sad part was, it was like being good on the accordion, no one gave a fuck. But the first thing she had done with the car Mr. Ott gave her was put the bumper stickers on the back and he never had been able to figure that one out. He was about to go on when a peculiar sound came to his attention.

The sound had come from somewhere behind him and he looked back in the direction from which he had come. What he saw was the bright flash of sunlight on chrome and glass—a spot of it moving down out of the hills. Car, he guessed, coming down off that little old back road, which was unusual these days because there wasn't anything back there but an overpriced whorehouse across the line and no one that he knew of ever drove in. It was a businessman's sort of place and they flew in. The car had raised a halo of dust to hang in the sky above the flash of metal and sun, but he could see now, too, as the car got closer that it was smoking as well, steam leaking out of the grille and joining the dust, and he guessed that was the reason for the peculiar sound. Assholes had probably broken something on that bad road and he guessed Floyd would probably figure a way to ream them still further before they got out of this place. He thought about that for a moment and it almost made him smile but then he thought again of those boys waiting for him and the smile was short-lived.

D elandra Hummer listened to a cat on the sheet metal roof. She put a pillow over her head and tried to go back to sleep. Then Bob Holt's shepherd began to bark and she gave it up. There was a warm yellow light breaking through the blinds which covered the room's only window. The light only looked warm, however; the room was still cold as hell. She kicked back the covers and sat up on the edge of the mattress. The mattress was on the floor. There was a straw mat alongside the mattress but the cold rising off the concrete came through it and made the bottoms of her feet ache.

She sat there for a moment in an effort to get her bearings. She'd been living in the room for a month now and every morning she looked it over like she was seeing it for the first time and was surprised to find herself there. Her father had built the room years ago when he'd first moved to the desert. It was what he and Rex had lived in until the trailer came. He'd built it over a concrete slab he'd found behind the station. The walls and roof were made from bits and pieces of things he'd taken from local mining sites. It was amazing that the structure was still standing. What was even

more amazing was that she had come back to it. A month ago she'd
been sleeping on a king-size water bed surrounded by mirrors and
oil paintings of plump naked women. Now she was surrounded by
clapboard and tin, with nothing more interesting to look at than
the dust-covered rocks she had collected as a child. And the rocks
made her blue. Looking at the rocks she was forced to think about
Sarge, to reflect upon the fact that he had—God only knew why or
when—taken the trouble to move the things up here from the
trailer where she had kept them, to arrange them in neat rows
upon the pieces of pine he had nailed to the walls to serve as
shelves. It was an image to boggle the mind and to think about the
why of it was to invite a depression which might linger for days.
"Never thought I'd fall, but the bottle took it all," she said—they
were the lines to a song. Except that in her case it wasn't the
bottle. It was something else and she had yet to put her finger on it.

She'd slept naked and when at last she managed to get her ass off
the mattress she moved quickly around the room, picking up
whatever article of clothing she happened to see and putting it on.
She found a black-and-white zebra-striped cotton dress, a pair of
red-and-yellow cowboy boots. She added a black pullover mohair
sweater against the cold. When she picked up the sweater she
found there was a rock from her collection beneath it. She picked
the thing up and looked at it in the illusory light. She could still
remember finding it. Actually, she could remember finding them
all. For the most part, there was little of real value in her collection. Some quartz and fool's gold, a few geodes. Mainly there were
rocks that looked like something else. The rock in her hand, for
instance, had reminded her of a fat woman's ass. There had even,
at the time, been a particular fat woman in mind—someone she
had seen with Sarge when he thought no one was looking. The
geodes were really her favorites, however. It was because they
looked like one thing on the outside and like something else when
you opened them. She placed the fat woman's ass on the shelf next
to her diploma from the Rainbow Beauty College and jerked the
blinds. She was treated to a peculiar sight.
There were two cars headed down the main drag from opposite
directions. One was a baby-blue Buick, the other, a red Cadillac
convertible with the top down. Both cars had California plates and
both were streaked with dust. The Buick was smoking.
The next thing she noticed was the unusually high number of
Negroes suddenly converging on the junction. There appeared to

be several in each car. She took a Kleenex from the pocket of the
dress and blew her nose—painfully. She seemed to recall having
mashed it against something, possibly a fireman. Lurid fragments
of one more lost night rose suddenly like a gritty haze across the
morning. She deliberately avoided remembering any more and
noticed—as the cars below her drew closer—the most peculiar
thing of all. It was her brother, Rex Hummer. He had managed
somehow, together with the three Negroes, to squeeze himself
into the front seat of the de Ville. And there he sat, hopelessly
contorted in an effort to accommodate his companions, his big
white face shining in the sunlight. The blacks were wearing hats
and shades. Except that one of them wasn't a black man. That was
the next thing she noticed. He was almost as dark as the others but
as the car passed below her she saw that he wore the kind of hat
the Indians wore and that there was in fact straight black hair
hanging out beneath the brim in back, covering the collar of his
jacket, and seeing that made her uneasy because he had the look of
someone she had not planned to see again.

The cars, which were moving quite slowly, stopped as they drew
alongside one another and Delandra could see a white man in the
Buick asking for directions. It looked as if Rex was trying to answer
him. She could not, of course, hear what was being said, but once
she saw Rex gesture back over his shoulder in the direction of the
station—as if that was what the man had been asking about. Delandra wiped her nose and chucked the Kleenex. She went to a small
refrigerator at the foot of the bed and took out a beer. "Hair of the
dog," she said. Then she moved back to the window.


The Buick had by now reached the gravel drive which circled
the pumps. The red de Ville had reached her father's museum.
There was a young man sitting behind the wheel of the Buick. She
guessed that he was in his early twenties. He had blond hair and
she found that he reminded her of a lifeguard she had once known
in Manhattan Beach. The memory was a pleasant one and she
decided the young man looked like someone she should probably
fuck. On the other hand, the man she had seen in the Cadillac was
now standing at the entrance to the museum with his back to her
and he looked like someone she should probably get closer to. It
was the kind of dilemma her life had thus far been made of and she
felt her heart quicken in her chest. When she stepped outside into
the morning she found that the blond-haired boy was standing in
the sunlight staring at her and so she supposed it was a case of first

things first. She smiled down on him from the concrete ledge which skirted the station's metallic walls just as a sudden gust of wind pinned the cotton dress to her legs. She could see the wind moving across the face of the grade. She saw a patch of wildflowers turn their faces to the road. She saw pollen dust and the luminous white petals of the Joshuas floating in the sunlight, drifting like snow above the desert floor.

# II

---

*Martians at the window*
*and you in my arms*
*put down that antenna*
*don't broadcast your charms*
R.F.F.
*Groundhog Day on Mars*

It was late Sunday afternoon before Neil Davis got through to Harlan Low at the Tonopah Hotel. Harlan stood in the hotel's lobby, the telephone receiver pressed to his ear, and looked out across the soiled red carpet, the flagstone steps, and the street beyond them. The street looked white and dusty in the full heat of the day. Above the buildings which lined the street across from the hotel Harlan could just make out a thin sliver of sky.

"Davis," he said. "Get hold of yourself, brother. Just give me the facts." He had not had to speak that harshly to anyone in some time. The last part, about the facts, even sounded corny to him. He wondered where he could have picked up such a line. Television perhaps. There was a television in the lobby of the Tonopah Hotel. Harlan could see its dark screen now—a dull thick mirror above the bar. He could make out his own reflection—the white dress shirt he wore standing out quite vividly in the gloom. He had to look up to see the screen and the angle from which he observed himself served to make him look even heavier than he already was. He looked like a cartoon. "What?" he asked. He was not sure if he had heard correctly. He continued to study the image above him with a kind of contempt. Neil Davis repeated what he had just said and Harlan realized that he had heard correctly after all. He looked away from the television set and into the scarred wood of the booth. He studied his free hand, the short thick fingers and neatly trimmed nails. He discovered that he was nodding his head, as if Brother Davis were standing in front of him. "All right," he said at last. "It's going to be all right. You stay there. I'll leave the others here and come down there myself. What was that?" He had to stop once more as Neil asked him about transportation. "No," Harlan said; he found that it was necessary to keep cutting Brother Davis off in order to speak himself. "It will be okay. I'll rent something." Neil started to say something else but Harlan cut him off right away. "Just wait for me, Neil. Understood?" He waited for Neil Davis to understand, then replaced the receiver and walked outside, into the heat.

Within two hours Harlan was back on the road in a rented Ford. He'd only told the others about the missed turnoff and car problems, had said that as much as he regretted it he was going to have to cut his stay short, that he was going to help out Brother Davis with the car, and that he would no doubt be seeing them all at a later time. He said good-bye in front of the Tonopah Hotel where Ruth Bishop provided him with a bologna sandwich and a bottle of beer.

The beer and sandwich sat next to him now, the dark bottle sweating against the pale green fabric of the Ford's seat. In spite of the fact that he had not eaten since breakfast—one greasy pair of eggs and hash browns in the Tonopah Cafe—he could not quite bring himself to start on the food. His stomach had been feeling rather queasy in the heat and he had begun to develop a headache. The headaches, he had found, seemed to begin with a kind of tic around his right eye. There were pills in his briefcase for just such moments—pills for his stomach, others for his head—but he did not stop to sort them out. He stared instead into the heat waves, the thin asphalt ribbon which stretched before him for as far as he could see, and he put the pedal to the floor.

He didn't open the beer until dark and by then it was warm. He drank it anyway, using it to wash down a pain pill. He looked into the headlights of a passing car. He'd seen it coming for a long time and when it was gone the road ahead was black and unbroken. He continued to think about the lights and found they reminded him of the spotlights the Liberian soldiers had rigged above the compound to prevent them from sleeping. They were made to stand, staring into the lights, as they had been made to stare into the sun that afternoon. The guards had circled them, making sure that all were doing this. To be caught looking elsewhere meant a butt stroke from a rifle. He finished the beer and let the bottle drop to the floor. He didn't like thinking about Africa very much and silently cursed the lights which had reminded him. When he let himself think about it at night he usually dreamed it as well—would wake up drained and angry and afraid. The fear was connected to more than a fear for his own life. It had to do with being needed—the way those African brothers had needed him, wanting more than a man could give. He didn't want to be needed in that way again.

He took one hand from the wheel and ran it back through his hair, squeezed the back of his neck and tried to shift his attention to the task before him. When he thought of the story Neil Davis had told him over the phone he did not know whether to be angry or saddened. The truth was, such a complete ration of horseshit he had not heard in quite some time.

Neil's car, it seemed, was in pieces with some bully of a mechanic making outrageous demands for repair. There was something about spending the night in the car, out on some back road at the door of a whorehouse—Panama Allen's daughter actually sleeping in the whorehouse. Neil had also lost his wallet and yet even that was not the capper. That Special Service boy, Obadiah Wheeler, had provided that. He had apparently—and Harlan was still not sure he had all this correctly—run away with some woman. Not only had he run away with her, they had stolen something as well, a relic of some sort as near as Harlan had been able to tell from what Neil had told him, something at any rate from a museum. It really was one of the oddest stories he had heard in some time, and Harlan Low had heard some odd stories. It went, more or less, with the position. A visiting Elder served about a dozen congregations at one time, roughly two thousand people, and was privy to all manner of confessions—some of it hopeless and sad, much of it unlooked-for and ridiculous.

Harlan picked up the bologna sandwich at his side and tested it once more for weight. At last he put it down still untasted and wished instead for another beer—a cold one. He noticed another set of headlights in the distance and hit his dimmer. The approaching lights did not reciprocate; they rushed toward him, high and bright out of the blackness of the desert. Harlan stared hard into their glare. As the truck passed he hit his horn, feeling the Ford rock in its wake. He gripped the wheel and tried to quiet the tic which had begun to pick up speed around his right eye, tried as well to imagine what in the world that poor dumb-ass boy had gotten himself into.

The orange neon of the A & W sign did funny things to the green of Delandra's car. Obadiah Wheeler looked across the resulting purplish tint on the hood and watched the last of the sun's light drain from a darkening sky. At last there was only one thin band of red—an airbrush job above the hills, and then that was gone too and he was alone with the night.

There was a greasy-looking burger sitting on a dark blue tray in front of him along with a large root beer in a frosted mug. He could not quite bring himself to start on the burger but watched instead as small drops of perspiration gathered on the mug, running slowly down its sides to form a wet ring on the paper place mat. The place mat had a map of the western half of the United States on it. There were small orange stars on the map to indicate the locations of various A & W franchises. Obadiah studied the map. He was waiting for Delandra to come back from the rest room. He sipped on the root beer and tried not to imagine that the man next to him in the blue pickup was staring at him.

The man, from what Obadiah could see of him, looked big. He had a large, round head and thick dark-rimmed glasses and every few seconds he seemed to look over in Obadiah's direction. He had pulled into the lot shortly after they had and had parked right next to them, in spite of the fact that there were a number of other spaces available. Obadiah stole another glance at him now. The man was shoving a burger into his face. Obadiah looked quickly away, out across the purple hood, and then back over his shoulder, along the length of the case which pressed against his seat. He would feel less uncomfortable, he thought, had Delandra been content to steal something smaller.

As it was, they had been forced to take the backseat out of the car, then to tie the trunk lid to the bumper to keep it from flopping up in the air and blocking visibility altogether. Inside, they had slid the front seat all the way forward and still the case was pushing against the backs, holding them forward just enough to make riding uncomfortable and driving worse. They had wrapped the case in a canvas tarp. But the Thing was too damn big to hide and the tarp was mainly to save them from having to look at whatever it was that lay looking back at them from beneath the glass.

There were apparently two possibilities: Sarge had made it or he had found it. Put another way, the Thing was either sacred or profane. It was difficult to know what to believe. Nor was it especially easy to reach a conclusion about what Delandra had told him they were going to be able to do with it—that there really was a buyer waiting for them out there beyond a dark horizon. But then, really, the events of the past few hours had been so extraordinary already, he was no longer sure how many of the old rules still applied. He was a man who, in a single stroke, had repudiated a lifetime, a system of belief, a family, friends. He was a man for whom the lines had been cut and he saw himself now—a tiny weightless figure from some sci-fi scenario, his arms flapping slowly about his head as he slipped into deep space. It was a grim picture and to contemplate it too deeply seemed to invite insanity. He had accordingly devised a kind of formula. Contemplation required time and rest. Speed and motion, on the other hand, did little to invite it. And so far he had been lucky; he had been able to keep things happening at such a pace that many of the implications of his actions were still behind him—scattered in his wake like the debris of a lost ship.

At rest the debris caught up. At rest he was inclined to review the series of events which had gotten him here, to look for the rational sorts of connections one always hopes for but which, in this particular case, seemed to be missing. This, he decided, was more like a dream. It had certainly begun with an image worthy of a dream—the dark-haired girl before the white metal wall, the day drained of color and shot through with a high white light born of heat and emptiness and vast distances. And when he did stop long enough to think about it, as he had just now, he did so with a kind of dumb wonder that any of it had happened at all. But it had and unlike that scene played out in the Pomona Hotel some forty-eight hours previously there were no missing parts; if he tried he could remember everything. He could remember the line of shadow drawn across the dusty hood of the Buick by the roof above the pumps. He could remember the crackling of the hot metal and the hiss of steam and he could remember what Neil Davis said to him when he thoughtlessly turned the key, killing the engine. Neil Davis had called him a fool and it was just about then that he'd seen the girl.

* * *

She would have been difficult to miss—black-and-white zebra stripes above red-and-yellow boots, a black mohair sweater and white-framed wraparound shades. There was a wraparound smile as well with too many teeth in it and which, beneath a desert sun, Obadiah found reminiscent of the grille belonging to a certain Buick Century the family had once owned. She was standing before a white metal wall above whose uppermost edge a red, white, and blue chevron floated lazily upon an empty sky. Her hair was black and thick, parted in the middle and just long enough to touch her shoulders. The face which held the smile was remarkable as well, Obadiah thought, not so much for what one would immediately call great beauty, though it was true she was not unattractive, but rather for the way in which it seemed to suggest something—an attitude perhaps, a certain level of audacity he could not recall having run across before and he knew almost at once, or at least later would believe that he had known, it was a face which might change his life.

He had gotten out of the car and walked toward her, up a steep gravel drive. The blackness of her hair, the black sweater, the black-and-white dress, the black-and-white sunglasses—it all seemed to vibrate before the stark white wall at her back as if she were the work of someone interested in optical illusions. He had meant to ask her about something but his mind seemed to have gone as blank as the sky above them. What in the end he asked her about was food. He asked her about breakfast and she had pointed out a place. They could see it from the station—a green-and-white sign with a name at the top like Mom's, or Pop's. It eluded him now. They had been standing side by side at the edge of the platform, looking back toward the town as Neil Davis reached them. "You're asking her about food?" Neil had asked of Obadiah. From the girl he wanted information. He wanted to know about mechanics and tools, the nearest Buick dealer. The girl had told him this was her uncle's department, that the man would not be down for another hour or so, at which point Neil had rested his hands on his hips and looked back toward the town. He had looked at the sisters waiting in the car and finally at Obadiah. "Well, crap," he said, "we may as well eat while we wait. The sisters are probably tired."

It was as Neil was walking back toward his car that the first in a series of really remarkable things happened. The girl had suddenly taken a step closer to Obadiah and covered his forearm with her hand. "Let me tell you something," she said. "That place down there is really a dump. Know what I mean? Stick around and I'll cook you some eggs."

Obadiah's face had widened in a foolish grin. At least he had assumed it to be foolish. He had walked back down the gravel drive to tell the others that he was going to hang around the station for a bit and they had looked at him in the way that Neil Davis had looked at him when he killed the engine.

Neil had stared at him longer than the others, an odd series of expressions dancing across his face. The dance had ended in disgust and they had indeed left him. He had watched them walk away, growing smaller as they descended the drive, and he had turned to the girl.

She was as tall as he was. When the wind pushed her dress back against her legs he could see that they were long and well muscled. And so, scarcely knowing what he was doing, knowing exactly what he was doing, he couldn't decide, he had followed her along a steep, rocky path toward a peculiar-looking shack, something built of wood and tin and corrugated fiber glass sheets which appeared to float above the hump of the hill in a sky burned white at the edges. "So tell me," she asked. They were by then at the door. "What's with the sister stuff?" She was pointing with her thumb toward the blue speck of Neil's car.

"What sister stuff is that?" Obadiah asked.

The girl had only looked at him and laughed. "See," she said, "you think like I do. I saw it right away. Come on in and I'll show you my rock collection."

Once, following her along the path, Obadiah had prayed for heart failure. Upon reaching the shack, however, and with one foot already in the door, it seemed clear to him this prayer would go unanswered. "I'd like that very much," he said. He had ducked beneath a chunk of wood the size of a railroad tie and the door—it was made of what appeared to be flattened oil drums—swung shut behind him with the kind of sound the pop-top makes on an aluminum beer can and the vast, colorless morning passed from sight.

The eggs, of course, had never materialized and what got cooked up in their stead was a mix of something Obadiah Wheeler had not experienced before. The one thing about it, however, when it was over, he did not have to wonder whether his virginity had been lost or saved. It had in fact been lost with a vengeance in back of a Chevron station in the middle of unassigned territory and he had been wide-awake through the whole thing. It was true there had been times when certain thoughts had intruded upon the moment. At one point he suddenly found himself imagining Neil Davis telephoning his father. At another he imagined doing so himself. Once, he had seen the face of Harlan Low. At last, however, it had all slipped away and there was only himself and Delandra Hummer, her face drawn up so close to his own, her sleepy, half-closed eyes and her warm breath on his neck. A twenty-two-year-old virgin was one of the funnier things she had run across in some time and she had laughed and scolded and whispered to him in a voice which was not unlike that first voice he had heard in the Pomona Hotel as soft and warm as any desert wind, and then she had guided him inside her and swung her legs up and over his shoulders, hooked a finger in his asshole and he had come so hard it was a kind of religious experience.

When it was over they sat around the shack and talked and Delandra got some beers out of the refrigerator. A couple of times she had gone back outside, telling him she had to check on something at the station. The first time she did it he was afraid she wasn't coming back. She was, after all, his first lover and it was not unlikely that he had done something wrong. The thought depressed him and he found that the idea of being alone terrified him. The alternatives he had once envisioned as mutant shapes seemed now to have found life in the desert. Through a crack in a sheet metal wall he saw what lived in unassigned territory—their bright, sluglike bodies awash in light, they crawled toward him from the desert floor, sticky snail trails of spent saliva smoking in their wake.

But she had come back and there was more beer and more talk and Obadiah, scarcely knowing what he was saying, had begun a ridiculously incoherent version of his life's story—just as if this person he barely knew would be interested. He told her what the sister stuff was about. He even told her what Special Service boys did. He told her about his deferment and his draft board. He tried to give her some indication of what the morning's activities were going to mean for him and in the same breath mentioned the possibility of his going to Canada to escape the shit which was bound to hit the fan. It was the first time he had actually expressed this idea verbally and he was quite taken aback by Delandra's response. She appeared to think it an excellent idea and before Obadiah stopped to think about it further himself, the two of them were talking it over just as if it were going to happen, just as if it made perfect sense that the two of them do it together.

And yet, somehow, even all the talk had not served to make it real, not for him. It was the kind of stuff you made plans out of when you were drunk. It had no weight—not even when Delandra said she had an idea about how they could raise the necessary money and Obadiah had begun to put his clothes on, just like he was going to do something about it. And later, after he had gotten his first look at the Mystery of the Mojave—which in itself was enough to detract from the reality of almost any situation—and they were wrestling the Thing into the back of Delandra's car, it hadn't seemed real even then. He still thought somehow that it was the booze, or the sex.

Actually, it wasn't until Delandra was seated behind the wheel and he was standing at the door, his hand upon the roof, that he realized what was coming down was indeed the real thing, that he was in the act of making a choice which would radically alter the rest of his life and he had for the first time considered the moment. It was, he imagined, the kind of moment which came for people with their fingers on the triggers, and for the first time that day everything seemed to grind to a halt, to achieve form and weight all at once so that it was in something like slow motion that he observed his own final move: his hand slipping from the heated metal of the roof, trailing as it dropped a tiny vaporous trail from the tip of each finger—as if each contained a miniature jet engine —something he did not imagine it was possible to see, until his hand had in fact reached the pitted chrome handle, had taken it into his grasp, and Delandra had whooped and banged on the wheel, put it in *D* for Drive and Obadiah had begun to appreciate the beauty of speed. The town had flown by them—a string of images, like frames off a scrap of film held to an open window: a clump of cactus, a desert museum, the white smudge of dust upon a turquoise sky. And it was only necessary to sit there to make it happen.

Obadiah was driving when they left the burger stand and he was certain the lights behind them belonged to the blue pickup. The truck, he believed, had followed them out of the parking lot and back onto the narrow highway. After a mile or so of staring into his rearview mirror he said as much to Delandra. Delandra jerked around in the seat to look out the back window. She never did anything slowly, Obadiah had noticed. If you told her to look at something, she would not just turn her head. She would swing her whole body around, and maybe bump into something in the process, or kick something with her boot. It was not that she was graceless. It was just that she seemed to have too much energy. It was like she had to keep looking for ways to throw some off. Obadiah was not ungrateful for this. It was her energy, he was certain, which fueled him now. When she swung back around it brought her face up close to his own and he could smell the burger and grilled onions on her breath. But it didn't matter. Her hair was loose and wild about her face—which appeared to him, by the poor light of the dashboard, to be slightly flushed. He felt flushed himself, a bit feverish. He guessed that he was feverish. Perhaps he was sick.

"Well, it could be the pickup," she said. "You can only go two ways out of that dump so it's fifty-fifty. Don't worry about it." She put her arm up over the back of his seat and he could feel her fingers on his shoulder. Her fingers were rather thick and strong for a girl—but nice, too, smooth tanned skin, short, clean nails. He liked feeling them on his shoulder. He liked the way she sat close by his side. Other girls had sat that way, on dates, if you wanted to call them that, but they had only been girls from the congregation and there had been nothing between them. This girl was his lover. It made all the difference. It made him different too. Or perhaps it made him the same. He had always been different; he had been raised to be. In the world but not of it. A pilgrim and a stranger. Now he had a lover and he was like the rest of them. It was a cause for both celebration and sadness.

"You've got to eat something sooner or later," she said. He had been turning down food since he'd met her. He had passed on lunch at a place called The Desert Inn and somehow he never had been able to get started on the A & W burger. Delandra had had a few bites of it, after finishing her own, then thrown the remainder at a sign. There was a six-pack of tall cans on the floor between her feet. She broke it open. "Let's drink them one at a time," she said. "And share. They'll stay colder."

He liked sharing with her. They passed the cold, sweating cans back and forth between them. He took long drinks and the beer burned in his throat, moving quickly to his head. "I don't know," he said after a time. He was looking into the rearview mirror. "I would feel better, I think, if I knew who that was, Delandra. I'm not kidding; that guy in the place was looking very weird."

"Well, shit," Delandra said. She shook her head. "You're a nervous boy, Obo. Why don't you just pull over and let him go by." She shot out a booted foot and hit the brakes. The car swung into a skid. They were going down the road sideways for a moment— Obadiah fighting the wheel, trying to remember if you went with it or against it. He jerked the wheel back in the direction of the skid, hit the gas, and the car popped back around, ran off the pavement and onto the shoulder, finally sliding to a stop in a shower of dust and sand. "Jesus Christ," Obadiah said, and killed the engine. The headlights drilled two holes into the night. The holes were pale yellow and filled with swirling clouds of dust. Delandra reached across his chest to kill the lights and everything went dark and quiet except for the sounds of their breathing and the popping of a hot engine.

Obadiah looked into the mirror. He could see those lights almost on top of them now. Suddenly a dark pickup shot past them and then hit its brakes. They could see the taillights come to a stop and what looked like the dark head of the driver turning to look back toward them. Obadiah remembered the large round head and thick glasses. Delandra still had one arm over his shoulders and he could feel her fingers digging into his flesh. He waited for back-up lights. The back-ups did not materialize, however, and suddenly the taillights were moving away from them once more, at last vanishing in the darkness.

"He just wondered if we were hurt," Delandra said.

Obadiah sat watching the empty road. The black, tortured shapes of several Joshua trees stood grouped near the side of the car. In places their branches were touched by moonlight and stood out like silver against the night sky. Obadiah looked into Delandra Hummer's face. "Don't be too sure," he said.

Delandra took a drink of beer. "Come on," she said. "Who would it be? There's nobody interested in this thing but you, me, a carload of niggers, and this fool I'm going to sell it to."

When Obadiah looked away he felt her teeth on his neck. "It's wired," she whispered. "Wait and see." And then her fingers were at his fly. When he looked at her she laughed. He tried crawling on top of her there in the front seat but got his feet tangled up in the wheel. They wound up stretched out on top of the case in back of the seats. "This glass is really thick," Delandra said. "Just do it slow and deep." Obadiah could feel her fingers back up under his shirt and her breath on his neck. He felt something give a bit beneath him. The movement was accompanied by the sound of cracking glass. He buried his face in her hair.

He didn't open his eyes until he'd come and when he did he found that a corner of the canvas tarp had been pulled back beneath them and that by the moonlight slicing in through the rear window above their heads he could see something beneath the glass—what looked to be the dull gleam of two yellow eyes staring up at him. When he saw it he kicked something with his foot and the trunk lid sprang up suddenly behind them. Delandra screamed and Obadiah fought to get his pants back up over his ass before someone's headlights could find it. He somehow wound up outside on all fours, crawling along a sandy shoulder—feeling that he was about to be sick once more while Delandra Hummer said something about roadside affairs and opened up on the Joshuas with the handgun she kept in the glove box.

Obadiah continued to crawl through the night. He couldn't decide if he was ill, insane, or just very drunk. What he knew for certain was that he was moving much too slowly and something was gaining ground—the enormity, perhaps, of what he had done. He had broken his parents' hearts. That was the worst part, he thought, about the kind of break he had made. It was not simply the wrestling with yourself, it was the people you hurt, the people who had given you love and yet were bound to see any wandering from the path as being somehow a rejection of that love. It occurred to him that this was not fair on their part, but there it was. Perhaps, he thought, this was after all the darkness outside—a dead spot in the soul, without equilibrium or pride, punctuated by gunshots and the dull gleam of monstrous eyes. Living on Bug House time. God have mercy.

Part of the trouble, it occurred to him, with the way he had been raised, was the odd blend of innocence and cynicism it fostered. The Friends had no problem with something like Vietnam. They'd known the score for some time now. The world, brother, was in the grasp of the Wicked One, and he guessed maybe he could not quite stop believing in that. His faith in a counterfeit world was quite strong. He accepted its imminent demise and believed it was earned. He had no quarrel with man's fall. It was somehow redemption and the straight and narrow he had stopped believing in. It didn't leave a lot to fall back on. He supposed he was not the first to contemplate this abyss—though that thought did little to comfort him now. He clutched at a handful of sand, hoping to calm the dry heaves which had taken him. He imagined once more the pink, sweating face of Bug House leering at him from an immense sky—the skin stretched tight from the scarring, the government-issue bridgework which allowed the mouth to sag in inappropriate places, the eyes glassy, red rimmed, a trifle wild. It was, he saw suddenly, the face that ordered the world. Not God or the devil. It was Bug House himself, the pudgy little son of a bitch. It was a kind of epiphany and he likened himself to Saul of Tarsus struck blind on the road to Damascus by the sight of his Savior. The immense face of Bug House, however, emitted no great radiance and rather than struck blind he found himself only slightly nauseous.

Delandra Hummer had put away the gun and taken up a red-faced Gibson Hummingbird. She was sitting on the passenger side of the seat with the door propped open and her legs stretched out in front of her so the moonlight could hit her boots. A simple three-chord progression wafted across the land. Obadiah imagined the softly glowing eyes of whatever it was they had stolen staring back at him from the glass-and-wood coffin. He imagined the eyes of the Mystery of the Mojave finding the Thorazine-blasted eyes of Bug House far above him and he felt himself gone weightless once more, strung like catgut between them. Delandra plucked the guitar and he himself was the sound—the waterfall of notes dissipating in the darkness. "Well Obo was a good old bo," Delandra composed in country twang. "But I don't know where he's been. Obo why don't you crawl on over and play with me. Obo why don't you crawl on over and we'll have a partee."

Obadiah lay on his stomach in the cool sand, little bits of gravel sticking to his face and hair. He rolled onto his back and looked

down the length of his body, across the tips of his shoes. He
watched Delandra Hummer at the open door of the Dodge. Her
song seemed to have driven his image of Bug House from the sky,
leaving only the night, and it occurred to him that he was, in spite
of everything, a lucky man. He thought about pulling himself
together and getting to his feet but he let the idea slide. He was
vaguely worried about scorpions and snakes but even that fear was
not enough to overcome the inertia of the moment. He called out
to Delandra across the tops of his shoes. "Delandra," he called, and
she stopped singing. He saw her turn in his direction though he
imagined he would be hard to see—given his distance from her
and his supine position. "What is it, Delandra? I mean, really.
What is that Thing?"

Delandra Hummer strummed a chord. "Beats me," she said.
"But I'll wager I can sell it."

W hen Rex found the Thing gone he had been
seized by something more than panic, by an
emotion as malign and ravenous as any he had
yet endured. In a cold sweat he had climbed the hill back of the
empty museum, boots sliding in the loose soil, a knot of white-hot
pain riding high in his chest. And there was nothing for it but to
run. And he had, driven by a dumb animal fear: fear of the men
who had threatened him, fear of a new and unspeakable emptiness at the center of his being. "You don't know what you've got till
it's gone," Rex said. By the dim light of his dashboard he could see
his miserable face reflected in the windshield of his father's truck
and it was to this flabby, translucent phantom that he occasionally
addressed himself. "Man's not stupid," he said, repeating what the
Indian had said to him. "Gracious no. Not this dumb suck butt. Not
Rex Hummer." The apparition grinned stupidly and Rex's words
came back to him like rain on a hard wind.

*     *     *

The men had been waiting for him in front of the bar, the two
black men, the Indian. They were driving a 1959 Cadillac de Ville.
The car was fire-engine red with white leather upholstery and so
bright it was hard to look at by the light of midmorning. There was
some kind of wooden chest riding lengthways in the backseat,
making it necessary for all four men to ride up front as they
returned to the museum.

It was a short, cramped ride and on the way the cadaverous
black man offered an explanation. "My boss runs a business out of
L.A.," the man told him. "I make trips all over and I buy things.
Take them back to the city. The Man owns a shop; he fixes them
up, sells them."

"Kind of an antiques dealer," Rex offered.

"That's it," the man said. "But it doesn't have to be antiques, just
something I think people will go for."

Rex had given this some thought. Somehow the man did not
look like what you would expect an antiques dealer to look like.

Later, in the musty gloom of the museum, the man told Rex he
believed his boss could use the Mystery of the Mojave. Knowing
what his people needed, that was the thing, he said, the key to
success. And it appeared the Creature would fit quite nicely at the
intersection of Pico and Sepulveda where a second cousin's eatery
—Monster Burgers by name—could use a gimmick. "Stand him
right there on the corner," the man said. "Put a double double
burger in his hand." At which point the Indian had laughed out
loud and the black man had offered Rex the absurd price of one
hundred and fifty dollars for the culmination of his father's life's
work.

They were, by this time, standing in the back room of the museum. The light, which had been so brilliant on the spines of the
ridges, was now weak and pale, the color of soured milk as it
spread across the wooden floor at their feet. "The Creature's not
for sale," Rex had told them.

The cadaverous Negro turned to look at his two companions.
"Thing's not for sale," he said. "Now ain't that about a gas." He
reached inside his coat and produced a white envelope. Inside the
envelope there was a yellowed piece of newsprint. "Then what's
this?" he asked. He passed the newsprint to Rex.

But Rex didn't have to read it to know what it was. It was one of
the ads Floyd had run when he first came out from Texas, when he
had decided something as useless as the Desert Museum ought to

be sold and had run a number of ads to that effect, without bothering to say anything about it to Rex. The ads said: "For sale: Sarge
Hummer's Desert Museum. Object of Mystery included." There
had been virtually no response at the time and when Rex had
confronted Floyd about it, telling him the museum was his and not
for sale, Floyd had only shrugged it off and said, "Suit yourself,"
and, as far as Rex knew, there had been no more ads.

"This is a year old," Rex said. "The Object of Mystery is not for
sale. None of it is."

"Thing's not for sale," the man said once more. "None of it is."
He treated this as if it were a source of some secret amusement.
"Well, fair enough," he said at last. "But I must tell you, at some
point the man I work for may want to see this for himself. He may
want to make you an offer."

The man had removed his dark glasses upon entering the museum and Rex now stood looking into a pair of deep black eyes. He
said nothing.

"Just so we understand each other," the man said. "The Thing
may not be for sale, but we were here first. You won't forget that.
You won't go moving it, or selling it to anyone else. Am I right? No
funky numbers on the part of y'all. You wouldn't do this poor
nigger wrong?"

But it was the Indian who had answered—whose answer Rex
was hearing still: " 'Course not," the Indian had said. And he had
clapped Rex once on the shoulder, slapping him with a large, flat
hand that felt to Rex like the backside of an iron skillet. "Man's not
dumb."

Lord no, not Rex Hummer. And after that they had left. Confused, Rex had followed them as far as the porch, where he
watched them walk back into the street. He had been told that it
should be possible for him, during certain hot days in the spring, to
see auras. Someone capable of seeing such things herself had told
him this. He had yet to see any but the thought occurred to him in
the empty museum that now might be the time. He saw nothing,
however, except the heat waves on the red metal of the car and
the men's dark suits, which were like holes in the morning. On the
opposite side of the road he had seen his sister. She was without an
aura as well—though this did not surprise him. From her he got
nothing more than the yellow-gray rooster tails of dust tossed by
her bootheels as she climbed the hill, looking, he thought, like
someone in a hurry.

Before the day was over he came to know what she had been in
a hurry about. She always had been a sneak and he guessed that

she had been spying on him, that quite probably she had heard everything that went down between him and the men, that from what was said she had gotten the idea that the Thing might be worth something and she had grown just desperate enough to steal it. And yet oddly enough his very first impulse was not toward rage but toward self-deprecation. He had in fact done what only hours before he had sworn not to. He had done a poor nigger boy wrong.

As the day wore on he saw of course that there was a good deal more to it. There was, for instance, for the first time in Rex Hummer's adult life, an empty museum. There was also a silent museum, for at some point it had come to him that for the first time since that night he and Delandra had snuck in to find their father's last version of the Thing, the peculiar sound failed to play in his head. And it was then, alone in the silence, that Rex had been set upon by something worse than fear.

And yet with this feeling had come another kind of revelation as well. In the time he'd spent alone with the Mystery of the Mojave, Rex had on occasion contemplated the possibility that this last version was not something Sarge Hummer had made. It was a repugnant possibility. He preferred to think of the Creature as Sarge Hummer's final word to a world which had paid him no mind. What he saw now, in the terrible silence of the museum, was that none of that really made any difference. It was what it was and there was nothing more to say. And now a task lay before him. He could not say precisely what the task was. It seemed to hover there, just beyond the range of his vision—a shape in a sandstorm. And yet to see the shape clearly would be to understand the purpose for which he had remained in the desert, for which he had been forged in her enormous heat. And he knew it was time to see the woman.

It was where he was going now, to see the woman. He drove on little white pills and coffee laced with Old Crow and the resulting combination lit the landscape perfectly. He had, after all, to stay sharp. There was no way around it. Signs and portents would guide him now. This understanding had manifested itself to him on a desert highway. So far the closest thing to a sign he had seen was a dead owl, but he was not without hope, even if what lay before him was nothing more than a huge empty hole, as cold, as black, as silent as space.

It was well past midnight when Harlan Low found the place Neil had described to him. It wasn't much of a place. He took a paved road from the interstate, which soon turned to gravel, then to smooth, hard-packed dirt as it entered the town. The road bisected a pair of dark, rocky ridges, running in a gently curving line at their base. Above the road, scattered along the high ground, a sorry collection of trailers, stores, and mining shacks were visible in the moonlight.

Harlan drove the length of the road. He started at the museum and ended at the bar. He saw the blue roof of Neil's car through the windows of the Chevron, but no sign of his people. He decided to stop at the bar and ask. He decided a cold beer wouldn't hurt anything, either.

He knew the bar had been a mistake when the bartender, a large, belligerent man sporting tattoos and a greasy black flattop, correctly identified him as one of the Bible thumpers who had robbed the local museum. "I suppose," the man said to him, "you'll want to make restitution." He turned to grin at a number of his friends who had arranged themselves at the bar. The men wore T-shirts and trucker's hats. They appeared to be in uniform. One, a man with a gap-toothed grin and the face of an idiot, said something Harlan could not quite catch. It sounded like fuckin' A.

"I will want to know more about it," Harlan said. "I understand the boy left with the sister of the owner. I was hoping I might speak with him."

"No can do," the bartender said. "Owner's gone already. Went out after them himself. Had the gun in the rack too, didn't he, Jim?"

"You bet," someone replied.

The bartender seemed to find this amusing. Harlan was not sure about how much of it to believe, but it was clear no one was going to tell him anything else.

"Maybe," the bartender said—he appeared to be giving it some thought. "I could just figure in what you people owe with what you already owe for that car down there."

Harlan was leaning slightly forward, his hands flat on the bar. It was the position he had assumed upon entering and he found that the wood was suddenly slick with sweat beneath his palms. "I thought maybe you already had," he said, and then regretted it right away. He was, after all, a long way from home. He had been more than a year now without a beating and he was not looking for another. The situation had the look of something both ludicrous and potentially dangerous. The trick was in not making it more of either.

The bartender put down his towel. "You trying to be funny?" he asked.

"No," Harlan told him, "I wasn't." He had begun to look for the the door. He wondered if anyone would try to stop him. He felt pissed off and foolish by turns. And why, he asked himself, hadn't Neil Davis been smart enough to keep his mouth shut in front of some ape like the one before him? The question made him angry. The anger was accompanied by guilt.

The bartender grinned at the man with the space between his front teeth. "What'd I tell you?" he said. He looked once more at Harlan. "I seem to recall the good book having something to say about liars and thieves."

"It says they will not inherit the Kingdom of God."

The bartender continued to grin. "Looks like your boy lost his spot."

Harlan forced a grin of his own. He looked toward the yellow light in the window and the black slice of bad road beyond it. He lifted his hands from the bar. "I'm sure we'll see each other again," he said. He turned slowly. The man closest to him stepped to one side. Harlan fixed the door in his sight and started toward it.

"Hey, I'm sure of that my ownself," the bartender called after him.


Harlan had grown up in The Way. His father had picked up on the movement and the family had followed suit. He had seen earlier, more radical days when the brothers had not been content with just knocking on doors but had gone looking for all of the confrontations they could get. They had often spent Sunday mornings picketing churches with signs which said things like RELIGION IS A SNARE AND A RACKET. They had staged their own parades, using sound cars and signs. Harlan and his brother had always managed to stay at the back of the parades just in case there were any fistfights to be had with hecklers.

It was what he thought about as he swung the car around in front of the bar and headed back down the road. He also thought about something he had recently read in one of the magazines. It was something one of the missionaries had said about the incident at Gbaranga—how for an entire night she had listened to the sounds of a brother being beaten, how the blows had echoed across a dark compound as loudly as the barking of a gun, and how when the brother was not receiving abuse he had led a number of the other brothers in song. Harlan Low had been the brother and when he read about it he thought of something he'd once heard a boxer say about seeing himself knocked out in the film of a fight. The guy said he didn't get scared until he saw the pictures. What Harlan thought of now when he thought of that night was what the woman had said about it. He found that what she said scared him. He couldn't remember anything at all about the song.

He drove slowly along the road. Africa had left him both gun-shy and quick to anger. It was a ridiculous combination. He found that the man in the bar reminded him of a certain Liberian soldier and he felt it was important to remind himself that rearranging the man's face with the toe of his shoe would not bring lasting happiness. He reminded himself as well that the parades and fistfights had taken place a long time ago, that he had been a good fifty pounds lighter in those days and not nearly as smart as he was now.

He was still thinking this over when, on his second pass of the Desert Museum, he noticed a shadowy figure standing on the porch waving its arms.

"Had an idea that might be you," Neil said as he approached the car.

Harlan sat behind the wheel, his window open to the night air. He found the sight of Neil Davis produced in him a certain weariness.

"We found it open," Neil said, jerking his thumb in the direction of the museum. "Seemed like as good a place as any to spend the night." Then he shrugged. "No hotels in this burg," he said.

In spite of the weariness Harlan was not ready for sleep. Nor was he eager for conversation. After encouraging the others to turn in he returned to the porch. He sat alone on a rough plank step and stared into the darkness of the road. He was worried that the men in the bar might get drunk enough to work themselves into something and come looking for them. It was the kind of thought he entertained more readily now than at any time in the past. That he should entertain it at all made him angry. The anger did nothing to lessen the fear, however. It was just something he had come home with.

He sat on the porch until the bar had closed and he had seen the headlights of half a dozen pickups bounce down the wash and turn toward the highway. He continued to sit on the porch. He listened to a pack of dogs yapping somewhere at the north end of town. Finally he got up and went inside. He decided to see what he could of the place Obadiah Wheeler had seen fit to rob.

The building was without artificial light but there were long, empty windows along both walls and with the shutters thrown open Harlan found the moonlight sufficient for obtaining a general idea of what there was to see.

There wasn't, it first appeared, a lot. Neil had arranged some long, narrow boxes on the floor of the main room upon which the others now lay sleeping. In the moonlight Harlan found that the sleeping figures reminded him of corpses in a makeshift morgue. He walked quietly around them. He passed through two smaller rooms, both empty save for a number of empty glass cases, before arriving at a third room above whose entrance someone had nailed a piece of wood with the words THE THING written on it. The Thing, apparently, was what Wheeler and the local girl had taken and the room was indeed empty. Harlan stood for several minutes at its center, in the darkness. He was trying to figure it but found he hadn't enough to go on. An affair of the heart, perhaps. Harlan had given in to an affair of the heart once. He had been eighteen years old at the time. He had run away with a neighbor's wife and they had gone to Kansas City. His father and the woman's husband had come looking for them. It was an absurd story. At least it seemed absurd to Harlan. The woman's husband wound up pulling a gun on him in their apartment. He wasn't very good with it and Harlan had taken it away from him. Then his father, who had been looking in another room downstairs, had come up and Harlan had fought his father. He could have taken his father but he hadn't.

In the end—not the night of the fight, but in the end—Harlan had done what his father wanted—he had gone home. What he had found at the time was that living with the woman was doing something to him. When he had left with her he understood he was breaking a rule. But he thought it was only one rule; he had thought that he could violate one principle and yet still live by the others, and what he found was that it didn't work that way. Later he believed he had learned the truth of Paul's words when he said that God's Word was like a mirror in which a man might see not only the man he was but the man he might be, and he came to understand that the proper business of life was trying to do something about the difference. It was the revelation which had pointed him down the road he still followed. It was about keeping honest and as near as Harlan could tell, obedience to the Word was the only thing that worked.

Harlan went to an open window. The night air was cool against his face. He could see a bit of the road and above that the ridge which led to the interstate. Above the ridge the sky was filled with stars. He tried for a moment to imagine what the girl the Wheeler boy had run off with might be like. Neil Davis had described her as a common whore. The curious thing about that was, it was more or less the way Harlan's father had once described the woman Harlan had run away with. There were times when it suited him to imagine he no longer remembered the woman's name, but he did. He continued to stand at the window, to examine the huge black shape the ridge had cut from the starlit sky. The woman's name was Virginia. At one point during the summer of his eighteenth birthday she had given him a record as a present—the Paul Whiteman recording of "I'm Coming, Virginia." It was supposed to be a joke, something she had picked up in a secondhand store. The thing turned out to be something of a collector's item, however, as it contained a cornet solo by Bix Beiderbecke and there were times now, when Harlan thought of her, when he imagined he could still hear the pure tone of Bix's horn as it filled a cheap two-room flat complete with bamboo shades and colored lights, windows open upon hot summer nights.

The woman had died some ten years later, or so Harlan had been told, in a Memphis hospital of cirrhosis of the liver—an ugly death and what he supposed was the point of the story, what one ought to remember about the pursuit of empty pleasures. That he remembered more, that the cheap trappings of a romantic sentimentality still clung to the episode like the scent of a dime store perfume, was a nagging source of irritation. That the trappings were capable, on occasion, of generating actual tears, was worse than irritating. But then he supposed there was a point in all of that too. It had something to do with the stuff choices were made of. Though not a subject he ordinarily talked about, it was, he thought, under the circumstances, something he might take up with a certain Obadiah Wheeler, should the opportunity present itself.

There was one more room in the building. It was a small, windowless room stuck to the back of the one which had housed the Thing and when Harlan pushed through the door and stepped inside he found himself in complete darkness.

He stood for a moment just inside the door, fishing in his pocket for the penlight he had recently attached to his key chain. The penlight had been a gift from a brother who worked for a big brake outfit and got penlights with their advertising on them for free. It was exactly the useless kind of thing people were always giving him. When he had found it he pushed its frail light around the room—a workroom, it appeared. There were benches and a long table and a number of tools lying about as if no one had picked anything up in a long time. In one corner of the room there were what looked to be a stack of fiber glass castings.

The castings were covered with a fine white dust and he was trying to get a better look at them when he bumped something with his head. Stepping backward and tilting his light he found himself face-to-face with a large medallion which had been fixed to a beam above him. His bumping it had set it in motion and the thing now swung easily at the end of a thin golden chain. The piece was made up of two parts, a circle and a hand.

He saw right away there was something wrong with the hand. In a moment he saw what it was. The hand had six fingers. A closer inspection revealed that the ring which circled the hand had been filled with eyes—they had been etched into the surface of the metal. He took a step backward and bumped a sawhorse. This made him jump and he jammed his elbow into a vise. He managed, however, to keep the medallion fixed in the beam of his light, as though he were worried about it going somewhere on him. In fact, the thing had spooked him. Nor did the unpleasant sensation show signs of dissipating as he continued to stand there, watching the object shorten its arcs within the circle of light he had made for it. The problem was, this was not the first time Harlan had run across such an object. He had seen something very much like it on two other occasions. The last was in Los Angeles. The hand had been fashioned of neon and he had glimpsed it one evening from the Santa Monica Freeway. The brother he was riding with believed the building beneath the hand to be some sort of temple. There had been no circle around the neon hand, but there had been a sixth finger. There had also been eyes. The hand was full of them. But this was the second time and it was hard to say how much attention he would have paid it had it not been for the first.

The first was in Africa, in a slum on the outskirts of Monrovia where he and another elder had gone to visit the sick child of a newly converted couple. The couple believed their son had been cursed in some way. It was not an uncommon reaction. The land there was rife with secret societies, fetishes, and devils.

Harlan had squatted with the others, beneath a tin roof, between walls of bamboo and corrugated iron. It seemed to be a part of the city to which the sea breeze was unable to penetrate. The air was hot and foul, heavy with the scents of sickness and burning garbage. A search had begun for what the couple believed to be the responsible object. Clothes were laid out and gone through, boxes emptied, furniture moved. At last, buried in a shallow hole just beneath the boy's bed, they discovered a small wooden hand. The piece had been carved from a dark wood then covered with a thin coat of white paint. There was a wooden ring attached to the wrist. The hand itself had six fingers with an eye at the tip of each. It was agreed that the elders would take the object outside and destroy it. And Harlan had begun to do just that, was in the act of leaning forward to pick the thing up, when it occurred to him that he could no longer breathe. It was as if some outside force was preventing it. Sweat had broken upon his forehead. The warm, fetid air had closed in upon him in such a way that he felt certain he would faint and it had seemed to him as if something, the night itself perhaps, in the black rectangle of an open doorway, had assumed some form, as if it were the shadow of something else. He could not say how long this condition lasted. He did not faint. He took the hand in an abrupt movement of his own and lurched into the street, where he managed to toss the thing into the fire of a burning oil drum attended by some ravaged beggar.

Harlan turned off his penlight and went back into the museum. But he didn't sleep there. He told himself it was because he wanted to be alone. He returned to the lot. He crawled into the backseat of his rental car and, using his jacket as a pillow, did his best to get comfortable.

He had never spoken to anyone about how he had felt that night in Monrovia. None of those present had said anything to suggest his actions were out of the ordinary. Perhaps he only imagined that he had lurched into the street. Perhaps he had simply walked. Perhaps the feeling was nothing more than physiological, the re-

sult of too rich a meal and foul air, the muddy coffee it was necessary to drink there in order to appear polite. When he returned
home that night he had found his wife already in bed, asleep. But
then he doubted he would have mentioned it to her anyway,
fearing that it would only upset her. Instead he had made himself a
drink and gone out onto the narrow balcony which had bordered
their room to watch the starlight above the sea, to decide at last
that it must have been the food, to warn himself that in the future
he would have to be more careful.

There had been no comparable sensations the night he saw the
neon hand at the side of the freeway. Nor had any returned to
haunt him in the museum. So why, he wondered, was he here now,
bent like a horseshoe in the back of a rented Ford instead of
stretched out inside with the others? The last he had heard of the
Liberian boy was that he had risen on the morning following the
destruction of the hand, fully recovered. It did give one pause. An
exorcism or a bad case of indigestion? "We have a wrestling," Paul
had said, "not against blood and flesh, but against governments,
against the authorities, against the world rulers of this darkness,
against the wicked spirit forces in the heavenly places." At the side
of Sarge Hummer's Desert Museum, Harlan Low did what he had
done that night in Africa, having found his wife in bed and himself
alone. He watched the stars and he slept.

When Harlan woke the stars were gone and
there was sunlight coming in through the glass
and making him hot. There was a bad taste in
his mouth and his back hurt. He climbed out of the Ford and stood
beside it. He put his hands on his hips and began working his torso
in circles, first clockwise, then counterclockwise.

Doing the exercises he stared down on the paunch around his
middle. The roll of fat was still fairly new and still a source of
embarrassment. Beneath the paunch was a wrinkled pair of char-
coal-brown slacks and a dusty pair of new wing-tip shoes. Harlan

felt fat, sloppy, and out of shape. He realized that if he dwelt on this too long it would only depress him. He promised himself a better exercise program when he got back to the city, but then doubted the resolve as soon as he had made it and that depressed him as well. Harlan had grown up on a farm. He had always been a reasonably good athlete and he had always kept in reasonably good shape. The image of himself as an overweight, middle-aged man in baggy suits did not sit well and yet of late it was what he felt himself sliding toward. That before the morning was over he should have to confront the man he had met in the bar about Neil's car did not sit well, either, and yet there it was. The one prospect seemed to aggravate the other. What was he going to do anyway? Walk up the hill looking fat and sloppy and appeal to the man's sense of fair play? He looked across the street where the Chevron sat on the ridge—a low rectangle of gleaming white metal before a flat blue sky.

He was still looking at the station and considering his position when he heard the others arrive on the wooden porch of the museum. He turned in time to greet Panama Allen as she came down the steps.

"Morning," Panama said. "Some fix, isn't it?"

"Yes," Harlan said, "it is."

They crossed the street together, Harlan slightly ahead of the others. He felt absurdly like the leader of something. The man he had spoken to at the bar was there to meet them. Harlan could see him in the drive as they made their way up the slight incline. Behind him Harlan could see the pale blue hood of Neil's car gleaming in the sunlight.

The mechanic met them at the point where the incline flattened back out into a gravel drive which circled the pumps. "What can I do for you?" the mechanic asked. He was dressed in a greasy pair of coveralls, work boots, and a T-shirt. There was a small white oval sewn onto the front of the coveralls with the name FLOYD in red letters on the inside. The man's arms were thick and hairy and on each forearm there was a tattoo. On one arm there was a heart with a dagger through it, on the other a Betty Boop with a name below it which Harlan could not read.

Neil started to say something but Harlan cut him off. "My friend here says you won't take his check," Harlan heard himself saying. He was aware of how it sounded but the words seemed to slip out under some power of their own. He was aware, too, of the others

standing behind them. When he tried to look back in their direction, however, he was blinded by the morning sun and could not
see their faces. He was able to imagine them, though. They would
look blank and trusting—the faces of small children.

"That's right," Harlan heard Floyd say in answer to his question.
"I don't take checks from strangers." Behind him, Harlan could
hear Neil's shoes on the pavement. He felt a hand on his sleeve. "I
was thinking," Neil said, his voice just above a whisper. "With the
rented car, we could drive back to the nearest town and find a
bank. We . . ." There was something in the tone of Neil's voice
which Harlan found difficult to bear. He raised a hand, cutting the
brother off. When he spoke it was to make the voice go away.
"He'll take your check," Harlan said.

The mechanic, who had turned his back to them and set about
unlocking another door, suddenly stopped what he was doing and
turned to face them once more. "Say what?" he asked.

"The check's good," Harlan said. He was trying to sort things
out, to think on his feet. But for some reason it wasn't working and
he found himself somewhat astounded at the speed with which the
thing was turning to shit—it was as if he had absentmindedly
wandered into the stuff and was now unable to turn around and
waddle back out. "I can vouch for it," he said at last. It was of
course a ridiculous thing to say and he wondered what it was,
exactly, that had gone wrong. A man who cannot control his
tongue, he thought, is like a ship without a rudder: James 3:4.

"And who the hell are you?" Floyd asked.

"He's a minister," Panama Allen said, her voice issuing from the
morning light. Harlan's first instinct was to cringe, his second was
to giggle. The situation was worthy of a schoolyard. At Harlan's
side Neil Davis looked as if he was about to cry. Patience, Harlan
thought, and yet even as the word took shape in his mind he
grasped the problem. The problem was that on this morning in
spring, on the edge of a town which, as near as he could tell, no one
had thought enough of to name, his was gone. Somewhere between that compound in Gbaranga and the white heart of the
Mojave, between the deportation hearing and the sniveling voice
of reason, the stuff had been used up. The tank was empty. It was
that simple. You could suck as hard as you wanted to on the siphon-
ing hose. You could rock the car. The lousy tank was dry as a bone.

"If I want a nigger's advice, I'll ask for it," the mechanic said. His
voice seemed to come from an immense distance.

Harlan almost laughed. It was a damn dream. He squeezed the
bridge of his nose between a thumb and forefinger, wondering for

one brief moment as he did so if there was not still some way out. At which point Bianca Allen spoke up at his side and he understood the play was no longer his.

"Honky motherfucker" was what Bianca said.

Floyd Hummer grinned and dropped the rag with which he had begun to clean his hands while Harlan Low, moving as he might had it in fact been a dream, let fall the sharkskin sport coat he had till now carried slung over one shoulder. He feinted with a left hand he had not raised in violence in twenty years and followed the feint with a straight right. He was hoping to catch Floyd in the Adam's apple. It was a serious punch.

Unfortunately Floyd moved a bit and the blow caught him more on the collarbone than on the throat. It probably hurt. It might have knocked a smaller man down. It knocked Floyd backward and into a set of red metal shelves set on casters. With Floyd leaning on it, the drawers rolled back and crashed into the wall with a loud metallic thud. Floyd grunted, reached blindly into the top of the drawers, and came out swinging a long set of pliers designed for removing oil filters. Harlan would have liked to follow Floyd to the wall, possibly planting a wing-tip in his scrotum, but the wing-tips seemed to have other ideas and he was having a terrible time with traction. The shoes were still fairly new and the leather soles slipped wildly beneath him. It was, he supposed, no less than he deserved. He did, however, manage some forward momentum in Floyd's direction and got there just in time to catch a wild hacking swing with the pliers on his forearm. There was a bright flash of pain which seemed to run in both directions along his arm as his hand went numb. But he continued to press. He watched the fingers of his left hand wrap themselves around Floyd's wrist. He got his right hand to the inside of Floyd's left arm, grabbed a handful of T-shirt, some of the coveralls, and drove his head into Floyd's face. He brought his knee up at about the same time, hoping to catch Floyd in the groin, but caught instead what felt to be the metal edge of an open drawer. He felt the steel corner tear into his slacks and the skin beneath. He was aware of the warm trickle of blood down one leg.

Floyd pushed off the cabinet and for several moments the two men danced about the concrete floor like a pair of crippled dinosaurs. Stray coffee cups, someone's windshield, the antenna on Neil's Buick, all disappeared in their wake. Harlan was still fighting for traction while Floyd was managing a series of rabbit punches with the grip end of the pliers behind Harlan's left ear. At last Harlan was able to twist Floyd's wrist until he heard the pliers hit the floor. He dropped his head to Floyd's chest, dropped both hands and punched as hard as he could, one, two, on Floyd's ribs, one, two just beneath them, and then upstairs, hooking hard to Floyd's head and that was just about it. Harlan Low was out of something for the second time that morning and Floyd was still in front of him.

Harlan feared for a moment that he might go down without even being hit. His lungs burned and his throat ached. His head throbbed. The colors seemed to have drained from the room so that he was seeing in black and white. Floyd did not bother to pick up the pliers. He just set himself and swung—a great roundhouse right which exploded on Harlan's jaw. Harlan saw it coming a mile away and wished like hell he could have moved.

It was, as near as he could remember, the first time anyone had ever knocked him off his feet with his fists. He was considering some method of regaining them when Floyd put a work boot into his ribs and followed it with another to the side of his head. Harlan Low rolled onto his side, groaning, reminding himself of a beached whale he'd once seen near Cabo San Lucas. He was hurt and horribly disgusted. He was aware of the terrible spectacle he had made, and for the first time that morning he was scared. Floyd Hummer had grabbed a drawer full of tools. He was holding the whole mess over his head and Harlan Low was beginning to think about serious bodily harm—the kind of stuff you tried to live with when it was over—knowing every time you tried to walk that you had done it yourself, that you really had been stupid enough to pick a fight you never stood a chance in, that there really had been murder in your heart. Nor would it, he supposed, prove inspirational for those present—an incident not to be reported in the pages of the *Kingdom Progress Bulletin.*

His vision, which had already gone to black and white, now seemed to switch to slow motion as well. He watched stupidly from the floor as Floyd lumbered toward him, the metal drawer held above his head. The moment had just about arrived, when Harlan saw something moving quickly among the shadows. He saw one bright slash of color in the midst of gray—a kind of electric pink—and understood that it was Bianca Allen. She had gotten her hands on what looked to be some kind of jack handle and she was winding up with it.

She caught the mechanic in the side, just below the rib cage but with the end of the handle curved round, digging up and into his solar plexus. Floyd stumbled forward and turned the shelf. Tools rained in front of him—a silver shower glittering in the sunlight which filtered through an open door—and Harlan understood as well that he had been granted one last chance. He reached blindly behind himself, grabbed something cold and hard, and pulled himself to his feet. Floyd stood looking at him, the empty drawer hanging from one arm, a peculiar expression on his big square face. Harlan came a half step forward and kicked him in the groin. Floyd grunted and went to one knee. Harlan hooked hard to the temple and Floyd pitched forward, facedown, over the racks. It was a filthy business, Harlan thought. He staggered outside into the sunlight and puked on the gravel drive, where, as if to add to his already considerable chagrin, there was a car pulling into the pumps at just that moment. He was aware of a woman staring at him from the passenger-side window. The woman wore too much makeup and fake black hair. But he didn't have long to appreciate the sight. Apparently the driver had decided to look for a more reasonable place to buy gasoline, and the car, which had slowed, now picked up speed once more.

It slipped back down the hill to vanish in the sunlight and Harlan was left on his knees at the edge of the pumps with nothing to look at besides Sarge Hummer's Desert Museum on the far side of the road, and nothing to think about except what he had found there, swinging in the shadows. Thinking of that, he thought of something else as well. It was something from a book, a spy novel, from a period in which he had still permitted himself the indulgence. It was something he believed Goldfinger had once said to James Bond: "Once is happenstance," it went. "Twice is coincidence. Three times, Mr. Bond, is enemy action." For a moment he found himself pleased in a simpleminded way for having remembered such a thing. The moment passed quickly. What it left him with was particularly unpleasant.

# III

---

*You stay out here long enough,*
*you start to hear things. You*
*start to see things too.*
—a desert resident
*It Came From Outer Space*

Obadiah and Delandra spent two nights in a small motel on the outskirts of Baker. The motel was of the old motor-court variety. The buildings were of pink stucco with bright green doors and there was a green plaster cactus in front of each room. Inside each room there were two small rectangular paintings of the desert. Obadiah knew about the paintings because he had spent a fair amount of time pacing the gravel drive which looped through the court, had glimpsed the interiors of rooms not his own. Delandra had spent a fair amount of time at a phone booth in the parking lot of the liquor store across the street. From the telephone booth she had been able to watch Obadiah pacing the gravel lot. She had begun to worry about him. He still had not eaten and had taken to spending inordinate amounts of time contemplating the Mystery of the Mojave. As she leaned against the glass wall of the booth she had watched him stop with each round to stare into the back of the car. Later, when she asked him about it, he would only say that he was checking on the cargo. When Obadiah asked Delandra what she was doing on the phone, she would only say she was putting things together.

On the morning of the second day they went to a store in town and Obadiah bought some new clothes—he had till now been wearing the powder-blue slacks and Madras sport coat he'd left Pomona in. He bought a pair of Levi's jeans and two western shirts, also a cheap pair of tennis shoes. He changed in the front seat of the car, in the parking lot of the store, at which point, things apparently having been put together to Delandra's satisfaction, they purchased a six-pack and left town.


Baker was somewhere behind them now with the sun filling up the windshield and burning the last delicate colors of sunrise from the morning. Obadiah was growing accustomed to the lighting. In the morning and evening there were what seemed to be colored mists in the hollows of the ridges, across the bottoms of the salt flats and dry washes—mists of amber and ashes of rose, colors that ran to violets and blues. In the light of midday, however, the delicate hues vanished in the heat, replaced by shades of tan and gray, chalky whites and yellows. The mists, if in fact there were such things, gave way to another variety of aqueous illusion—the water mirages upon whose surfaces the tans and grays repeated themselves in silvery splendor.

It was a display which could, Obadiah had found, be particularly hard on the hungover—a club he seemed lately to have found a home in. He adjusted the sun visor before him accordingly. He dug Delandra's spare set of white-rimmed sunglasses from the glovebox and wrenched a fresh beer from the plastic ring which bound it to the others. He drank quickly, squirming in his seat, looking for a way to get comfortable, though experience told him there wasn't one. The new clothes didn't help. The shirt felt stiff and scratchy, as did the jeans. At last he gave up, trusting the proper amount of beer would do the trick. He drank with his eyes closed, the morning slipping by unseen beyond an open window, and he didn't open them again until he heard Delandra bitching about the bikers.

They had, at some point during the last night in town, been joined there by an invasion of motorcycles. The bikes were big, stock Harleys with all manner of machinery attached—windshields, roll bars, saddlebags, running lights, long, curving antennas that whistled in the wind. The riders seemed to come in pairs. They were middle-aged or older and on the backs of their matching leather jackets were names like John and Peggy, Ray and Rayanne, Pilot and Co-Pilot. Obadiah and Delandra had seen them earlier, around town, and now it looked as if they had caught them on the road. They were strung out for what looked to be about a mile and moving at about fifty miles an hour. Delandra had the Dart up to about eighty and she wasn't the kind of girl who liked to be slowed down.

"God damn it," she said. She hit her horn and moved out to pass the whole line. She got it up to ninety and she was cutting it pretty close. A couple of people yelled at them as they sped past. Obadiah slid down a bit in his seat. He wrapped his hands tightly about the beer can resting upon his chest and tried to imagine what kind of picture the two of them made, a pair of lunatics in matching sunglasses, pushed as close to the dash as they could get in a battered Dodge doing service as a hearse. "You could slow down a little," he suggested.

"These dumb shits," Delandra said, "will run every restaurant on the road out of food if we don't beat them to it." Obadiah turned in time to see one old man shout something at them—his face was all teeth and dark glasses. Obadiah grinned and waved. Delandra cut the Dart back into the right lane, forcing the man to swerve out of the middle of his lane and toward the shoulder. Delandra moved dangerously close to the shoulder herself before swinging them back on line. A mile or so down the road they came to a fork and Delandra swerved to the right, her rear tires catching a bit of the shoulder. Obadiah opened a fresh beer. "You know you really are the worst driver I've ever seen," he said.

"You love it and you know it," Delandra told him.


An hour or so later they came upon a settlement not unlike the junction—a collection of widely spaced shacks and trailers, their backs to a ridge of iron-colored stone at whose base had collected great white drifts of sand. The surface of the sand had been left rippled by the wind—perfect curving lines spaced at regular intervals as if the whole ridge had somehow been thrust down into a liquid earth.

Delandra swung the Dart off the road, parking before a small house bookended by a pair of railroad cars. The cars were in fact connected to the house, replacing its north and south walls. The entire structure had been painted a garish shade of yellow, trimmed in pink and green. An elaborate hand-painted sign running the length of the house's roof identified the building as FLO'S RAILROAD CAFE.

"I'm going to buy you something to eat," Delandra said, "and then I'm going to watch you eat it."

They went inside where it was cool and empty and Delandra bought him something called the Railroad Platter, and she did watch him eat it—at least she watched him eat half of it, which was just about as long as she could sit still in one place, and then she started looking around for a phone. There wasn't a pay phone but she finally pestered the old woman who served them into letting her use the one in the kitchen.

She was gone for some time and Obadiah, having done what he could with the Railroad Platter—the original weight of which he had placed at about six pounds—decided to pay the bill and go outside to have a look at the cargo.

It was a brilliant late morning with the air sharp and dry and dead still so that the sound of his new tennis shoes sinking into the sand beneath him seemed abnormally loud. Behind the restaurant the dark iron-colored ridge was like the broken blade of a knife against a pale, luminous sky.

The cargo was secure. Obadiah decided to crawl in anyway for a closer look. He went back on his haunches and turned a bit of the tarp so he could see the face. The Thing lay looking back at him from the gloom of its coffin. Sometimes he felt its eyes were following the movements of his. It really was the damndest thing he had ever seen. And he had examined it from all angles. Once when he was alone with it, he had even lifted the lid and tried rolling the Creature onto its side so he could see the back. The back looked like the front.

He was willing, if only because the alternatives still seemed at this point too farfetched, to accept Delandra's banal proposal that her father had built it out of junk. Still, there was something about it which seemed to defy this logic. Looking at the Creature made him feel something. He couldn't say it any other way than that and occasionally, trying to imagine what dark flower of the soul had opened to its touch, he would try as well to imagine something of the man responsible.

He would try to imagine him out there in his shed, building and discarding—to the ultimate exclusion of all else, as Delandra had said he had done. When he tried to imagine Sarge physically, however, to put a face, even if only in his own imagination, to the name, the only face he could come up with was that of his own father, which was rather long and narrow, punctuated by a pair of intense green eyes and capped by a patch of thinning light brown hair. Obadiah's father had spent half of his life on the porches of his neighbors, perfecting his door-to-door presentation—if not to the exclusion of all else, at least to the exclusion of a good deal—and he had, on more occasions than Obadiah cared to remember, taken the boy with him—this while Obadiah was still too young to have a presentation of his own—so that Obadiah sometimes recalled this part of his childhood as a kind of pastiche of porches and voices, of half-remembered faces and fragments of sensory perceptions: a certain slant of sunlight upon his face, an odd-shaped chunk of sky caught between bright stuccoed walls. And, of course, there were the words—fragments of scriptural debate. They rang now as a kind of litany in his mind: In the beginning was the Word and the Word was a god—not God, but a god. And while it is true that the original text did not make use of the definite article, the grammatical construction nevertheless implies its use, as in Acts 28:6, where Paul, bitten by a snake but unharmed, is spoken of as a god. . . . It was a shame, he thought, that his faith had failed him, leaving these things in his head—chains of Scripture aimed at everything from establishing the continuance of the seventh creative cycle, to debunking hellfire and the Trinity. They lay there now in his mind, the fossilizing vertebrae which had once formed the spine of some great beast. He put his hands together and rested his forehead against their heels. He stared between his wrists into the eyes of the Mystery of the Mojave. The Mystery of the Mojave stared back. He believed for a moment that the Creature was trying to tell him something. The moment was lost, however, as Delandra Hummer rapped at the glass behind him with her knuckles. Obadiah replaced the tarp. Caught again, he crawled rather sheepishly from the car and stepped out into the hot blue day.

It looked as if Delandra was about to tell him something when they were interrupted by the roar of motorcycles. The bikes were peaking a small hill and descending upon the breakfast cafe like a line of mutant ants. Delandra jerked her thumb in their direction. "See what I mean," she said. "We just made it."

The riders began bringing their machines to a halt in the dusty lot, couples dismounting and stretching their legs, pulling off helmets and patting hairdos. Obadiah noticed one old guy walking toward them. It looked like the guy Delandra had almost run off the road. "Hey," the guy yelled. His wife and another couple were standing behind him. More were beginning to move in their direction. "What the hell you think you were trying to do back there," he asked, "kill someone?"

"Damn straight," Delandra told him. "Cross me and you'll wind up like this poor son of a bitch." She jerked open the door, reached inside and flipped the tarp away from the case. The man and his wife came a couple of steps forward. With the car door thrown open, the seat forward, and the sunlight streaming through the glass, the profile of the Mystery of the Mojave was lit up like a jewel in the sun. The lady opened her mouth and put a hand on her husband's arm. The man stretched his neck and squinted. "It's some kind of fake," he said. But there was a funny kind of expression on his face when he said it and he did not seem inclined to move any closer. "Takes one to know one," Delandra said. She replaced the tarp and climbed in behind the wheel from the passenger side. Obadiah followed her. "I think we should call the Highway Patrol," he heard someone say as he slammed the door behind him. Delandra swung the car around and gunned it, leaving the motorcyclists to eat her dust. "Citizens," she said, "they make me sick."

I n another hour they came to another town. At least it was more of a town than the junction. Two-story brick buildings baked in the sun along a paved main street. Upon closer inspection, however, Obadiah could see that most of the windows were boarded, the buildings, like the mining shacks which dotted the hills, empty.

He might have taken the place for a ghost town had it not been for the dozen or so late-model cars he saw parked here and there as they drove along the street. At last Delandra pulled up in front of one of the buildings and killed the engine. The building was made of brick with a deep wooden porch which extended to the street. There were benches on the porch and a high wooden railing and several old men rested there in the shade. "Let's stop here for a beer," Delandra said. "I want to run something down for you."

They went up some steps and into the building. The saloon was deserted, dark, and cool. A bartender walked out of the back room as they came in. Delandra called him by name, ordered a pitcher, and then directed Obadiah to a table against the wall. "Look," she said after they had seated themselves, "I want to show you something."

She passed him a thin white piece of cardboard with a typed

message on it. The message had been typed in red ink, using all capital letters.

Obadiah took the card.

"It's from Sarge," Delandra said. "He always made up a little something to go with his newest version of the Thing."

Obadiah turned the card over. The back side was blank. He looked again at the red ink and began to read.

It seems that Sarge had gone to sleep one night in his camper at a roadside rest near a town called Trona, that sometime later, during the night, he was awakened by a peculiar wind. Looking from a camper window, he observed a strange light in the sky and what appeared to be a cigar-shaped craft descending toward some salt flats near which he was parked. Somewhat shaken, he gave it a few minutes thought, then grabbed a shovel—the nearest thing to a weapon he had in the truck—and went out to investigate. He did not get far. Somewhere on the dark flat he was set upon by a strange creature. The creature was large and powerfully built, though somewhat slow. There followed a lengthy battle—what felt like hours to Sarge Hummer. He swung his shovel hard and often, connected with blows he was certain would have killed another man, and then, finally, was himself knocked unconscious.

When he came to, it was morning. The weak light given by a quarter moon had been replaced by the light of a rising sun. Sarge stood and dusted himself off, amazed to find himself still alive. He retrieved the shovel, started back toward his truck, and that was when he made his remarkable find. His first guess was that it was the creature that had attacked him, though he could find no marks which might indicate a fatal blow. After getting the body to his truck, he retraced his steps out onto the flat, this time going much farther than he had the night before. He found no cigar-shaped craft. He did, however, find some strange crystals near a blackened ring of earth. Later, a friend examined the crystals and said they appeared to be sand particles which had been fused by a high heat. The card ended with the words AND SO THE MYSTERY REMAINS. WHAT IS IT? ALIEN BEING? MISSING LINK? YOU BE THE JUDGE! The card was signed: *Sarge Hummer, 1961.*

When Obadiah raised his eyes he found Delandra watching him, leaning forward across the table.

"Well?" she asked him. "What do you think?"

"Quite a story."

Delandra nodded. "That was my old man."

Obadiah was silent. He was trying to remember something. It seemed to him there was some biblical connection to be made.

Something from the Old Testament—one of the Hebrew prophets calling down fire from heaven to consume one of Baal's altars; years later archaeologists finding unusual crystal formations on the site. He could not remember any more. He looked back at Delandra. "So what do you think of it?" he asked her.

Delandra shrugged. "He made up things like that to go with all of them," she said.

The bartender crossed the room with the pitcher. "But you did say this Thing was different from the others?"

Delandra nodded. "You've got to give it to him there. Credit where credit's due. At any rate"—she tapped at the card with her finger—"this may come in handy yet. Let me tell you how I was thinking of financing our trip. About ten years ago this retired doctor moved out here from the East Coast and began an operation even crazier than Sarge's. He bought up a bunch of land around Table Mountain and began building things. He built something called an Electro-Magnetron, a Martian Museum; he even went so far as to build a landing strip for alien craft. I've never seen the stuff, but I've heard about it. He holds a big convention up there every spring and UFO freaks from all over the country show up. I don't know what they do. Wait for the Martians to come and carry them away, I suppose."

"Kind of like the rapture, in other words."

"The what?"

"Christ on the clouds to receive the elect."

Delandra nodded. "Christ on the clouds. I had almost forgotten about Him. Is that what you were waiting for yourself?"

"No. We believe He's returned already but no one knows it."

Delandra nodded once more. "I see," she said. "Interesting." He could see, however, that she wasn't in the least. But then neither anymore was he. He watched her take a drink of beer, following a bit of sunlight as it moved along the side of her face. He had never imagined that she was the kind of girl he would love. Pre-Delandra fantasies had never included anyone even remotely like her. And yet, sitting with her now, half looped in a town he could not name, studying the arch of her brow and the place near her temples where the dark hair joined the skin, he did not see how he could go on without her. It was a frightening thought and he reached for the beer.

"Dr. Verity is the guy's name," Delandra was saying. "I don't know what his whole rap is, something about being in contact with aliens, relaying messages, that sort of stuff. But I know one thing. I know that one time the old fart showed up out at our place and offered to buy a version of the Thing that wasn't anywhere near as good as the one you and I've got right here." She waved toward the swinging saloon-style doors through which they had entered. "You get my drift?"

"So there really is a buyer."

"I think so. That's what I've been up to on the phone. I've been trying to get through to the old fart. I wanted to set up a meeting."

"And?"

She shook her head. "I don't know yet. I got hold of some people but they've been giving me the runaround. I finally set up something for tomorrow. We're supposed to meet this guy at the landing strip."

"Verity?"

"I don't think so. Someone in his group. But I would say we've got a shot at connecting with someone who will want to buy. That's the main thing."

Obadiah was still holding Sarge's card. He turned it once more, looking at it in the dim light. "So why have you waited?" he asked. "Why didn't you and your brother sell it to him before?"

Delandra sat tracing a pattern in the moisture left by the pitcher with her finger. She was still wearing the white-rimmed shades, which sat just a bit crookedly on her face. "Rex wouldn't want to sell it," she said. "And, well, you know me. I am a sentimental girl."

Obadiah nodded. He could see that she was smiling back of the shades. The smile soon turned into one of those grins with too many teeth in it—the likes of which he had seen upon his arrival at the Chevron. This time, however, the grin was complicated by the crooked glasses. She looked just a bit wolfish and slightly crazed.

"And then maybe I never had a good enough reason to sell it before, either."

"And now you do?"

Delandra moved her shoulders. "I'm here, aren't I?"

Obadiah looked back toward the light and the doors. There were particles of dust caught in the light, and the light, as it moved toward the bar, took on a certain delicate glow because of them. It ran to golden and drew a slender brilliant vein along the wooden edge of the bar before splashing to a dusty floor. The bartender had gone somewhere out of sight, leaving Obadiah and Delandra alone with the dust and the light. He was trying, he found, to think of about six different things at once. He was trying to think about what Delandra had told him and how, or if, it changed things. He was trying to think about Delandra being here, because of him. He could not say he was unmoved by the thought. The idea that he was good enough reason for anyone to be anywhere seemed to him at the moment nearly as mysterious as the Thing in the back of Delandra's car. He poured the last of the beer into their glasses and sat looking at the note which still lay beween them, its red letters shining in the yellow light. "When we go to meet these people," he said, "will we be going anywhere near the town of Trona?"

"Right through it."

"And how about that roadside rest, the one Sarge mentions in the note. Will we get a chance to look at that?"

Delandra looked at him the way his mother might had he just announced the discovery of spots on his throat. "I suppose," she said. "But why do you ask?"

Obadiah shrugged. He was looking down at the note which still lay between them on the table. "I don't know. It might be interesting to have a look."

Delandra signaled the bartender for a second round while making an odd high-pitched whirring sound with her mouth, like she was doing sound effects for a grade B horror flick. "I'm sure there'll be a lot to see," she said.

T wo pitchers later they were back on a dusty street —much too bright after the dim saloon. It was Delandra's plan that she and Obadiah take a cheap motel she knew of on the outskirts of Trona. Not only would this give them a place to spend the night, it would give them a place to stash the Thing when they went out the next morning to, as Delandra liked to say, contact the contact. Since, however, they did not want to check into the motel until after dark, there was, at present, time to kill.

Unhappily, for Obadiah, who was now anxious to get back on the road, time does not die easily in towns like Rimrock. After Sarge Hummer's last note and testament there was not much to see. Or perhaps it was just that what there was seemed suddenly pale by comparison. Obadiah tried getting Delandra to tell him more about Verity but she had already told him what she knew. He tried getting her to talk more about her father but that subject did not seem to interest her. "What's there to say," she said. "Just some yahoo like the rest of them."

"The rest of them?"

"Nuts. The desert's full of people just like him. They get out here and pretty much do as they please. Build houses out of tin cans, wait for the aliens to come and carry them away, ride around in four-wheelers with six-guns on their hips like goddamn cowboys. Goofballs on the range. What can I say?"


The town of Rimrock lay on a grade, giving it a high side and a low side. The main street, which at one time had been paved, together with the brick buildings, sat on the high side, backed up against a squat, stony ridge. The rest of the town fell away in a southeasterly direction, ending in a sorry collection of shacks scattered about the edge of a dry lake. It gave one the impression that the town had once been perched at the edge of the sea but that the sea had deserted it. There also appeared to have been, at one time or another, an upheaval of some magnitude, perhaps an earthquake, for all along the western side of the main street there were places at which the ridge had given way and slid down to destroy a building or two. There were perhaps half a dozen such pockets of destruction along the quarter-mile stretch of road.

Obadiah and Delandra walked slowly along the street. It did not appear as if any effort had been made to restore the damaged buildings, so that Obadiah guessed the town must have begun to die before the slide came. He and Delandra looked into the windows of rooms which must have looked now very much the way they had when the rocks came pouring through their western walls. Broken pieces of furniture and various mangled appliances could be seen in some of the rooms, often half covered by mounds of earth and brick. The rooms were possessed of a heavy, musty odor and the shafts of sunlight which pierced the windows and ruined ceilings were streaked with dust, so that the rooms had about them something of that same dusty golden light Obadiah had seen in the bar, and he found that strolling among the wreckage made him unaccountably happy. There was a certain finality about the place he found oddly satisfying. He asked Delandra if people had been killed here but she pleaded ignorance. "You were never curious?" he asked her.

"About what?"

"About what happened here."

"The ore ran out and the ridge came down. That's what happened here."

They had by now reached the end of paved road. At their feet lay the desert, a vast expanse of land dotted with creosote bushes and mining shacks. The shacks ended after a mile or so and then there was just the creosote going on for as far as the eye could see. They turned back toward the town.

Obadiah, never having been a lover before, was at times uncertain about how to conduct himself. His interest in the town, for instance; Delandra seemed to find it boring. His interest in Sarge Hummer's note and the roadside rest at the edge of Trona she seemed to find irritating, so that he was somewhat torn between a drunken sense of happiness and the feeling that he was blowing it. He had wanted them to operate on the same frequency. He sensed instead that certain intangibles were slipping out of sync. Maybe it was just him. Maybe he thought too much about what all of this was costing him and it was making him weird. The odd part was, he was enjoying himself anyway, right here and now, and when by chance they happened upon Rimrock's lone barber shop, he was set upon by a sudden screwball notion to alter his physical appearance. Perhaps, he thought, one could learn to enjoy being weird.

They were by now halfway back to the car, standing at the side of an old-fashioned red-and-white-striped barber's pole. At their backs the street ran downward, past a smattering of houses toward the white, shimmering surface of the dry lake.

"Flattops with fenders are always hip," Delandra told him. He was pleased to see the prospect of a haircut amused her. Perhaps they were on similar frequencies after all.

Obadiah counted change in the palm of his hand. "You know," he said. He had been thinking about the conversation in the bar. "It would be funny if this one turned out to be the real thing."

"Your haircut?"

"The body we've been hauling in your car. I mean I was thinking about that note. I was thinking it would be funny if this time Sarge was telling the truth."

Delandra nodded but she wasn't smiling. "I guess it would depend on your sense of humor," she said. "But anyway, so what?"

"So what?" He repeated her question. It was somehow not the response he had expected.

Delandra looked up and down the street. "Must be an echo out here," she said.

\*    \*    \*

She waited for him in front of the shop. He could see her out there, seated on a bench while the old man worked on his head. Her face was turned toward the street and the sunlight lit her throat and the underside of her jaw in such a way that made her neck look long and sleek. It was like he was seeing her for the first time and found that she reminded him of a bird of prey.

Obadiah had asked the barber to take it all off. He waited now impatiently as chunks of blond hair covered his shoulders. "Funny," the old man said—he was probably in his seventies, thin and wrinkled with a full head of white hair that was streaked here and there with strips of yellow the color of tobacco stains. "Most young folks nowadays want it long. You're not one of those hippies, I take it." The old man seemed to find the whole idea of hippies somehow amusing. Obadiah assured him that he was nothing of the sort. "In fact," Obadiah told him, "I'm a full-time minister."

"You don't say," the old man said.

"Yes, I am."

"What denomination?" the old man wanted to know.

When Obadiah told him the old man shut up and didn't say anything else. When he was done he whirled the chair around so Obadiah could see himself in the mirror. His hair was short enough to have been a butch—except for the top, which was still a bit too long for that. He was pleased to see that the old man couldn't cut hair worth shit and that the sides did not match. His mustache, he saw now, should go as well. He suggested this to the barber and the man removed it with a straight razor. When it was done, Obadiah crossed the street for a pair of fifty-nine-cent sunglasses before allowing Delandra to examine him. She did so from all angles, at last deciding he no longer resembled the lifeguard from Manhattan Beach. "The new Obo," she said. She put a finger to her chin in mock concentration. "It's different. You've got to give it that."

Obadiah found a piece of dusty plate glass and studied his reflection. The shades and haircut gave his face an odd gaunt look he had not seen before. His body looked different, too, he thought—though how much of this was due to the glass and how much to the weight he had lost in the last few days, he could not say, but he definitely looked longer and thinner, more angular somehow in his stiff western shirt, the dark jeans which still had not been shrunk to fit. Delandra joined him in the glass so they could look at each other together. He watched as her reflection broke into a smile beneath the dark glasses which he had tilted, stems way up, above her ears, so they rested on her face at a crazy angle. Obadiah laughed out loud. He had, during the haircut, been thinking about the question Delandra had put to him going in and an answer had presented itself: The world was a different place, that was what. If Sarge Hummer's note was true, then the world was one kind of place. If the note was a lie, then it was another. It was a little like having religion. The world was a more interesting place if there was more to it than what met the eye and he wondered now if a man who had stopped believing the Word had become flesh might take a chance on Sarge Hummer. He said nothing to Delandra, not wishing to disturb the festivity of the moment. Still, he was certain there was something at the core of this idea which had accounted for that feeling of euphoria with which he had left the bar and it occurred to him as well that if motion had been the first part of his most recent equation for happiness he had, just now, on the streets of Rimrock, stumbled upon the second. It was, after all, he thought, what every man needed: something to hope for, something to do, and someone to love.

I t was near dusk by the time they reached the roadside rest on the outskirts of Trona, and Obadiah's disappointment was immediate. In the miles between Rimrock and Trona he had imagined it all a bit differently—more mysterious somehow. Confronted with the reality this whole idea seemed so silly, he wondered how he had ever arrived at such an expectation in the first place.

Delandra, on the other hand, seemed quite pleased with herself. She sat eyeing the desolation with a satisfied smirk as Obadiah stepped from the car. A tepid wind tugged at his shirttail and a peculiar odor wafted across the flats. "Are you coming?" he asked.

Delandra was hanging her head out an open window. "Coming where?"

"I don't know. To look around."

"Look around where? You can see the whole fucking place from right here."

This was true. It was without a doubt the least inviting roadside rest he had yet seen. There was not a tree in sight, no line of wind-bent cottonwoods, no blade of grass. There was only a wide gravel lot at the side of the road, a tiny block building and a series of odd-looking picnic tables which appeared to be made out of fiber glass. Everything had been painted an ugly shade of dark brown and trimmed in orange—though by now the paint was chipped and weather-beaten and in places had begun to peel. On the west wall of the rest rooms someone had left a spray-painted message which read: *Welcome to the pitts.*

Obadiah crossed the gravel lot and entered the building. He relieved himself in a urinal someone had pulled halfway out of the wall and which, when he flushed it, quickly deposited a gleaming pool of water on the concrete floor. Then he went back outside and looked toward town. Trona, Delandra had told him, had been built around a chemical plant and standing now at the edge of the lot he could just make out a series of tall, rectangular structures rising above the remnants of a mirage which still ringed the flats. Above his head the sky had taken on a depth of color he did not believe he had seen before. A deep cobalt blue of neon intensity arched above him like some immense circus canopy. The only break in this illusion lay toward the western horizon where a thin band of orange light had begun to spread above some ridges. As he came down the single step he felt once more the tepid wind laced with the peculiar smell. Delandra was still watching him from the car, an arm out the open window, her chin on her bicep. He felt that some show of looking around should be made, though rarely had he found himself in a spot where so little seemed to present itself for inspection. The rest area occupied a gravel strip at the edge of the road and was shaped roughly like a quarter-moon. The highway curved through one side and on the other lay the flats.

Obadiah glanced once more in Delandra's direction and then turned toward the desert. He wandered rather halfheartedly toward the edge of the gravel and then eased himself down a slight embankment. The embankment turned out to be steeper than it had first appeared and when he reached its bottom he was standing upon the flats and a change he had not counted upon was immediately apparent. From the rest area you could see the flats and it all looked very desolate and empty with nothing much to see. From the flats at the base of the incline, however, you could not see the building or picnic tables or the rest area at all. With the rest spot removed, Obadiah was alone with the landscape and suddenly quite aware of himself in relation to it—the scale of things, as it were. He became aware, too, of the ground itself. It was composed of a kind of dried mud which had cracked into great hieroglyphic patterns. The fissures between the chunks of ground were deep, the chunks themselves of a remarkably uniform size and shape, composed of a substance which, in one place, would pop like crockery beneath his feet, while in others it seemed to absorb his steps completely, giving back no sound at all.

He walked for some time, taken in by the great distances, the peculiar relationship of space and light, the proportional scale of his own body. He walked until he came to a fence. Somehow the idea of a fence running across the middle of a salt flat did not make much sense. Upon closer inspection he found that it was a government fence. It was low—maybe four feet high, made of barbed wire run between a series of short dark posts. On one of the posts he saw a sign which read: NAVAL WEAPONRY SITE ONE HUNDRED YARDS AHEAD. STAY CLEAR! Looking farther, he saw another fence. The second fence was taller and there were small red lights at the tops of the poles which supported it. There was nothing else. The fences ran in either direction for as far as he could see. Could naval weaponry account for the cigar-shaped craft and strange light Sarge had seen from his camper? The discovery of the site certainly suggested one kind of explanation, and yet, in a crazy sort of way, it was an explanation contradicted by the land itself, which seemed, since distancing himself from the pathetic rest area, to suggest quite another and he felt once more a rising of his spirits, some surge of that same excitement he had felt in the town. He had, after all, seen the Thing, the existence of which seemed to him more meaningful by the hour, less likely to be explained by ordinary occurrences. Or was it just that he wanted extraordinary occurrences? Perception is an embrace. He had read that somewhere. The phrase came back to him now on the dried mud of the great flat.

Above his head the blue had gone to purple while the thin line of orange light which had earlier lain to the west had erupted in a brilliant display of reds and pinks and yellows. The colors swept upward from the horizon in a series of luminous arcs. To the north the towers of Trona had caught the light in such a way as to make of the town a golden city at the edge of the plain and he wondered if there was not, somewhere in these acres of light, in the hieroglyphics at his feet, or even somehow, in the silence itself, an attempt to communicate. It was a peculiar idea and yet one which seemed to dissipate upon articulation until that sense of euphoria he had felt only moments before was all but gone and in its place there was only an unpleasant sense of emptiness. What, he wondered, in the fuck was the matter with him? Had he really made some significant discovery in the least expected of places or was he simply losing his mind? A kind of theory formed: a mind weakened by years of self-abuse, broken at last beneath the truckload of guilt brought on by a series of rash acts. He stumbled once in the mud, cursing an upbringing which in the end had managed only to bring him to this. Perhaps, he thought, all he was really after was something not that far removed from what his parents must have felt when they had found The Way. For they must, he thought, have had their moment—something the likes of which had just now eluded him, that recognition, sudden or gradual, of another reality. For him it had not quite worked that way. For him the answers had always been there. He could see now, of course, that the answers had been their answers, that his journey had worked as a reversal of their own, a working of his way back through the system they had given him in a process of undoing until the pattern of meaning had broken down, the code dissolved into simple noise once more. Still he envied them their vision and he would, he thought, have gladly welcomed any revelations which might care to visit themselves upon him at this moment, here, on a quickly cooling patch of earth one might as easily see as biblical as otherworldly, and he found himself standing still once more, mute, receptive, awaiting the Word, or perhaps the arrival of one more cigar-shaped craft and the intrusion of another order of being. Anything, really, to sweeten the pot. It did appear, however, that he was, on the evening in question, shit out of luck and with nothing more interesting than the ever-present noise of his own breathing mechanism rattling in his ears he started out once more across the flats, moving this time in the direction from which he had come, back toward the rectangular shapes of the rest rooms and the impossible shapes of the picnic tables which had come to resemble something like gallows above a black horizon.

He had not yet reached the rest area, however, when he too, like Sarge Hummer before him, was set upon by a strange creature. In Obadiah's case the mystery was short-lived—the creature soon recognizable as the offspring of Sarge himself. It was wearing a dress and cowboy boots.

It had grown dark quickly, with the moon not yet risen much above the surrounding ridges, so that upon reaching the base of the incline leading back to the road he was for several moments immersed in shadow and it was here that he nearly collided with Delandra Hummer, who was by now making her way down the incline in an effort to locate him. She loomed suddenly in front of him and he actually dropped to one knee in an effort to avoid collision. In spite of the fact that he had only recently been hoping for some brand of remarkable encounter, it scared the shit out of him. Judging by her response it scared the shit out of her, too, and for a moment they sat side by side on the ground, breathing hard, and it took a moment for him to realize she was crying. At least he thought she was crying. He could feel her shoulders shaking and something in her voice made him glad he could not see her face.

"What in the fuck were you doing out there," she asked him. "What are you, crazy like the rest of them?"

He was somewhat taken aback by her reaction and said nothing. He was trying to think of something witty to say, but nothing came to mind.

"You're not funny," she told him. "I told you. He built it out of junk."

"Delandra," Obadiah said. "I've seen it, remember? He might have made it. But he did not make it out of tin cans and hubcaps."

"Who said he did? He used all kinds of stuff. Fiber glass, resin, a special rubbery stuff some guy used to deliver in big canisters."

"What rubbery stuff? What guy?"

"How should I know?" She had him by the shirtfront now and he could feel her knuckles against his chest. "All I know," she said, "is that I'm going to sell the son of a bitch to these goons at Table Mountain and I don't want anybody to queer the deal." Her nose was about half an inch from his and her hair was all over her face and he fancied he could even see her pulse in that little hollow spot below her throat and what he really wanted, he thought, was to make love to her, to get his pants down and hers off, to pull her down on top of him with her dress and cowboy boots still on and his cock inside of her and fuck her by the light of the moon.

"Hey, come on," he said. His hand was on the wrist that held his shirt. "The material, the material."

Delandra released her hold. She had one leg out straight next to his and one drawn up and he could see in the moonlight the pale smooth skin of her thigh. "I should feed you to the fishes," she said.

It was, Obadiah believed, something John Wayne had said in a movie called *In Harm's Way,* and he, in turn, repeated something Delandra Hummer had once written on one of Sarge's cards: "Beat me, fuck me, call me Ruth."

Before it was over she had him on his knees with one hand on his cock and her tongue in his ass and the sweat was running down his neck and hitting the cracked earth of the Mojave with the sound of rain on glass and it wasn't, he supposed, anything at all like what had happened to Sarge Hummer. And finally the moon was high and white and they were side by side once more and Obadiah could feel the cool chalky ground on his bare back, and on his ass, and on his legs and he was very much aware that she was the only other living thing anywhere around him for miles and miles. Just the two of them, like the first astronauts marooned on Mars, like Adam and Eve, for Christ's sake, somewhere east of Eden.

He could have gone on casting about for comparisons for hours but was interrupted by Delandra. She had rolled toward him with one leg over his and her thigh against his groin. She had one hand on his face and he could feel the dust on her fingertips as she turned his face toward her own. "You've got to understand something," she said. "I've had enough crazy people in my life. You know what I mean? And there's just no percentage in it." She tightened her grip on his jowls so he could feel his cheeks pressing against his teeth. "Just don't you go crazy on me too, you little fucker. Go crazy on me and I'll kick your fucking ass."

Obadiah was looking into her eyes and once he fancied that he could see the stars winking behind them. He didn't want to go crazy. He really didn't. He was, after all, a personal friend of a certain Bug House, and he'd seen where that got you.

The approach to Porkpie Wells was rough and rocky and when he entered the town Rex Hummer felt he had entered the skeletal remains of some huge beast. To his left a beaten black-and-white sign hung from a post.

The sign said: PORKPIE WELLS. ELEVATION 12 FEET. POPULATION 26. The centerpiece of the town was an old hotel some business-men from Los Angeles built in the twenties. It was empty now. Twenty years ago someone with renovation on his mind had painted everything white. It was a two-story building, shaped like a U. There were arches on the first floor and tall rectangular windows on the second. The shaded arches and dark interior walls which showed through the open second-story windows stood in sharp contrast to the bone-white stucco and were what in particu-lar gave Rex the illusion of having penetrated the rib cage of an animal long dead. There were a few cottonwoods making a mess around a cracked stone fountain where a ceramic boy stood clutching his tiny ceramic penis. But there was nothing taller than the hotel itself, nothing to break the sharp angles of white and black before a blue blaze of sky.

It was the second time in as many days that Rex had made the trip. He was still looking for the woman. When on his first pass he had found her gone, he'd driven as far north as Goldfield, Nevada, where the woman owned a mining claim and a shack. When she wasn't there either he'd driven back to Porkpie Wells. He in-tended to camp here, in the ruins of the hotel, until she showed.

He parked by the cottonwoods. The radiator made a soft hissing sound when he killed the engine and a pale cloud of steam rose from beneath the hood. As he climbed from the cab he could hear the soft patter of water as it dribbled beneath the front of the truck. He stood for a moment in the shade of a wall, watching the puddle, then turned and started along the courtyard toward the back of the hotel. He kept to the narrow strip of shade provided by the wall, down along one long wing until he came to the steps which led upward onto a wide stone porch and the entrance to the opera house. If the centerpiece of Porkpie Wells was the hotel, then the centerpiece of the hotel was the opera house. It was the tallest part of the building and sat at the center of the two wings. It, like the hotel, stood empty for most of the year, but during parts of the spring and fall when Porkpie was likely to see a fair number of tourists passing through on their way to the ranch and inn near Furnace Creek, the opera house was open to the public. It was the woman who ran the place. Her name was Roseann Duboise. She billed herself as the Buffalo Woman and performed what were supposed to be authentic Indian dances. She sang songs, played a respectable ragtime piano, and served imported German beers. In the off-season, when she wasn't making a fool of herself with the dances or working her claim in Goldfield, she lived in a tiny dilapidated trailer perched on the side of the ridge back of the hotel. The trailer was open to the public year-round, whenever she was there. In it she read palms, told fortunes, and saw auras, though the manifestation of auras was limited to certain months of the year and particular atmospheric conditions.

Coming out on the back side of the inn, Rex could see her trailer against the side of the ridge. It appeared to be strewn rather than built there—the wreckage of some light craft, most of it an oxidized shade of pale yellow. At one end there was a black and silver sign with a hand and the word FORTUNETELLER painted on it. Rex figured he might as well check the trailer one more time before checking into the hotel. His heart thumped heavily, however, as he began to climb. To see the woman had not been an easy decision for him. He was afraid of her and harbored certain peculiar ideas about her true identity and the reason she seemed to know more about him than anyone should. It was either, he had decided, that she was what she said she was, a reader of secret signs or—and it was difficult to be sure, twenty some odd years having elapsed in the interim—she was the woman who once lived with Sarge Hummer just long enough to provide him with a baby girl.

The day was hot and bright and Rex made his way slowly along the steep path toward Roseann's trailer. To the east he could see thunderheads. He had hit rain in Goldfield and now it looked as if the storms were moving west. Once, while pausing to wipe his brow, he thought he heard a distant peal of thunder, though it might have been a navy fighter—sonic booms not being an uncommon occurrence in Porkpie Wells.

The path Rex followed was bordered by a variety of red and black stones. As he neared the trailer he began to find an occasional cow skull among the rocks. The things lay grinning up at him with broken teeth. Back of the trailer the ground continued to rise, up toward the lip of a dun-colored ridge which swept across the sky in a long jagged line. And back of that ridge there were others—bits and pieces of which were visible from where Rex stood. The bits and pieces jutted still farther skyward in broken bands of sun-washed earthtones. On the other side of all that was Death Valley.

By the time Rex reached the trailer he was somewhat winded. He stopped to rest by the black and silver sign. Looking back toward the hotel he was once more reminded of the carcass of an animal. Among the permanent places of business in Porkpie Wells was Charlie's Bar. The bar had once served as the Porkpie Lounge and was attached to one end of the building. Looking down on it from this height Rex could see a slender ribbon of smoke curling from the roof and what looked to be three souped-up motorcycles he had not seen the day before. The motorcycles had a lot of chrome on them which flashed in the midday sun.

Rex found the door of Roseann's trailer closed and locked from the outside. It was the way he had left it. A large brass padlock which looked like it was probably worth more than the trailer hung solidly against the chalky yellow paint. The curtains were drawn and the place had a quiet dusty look about it, as if no one had been there in some time. Rex dragged a hand across his brow.

Since losing the Thing he had become prey to mind-numbing headaches and spells of dizziness. He felt dizzy just now and sat to rest on the wooden crate which did service as the trailer's front porch. Waiting for the spell to pass, he thought of the day upon which a combination of atmospheric conditions and high-intensity heat had made possible the manifestation of his own aura.

It was in the parking lot of a McDonald's burger joint at the edge of Baker. There were golden neon arches there and a sign with a lot of zeros on it and Roseann had observed his aura—arching between the golden arches like an electrical current jumping between poles. She said it was something to see. It meant, she said, he was without question intended for something special. She was a large dark woman, dressed that day like a man—a flannel workshirt, in spite of the heat, jeans and boots, a black hat with a beaded band. She had been sitting alone on a plastic bench drinking Coca-Cola from a paper cup. Rex had heard her whooping at him as he waited in line.

Later she had read his palm in an effort to figure out exactly what the something special was. She had seen a lot of things but the special part had been kept from her. She wouldn't say by whom.

"You're Sarge Hummer's boy," she had said.

"You saw that in my hand?"

"Your whole fucking life is in your hand," Roseann Duboise had told him. "Your old man still in the monster business?"

Rex admitted that he was. He was seated by then on the bench beside her, looking at her in the heat and it was there he had begun to entertain the notion that he had seen this woman before

—though in another guise. He had tried to picture her with lipstick and red hair. "Have you and I met before?" he asked her.

The woman ignored his question. He later understood it was a way she had. "Your sister shot your eye out with a pellet gun," she said.

He had to admit to being somewhat astonished at hearing this piece of information. "It was an accident," he said, "and she's my half sister."

Roseann had only shaken her head. "She's no good," Roseann told him. "I'll tell you that right now."

He'd seen her a couple of times after that. He'd driven out to the opera house and caught her Indian dance routine once. And later, when Sarge was dead and he was at work on the Hum-A-Phone, he'd remembered her load of junk and gone out to see if she had anything he might be interested in collecting.

And that was the last time. He'd caught her one evening, drunk on her ass and still in the buckskins she wore at the opera house. She'd brought him back up to the trailer and he had gotten a look at what was inside. The place was full of all manner of weird-looking stuff—teeth, scalps, knives, horns, beads, and Indian dolls. What she was most proud of, however, was her collection of sacred stones. The stones were round and smooth. Some were the size of baseballs, some more the size of golf balls. Some were dressed in little knit sweaters Roseann Duboise had made for them herself. She explained to Rex how the rocks were capable of travel. "You lose something," she said, "you can send one of these stones to find it for you." It sounded handy enough to him. He had been about to ask how he might become the owner of one himself when he caught sight of something else. It was in a shoe box beneath some rocks. It was a photograph of Sarge Hummer. The picture had been taken when Sarge was in the Marines. Rex had never seen it before. His father was standing by the wing of an airplane. He wore a leather flight jacket, a T-shirt, and khaki pants. And he was laughing. Rex had not seen his father laugh that often. When he asked Roseann about it she said she'd picked it up in a thrift store somewhere. She said she collected photographs—but only of strangers. She said she had no interest in photographs of people she knew. She told him he could take the one of Sarge if it would make him happy—which he was considering doing when she made a pass at him. At least he had always assumed it was a pass. She'd asked him to take a look at something and then she had shown him her twat. She'd hauled up her buckskins long enough for him to see that the thing had been shaved bare and tattooed—

decorated with what appeared to be a ring of teeth. He had declined to examine the object at closer quarters and the last he had seen of her she was standing on the crate upon which he now sat. "Send your old man out here sometime," she had told him. "I'd like to meet his ass."

"Sarge is dead," Rex had told her.

She'd stood there looking at him for a moment. She was a large woman and given the elevation of her porch and the white buckskins gleaming in the moonlight she'd managed to look more like a water heater than a person. She hadn't said anything. She'd just gone back into her trailer, letting the door swing shut behind her with a loud, hollow pop, and that was it—the last Rex had seen of her and the last he expected to until, that is, he came upon hard times, until the weird music stopped playing in his head and the Desert Museum was standing empty and silent as the grave. He'd come back then. Perhaps this time she would tell him what he was meant for. There had to be something.

At last he rose from the porch and dusted his palms on the seat of his pants. He went back down the narrow walkway, past the skulls and the rocks, and the silver and black sign with the hand painted on it, noticing for the first time and with no small amount of disgust, that she had given the thing six fingers. On her ass, he thought, or perhaps it just had something to do with not being able to draw any better than she could dance.

B y the time Rex got down from the ridge the shadows in the courtyard had begun to lengthen and had taken on a slightly bluish hue in the warm orange light. The bikes he had seen from Roseann's trailer were still in front of the bar. They were big, chopped Harleys with long chromed forks and high-gloss tanks. He paused for a moment to admire the work before moving past them and into the building.

He hadn't been in Charlie's for close to two years but it didn't look as if much had changed. The place was still dark and musty, still smelled of spilled beer and stale tobacco. Charlie was back of the bar. He looked up as Rex came through the door and greeted him by name. Charlie was a tall, skinny desert rat in his late forties. He had light brown hair which was long and stringy and which he wore pulled back tight against his skull with a ponytail in back long enough to strike him between the shoulder blades. He had a large mustache and a graying, pointed beard and sometimes reminded Rex of old photographs he'd seen of Buffalo Bill Cody. Except Charlie was skinnier. Buffalo Bill on speed. Charlie fancied himself a guitar player and occasionally showed up at the junction for talent showcase nights. He probably would have showed up more often if Floyd hadn't proven himself partial to giving Charlie a bad time and yelling things like "Hey, Pencil Dick" at him when he was trying to perform.

"Heard about your new invention," Charlie said as Rex crossed the floor. "First place, huh. The man's a Hollywood star." He said this as if he were speaking to a roomful of people. In this case, however, there was no one there but a scrawny Mexican at one end of the bar and the owners of the Harleys hunkered down in a booth way at the back and none of them looked particularly interested in the news.

Rex shrugged it off. "Seen anything of the Buffalo Woman?"

Charlie set a beer down in front of Rex. "On the house," he said, and then: "Fuck no. I hear the old whore's got herself a new beau, though. A real Indian if you can believe that. Jesus, can you imagine tying into that wench?"

Rex took a drink of the beer. "You ever seen the guy?" he asked.

"The Indian? Hell no. The guy's from Victorville, I think. The only reason I even know about him is that he showed up at one of her gigs at the opera house"—Charlie jerked his thumb in the direction of the courtyard—"and wound up beating the shit out of a couple of tourists. Great for business, huh?" Charlie paused to shake his bony head. "Why you interested?" he asked.

Rex ignored him. He was staring into the bottles back of the bar and thinking about Indians.

"Hey," Charlie said, his face lighting up noticeably. "I hear Floyd got beat by some nigger."

Rex nodded and Charlie began to laugh. The laugh turned into a cough and he stomped around behind the bar for a full thirty seconds trying to get hold of himself. When he returned to where Rex was sitting, there were tears in his eyes—of joy or physical discomfort, it was hard to say. "Wish I coulda been there, man."

"Do yourself a favor," Rex told him. "Don't ever let him hear you laughing about it."

Charlie wiped his nose.

"You ever get that piano tuned?" Rex asked. There was an old white upright in one corner of the bar. It had been badly out of tune the last time Rex was here, but he was thinking he might like to fool around with it. The piano was at the same end of the room as the bikers, though on an opposite wall. He looked back in their direction now. "Fucking lowlifes," he heard Charlie whisper, "been holed up over there in the north wing for close to a week now. Got this little pussy with them, though." He raised and lowered his eyebrows several times in rapid succession before casting a sly smile in Rex's direction. He then paused, as if to add weight to what would follow. He leaned slightly forward on the bar and reduced his voice to a gravel-laden whisper. "And guess what else?" he asked. "The little dirt bag was in here the other night dancin' on the tabletops, showin' off this fancy dye-job she'd done on herself. Now let me tell you something about the location of this little item." He wiggled his thumb in the direction of his own crotch. "She's got the little beggar dyed red, white, and blue." Charlie slapped the bar and chuckled beneath his breath. "Yes indeed," he said, "one patriotic pussy comin' right up." This time he laughed out loud. His laughter charmed like the death rattle of a wounded animal and Rex turned away from it. He left the bar and crossed the room. He went to the piano and sat down.

Behind him the two largest bikers, a bearded blond and a brunet appeared to be arguing over whether or not the brunet had ever been a cop. "Sheet, man," Rex could hear the blond guy saying, "you were never a cop, man."

"Hey, fuck you, man," the brunet said, "I was, too, a cop."

Rex played several tentative notes on the instrument. He was strictly self-taught but he liked fooling around with it. Perhaps it would help him relax. He began by trying to pick out the melody line to "Hong Kong Blues." Behind him he was aware of the bikers getting quiet. "Hey, rock and roll, man," someone said. "Shut up, Dick Head," came a reply. Rex ignored them. He was trying to remember the words: "This is the story of very unfortunate colored man / got 'rested down in old Hong Kong / he got twenty years privilege taken away from him / when he kicked old Buddha's gong."

Finally the bikers got up and left. Rex could hear them clomping across the floor behind him. For a moment sunlight flooded the bar, then a door slammed and it grew cool and quiet and dark once more.

He played for what was perhaps an hour. At some point the door opened again and soon Rex was aware he had attracted an audience. There was a girl listening to him. She was seated at the table where the bikers had sat earlier and he wondered if she was the girl who had been keeping them entertained in the north wing. She was a small boyish-looking creature. She wore oversize khaki pants and a loose-fitting white tank top. She had short black hair, a small nose, and large dark eyes.

Later, when Rex stopped for a little break, she walked over to where he was sitting. "You're okay," she said.

Rex was not used to being approached by women—at least not the kind of women he imagined he could ever be interested in. This girl was something different and she made him nervous. He could see upon closer inspection that she was recovering from a very righteous black eye. There was still a good-sized bruise running down into her cheek, accentuating the darkness of her eyes and the whiteness of her skin. She wore large gold earrings and a small dark tattoo on one shoulder—a little cross with beams of light spreading out from the top. She pulled a chair away from the table and tossed herself into it. She landed with one leg drawn up, a foot on the seat, a forearm resting across one knee. It was a position which revealed an armpit and most of one small breast.

"That your truck out there?" the girl asked.

Rex said that it was.

"I was wondering," she said, coming right to the point, "you going anywhere near Table Mountain? Like maybe you could give me a ride?"

Rex had not been thinking of going there. He looked away from the patch of soft dark hair beneath her arm, the white curve of skin. "I might," he said, having discovered that his heartbeat was something he could hear.

The girl nodded. She had an odd voice—Betty Boop with a whiskey throat. "I've been trying to get up there for two weeks now," she said. "These pussy bikers were going to take me. Now they don't want to."

Rex took the news that she was in fact the girl with the bikers without flinching. But he was not unaffected. On the one hand, he wanted to tell himself that he'd best think twice about taking her anywhere. On the other hand, there was what Charlie had told him. He had encountered decorated pussies twice now, both times in Porkpie Wells. The coincidence appeared pregnant with meaning.

"Yeah, I really want to get back up there. You know, to look at these guys you wouldn't think they were such pussies." Rex assumed she was referring to her traveling companions but it sounded like dangerous talk to him and he left it alone.

The girl proceeded into a lengthy rap about Table Mountain, how she and some other people had gotten into renovating this old mining town and how there was this doctor up there who had built all this righteous stuff. She had been stupid to leave. Her sister, with whom she had been traveling at the time, had talked her into it and they had gone to San Francisco where it was nowhere near as righteous as Table Mountain and she had been trying to get back ever since. She stopped for a while and looked at her hands. "The doctor died," she said suddenly, "but he left everything to the Table Mountain people—that's what we started calling ourselves. The only thing is, the doctor had this daughter—a real asshole, and she says she's taking the will to court." The girl stopped to laugh. Her laughter was rather deep and throaty—not at all what Rex had expected. "She's going to take a will to court," she repeated.

Rex nodded and looked at the way the girl's big golden earrings flashed in the light now slicing through a narrow window near her head. The Table Mountain stuff was not news to him. He'd even met Dr. Verity once himself—a large, red-faced man with a paunch and a balding head. The guy had driven out to the Desert Museum years ago in a big pink Lincoln and offered to buy one of Sarge's Things. He said nothing about this to the girl.

"It was fun when Verity was around," the girl said. "When he died it was sad. We took his body out to this ridge and the aliens came and got it. I left after that. But I shouldn't have. I got this letter a few weeks ago from one of the sisters. She says Verity has come back. He has begun to appear."

"Begun to appear?" Rex asked. He wasn't sure that he cared for the sound of it.

The girl shrugged. "I don't know that much about it yet. He's gotten beyond the human form. He's going to teach us how to use the Electro-Magnetron."

Rex had heard about the Electro-Magnetron too. It was something of a joke among the locals. He'd heard that it had been built to reverse the aging process, but that there was a part missing. "I thought there was a part missing," Rex said.

The girl looked at him for a moment. "There was," she said. "Did you know there was a race of people at the center of the earth?"

Rex said nothing. In the courtyard the shadows had begun to lengthen. He tried to picture in his mind what a red, white, and blue pussy might look like.

The girl wrapped her arms around herself as if she had taken a sudden chill. "It's like another dimension down there, and these people, they're like gods or something." She stopped suddenly to laugh. "It sounds crazy," she said, "but can you imagine it? If there was a way to bring them back?" She smiled sweetly at the thought. "Blow some fucking minds, or what?" She hugged herself once more and her smile seemed to spread out to include things. It included Rex in such a way as to make him feel he had already agreed to take her where she wanted to go. He could not say the feeling was unpleasant. But then he thought of an empty museum at the side of a pitted asphalt road and the feeling died on the vine. He would have taken this girl there, he thought. She would have seen the Thing. She would have heard the Hum-A-Phone. Blow some fucking minds indeed. There was suddenly sweat on the back of Rex's neck, a dull, drumlike thumping back of his eyeballs. "Tell me," he said, "why don't these guys want to take you anymore?"

"I told you," she said. "These guys are wimps. These guys wouldn't know a large time if it came up and buggered them in the ass. I mean they're not even real bikers. Shit, I lived in Oakland with some Angels once. These guys are dildos."

"Yeah, but what are they afraid of?"

The girl looked him in the eye. The orange light gave the bruised flesh of her cheek a faintly iridescent quality. "They think the people up there are devil worshipers," she said. "Some fuckhead they met told them he'd heard some very weird stories. Like if these people don't think you're right on they might cut you up and sacrifice you to somebody." The girl continued to look at him. Then she smiled. "It's strictly bullshit," she told him.

Rex nodded but he was paying little attention to her now. A thought had come to him. It had appeared among his memories like a blade of grass upon parched ground. It had to do with the profound sense of disappointment once expressed on the part of Delandra Hummer over her father's refusal to sell Dr. Verity one of his Creatures, and Rex returned the girl's smile with one of his own. From somewhere beyond the wall came a sound—music turned up real loud but so far away that only the bass line could be heard in the bar, a dull throb like the sound of blood.

That he was a man of some destiny was something Rex had never doubted. He'd believed it when Roseann Duboise had told him he was meant for something special and he had known in his heart he would not be forsaken. That simply was not his fate. He had after all come to Porkpie Wells seeking a sign. He looked once more at the girl and then back into the courtyard where the orange light lay gleaming on the snowy walls, and finally back toward Charlie at the far end of the room where the bartender, at last having caught his eye, was busily finger-fucking the fist he had made out of one hand with the forefinger of the other. He was holding the whole business high enough over the bar for Rex to see and grinning like a demented rodent.

When they entered Trona on the following morning the weather had turned muggy and the sky the color of pearl. The Thing, for the first time since they had stolen it, was no longer in the car. They had left it in their room at the Blue Heaven Motel, the bedspread covering the case, a DO NOT DISTURB sign on the door.

The golden city Obadiah had once glimpsed from the edge of the flats was, it appeared, a hoax of the cruelest variety for he did not believe he had seen an uglier town. Searching for some set of images with which to compare it, he was at first reminded of certain old photographs of eastern mill towns—those black-and-white portraits of industrial desolation. Tortured landscapes wherein sorry company towns hunkered on treeless hills in the shadows of smoking factories. They'd had, of course, to do something about the color scheme in the Mojave. The dirty grays and blacks of hard eastern winters had given way to the red-shaded earthtones of equally hard desert summers. As for the company town, its houses were of faded stucco pastels—pinks and greens and yellows, but bleached and dusted with a fine gray dust until they had taken on something of the quality of old work clothes washed too many times, bleached by long days beneath the sun. The houses were single-story structures, each one identical in design to its neighbor—low rectangular buildings with peaked sheet metal roofs that fanned out into a ten-foot overhang all around, making for deep porches and shade for the coolers which sat stacked in their shadows. In front of the houses there were makeshift fences of wood and wire and yards of sand.

As for the rest of Trona—the Corner Pocket Bar, Frank's Liquor, a pair of large mustard-colored buildings which turned out to be the school, a church made of concrete blocks, a theater, a handful of thrift stores and junk shops—it all lay scattered among the loops and curves of the highway as it meandered in the dusty blue shadows of the Trona Chemical Works before straightening itself out and making like a streak, one slender arrow of sunlit pavement running in a rule-straight line toward the eastern rim of Death Valley, as if its builders had at last remembered what was what and gotten the hell out in a hurry.

And there was one final detail he noticed that morning, a kind of coup de grace he picked up on after rolling down his window for a breath of fresh air. It was the peculiar and noxious odor Delandra told him was a product of the chemical plant and one of Trona's— together with the weather—more or less constant features. And with the discovery of this last bit of news he was set upon by a second set of images for which he was at once willing to abandon the first. The second set had nothing to do with documentary films or old photographs but was drawn instead from the reading he had done between the ages of about twelve and fifteen—the years in which he had worked his way through the entire Winston's SF-for-young-people series he'd discovered housed in the Pomona Public Library—so that what he was at last able to see in Trona was not really a town at all but an outpost of some sort. A Martian mining complex. A penal colony on Equatorial Mercury. The last uranium works of the fifth moon of the planet Tractar. The image was particularly satisfying when thought of in light of what he and Delandra Hummer had come to find: a landing strip for alien craft.

"I didn't tell him I didn't know where it was," Delandra said. "I kind of wanted to sound like I was familiar with the setup."

Obadiah nodded. It made sense to him. "Why the hell not?" he said.

"Anyway," Delandra went on, "it should be easy enough to find. All we have to do is ask someone about where they hold the UFO conventions. It's all in the same place. I know that much."

They wound up at a small thrift store on the eastern edge of the town. It was a white Quonset hut type of building situated on a wide gravel shoulder at the side of the interstate. There were perhaps half a dozen people inside, not counting the two old women in yellow aprons who appeared to run the place. Everyone stopped what they were doing and looked up as Obadiah and Delandra came through the door.

Obadiah, immediately uncomfortable beneath their collective gaze, drifted off toward a rack of aging sport coats and assorted Hawaiian shirts as Delandra approached one of the women seated behind a desk. He was not so far away, however, that he could not hear their voices. He heard Delandra ask about the Martian Museum and then he heard one of the women laugh. "There's nothing like that here, honey," the woman said. "I guess you got the wrong town."

"Nonsense," Delandra said, "I know there's something like that here. I don't live that far away. I've heard about it for years."

"Well, I can't say what you've heard, dear, but I've lived in Trona for fifteen years and I know there's nothing like that around."

"And you never heard of an airstrip for flying saucers?"

The woman laughed again. "Someone's been pulling your leg," she said. The other woman laughed with her.

Obadiah had by now drifted farther toward the rear of the store, where he found himself suddenly staring into the sunken face of a thin middle-aged man. The combination of the man's height—his head only barely rising above the rack of coats—together with the dull used look of his clothing had caused him to blend in so well with the used sport coats that Obadiah almost passed him without seeing he was there. For a moment the two men stood facing one another. At which point the man smiled, displaying a set of ragged yellow teeth, and disappeared as if he'd been caught at something. Obadiah returned to the shirts. But there was something about the man. It took him a moment to decide what it was. It came to him while holding a brown and yellow polyester item to his chest before a thin rectangle of mirrored glass. It wasn't the man. It was him. He'd been thinking the guy was weird, but looking into the mirror, what he saw was that the man looked no weirder than he did himself. Perhaps it was the new haircut, the stiff clothing, the missing mustache, the lost weight. . . . The real revelation, however, was satisfaction this sense of camaraderie aroused in him. It was true he had long ago grown accustomed to feeling on the outside of things—having grown up in The Way. But that, at least when he hadn't been out knocking on doors, was a kind of secret difference because no one had grown up looking any straighter than he had. But now, staring into this bit of mirror in a desert thrift store, he was remarkably pleased to see he had at last achieved a certain harmony between freak sympathies and outward appearances. He had never had a problem believing in a world that was passing away, it was looking like he might give a shit that had always bothered him. It had never been a world he'd had a stake in and now, suddenly, he looked the part. He no longer looked like a scoutmaster—or some guy who had played basketball in high school. Nor, he was equally happy to note, did he look like those of his generation now camping in The Haight. No uniforms for Obadiah Wheeler. He looked like what for some dark reason he had always been drawn to—like something you might find lurking in the shadows of the Pomona Hotel—and he knew in his heart that there had always been just a trace of something in Bug House's twisted smile which he had found to admire.

He brought the brown and yellow shirt for fifty cents and by the time he got to the cash register to pay for it Delandra had concluded her business with the old woman and was standing on the porch in the sunlight. She had her arms folded across her chest and was looking back into the store. When she spoke it was loud enough for the woman at the cash register to hear. "The old whore won't tell me a goddamn thing," Delandra complained.

The woman gave Obadiah a sour look. Obadiah smiled and handed her a pair of quarters.

They were crossing the dirt lot when Obadiah suddenly noticed someone coming out from in back of the store, angling across the lot to meet them. It was the man with whom he had recently shared a brief moment of recognition at the rear of the shop. "I know what you're looking for," the man said when he reached them. He sounded a bit out of breath, as if the trip across the lot had taken something out of him. Perspiration beaded along his hairline and streaked down one sunken temple. He stopped after he said it and stood looking at them in the heat.

"Well?" Delandra asked.

"She's right," the man started up again. He jerked a thumb toward the shop. "There aren't any of those things anymore. But there used to be. Used to be a landing strip, and the Electro-Magnetron. Dr. Verity died." He stopped again, for a moment, and looked toward a line of rocks back of the store. "When he died the people stopped coming. Then some vandals got in and tore up most of what he'd built."

Delandra stood with her hands on her hips. She was several inches taller than the man and she stood looking down on him, the sun glancing off her hair and the edge of dark glass where it joined the white plastic rim of her shades. "Well, somebody is still around, somewhere," she said. "I've talked to someone on the phone."

The man looked once more toward the rocks, as if that was where it all was. He shook his head slowly. "There's someone out there," he said. "The Electro-Magnetron is still there, and someone's taking care of it."

"Can you tell us where it is?" Delandra asked him.

The man pointed back the way they had come. "You go down there until you see the post office, then you make a left. It's a dirt road and you stay on it for about two miles."

Delandra looked at Obadiah. "Okay," she said.

"There is one thing," the man said. And then he was quiet, waiting to be asked.

"And what one thing would that be?"

The man's shoulders were thin and bony and when he shrugged them the cloth of his shirt hung back against his chest like a loose sail. "Dr. Verity was real nice," he said. "People went out there to see him all the time. It's different now." He paused and brushed at something on his upper lip with his finger. "There's some funny people around now."

"Funny ha-ha or funny peculiar?" Delandra asked.

The man looked at her for a moment and moved his shoulders once more. "You know," he said. "Funny."

O badiah looked east, toward Death Valley, where a group of thunderheads had begun to collect above a line of red rock. He was still trying to come up with some reassuring way of defining for himself what the oddball from the thrift store might have meant by funny, but he wasn't having much luck. If the Mojave was capable of fueling the fantasies of UFO fanatics and fundamentalists alike, it was capable of producing fantasies of another kind as well—a peculiar brand of paranoia. Maybe it went back to the idea of scale, of vulnerability in a landscape without concessions to the notion of comfort. What at any rate Obadiah found himself imagining with mounting clarity as the car swerved through a sand bog was the exotic variety of funny people he and Delandra might find at the end of the white, dusty road—the guardians of Ceton Verity's Electro-Magnetron. And this, in fact, if they were lucky enough to even find the thing before being caught in the lowlands by the unseasonable thunderstorm that had been building all morning along the peaks separating them from Death Valley.

Delandra had noted the clouds before setting out on the un-paved road but seemed to think there was time. "I just want to see who these people are," she said. "I mean I talked to somebody and they acted interested. Shit, I don't care if we sell it to the old man or not. Anybody with money will do."

Obadiah had nodded, looked once more toward the clouds, and wondered if that was what he wanted too.


The man from the thrift store had given them directions which were vague at best and after half an hour on the dirt road they still had not found anything which looked like it might pass for an alien landing strip. At last, rounding the end of a long finger of iron-colored stone, they decided to stop the car and climb to the top of the ridge. "If we can't see anything from up there we'll start back," Delandra said.

Obadiah sat listening to the silence which had filled the void left by the engine. He wondered if it was anything you ever got used to. The silences, the high white heat, the hurtful light.

It was slow going in the rocks and by the time they reached a ledge near the top Obadiah found that he was breathing hard, that his shirt was damp with sweat. They looked around at the empty flats beneath them. A sudden burst of thunder boomed out of the ridges to the east and rolled down across the desert floor. Above them a lone hawk circled and then wheeled away toward the west, along the stony spine of the ridge they had climbed. There were patterns on the flats below them—what looked like jeep tracks—another road which intersected with the one they had taken, but nothing else. Delandra slapped at a flat piece of rock with the palm of her hand. "Well, fuck it," she said.

Obadiah nodded toward the clouds. "Storm's getting closer."

Delandra looked east, across the top of her shades. "Let's get back," she said. "But let's try the other road." She gestured toward the place below them where the road they had taken crossed another just like it, one which seemed to run back the way they had come but on the other side of the ridge they were now on.

Obadiah looked at the thin white line. "You sure it goes back to town?"

"Reasonably. There's not much else in that direction."

The road hugged the ridge which obscured their western view. "It's worth a shot," she told him.

Obadiah regretted the choice of roads almost at once. The new road seemed softer than the one they had taken out and every few minutes they would hit a sand pit. Delandra would gun it, hitting the pit at about fifty miles an hour, exiting the other side amid clouds of swirling sand and dust at about ten miles per hour. "It's the only way to make them," Delandra told him. "You've got to hit 'em fast."

"I'll remember that," Obadiah said. He was hanging on to the dashboard, watching the hood go white with dust. He was about to venture some gloomy prediction as to what the pits were going to look like when the storm hit when, suddenly, emerging from the longest bog yet and rounding a tight turn, they came hard upon a section of paved road and what could only have been, even if it had not been so marked by a large black-and-white sign, Ceton Verity's Electro-Magnetron. "Wa, la," Delandra said.

Obadiah found it difficult to assess the immediate impact the sight of Verity's Electro-Magnetron in its natural habitat had upon him. The building itself was almost comical—as if they had stumbled upon the sight of some cheap sci-fi set. It was a circular building with a dome-shaped roof. The walls seemed to be made of wood, while the roof looked to be made of aluminum. The place might have passed for an observatory of some sort had it not been for the color scheme. The Electro-Magnetron was painted red, white, and blue, with gold and silver trim. There was one tall antenna at the top of the domed roof and all around the sides, at about that point where the roof and walls met, there were what Obadiah took to be antennas of another variety. These were shorter and thicker than the one on the roof. They were set paral-

lel to the ground and were evenly spaced around the circumfer-
ence of the building. Each arm was silver in color and capped with
a red ball.

The oddest part of the scene, however, was the way in which the
Electro-Magnetron interacted with its immediate environment—
setting up a certain tension between the comical aspects of the
building and its stark desert surroundings, which worked to lend a
certain dignity to the whole affair. Obadiah was not sure if he
should be amused or impressed. The Electro-Magnetron was of
respectable scale. Its shining metal roof rose perhaps forty feet
above the desert floor, cutting a great silver arc across the face of
the ragged, blood-red stone which reached out to surround it on
three sides, and one might have been willing to believe, had it not
been for the zany paint job, that the structure had really been built
there for some meaningful purpose. And yet, just as he was about
to dismiss it as one more crackbrained attraction, he was forced to
recall it was the same label he had once hung upon Sarge Hummer's Desert Museum.

Delandra let the Dodge roll to a stop near what looked to be the
front of the building and from this vantage point they could see
the Electro-Magnetron was not entirely alone. Perhaps fifty yards
down the road someone had set up a pair of aluminum house
trailers. The trailers were surrounded by a chain link fence and
within the compound created by the fence there looked to be a
couple of trucks and one or two cars. The vehicles were all parked
behind the trailers, in the farthest corner of the lot from where
Obadiah and Delandra sat, and it was hard to see for sure just how
many there were. Someone had also erected a fence around the
Electro-Magnetron—this capped with barbed wire—and near the
gate someone, perhaps, Obadiah thought, Verity himself, had
posted a black sign with silver letters. The word ELECTRO-MAGNE-
TRON was printed at the top and below that there was some kind of
explanatory note. Obadiah read through it several times without
coming any closer to knowing what the odd-looking building was
all about. It apparently had something to do with the collecting of
electromagnetic impulses which were to be used in the manufac-
ture of mana rays, which in turn were to be used for the further-
ance of life, energy, and harmony. Delandra killed the engine and
they climbed from the car. There was moisture in the air now and
the smell of rain. But at least they had found the paved road which
Delandra was sure would get them back to Trona.

They were moving closer to the gate and sign when they heard the distant popping of a trailer door. They looked toward the second, smaller compound in time to see a man moving down the steps which led to one of the trailers. He did not appear to look in their direction but moved around the end of the trailer, walking toward the trucks and cars. He had a rifle in one hand. He carried it loosely, even with his thigh, parallel to the ground. A moment later they heard an engine start up and soon a pickup was bounding across the rutted dirt of the compound, hitting the piece of road upon which Delandra had parked the car and moving toward them, a thin trail of white dust floating in its wake.

Delandra and Obadiah were standing between the Dart and the gate. "We could make a run for it," Obadiah suggested. He smiled to let her know he was kidding but the smile had not been an easy thing to muster and was probably, he thought, not very convincing.

"Relax," Delandra told him. "All these assholes out here carry guns. They like to play games. But we've got the Thing. Right? Just act cool."

"Right," Obadiah said, and might have found it an easier pose to assume had he not suddenly noticed that the approaching truck was painted a dark blue and looked very much like the one he had seen that first night at the A & W burger joint.

Back at the compound, behind the truck, a pair of large, gangling dogs had run to the edge of the road and begun to bark. The barking had an odd, flat ring to it—a kind of metallic popping upon the heavy air which preceded the storm.

T he man driving the truck had little crosses tattooed on each hand, in the skin between the thumb and forefinger. Obadiah noticed the crosses because of the way the man stood when he reached them. He stood with his thumbs hooked in his belt loops.

He was not the man Obadiah had seen at the root beer stand. He was tall and rangy with a narrow white face and long white hair pulled back in a ponytail. His brows and lashes were white too. He was almost an albino. He might have been thirty or he might have been forty. The white hair made it difficult to tell. He was dressed in work boots, jeans, and a dirty white T-shirt without sleeves. The cut of the T-shirt worked to accentuate the length of the man's trunk. His torso and arms appeared slightly longer than what they should have been and Obadiah found that the man reminded him of the kind of lizards he used to catch in his aunt's woodpile. Alligator lizards, his aunt had called them. And the guy did look like he'd been under something for a while. He looked like being out from under it made him uncomfortable.

"Something you need?" the man asked.

"We're looking for Dr. Verity," Delandra told him.

The man studied them for a moment. "He died. You the woman who called?"

Obadiah glanced at Delandra. Her eyes had narrowed behind the shades. "I might be," she said.

The man smiled for the first time. "I might be," he repeated. "I like that."

They followed him back to the compound in the Dart. A kid and two dogs met them at the gate and then chased them toward the trailers. The guy in the truck stopped as he entered and shut the gate after them. Storm clouds were overhead now and as they stepped from the car they felt the first full drops of rain on their faces. By the time they got to the red wooden steps leading up to the nearest trailer, the compound had gone to mud.

The man Obadiah had first seen at the A & W was waiting for them in the trailer. It was the same man or it was someone who looked very much like him. No one said anything about it and it soon became apparent that none of those present were going to cop to much.

The man was seated in a large green rocker which filled up most of the trailer's living room. On the other side of the trailer from which Obadiah and Delandra had entered there was a sliding glass door which opened onto a deck built of two-by-fours beneath an aluminum awning. The glass in the sliders was greasy with nose prints and hand prints. The child who had run after them in the yard was there now, on the deck, one hand on the glass, the other down the front of his pants. Behind him, framed in the open doorway of a storage shed, there was a fat woman doing something in front of a large tub.

The man in the green chair introduced himself as Jack. He called the blond man Lyle.

"You're Sarge Hummer's girl?" the man said when Obadiah and Delandra had seated themselves on a bench seat at one end of the glass door.

Delandra shrugged. "You could say that," she said.

The man laughed and showed a mouthful of bad teeth. His head was as big as Obadiah had remembered it and the body that went with it was big as well—fat, but the kind of fat you expected covered a good deal of muscle. The man wore a dirty pair of jeans and a black T-shirt which said "Who needs niggers?" on the front. "He was a crazy son of a bitch, wasn't he?" the man asked.

Delandra had settled into the seat with one arm up and resting along its back. She had her legs crossed in front of her and her glasses pushed back on her head. "You wouldn't have said it to his face," she said. Her eyelids were still propped at about half-mast. All in all it was, in the opinion of Obadiah, a fine pose. She looked, he thought, a bit sleepy and a bit bored, maybe just a bit contemptuous of what was around her. It was a pose he very much admired.

Jack laughed again.

"Who's your friend?" he asked.

"Just a friend."

"He have a name?"

"I don't know," Delandra said. "You'll have to ask him."

Jack looked at Obadiah. "Obadiah Wheeler," Obadiah said.

Jack repeated the name. "Sounds like some sort of toilet bowl cleanser."

Lyle grinned at Obadiah. "You don't have to sit still for that shit," he said.

At his side, Obadiah felt Delandra moving on the bench. "So come on," she said. "Let's talk business. Are you the guy I talked to on the phone or aren't you?"

"You were supposed to be here this morning," Jack said. "You're late."

Delandra shrugged. "We had some trouble with the car."

Jack just looked at her. Delandra stared back. Obadiah looked at Lyle and then outside, toward the fat woman in the shed. The rain was coming down in sheets now, tearing miniature canyons out of the mud and sand beyond the aluminum awning. As Obadiah watched, a brilliant pattern of lightning raced across the sky above the shed and the woman. The rain in the trailer was like hail on a tin can.

"So what, exactly," Jack asked, "do you have?"

"Something Dr. Verity expressed interest in before he died," Delandra said.

"Not one of those bullshit things your old man was always building," Jack said. "You wouldn't be trying to push off one of those?"

"Something he found," Delandra said. "I don't know what it is. I know Verity was interested. I know some other people are interested now."

"What other people?"

"I don't know. Some black guys from the city."

Jack looked at Lyle. Obadiah, seated just a bit forward now on the bench, was able to look down the length of the trailer, past the cooking and dining area toward the back bedroom. There was something on the wall there, at that end of the trailer. It looked like some kind of little shrine. It was painted the color of the Electro-Magnetron and had light bulbs around it. Somehow the sight was not comforting. He looked back at his shoes upon the soiled floor.

"And you want to auction it off. Is that it? Highest bidder gets it?"

"Something like that," Delandra said.

Obadiah had inadvertently let himself get caught staring at Lyle. "Dr. Verity was Jesus Christ," Lyle told him.

Obadiah felt a slight chill run along his spine. "That's cool," he said.

"You bet your ass it is," Lyle said. He sounded mad about something. Obadiah didn't think that Lyle mad was something he wanted to see.

"So when do we get a look?" Jack asked. "You have it now?"

"No," Delandra said, "we'll have to get it."

Jack looked at Obadiah. "You've seen it?" he asked.

Obadiah said that he had.

"What is it?"

"A body."

"What kind of body?"

"I believe it's the body of an alien being," Obadiah said. He made sure he looked Jack in the eye.

Jack's face did not change with the news. "Maybe you should go get it," he said. "Your girlfriend can stay here; just to make sure you come back with it."

Obadiah continued to look the fat man in the eye. It was true. He really wasn't ready for this.

"Cut the crap," Delandra said. "If you've got the money and you want to talk, let's set up a time and place. If not, we're out of here."

Jack looked at the two of them, first Obadiah then Delandra. "You're a tough one, aren't you?" he asked.

"Business," Delandra told him.

"Listen," Jack said as they were leaving. "Your old man was an asshole. I would've said that to him anytime."

Delandra just looked at him. They were at the door now. The rain had stopped as suddenly as it had begun, and beyond the wooden railings of the porch the mud was strewn with puddles the color of the sky. "Whatever you say," Delandra said.

"Hey, Sweet Meat, that's my style. Remember it." In the background Obadiah could hear Lyle chuckling. "See you soon," Jack said.

A huge rainbow had sprouted above the iron-colored range by the time they hit the asphalt which led to Trona. Delandra dragged a hand up over her forehead and back through her hair. She glanced at Obadiah in the seat next to her. He had one hand on the armrest. The other was rolled into a fist, resting on his thigh. His profile had a pale, drawn look to it beneath the black arm of the shades and the regrettable haircut. "Just a couple of regular guys," she said. Obadiah looked at her but she could not see his eyes, only her own face in the shades. She looked away, back across the rain-streaked hood. "You were all right," she said. Obadiah did not respond. She was trying to decide if she wanted to ask him about what he had said in the trailer. He had managed the right line at the right time with sufficient conviction and it was about this conviction—or the illusion thereof—that she was curious. She was just at the point of asking and then changed her mind. Perhaps she thought it would be better not to know.

Harlan's room had no view. A bulky cooler filled its only window and if he wanted to know what the day was doing he had to do one of two things. He could go to the cooler and peel back the strip of aluminum foil which had been attached to the top half of his window, or he could leave his room and walk down the hallway to the living room, where a large picture window looked out upon a yard of sand and cactus. On the other side of the same room there was a sliding glass door which opened upon a small patio. Standing on the concrete slab one could look west across a new redwood fence, and see part of the Las Vegas skyline.

For the most part, Harlan preferred peeling the foil. He couldn't really see much that way and was reminded of TV dinners, but it was enough to tell him something about the weather and was preferable to stalking about the house where he might be stopped for conversation by one of its three occupants. Harlan was interested in the weather because as soon as the storms stopped, he intended to leave.

The house, part of a new development on the eastern edge of Las Vegas, was owned by a young couple, acquaintances of Neil Davis, and it was where Harlan had been brought to recover from the beating he had taken at the Chevron. He had been here since Monday afternoon. It was now Wednesday afternoon and it was raining. Hard. Neil Davis and the sisters Allen had already left. They had gone on up to Tonopah. Harlan had wanted it that way. He wanted to be alone. He had told them he would rent something in Vegas and drive it back to L.A. If, however, he had intended to get back to Los Angeles immediately, he would not have bothered waiting out the storm. As it was, a number of factors contributed to his still being here. For one thing, he hurt more than he cared to admit and had, in fact, blown one day—Tuesday —in bed. For another, he had no intention of returning to Los Angeles, not just yet. He had some looking around to do and that would be made a good deal easier by dry weather. He also needed some information; he needed a phone and a place where he could be reached. Still, he was not comfortable here, and as he stood at the window staring past the foil into a rain-slick street, he was anxious to be gone.

Normally, staying in someone else's home would not have been a big deal for Harlan. He had lived most of his adult life in homes not his own. He had gone into the circuit work in his twenties and that was how visiting elders lived in those days. Now many owned house trailers, which could be moved from place to place, or even, in some areas, kept in a central location, allowing the brother to drive to the different congregations he served—almost a normal life—and a few Harlan knew of even had children, something which was pretty much unheard of when Harlan had started. The governing body had felt then it was important for the elders to stay in the homes of the brothers. And so Harlan had, at first as a bachelor, later with his wife—sleeping in someone else's bedroom, eating in someone else's kitchen, kicking off one's shoes in front of someone else's TV, figuring out which people you could relax with over a couple of cold ones and which ones would take offense, or pester you night and day with silly questions. You tried, of course, to weed the latter off your list, but there always seemed to be one or two you couldn't get rid of. As a bachelor it really hadn't been that bad. He had always adapted to things pretty easily—go outside with a beer and toss the football around with someone else's kid. With a wife it had been harder. Takes an unusual woman, he supposed, to be content in other people's houses, and Judith had never been. Later, when they had moved to Africa, they had lived in the branch home with other missionaries and that was better— more like having your own place, but then in Africa there had been the country to contend with and by that time Judith's health was not so great.

Harlan sighed. He tucked the aluminum foil back into place and the sliver of rain-slick street and gray sky went away. He seated himself on the edge of his bed and rubbed his face with his hands. He thought of checking the refrigerator for a beer, but that, like getting to the patio, would mean risking some sort of meeting. It was stupid, really. He didn't know what Neil Davis had said to the people about why he was there, and they had been nice. Still, the subject had been carefully enough avoided to leave him suspecting it was probably something not that far from the truth. And that was embarrassing. It was worse than embarrassing. And it was certainly not going to end here, in the desert. It was quite likely that at some point upon his return to Los Angeles, he would be asked to step down. They would no doubt be nice about it. The incident would probably wind up being connected in some way to what he had gone through in Africa. He would be told that a good rest was in order. He would still be asked to step down.

This was not, in his opinion, out of line. Visiting elders didn't go around getting into fistfights. And there was no question in his mind that it was something he could have avoided. He had swung on Floyd Hummer with murder in his heart. And that was the bottom line. There was always, Harlan believed, a bottom line.

When he thought of stepping down, however—of what in plain fact that was going to mean for him—he was faced with a series of conflicting responses. In a way he was relieved. He had carried a lot of responsibility for a long time. On the other hand, there was something depressing about the direction in which he had begun to move. Missionary to Elder, finally back to simple publisher. Not exactly the rising star he had been in his youth. It would just be digging in somewhere now, he and Judith. Perhaps if there had been children, but there was little chance of that now and when he thought along those lines he could see a whole section of his life closing off behind him in some inexorable way. He would even have to hold down some job. He grinned at that prospect and rubbed his face once more. He would try to get something outside, maybe work himself back into shape. His fear was that some brother would offer him something in sales or some damn thing he would no doubt be good at and the money would be too good to turn down. He would grow old and fat and even softer than he was now. At the heart of it, of course, there would be his relationship with his Creator. There would be accountability. A bottom line. And so, if he was imaginative enough about it, he might just see all of this as having a kind of streamlining effect—a cutting back to essentials. He found the prospect at once promising and unrelentingly bleak.

Bleak enough, Harlan decided, to at least warrant a beer. Confrontations be hanged. He rose slowly from the bed. He was dressed in a large terry cloth bathrobe with which the man of the house had provided him. After seeing to it that the garment was securely tied about his middle and pausing at his door long enough to satisfy himself the coast was clear, he left his room and headed for the kitchen.

He was on his way back, beer in hand, nearly home free and congratulating himself on his stealth, when he came close to tripping over the couple's young son. The boy had taken up a position in the hall near Harlan's door. He was seated Indian style upon the floor. "Who was the shortest man in the Bible?" the boy wanted to know.

"Beats me," Harlan said. He had, of course, heard all the jokes before, but the boy seemed to have just discovered them and was always disappointed if he couldn't deliver the punch lines himself. "Bildad the Shuhite," the boy said, grinning. "Job 2:11."

Harlan guffawed several times. "Did you know people smoked cigarettes in Bible days?" the boy asked. This time he didn't wait for the reply but went right ahead. "Genesis 24:64: 'And Rebekah lifted up her eyes, and when she saw Isaac, she lighted off the camel.' "

Harlan haw-hawed his way toward the safety of his room. The boy was standing now. "Here's one for you," Harlan said. "Who was the man with the stretchiest skin in the Bible?"

The boy looked stumped. "Balaam," Harlan said, "once tied his ass to a tree and walked five miles."

The boy looked slightly dumbfounded for a moment then burst into laughter and ran off in the direction of the living room.

Harlan stepped inside and closed the door behind him. At the far end of the hall he could now hear someone in the kitchen, banging pots and pans. He looked at his watch. It would be dinner-time soon. He went to the window and looked outside. The rain had stopped but the sky was still filled with clouds. Harlan sat on the bed and opened his beer. He glanced at the phone on the dresser and closed his eyes. Hopefully, before the evening was over the long-distance calls he had made that morning would bear fruit. There had been one to Los Angeles. Another to New York. He was hoping the phone calls would give him some sense of what his next move should be, for if part of what had been occupying Harlan's mind since the fight had to do with the shape of his life, another equally substantial part had to do with what he had begun to think of, in an almost obsessive sort of way, as his last official act as a visiting elder. He took some satisfaction from the fact that it was an act at least grounded in Scripture: "What do you think?" the text asked, "If a certain man comes to have a hundred sheep and one of them gets strayed, will he not leave the ninety-nine upon the mountains and set out on a search for the one that is straying? And if he happens to find it, I certainly tell you, he rejoices more over it than over the ninety-nine that have not strayed." Harlan Low could not take back his acts at the station. He could still, however, go after Obadiah Wheeler.

Harlan woke on the following morning to the sound of thunder. When he looked out the window it was the same old thing. He donned the terry cloth bathrobe and went into the kitchen to help himself to some coffee. When he returned he sat on the edge of the bed and looked over the notes he had made the night before. His long-distance calls had indeed borne fruit. The stuff was strewn all over his sheets—a litter of hurriedly scribbled notes.

With no real idea of where to begin looking for the Wheeler boy, he had elected to begin by trying to find out something about this image which seemed of late to keep popping up in one form or another under his nose—this hand. The hand was what the notes were all about.

The building he'd seen from the freeway was indeed a temple: The Temple of the Sons of Elijah. When he had found this out, he contacted a friend in New York to see what they had there on the group. The man he spoke to was a brother by the name of Mitchell. The man had been one of Harlan's instructors at the missionary training school. He had checked the file, called Harlan back, told him there was a fair amount there, that he could give him a few of the basics but that if he wanted more they would have to talk again, later, as Mitchell was on his way out of town. The basics turned out to be mostly information on a man by the name of Leonard Maxwell, the founder of the Sons of Elijah. It was enough to get Harlan interested.

Maxwell was a black man. He was forty-eight years old. He had soldiered in the war, had dabbled in interests as diverse as script-writing and gold mining before getting into religion. His entrance to the field was marked by the publication of an article in a magazine called *UFO Alert!* The article presented Maxwell's assertion that evil was a magnetic phenomenon about which something might be done through magnetic manipulation.

The *Alert!* was the first magazine to touch any of Maxwell's ideas, but when it did the reader response was astonishing. The

article became a series of articles and soon Maxwell had invented a
whole lost epoch of the earth's past—something he referred to as
the Elder World. There was even a book, a collaboration on the
part of Maxwell and the editor of *Alert!*

Maxwell claimed to have come by his information with the aid of
a Geiger counter–like device capable of decoding what he called
the Language of the Spheres—ancient coded messages left in
stone by the Celestial Visitors.

His following grew, up until 1953, at which point he screwed up.
He tried to market one of his magnetic devices and wound up
doing eighteen months in a California prison for fraud. The incident apparently ended his relationship with *Alert!* because when
he resurfaced he was on his own—this time claiming to have
become a contactee. A contactee, Mitchell explained, was anyone
claiming contact with aliens. In 1965, Maxwell set up headquarters
in Los Angeles and filed for tax exemption as a church.

This was what Harlan had gotten from Mitchell. The rest of
what was in his notes had come from a brother in Los Angeles, a
black man who lived near the temple. Harlan had been put in
touch with the man because he was supposed to know something
about the Sons. The man's fleshly brother, Harlan had been told,
was one himself.

"Know more than I want to about those people," the man had
begun by telling him. "Talking to them is like watching cartoons.
It's all Batman and Robin."

When Harlan asked for specifics the man had begun to elaborate. "Well, first," he said, "you got your Elder World and you got
your Ancients."

Harlan now had them in his notes. The Ancients were the controllers of the Elder World, the creators. Unlike the Creator, with
whom Harlan was familiar, these had simply done it for sport. It
was the kind of sport a demented child might take with bugs in a
jar.

You also had your Zedroes, Drones, the Super Race, and the
Celestial Visitors. It was, Harlan had to admit, a little like watching
cartoons. The theology was upside down, with the creators as
villains and life fallen from the start. The messiahs of the Elder
World were the Celestial Visitors, a small group of ancient astronauts who had come to earth after their own world had been lost
in a great cataclysm. In general, the story was as follows:

The Ancients had created life for sport. The trouble was, it got
away from them. Or threatened to. New life in all its raw vitality,
its utter wildness, was something the stodgy old bastards hadn't

counted on. More than a little annoyed, they even created a race of Zedroes—also known as Half Things, to help keep it in check. Enter the Celestial Visitors. If the Ancients were antilife, the Visitors were for it. They saw its wondrous potential. Too few in number to challenge the Ancients directly, they set about breeding with the daughters of men to produce a super race. It was, according to Maxwell, an incredible period. The new race, beneficiaries of both the Visitors' wisdom and their own immense vitality, were indeed something to behold. Even the Ancients were impressed, so much so that in one desperate move—an act demanding all of their terrible power—they effectively brought an end to the Elder World and the first age of men.

To ensure their own survival, the Ancients passed into a state of dormancy within another dimensional plane, from which they had counted on the surviving Zedroes to wake them. The Elder World had not passed quietly into the void, however, and the violence of its passing had created changes in the earth's magnetic field which even the Ancients had not foreseen. In short, they were stuck. Zedroes were stuck, too, some in the realm of the Ancients and some in the world of men. Those in the realm of men—the conscious realm—were now too few in number to wake the Ancients on their own. It was going to take time. Magnetic tidal flows would have to shift. Stars would have to align themselves. And the Zedroes would need help. They would need Drones.

Drones were humans, either demented, naive, or simply weakwilled enough to be used by the Zedroes. Adolf Hitler had been a prominent Drone. Billy Graham was another. The locating and exposing of Drones was of primary concern to the Sons of Elijah.

"This," Harlan had asked, "is where it gets like Batman and Robin?"

"Batman, Superman, the Green Hornet, all rolled into one," the brother had told him.

It wasn't the first time Harlan had seen this kind of thing. What he had not run across before, however, was the twist Leonard Maxwell had put on the Super Race routine.

Without the Visitors to guide them, the fledgling race soon lost the use of their powers. Ignorantly they toiled with the rest of mankind to emerge from the Great Postwar Darkness. But the Visitors had left messages coded in stone. To break the code was to learn the truth of history. The task had fallen to Leonard Maxwell and Maxwell had learned a number of interesting things. He had learned that the Visitors were black. The race they fathered was black as well and what lay behind the suppression of the black man in the modern era was nothing less than the efforts of Zedroes and their Drones to prevent the race from rediscovering and using their powers.

What it came down to in the end was a kind of race. Would men rediscover the secrets of the Visitors? Or would the slumbering Ancients, aided by Zedroes and Drones, awake?

It had seemed to Harlan, in the beginning, that there were at least three reasons for being interested in all of this. One had to do with the fact that the Sons were a group active in his territory— whether the medallion in the museum had anything to do with them or not. A second reason was that if the medallion was theirs, it might mean the Wheeler boy had gotten involved with them in some way—whether he knew it or not. The third reason was personal. It was based upon speculation that there might in fact be some connection between the hand Harlan had seen in Africa and the two variations he had seen since returning to the States. So far everything he had learned about the Sons of Elijah seemed to work against this—the stuff was too absurd. Connected to the second possibility, however, there seemed to be a legitimate reason for concern. The brother in Los Angeles seemed to think so. "This boy black or white?" he had asked when Harlan mentioned that a boy from his circuit may have become involved with the Sons.

"White," Harlan had replied. "Is that bad?"

"It's bad if he's done anything to make them mad," the brother said. "Let me put it like this. These guys take the Zedroe, Drone stuff real seriously, if you know what I mean. I mean my own brother's got himself a pair of Dobermans and a house full of automatic guns. He's got a license-plate holder says 'Search and Destroy.'"

"In other words, you wouldn't want these people to get the idea you were a Drone."

"I know I wouldn't," the brother told him.

Harlan was about to hang up when it occurred to him there was still something important he had forgotten to ask. He wanted to know about the name and he wanted to know about the hand.

"They say Elijah was one of the Visitors," the brother said. "They think Melchizedek was the other. They think maybe there were only two."

Harlan thought for a moment. "Melchizedek because he was

without genealogy. Elijah because he ascended in a chariot of fire. Am I close?"

"On the button," the man told him.

Harlan shook his head against the receiver. "Except that Elijah wasn't a black man and his ascension was in fact a transference. The Bible shows he was still alive, on earth, at a later time."

"This is true," the brother said, "wouldn't do any good to tell them, though. It would be like trying to talk to them about that finger thing."

"The finger thing?"

The man proceeded to tell him that the Sons had a bible of their own. *The Book of Stones.* It was suppose to be older than the Bible. It was what the Visitors put down and what Maxwell translated. Some of the stories in the Bible were in fact, according to the Sons, bastardized versions of incidents originally recorded by the Visitors. Ezekiel's vision of the wheelworks was a case in point. The incident here was the arrival of the Visitors. The Bible called them cherubs. It failed to mention that their hands, as well as containing a number of eyes, also had six fingers.

This was not an idle omission. Zedroes and Ancients had, toward the end of the Elder World, tried many times to assume the form of the Visitors in order to trick men. Such was the Visitors' power, however, that neither Zedroe nor Ancient could accomplish this completely. There was always something just a little bit off, one detail they could not manage, something apparently to do with the hands—and hence the symbol of the Sons of Elijah.

"The thing is," the brother told him, laughing a bit into the phone, "they do have a tricky little point there about those hands."

Harlan had asked him what the tricky little point was.

The point was this: In the twelfth verse of The Book of Ezekiel it says that the creatures had eyes in their hands. In the twenty-first verse it says that their hands had the likeness of those of earthling man. Now when (it was a question the Sons were fond of asking) was the last time you saw someone with eyes in their hands?

Harlan sat looking at the verses now, in the white glare of the room's single overhead light. The verses did not represent a contradiction to him. And yet he could see how it was just the kind of thing some yo-yo like Leonard Maxwell would make something of. He listened to the metallic pinging of the rain upon the cooler at his window. He looked at the text. He would leave in the morning, he promised himself. Rain or shine.

Obadiah was up early. The air was cool and bone-dry with the ridge in back of the motel shining like metal filings before an empty sky. It had been agreed, upon leaving the compound, that he and Delandra would meet Jack and Lyle on the coming evening at the Blue Heaven Motel.

Delandra, optimistic, did not believe the boys would misbehave. Obadiah was less certain. He was still entertaining the idea that Jack was in fact the man he had seen at the A & W—though Delandra had dismissed this notion so quickly, Obadiah had begun to wonder. It had, after all, been dark. He had been in a weird state of mind. Perhaps the session at the trailer had only fueled his paranoia. And yet either way he was not happy with the scenario. Either Jack was the guy at the burger joint, which suggested connections neither he nor Delandra knew anything about. Or Jack was simply Jack—which in itself was bad enough. Selling the Creature to Verity, if in fact he had proven to be the eccentric old fart Delandra had described, was one thing. Jack and Lyle were something else. Obadiah found that sitting in their trailer had made him slightly nauseous and he did not look forward to seeing them again. Nor was he much impressed by Delandra's plan for avoiding bullshit—should her optimism prove ill-founded.

The plan—alternate plan B, Delandra liked to call it—had Obadiah stationed just outside the rear wall of the motel, ear cocked beneath an open bathroom window, Delandra's pistol in hand. If there was trouble he could . . . and there was the tricky part. Come through the bathroom window, gun blazing, bullets ripping bloody holes from Jack's fat chest? Obadiah had tried to envision how this would work. He thought of it again now as he leaned against the fender of Delandra's car in the stillness which had followed the storm. He tried to imagine jumping bad on the likes of Jack and Lyle. With the exception of one twenty-two-caliber rifle he'd once used for target practice at a summer camp at the age of eight, he had never handled a weapon of any kind. Which is why he was here now, why they were up early instead of sleeping late in one another's arms. Delandra had determined he should practice with the gun.

When she came out of the motel she had the gun with her. She gave it to Obadiah as she got into the car and he held it now, in his lap, the barrel pointed at the floorboards between his feet. The thing made him nervous. He kept waiting for it to go off and destroy his foot. It made him feel guilty and more than a little foolish.

Nor was the gun the only thing bothering him. The rest of it had to do with their intended sale of the Mystery of the Mojave, and as the gleaming towers of the Trona Chemical plant slipped from view he tried to decide how the subject could best be approached. He waited until the town was well behind them. He waited until Delandra had found a half-dozen junked cars rusting in the sunlight at the end of a narrow dirt road. The cars were at the bottom of a shallow sandy bowl at which the road had ended. Delandra parked at the lip of the bowl and got out. Obadiah followed her. When he got around to speaking he found that his voice had the odd, flat quality voices often did in that climate. It was a quality of sound he now associated with the barking of Jack's dogs. "I've been meaning," he said, "to talk to you about this sale."

Delandra's only response was to cast a sideways glance in his direction. It was pretty much what he had expected. He continued to follow her. She was headed into the bowl, taking these big long strides, throwing her boots out in front of her, skidding with each step, kicking up clouds of dust and sending small rockslides ahead of her, into the cars. She reached the bottom ahead of him and stood there resting, bent at the waist, hands on her knees. Obadiah did the same, winded from the speed of the descent. At last he put a hand on her arm. "Delandra," he said. "I'm serious about this."

She turned her head to look at him, the sunglasses perched crookedly on her face. "Give me a break," she said.

"Come on, I want to talk. I want to talk seriously about this thing before we sell it to somebody and it's too late."

"You want to talk seriously about the Mystery of the Mojave?" Delandra laughed.

"Seriously. Is that too much to ask?"

"Yes. I'm not a serious girl, Obondigas. You should know that by now."

What Obadiah wanted to say was that having seen the Mystery

of the Mojave, he believed he had incurred a certain responsibility for it. "You're responsible for what you see," he said.

"What are you talking about?"

"I'm talking about that thing we've been dragging around with us for the past three days. I mean I don't care what you say about your old man making it, I say it's no ordinary thing and what I'm suggesting is that we make some serious attempt at finding out what it is. You admit it is different from the others. So what if he didn't make it? Aren't you just a little curious? Wouldn't you like to know for sure?"

"No," Delandra told him. "I wouldn't. And anyway, how would you suggest that we go about doing this?"

"Get somebody to look at it."

"We're getting Jack and Lyle to look at it, remember?"

"I was thinking of somebody who just might know what the fuck they were talking about. You know? Lyle thinks Verity was Jesus Christ."

Delandra smiled at the thought. "Lyle's a good boy," she said. She took the gun from Obadiah and began putting shells into the chamber. She held the gun out in front of her while she did this. She held it turned on its side, pointing slightly downward. When she was finished she gave the cylinder a spin. It made a soft clicking sound which she ended with a flick of her wrist. "When the hammer's down, that's like the safety," she said. "You have to pull the hammer back to cock it and you have to recock after each shot. It's an old gun. It belonged to the Sarge. He had the oversize grips put on. When you fire it use both hands." She brought the gun up quickly, pulling the hammer back with her thumbs. The following blast was deafening. Obadiah flinched and looked away. He had no idea what she was aiming at.

"Your turn," she said. She passed the gun to Obadiah.

He found the dark wooden handle still warm from her grip. "I don't get it," he said. He could barely hear himself speak. "I can't understand why you're not more interested in this."

"I thought you wanted to go to Canada," Delandra said.

"I do."

"So all right. So let's raise some cash and do it."

"Maybe we could do both."

"Jesus." She was standing with her hands on her hips now, her glasses still crooked on her face. "And who in the fuck do you think you're going to get to look at that thing? The cops? Shit, you show that thing to anybody like that and they're either going to laugh in

your face or they're going to confiscate it for some damn reason
and that will be that."

"I wasn't thinking about the cops."

"Who, then?"

"I don't know. Somebody at a university or something."

"For Christ's sake," Delandra said. "Shoot at something, will
you?"

Obadiah looked around for something to aim at. The gun felt
like a lead weight at the end of his arm. He aimed the thing in the
general direction of a rusting Plymouth station wagon and pulled
the trigger. The gun kicked in his hands, jerking his arms upward.
When he looked back at the car he found that there was now a
bullet hole in the panel above the rear wheel.

"Maybe you could aim at something smaller," Delandra suggested.

He picked out a carton of beer bottles perhaps twenty feet
away. The first two shots did nothing but send chunks of earth
flying into the sky. The third shot hit the carton and sprayed the
ground behind it with shards of broken glass. He left the hammer
where it was and lowered the gun. "I think," he said, "that we
should show it to someone who could look at it and tell us if it's
man-made or not. I mean, think about it for a minute. Maybe your
old man wasn't as crazy as you thought; maybe he really did find
something. Who knows, you might put his name in the goddamn
history books."

"Big deal," Delandra said. "Sarge didn't read books. He hated
fucking books." She was walking away from him now. Obadiah
followed. They walked past the cars and out into a clearing on the
other side. There was a pile of rusted oil drums in the clearing and
when Obadiah caught up to her she was looking at something on
one of the drums. "There," she said, "shoot that."

There was a large gray lizard sunning itself on a scrap of rusted
metal.

"You're kidding me."

Delandra took the gun from his hand and set the hammer.
"Don't be such a goddamn wimp," she said. She raised the gun
toward the drum. Obadiah grabbed her wrist. He did it just as she
was in the act of pulling the trigger and the bullet slammed into
one of the drums. The lizard disappeared. "Don't be such an
asshole," he told her. "There are enough assholes around already."
He stood close beside her, his hand still on her wrist.

"If you can't shoot a lizard," she asked him, "how will you shoot
your old friend Lyle?"

"I was hoping it wouldn't come to that."

"Oh, no," Delandra said. "Heaven forbid that the game get rough. Maybe you could quote him a few Scriptures." She jerked away from him.

He stood for a moment, watching her go. She disappeared among the cars. When he saw her again she was already moving back up the grade on the far side of the bowl. The gun was pointed at the ground, swinging at the end of one straight arm. The sunlight was bright in her hair and suddenly what he was thinking about was how it felt to be inside of her in a dark room with just the scent of their bodies in the darkness and her breath on his neck and how she could work a kind of magic he had only, until the recent past, barely been able to imagine. He thought of her on top of him with just the moonlight on the side of her face and that sleepy kind of half smile that was part of the lovemaking and he thought of how when he had come in off those flats at the roadside rest on the outskirts of Trona he had found her crying and he started after her.

He caught her at the car. She was already inside, behind the wheel. Obadiah got in next to her. It was the way they had begun. "What's the matter?" he asked. "What's going on?"

Delandra only shook her head and started the car. She was starting to feel tired and feeling tired made her angry. "Don't even ask," she said. "You wouldn't want to know."

D elandra drove without speaking. She drove without doing anything except stare at the road and by the middle of morning they were back in Trona, where nothing seemed to have changed. The town still looked like no one was home. Delandra turned off the highway and down a short stretch of paved road. The road ended between a deserted theater and the bar called the Corner Pocket.

The bar was nothing but a small stucco box which had been painted the color of pea soup. There was a white pickup truck in

the parking lot with a sign on the door which said TRONA CHEMI-
CALS. The theater was a much grander piece of architecture and
had something of an art deco air about it. There was a large tiled
entry and a ticket booth made of glass and polished aluminum.
There was scrollwork in stone at the edges of the building and
above the sidewalk there was an empty marquee which someone
had thrown a couple of rocks through. There were still bits and
pieces of whatever the marquee was made of strewn along the
walls beneath the stonework where the wind had left them.

Obadiah and Delandra sat in the car for some time. Neither of
them said anything. Obadiah sat with his arm out the window, his
elbow pointing at the empty theater. He was thinking once again
about what this was costing him. It was costing him too much not
to know everything. "You're going to have to tell me," he said.
"We're in this together and I ought to know."

Delandra turned to face him. She was sitting with her wrists on
top of the wheel. Her hair was still mussed from the wind. "I
thought you said that if you don't go home your people will have to
notify your draft board. The government will issue a warrant for
your arrest."

Obadiah nodded. This was true.

"Then we haven't much time, have we? And finding someone to
look at the Thing would take time. You really want to go to jail for
it?"

Obadiah studied the heat waves which had begun to chew at the
edges of the hood. "No," he said, "but then all of that will take time
too. At this point I would be willing to take the chance."

"Oh, boy," Delandra said. She sat for a moment looking at her
wrists. "The trouble," she said, "is that I don't want to take the
chance. You see, yours is not the only ass on the line."

Obadiah pulled himself into a more upright position. "I take it
this is the part I didn't want to know?"

"This is the part you didn't want to know. The thing is, I put up
my share of the Desert Museum as collateral with this
bailbondsman. Now I've got less than a week before the court date
and I don't plan on being around."

Obadiah removed his glasses. He wiped the sweat from the
bridge of his nose. He supposed that he should hear the whole
thing.

Delandra shrugged. "I got busted for possession one night in
Victorville. I was a little short at the time and I had to use this
bailbondsman a friend of mine knew about. You know how that
works. The man puts up the money. You put up some collateral. I

put up my share of the museum. I assured him the Mystery of the Mojave was included, though I don't know why anyone would care. At any rate, you remember those guys you passed in the street the morning you came to the station?"

"The black guys in the red Cadillac?"

"Two black guys and one Indian."

"I hadn't noticed."

"Well, I did. And I think the Indian was the bailbondsman from Victorville."

"You think?"

"It gets complicated," Delandra said. "You see, there are these three brothers. They're bondsmen. They have an office in Victorville. I talked to one of them. But they all sort of look alike, if you know what I mean. Now what I think is that this guy in the red car was one of them. I don't know which one. I tried to get a better look at him but he never took the hat off and I never got that close."

Obadiah sat staring into the dashboard. On the metal grillework over the speaker someone had lined up a row of toothpicks. They pointed toward the windshield like a miniature row of spears. "And you were willing to go out on this limb because I needed bread for Canada. You were going to walk on your trial date, get this bailbondsman down on your case, leave your brother holding the bag on the museum, all because I show up and you decide it might be fun to see Canada?"

"It's the way my mind works," Delandra said. "What can I say?"

Obadiah continued to examine the toothpicks. The sun had moved just far enough to be visible at the edge of the windshield. Soon the front seat would not bear sitting in. He shook his head, as if to make something go away. The something stayed where it was. Like the sun moving at the edge of the glass, it filled the car with unwanted light. "What I think," he said, "is that you were planning to walk on this thing all along. I think you were planning on selling the Thing, too, to the UFO freaks at Verity's convention. And that's what you were waiting for. Then the Indian showed up and it forced your hand. And there I was, standing around with my thumb in my ass, and you did need a hand getting it into the car."

"You're pretty smart, Obo." She was giving him one of her more wolfish grins. "Except I never noticed that, about your thumb, I mean."

Obadiah wanted to punch her in the teeth. "What I don't get," he said, "is why you were willing to walk on a possession charge. I mean that's not that big a deal, is it?"

Delandra abandoned the smile and let herself slide back down into the seat until her face pointed at the roof. She was getting tired of making a joke out of it. It was really only marginally funny anyway. But then he had asked to hear the whole thing—as if that was something she knew more about, really, than he did. Still, focusing on the stained headliner already sporting a three-inch tear above her face (soon, she knew from experience, the thing would be hanging down, obscuring vision, a certain symbol, like some white-trash tattoo, of one's station in life) she was willing to take a crack at it. She told him about how up until a month ago she had been married to this used-car dealer from San Bernardino by the name of Fred Ott, the owner of Ott's Used Auto, actually two Ott's Used Autos, one in Victorville, and one in San Bernardino, and how the guy was twice her age but how for the first time in her life she'd had some bread and someone willing to finance her excesses and so how it wasn't so bad, at least not in the beginning. Toward the end there, however, things had begun to get a little weird. Fred believed he had been granted a vision and had taken to lying about the house all day in a pair of polyester shorts.

"A vision?" Obadiah asked. He was mildly curious.

"A small metal-headed man from the center of the earth appeared to him," Delandra said. "He told Fred how the world was going to end. After that, Fred quit going to work. He stayed around the house writing letters, making phone calls. Occasionally he would go out to the library to look something up. Nobody would pay any attention to him, of course.

"Finally he became despondent and just took to staying home, lying around the house all day on the couch in front of the television in a pair of these polyester shorts."

It was funny how those shorts had worked on her. Perhaps they were only a symbol—like the torn headliner and the tattoos. "Finally," she said, "I began to see this guy who dealt a little. Fred found out about it and got even weirder. Until one night I went out in front of the house to meet Tom."

"Tom the dealer?"

"The very one." She did feel like she was telling him a joke. It was the way she always wound up feeling when she tried to say anything to anyone that meant something. "It was late and it was dark and I was out on the street talking to Tom when all of a sudden Fred comes running out of the house. He's yelling. And he's waving a gun. I knew it was Fred right away. He had his shirt off and I could see his white stomach and the polyester shorts shining in Tom's lights. Tom thought it was a narc and hit the gas. Later, he said he thought he had it in reverse, but he didn't.

"I wound up getting charged with possession. But then I heard that Fred's mother had hired a lawyer and was going to try to get the charge upped to accessory to murder. And that's when I started thinking about that convention, about selling the Thing and walking on the whole deal. And that's when you showed up and started talking Canada."

Obadiah looked into the empty plate glass of Trona's fanciest building. He felt as a fish might which had just been gutted, quickly, so that there was just the one sparkling moment of awareness—the sun, the sky, what had been lost. "You make it sound like a fucking joke," he said.

"I guess you had to be there."

Obadiah said nothing.

Delandra went on. She didn't seem to be able to shut up now, or to make herself sound anything but cheap. "But you know, I really don't think the old lady cares that much about getting the charges changed. I think she just wants me gone. I think she just wants to make sure I don't fight her for the car lots. So I decided maybe I would be gone. I didn't want the car lots anyway. I figured I would just sell the Thing and split. Rex could work it out with the bailbondsman. It would do him good to be shed of the whole mess, anyway. Then that fucker showed up and saw what was there."

"Except that maybe it wasn't him and you don't know because you couldn't get close enough to get a good look. You told me before that you thought those guys were just some high rollers on their way to Vegas."

"Listen," Delandra said, "what we're talking about here is the very possibility. Let me point something out to you. You seen many police stations in town here?"

Obadiah looked into the empty street. "No," he said.

"You see any around the junction?"

"No."

"You seen many cop cars on the road?"

In fact, he had not.

"That's because there aren't any," Delandra said. "I mean, they've got them in the real towns, in Victorville, Ridgecrest, places like that. Out here, it's just a sheriff's department somewhere, or, if things get radical, the highway patrol. But a lot of the time it's people like the Corasco brothers. And they have ways of getting things done."

Obadiah used a hand to wipe his brow. "So why is this Indian—if of course he's one of the Corascos—so interested in the Thing?"

"I believe it's the principle that counts."

"The man has his rep. Is that it?"

"The man has his rep. They were talking about one of his clients while I was in Victorville. Seems the Indian had done some chiropractic work on the guy with an ax handle. They had him in traction in the hospital across the street from the jail. They had a steel pin in his head to keep him straight."

"Some rep."

"It's the kind of rep," Delandra said, "that will make one think twice."

Obadiah was going to say something else but he didn't. He was going to say something clever about frontier justice. What he found himself doing instead was thinking for a second time about the bailbondsman from Victorville. He had to admit it did put a certain slant on things.

"Well, don't look so disappointed," Delandra told him. "We can be wanted together. You know that song? I want to be wanted?"

"Just like Bonnie and Clyde."

"Exactly. Now let's go across the street for a drink."

"Go ahead," he told her. "I'm just going to sit here for a while."

Delandra opened her door. For a moment neither of them spoke. "Look, Obo, what did you expect, anyway?"

"I don't know," Obadiah said. "I don't know what I expected."

When she had left him he watched her cross the street. It was quite a picture: the tight, faded jeans, the red-and-yellow boots, the black T-shirt and black hair, the sunlight and the sound her boots made on an empty street. He noticed she had left her keys in the ignition and her purse in the back. It was fucking typical, he thought. He could see that now. Disaster clung to this woman like static electricity. A short life of sorrow was written all over her. But then what, he wondered, had he expected? What communion was there, after all, between light and darkness? Eventually he got out from behind the wheel and stood for a moment at the side of the car. The street, paved in asphalt the color of dried blood, was empty and brilliant, filled with a light he found difficult to bear. Crossing it, he followed her into the bar.

The Corner Pocket was about what he had expected. It was dark and gloomy and smelled like the customers had been pissing in the corners. There were a couple of guys standing around a quarter pool table and a fat man in a polo shirt sitting behind a counter next to a little oven with a glass door. There was a white cardboard menu above the oven with half a dozen items listed on it.

It took him a moment, after the brightness of the street, to find Delandra in the gloom. She was alone at a corner table. There was a pitcher of beer on the table and one glass. Obadiah was aware of the men watching him. He stood just inside the door. He was holding Delandra's purse. He was tired and angry and he couldn't decide if he was angry with her or with himself. It was, of course, ridiculous to imagine that one could pull into a place like the junction, jump into the sack with the first woman one saw, join her in robbing the local museum and still expect everything to come up roses. Everything he had been taught told him this was not the way it worked. On the other hand, he had grown up believing in miracles. He'd grown up believing in a new order, the end of death, and the eventual triumph of justice.

He crossed the room and placed her purse on the table. "You know what I don't get," he said. He was seating himself next to her. "Is why Fred Ott? Why not someone you loved?" He knew it was the wrong thing to say and he was mildly surprised at how quickly his resolve not to ask her about any of it had withered to nothing. He wanted to know everything. It was like staring into a wound.

Delandra had smiled at him as he crossed the floor. The smile died as he spoke. "Oh, come on," she said. "Let's not talk about that now. Let's play some pool."

"I want to talk about it."

"About Fred Ott?"

"About you."

"About the Mystery of the Mojave?"

"Among other things."

"That's what I was afraid of," she said. "Screw the Mystery of the Mojave. I'm sorry I ever introduced you. I wouldn't have if I'd thought you were going to go fruit over it." She sat there for a moment looking at him. "Look," she said, "I'm going to shoot a couple of games. You want to come with or what?"

"No," Obadiah said. "I don't. Why don't you at least wait until those assholes are done?"

Delandra looked at the men at the pool table. "How do you know they're assholes?"

"I have a hunch."

Delandra grinned at him. She took off her dark glasses and left them on the table, then sauntered off alone to get her quarter on the rail.

Obadiah sat watching her amid the stale cigarette smoke and the gloom, inhaling the variety of rancid odors which seemed to permeate the corner in which he sat. The blood burned in his cheeks. The men at the pool table wore jeans and blue work shirts. One of them wore a white windbreaker that said something about a softball team on the back. Every now and then one of the men would look in Obadiah's direction, as if they were trying to figure out what kind of loser this young whore was dragging around with her. When they weren't staring at Obadiah they were watching Delandra lean over to sight down her cue like it was their lucky day. Soon all three of them were whooping it up, poking each other in the arm and ordering more beer.

Obadiah finished what was left in the pitcher and then he began to get scared. He had just enough of a buzz on and he was just pissed enough to do something he was certain would make everything worse. He wasn't sure exactly what this was but he was just sober enough not to trust himself anywhere near the pool table. The trouble was, he couldn't just sit there and watch it anymore either, so at last he got up and walked out. He made a fair amount of noise doing it. He banged his chair against the floor and then against the table. He even bumped into a few things on his way to the door. Delandra never even looked at him. Neither did the two men. They all just stood there, looking at a shot. The only person who seemed to notice him leaving was the fat guy in the polo shirt and he had such a simpering grin on his face, it was all Obadiah could do to keep from swinging on him.

Once outside, he realized he had left the keys to the car with Delandra's purse but he couldn't quite bring himself to go back inside. And anyway, he was within walking distance of the motel.

It was hot and quiet and maybe, he thought, the walk would do him good.

He walked along the edge of what appeared to be the town's main drag, a ragged stretch of asphalt which paralleled the interstate. The theater and the bar were more or less alone at the east end of the street. But then the road curved a bit and soon he was walking past other stores and businesses. He passed a junk shop and a trading post, a used-book store. The bookstore caught his attention. It appeared to specialize in old comic books. Obadiah left the street and walked inside. The comic books were along one wall, arranged in racks and laid out flat on the floor so you could see the covers. On the other side of the store were used paperbacks—the kind with scantily clad women on the covers. Often the women were screaming, chased by men with knives. Toward the rear of the store there were a few dusty-looking hardbacks stacked against a wall.

The store consisted of one long rectangular room. The room was bright at the end which faced the street but ran quickly to shadow as the sunlight failed, replaced by the light of a single neon tube. An extremely large woman accompanied by a small brown dog sat near the door behind a metal desk. There were books stacked on the floor behind the desk and a lot of paperwork strewn across the top. There was also a small black-and-white television on the desk with rabbit-ear antennas. The woman was watching a game show. She looked up as Obadiah came through the door.

He browsed for a few minutes on his own, up one side past the comics, and then down the other, past the naked women and the men with knives. He imagined that several of the men on the book jackets bore a striking resemblance to the men he had left Delandra with in the Corner Pocket and was set upon by a hot wave of guilt. No stranger, however, to such moments of dread, he fought the impulse to rush out of the store and back to the bar. What he did, instead, was approach the woman behind the desk and inquire after Ceton Verity. It had occurred to him that it might be interesting to collect another opinion. So far the only people he and Delandra had spoken to were the people from the thrift store, aside, of course, from Jack and Lyle.

At the mention of Verity's name the woman turned off the television. "Dr. Verity passed away," she said, and then smiled.

"Yes," Obadiah went on. "I heard that. I was just curious about what he built here."

"The Electro-Magnetron. The landing strip. The Martian Museum."

Obadiah, encouraged, nodded his head.

"Dr. Verity did many wonderful things," the woman told him. She folded her plump hands, which were heavily decorated with turquoise jewelry, on the ink blotter before her. "The museum was filled with interesting things—gifts from alien visitors, things he'd picked up on his travels to other worlds." The woman said all of this in a very matter-of-fact voice, as if the news was nothing out of the ordinary. Perhaps she took Obadiah for a believer. "I've heard there were conventions here, too," he said.

"Yes," the woman nodded. "Once a year. The most wonderful conventions. People would come from all over the country."

"What did they do?"

"At the convention, you mean?"

Obadiah nodded.

The woman smiled once more. "They would talk," she said. "People could enter the Electro-Magnetron. Dr. Verity would tell about his most recent travels."

"What do you know about the Electro-Magnetron?" Obadiah asked her. He was greatly encouraged by her willingness to talk and was beginning to wish they could have stopped here instead of the thrift shop on their first visit.

"I know it is capable of reversing the aging process," the woman said. "Or at least it would have been. There was a part missing. Dr. Verity died before it could be found. It was a great tragedy."

Obadiah said that he was sorry to hear it. "You wouldn't happen to know how Dr. Verity died, would you?"

The woman shook her head. "They just found him," she said. "One morning in back of the museum. He had asked that he not be buried, you know. He was donating his body to the Interplanetary Federation and he asked that it be left on top of that ridge." She waved toward one wall of the shop.

"And what happened? Do you know?"

"Oh, he was taken," the woman said. "They came for him during the night."

"Do people still come here? Are there still conventions?"

The woman, who had been looking him in the eye, now turned her face toward the desk. The sunlight coming in through the glass lit her hair, which was dark and streaked with gray. Obadiah guessed she was perhaps fifty years old, though her hair was worn more like a younger woman's, simply, pulled back against her skull and braided loosely in the back. Obadiah waited. He stood looking down on her hair, the round hump of her shoulders. He found that he wanted suddenly to touch her, to place a hand on her arm. He had talked to people like this so many times, stood on so many porches, listened to so many crackbrained ideas, watched their owners cry—for any number of reasons. He was suddenly afraid this woman might cry now, for Ceton Verity, for the Electro-Magnetron with its missing part, for something that had passed from her life and for what had taken its place. "No one comes here anymore," the woman said at last, looking up. "Most of what the Doctor built is gone now too. The Electro-Magnetron is still there. But they have it now."

"They?"

The woman shook her head and made a face. "They," she repeated. "I don't know. No one goes out there anymore. They won't let anyone in. They wouldn't even let Mrs. Verity in."

"He had a wife?"

"Yes, and a daughter. They're both still alive, though his wife now spends most of her time in the East. That was where they were from, you know, the East."

"What about his daughter?"

"I wouldn't know. If you wanted to reach her, or his wife, for that matter, you might try through his publisher."

"He was a writer too?"

The woman smiled again, for the first time since the mention of They. "Oh, my, yes," she said. "He published many books on all kinds of topics."

Obadiah looked around the store. "You wouldn't happen to have any, would you?"

"Why, yes, I do," the woman said. She hauled herself out of her chair and reached behind herself for a cane. "Broke my hip last summer," she said by way of explanation. She wobbled out from behind the desk and started for the farthest wall. She was followed by the dog. Obadiah followed the two of them, trailing the dog's pink ribbon into the gloom at the rear of the shop. The air was mustier there. It smelled of dust and old paper. The woman pulled a slim blue book off the shelf and placed it in Obadiah's hands. The book was entitled *The God Within* and was the first in a series called The Books of Bueltar. "It was what he was working on when he died," the woman said. The books were apparently transcriptions of a series of conversations Ceton Verity had had with an alien he'd met in New York. It was in fact the alien, according to the woman, who had sent Ceton Verity west, to build the Electro-Magnetron.

When Obadiah inquired after the rest of the series, however, the woman told him this was all she had.

The first volume of the Books of Bueltar was two dollars and fifty cents—used. When Obadiah had finished collecting change from a five, he asked once more about the They who now guarded the Electro-Magnetron.

The woman made the same face she had made earlier. "You don't want to know anything about Them," she said. When Obadiah persisted, the woman asked him if he remembered the wildlife mutilations of a few years back. Obadiah said he thought he had read something about it. In truth he thought he had, but the memory was vague at best.

"It was a terrible thing," the woman said. She paused. "Someone was mutilating animals," she said. "All kinds of animals, cutting out different organs, you know." She looked toward the floor for a moment. "Mostly I guess they were sexual organs." She said this as if the idea embarrassed her. "It was a big thing," she went on. "The government even got in on the investigations because a lot of these mutilated carcasses were being left inside some of these top-secret weaponry sites around here. I mean left right on the doorsteps with no trace of how they got there, no tire tracks, not even any signs that the carcasses had been dragged."

Obadiah looked through the glass window, into the street. The asphalt looked hot and dark; the colors of the buildings were sharply defined in the clear desert air.

"It went on for about six months," the woman said. "They never really found out all there was to know—at least if you ask most people around here. But at one point some government men came out and arrested those people out at the Electro-Magnetron."

"How many people were there?"

"I wouldn't know. A dozen maybe. The cops wound up letting them go. Couldn't prove anything, I guess."

"When was all of this?"

"Last summer."

"Verity was dead then?"

"Oh, yes," the woman said. "He would never have allowed the kind of things that have gone on. Those people have just taken the place over." The woman paused, looking past Obadiah, toward the window. "It's been different around here ever since," she said. "You know, the whole atmosphere of the place. Most people don't want to talk about it. I mean, those people are still out there. And no matter what happened at the trial . . . Well, let's just say folks are scared. You're not planning on going out there yourself, are you?" Suddenly what Obadiah had dreaded transpired. The woman began to cry. A large tear formed on her cheek and rolled to drop upon the ink blotter. She wiped her nose with a ringed finger. Obadiah waited, shifting his weight. There was one more thing he wanted to know. He wanted to know the exact date of Verity's death. When the woman told him, he jotted it down on a blank page of his book. He did it quickly, scarcely looking at what he was writing. "Also there will be signs in the sun and moon and stars, and on earth anguish of nations, not knowing the way out because of the roaring of the sea and its agitation," he said softly, the words seeming to come from a long way off. It was a kind of conditioned response: the search for something that might prove comforting. "But as these things start to occur, raise yourselves erect, and lift your heads up, because your deliverance is getting near."

The woman looked at him. "The Bible?" she asked.

Obadiah admitted that it was.

"Dr. Verity could quote the Bible," she said. "He explains in the Books of Bueltar how much of the Bible was really written by early extraterrestrial visitors. Are you familiar with Ezekiel's vision of the wheelworks?" she asked.

Obadiah said that he was. On some morning from a distant past he might have gone on. He might have countered her interpretation with one of his own. They might have talked for hours while the sunlight heated the room. She looked hopefully up at him from her cluttered desk while Obadiah felt the palm of his hand go slick with sweat against the spine of the book, felt the too early drunk going sour on him. He groped for the front door with his free hand. The woman looked disappointed. "Promise me now you won't go out there," she said. He assured her that he would not, that speaking with her had been most enjoyable. She started up from her desk. Obadiah waved her down. He took his book, slipped once more into the street, and sucked down a few good lungfuls of desert air laced with whatever noxious substance it was which issued from the towers of the Trona Chemical Works.

Obadiah had intended to walk back to the motel, but when he left the bookstore he turned instead toward the Corner Pocket. He believed it had something to do with the covers of the detective magazines.

The sun was straight up and the shadows had fled the street. His shirt stuck to his back and the layers of heated air did funny things with the horizons. Ahead of him, where the road curved, he could see the theater and a piece of the lot but he had to make the curve before seeing the bar itself and when he did he was aware of an acute sinking sensation in his chest. Delandra and the three men, all considerably more intoxicated than when Obadiah had left them, had moved outside, where they now stood shouting obscenities at one another beneath a colorless sun. Mainly it was Delandra and the guy in the white jacket who were doing most of the yelling. At one point, as Obadiah moved up the grade toward the lot, he saw the man lurch forward and grab at Delandra's arm. Delandra responded by kicking the man in the knee. When he took a step backward she followed with a roundhouse right to the solar plexus. Obadiah paused briefly in his ascent, halted by some combination of disbelief and horror. The other spectators seemed to find the action quite amusing. By the time Obadiah had gained level ground, the others were clinging for support to the side of the white pickup and laughing hysterically. Meanwhile, the man in the jacket, obviously now in some pain, was standing red-faced about five feet in front of Delandra, wagging a finger in her face.

At Obadiah's approach, Delandra turned to look at him and the man took the opportunity of moving forward to grab at her hair. He succeeded in getting a fistful of it. Delandra shrieked and lowered her head. Her boots fought for traction in the gravel lot, looking, it appeared, for something like ramming speed. Which in fact she managed—at least enough to get her head into the pit of the man's stomach and knock him over, ass first, into the lot. The man still had hold of her hair and Delandra followed, sprawling on top of him, her legs still kicking. "Hang on to her, Bob," one of the men yelled. "Don't let go."

Obadiah approached the pile of humanity. He had in mind pulling Delandra to her feet. "You keep your ass out of it," one of the men yelled. "It's one on one." The other man laughed.

Delandra had her head turned now, one side of her face mashed against the guy's chest. She was trying to see Obadiah. "The gun," she said. "The gun."

"Whoa," one of the men said.

"Whoa yourself, shithead," Delandra yelled from the ground.

For a moment Obadiah stood looking at the men. The men looked back at him. It was a moment in which time stood still. And then they were moving toward him, to the left and right of where Delandra lay struggling with the man, and Obadiah began to run.

He reached the Dart ahead of them, jerked open the driver's side door, and dove into the front seat. He got the revolver out of the glove box at about the same time the men reached the middle of the street. He did not believe that he was actually going to shoot at anyone but it occurred to him that he'd best look serious about it. He pulled the hammer back and swung the barrel around so that it was pointing toward the street over his outstretched body. He was sort of lying on his back, sighting down his stomach. The men stopped running when they saw the gun. They both stopped at the same time and there was something almost comical in the effect. They appeared to stop themselves by digging their heels into the pavement. Then they started backing up, their palms turned toward Obadiah. The guy in the polo shirt backed into a curb and went down hard on his ass.

Obadiah slithered out of the front seat, legs first. In the act of doing this he managed to bang his forearm against the wheel and the gun went off. He wasn't holding it very tightly and it kicked with enough force to bring the barrel up against the roof of the car. The blast rattled his jaw. The man in the polo shirt put both hands over his head. Obadiah was standing by now, in the street at the side of the car. He could not believe the fucking thing had gone off. It was like some stupid thing he might have read about in the paper—one more moron blowing his own foot off with a gun he didn't know was loaded. In this case he was the moron. He half expected to see some local grandmother dead on the street. There was no one there but the men, however, and none of them appeared to have been hit. He felt that he was floating rather than walking toward them. He wanted to disappear. He wanted to tell the guy in the polo shirt to "Dance, motherfucker." The expressions on the men's faces were really something and there was a moment in which he considered spraying the pavement with hot lead. The moment passed.

All of this happened very quickly, though it seemed to Obadiah as if it had taken a very long time, as if Delandra would never regain her feet. But she was up now and running toward him, her breasts bouncing beneath the T-shirt, and there was a wild sort of light in her eye he had not seen since she first suggested breakfast at the Chevron station. "You should know better than to mess with the queen of the roller derby," she said to everyone.

"Come on back, sometime," one of the men said, "without your friend."

The man in the white jacket said something about fixing them both. Delandra gave everyone the finger and jumped into the car. Obadiah ran to the opposite side, the gun still in his hand. It was true, he thought, they were like Bonnie and Clyde. It was too fucking ridiculous to even think about.

Delandra drove like mad, laughing and hooting all the way. She tore through the ruined asphalt of the motel's parking lot and parked the car in the back, hiding it from the road. After that they got out and ran to the room. They started out walking and then began to run. Delandra got there first and she tried to lock Obadiah outside. She was still laughing, though, and still drunk, and Obadiah managed to push past her and into the room and once they were both inside she threw her arms around his neck and pressed her body against his and held him that way for a long time. Finally they made love, on the floor, and then on the bed, and every now and then a car would go by on the highway and they would stop and listen and try to figure out if it was the men from the bar out looking for them, or maybe the Highway Patrol. But all of the cars went on by and the room grew dark with shadow and the sun appeared at an open bathroom window, an orange blaze beyond the turquoise tile.

They lay on the bed for a long time when they were finished, watching the light. Their clothes were strewn all over the room, the floor, the bed, the case of the Mystery of the Mojave, which was also covered with a bedspread and which Obadiah had not once looked at since returning to the room.

"You know," Delandra told him. Her bare arm was pressed against his and her breath was soft and warm against his neck. "The thing is, we can't afford to get bogged down in all of this. Do you know what I mean? We've got to make a break and the break has got to be clean. I'm beginning to believe there is something between us."

Obadiah studied the ceiling. In one corner there was a brownish stain and the light from the bathroom lay across it in narrow golden rectangles. Once he felt Delandra shiver at his side. He thought about what she had said, about there being something between them. Sometimes he thought there was, and sometimes he didn't know. It was a difficult thing to get hold of. And then he started thinking about his conversation with the old lady in the bookstore and the date he had written on the flyleaf of Ceton Verity's book. He was considering saying something about it when the phone rang.

They both jumped. Finally Delandra sprang from the bed and grabbed at the receiver. "Yes," Obadiah heard her say, "this is Delandra Hummer." He propped himself up on his elbows and watched her at the foot of the bed. She had her back to him and the orange light caressed her hip and thigh and one naked shoulder and there was a long, curving shadow in the middle of her back so that she reminded him of a painting in which exquisite use had been made of light.

When she returned to the bed she looked upset about something. "Fucking Jack and Lyle," she said. "They can't make it until tomorrow." She lay down facing the curtains which blocked their view of the lot. "They're trying to fuck with me," she said. "I really hate it when people try to fuck with me."

At some point Obadiah noticed that she had begun to shake, softly at first, and then more violently. He moved his body up to hers, curving himself around her back and circling her with his arms and she lay there for a long time without saying anything and finally she stopped shaking and went to sleep. Obadiah didn't say anything either. He lay there holding her, feeling his heart beat against her back. He felt that he was protecting her from something, though he couldn't say what it was, but the very idea of it moved him to tears. He wondered if in the morning he would get around to telling her what he had learned in the bookstore, that Ceton Verity had died in a remarkably similar way to Sarge Hummer, that he had simply been found dead near the site of his museum within the same month that Sarge Hummer had been found dead in back of his.

Obadiah found that his arm had gotten numb and he realized he had been sleeping. At first he thought it was his arm which had wakened him. Then he realized it was something else. Someone was knocking on the door.

Delandra went from being asleep to sitting bolt upright at the edge of the bed. It was dark in the room and he couldn't see her face. He saw her head moving from side to side. She went to the corner of the window on her hands and knees and looked outside and for a moment a pale white light from the parking lot crossed a piece of plastered wall. Delandra let the curtain fall and crawled back to bed. "Shit," she said, "it's them." Someone knocked again.

"Them?" The first people Obadiah thought of were the men from the bar.

"It's Jack. I told you those fuckers were screwing around. We should have split. This is fucking stupid." She was pulling on her pants and then her T-shirt, seemingly all in one motion. She also managed to throw Obadiah his jeans. "Where's the fucking gun?" she said.

Obadiah was waking up fast now. It was like waking to a bad dream. He pulled on the jeans and started feeling around in the dark for the gun. He had remembered leaving it on the dresser. Delandra was now at the door. The door was still closed and she was saying something through it, waving at Obadiah to get into the bathroom and out the window. Alternate plan B. Obadiah couldn't find his shirt and there was not time for his shoes. He placed the gun on the windowsill. He stood on the toilet bowl and went out the window one leg at a time so that for a moment he was straddling the sill. He slid over onto the back of one thigh, squeezed his body through, and then dropped to the ground. The gravel bit at his feet and the night air was cold on his back. He was in the act of removing the gun from the sill when he heard a voice issue from the darkness above him. When he brought himself to look, what he saw was the twin black mouths of a double-barreled gun and above that the long, bony face of Lyle Blackledge grinning unpleasantly down on him from the roof of the Blue Heaven Motel.

Lyle's face was lit from the underside by a single naked bulb which burned at the rear of the motel. Behind him the night sky had acquired a faintly bluish tint from the neon which burned somewhere on the other side of the building. "Guess what?" Lyle said.

Obadiah shivered. He was still in the act of reaching, his hand still covering Delandra's pistol.

"Whatever you've got in your hand there," Lyle said to him, "put it on the ground."

Obadiah put the gun on the ground at his feet. It looked quite small, he thought, not anything like what had given him the power earlier that afternoon at the Corner Pocket Bar. It occurred to him that that was what he was paying for now.

Lyle swung himself from the roof and dropped easily to his feet. He picked Obadiah's gun up and looked at it. "Gee," he said, "let's go inside."

Together they walked around the end of the building. Obadiah entertained the hope they would run into something—the old woman who ran the place, new guests, anything that might change in some way what was coming down. They saw no one. The night was silent except for the wind and the distant yapping of some dogs. They passed beneath the neon sign which leaned toward the highway and for a moment both men were bathed in a delicate blue light. The moment passed. They reentered the land of shadow and started down the narrow concrete walkway which led to Apartment B. For Obadiah, it had been quite a journey. Reaching the room, he felt that they had been walking for days, across the most difficult of terrains.

Jack was there with Delandra. She was now wearing jeans to go with the black T-shirt and boots. She was seated at the edge of the double bed. Jack was seated by the door in a wooden, straight-backed chair. Obadiah sat next to Delandra.

"Dipshit here had this," Lyle said. He handed Delandra's pistol to Jack.

"Well, well," Jack said, "not expecting trouble?"

"Fuck you," Delandra said.

Jack laughed. "That's not a bad idea," he said. "I've heard worse. What do you think, Lyle?"

"Fucking whore," Lyle said. "I'll have her beggin' for mercy before I'm done." He looked serious about it. Obadiah felt something go slightly numb somewhere in the middle of his body.

"Let me tell you something about all of that," Delandra said. She was looking at Jack. "You try anything twisted and you're going to have to kill both of us. You understand? You kill both of us and you won't get far with what you came for."

Jack was leaning forward in his chair. He was dressed in a pair of dirty jeans, work boots, a faded cotton work shirt with the sleeves rolled up on his forearms. His dark brown hair looked greasy and uncombed and his glasses seemed to have slipped a bit toward the end of his nose. There was perspiration around his neck and across his forehead. Jack looked for a long moment at Delandra. The door to the room had been left slightly ajar and through the crack Obadiah could see the dark blue pickup. He could see the fat woman he had seen at the trailer sitting behind the wheel. The truck hadn't been there when he and Lyle made their walk. The woman must have parked somewhere closer to the highway, then driven up when she saw Lyle and Obadiah go into the room. It occurred to him that Delandra was probably wrong. Jack and Lyle could do something twisted and get away with it. They could haul them out into the desert somewhere and no one would ever know. This seemed so obvious to him he almost said something. But he didn't.

"Well now," Jack was saying, "I guess that all depends on just how far we want to get with it, doesn't it? I mean maybe we won't want it at all. Maybe it's just some damn pile of junk your old man threw together. What then, honey?"

Jack got to his feet and walked to the case. He pulled the sheet away from the glass. Lyle came a step off the wall he'd been propped against and looked down, his long neck held at an odd angle. Jack looked at the Thing for a moment without saying anything. Then he opened the lid. The hinges squeaked loudly and a peculiar though by now, Obadiah thought, oddly familiar odor seeped into the room.

Suddenly it was very quiet. Jack and Lyle stood side by side, staring into the case. Beyond the doorway Obadiah could see the reflection of blue neon on the fender of the truck. A moth which had become trapped between the window and the curtain fluttered against the glass. Lyle, Obadiah saw, had laid Delandra's gun on top of the dresser, in nearly the same spot it had been before Obadiah had taken it to go outside, and a certain sequence of action presented itself to him. A man might, he believed, throw himself at Lyle, knock him into Jack, grab the gun, and come around shooting. It seemed both suicidal and plausible. His heart beat faster and for a moment he felt himself coil for the move. Anything, he thought, but a shallow grave in the desert.

"I'll be damned," Jack said. He looked from the case to Delandra, then to Obadiah. Obadiah remained at the edge of the bed. The opportunity had passed.

Lyle was still arranged in the pose he had taken with his first sight of the Creature. There was a vein bulging out on the side of his neck where it arced toward the light and Obadiah fancied he could see it pulsing. He found himself wanting suddenly to laugh out loud. Seen many of those, hick? He kept his mouth shut.

Jack now turned to the half-open door and made a signal to the woman in the truck, then he closed the lid and covered it with the sheet. The lights came back on in Lyle's eyes. He cranked his head back down to a more realistic position. "Come on," Jack said, "let's get it in the truck and get out of here."

"What about them?" Lyle asked.

Jack looked at Obadiah and Delandra. "Fuck them," he said. "We got what we came for." He moved a step closer to the end of the bed. He looked first at Delandra then at Obadiah. "It's been fun," he said. "But I wouldn't ever want to see either of you around again. Is that clear?"

No one said anything. Obadiah could feel Delandra's shoulder, hot against his own. Lyle had moved a bit to one side, closer to the case. He reached out suddenly and hit Obadiah across the side of the neck with the shortened barrel of his gun.

Obadiah saw the barrel moving toward him and turned his head away. It hadn't looked as if the gun was moving that quickly and he was stunned at the explosion of pain. He felt himself start up and then sink back down. His ass slipped off the edge of the bed and hit the floor hard. "Somebody's talking to you, Dipshit," he heard Lyle say through a red mist. "You understand or not?"

Obadiah said that he understood. He sat on the floor with his hands at his sides while Jack and Lyle carried the case out the door and loaded it into the truck. For a moment the truck's headlights filled the room and then they were gone and there was just the night pressing in upon them from the empty lot and the flats beyond and somewhere in the blackness at the edge of town the pack of dogs Obadiah had heard as he walked around the building with Lyle were still yapping mindlessly at the moon.

"Well," Delandra said. "That's that."

# IV
---

*oh, daddy's way out there*
—R.F.F.

The girl Rex met in Porkpie Wells was named Dina and the possibility that it might be something good lasted roughly twenty-four hours. It survived a hard rain and one very drunk night and then it soured.

It all started to go bad in the bright sunlight at the foot of a dirt road leading into Table Mountain. The road, normally open year-round, was closed. There was one of the state's yellow and black barricades set up at the entrance together with a road's closed sign and a warning about flash floods. Rex and the girl sat at the side of the road, and looked at the sign. "Take a four-wheel drive to even try it, if the road's washed out," Rex told her. The only other way in lay far to the west—the road out of Ridgecrest, and that was something like a day's drive.

Dina did not take the news well. She called Rex a pussy and a dildo. She said that he was an even bigger pussy than the bikers she had left in Porkpie Wells and that she would go on alone, at which point it was necessary for Rex physically to restrain her from starting off down twenty miles of bad road with nothing more on her feet than a ninety-nine-cent pair of Flojos.

It was a grim scene and the beginning of the end. For such a diminutive person the girl proved herself capable of really horrendous amounts of noise. Rex drove with a pounding head as the girl railed at him, from the cutoff road at Table Mountain to the southernmost tip of Death Valley, where his radiator at last failed him in a town called Dry Creek.

                            *   *   *

In the end, Rex supposed, it could have been worse, his radiator
could have failed in the middle of nowhere. As it was, there was a
station in Dry Creek and a man willing to sell him another. It took
Rex the rest of the afternoon to get it on, and by sunset the girl had
become unmanageable. She'd been taking something all afternoon, popping pills she kept in an embroidered leather satchel. At
some point near sundown she complicated matters considerably
with the purchase of two bottles of mad dog 20/20. She eventually
followed that with a short dog of Silver Satin and at something like
one or two in the morning tried to commit suicide by banging her
head on the surface of an empty concrete slab behind the station.

    The commotion woke the station's owner and his wife, who
were able to help Rex in restraining the girl. It was an even uglier
scene than the one played out on the Table Mountain road and by
sunrise Rex had the distinct impression he was being held in some
way responsible for it by the residents of Dry Creek—all of whom
had by first light been drawn to the scene, very much, it appeared
to Rex, like flies to shit.

    The last he saw of little Dina she was seated on the back of a car
belonging to some local young stud. The car was a souped-up '59
Chevy with baby moons on the tires and a small stack of chromed
pipes in the rear window. Dina was seated on a rear fender, an ice
pack on her head. She was holding it there like a cap with one
hand and drinking a beer with the other and when Rex passed she
stuck her tongue out at him. It was the way he would remember
her—one more postcard from a collection whose meaning he had
yet to discern.


    He had driven for a good two hours, in the direction of the
junction, before he realized Dina had forgotten her leather
satchel. If she thought he was going to drive the two hours back to
give it to her she was crazy. He was going to dump it. He had
picked it up and was nearly in the act of tossing the foul thing out
an open window when something fell to the seat at his side. It
appeared to be a letter addressed to someone named Dina Vagina
in San Francisco. The return address was Table Mountain. Rex put
the satchel back down and drove for another fifteen minutes,
thinking about the letter, before his curiosity got the better of him

and he pulled off the road to read it. He stopped on a dusty turnout and parked in the shade of a large Joshua.

The letter was, as Rex had guessed it to be, the letter Dina had spoken of in the bar at Porkpie Wells. The gist of the letter was that Ceton Verity had indeed returned. He had appeared twice now to several of the sisters. He was dressed in white and had about him a special radiance. He said that he was only able to maintain his human form for short periods of time and no one was allowed to touch him. He said that the mystery of the Electro-Magnetron's missing part had been solved. There was no missing part. It had been revealed to the sisters that the Electro-Magnetron was a psionic device. That at the right time, the correct person would arrive. In the meantime the sisters were to become accomplished in the chanting of certain ancient songs, as the music, though not the key, would play a part in the operation of the Electro-Magnetron. On one page of the letter there was no writing but rather a crude drawing done in blue crayon of a fantastic-looking creature. It was also suggested that Dina find a story entitled "The Call of Cthulhu," by H. P. Lovecraft.

Rex read the letter twice. Then he looked at the drawing for a long time and once, when he was looking at it, it seemed to him that a peculiar sound had begun, very faintly somewhere above him, as if a wind had begun to whistle in the spines of the Joshua. When he looked up, however, the spines were still in a windless sky. On the bottom of the page there was an unusual word: *Mastamho*.

Rex folded the letter very carefully and placed it in the front pocket of his shirt and snapped the button after it. He examined the rest of what was in the satchel: pills, a switchblade knife, a delicate golden chain, some dirty Kleenex, a small change purse with about thirty-five cents in it. Rex threw the pills and the Kleenex into a trash can chained to one end of the turnout. He put the other things back in the satchel. He put the satchel under the seat and drove away.

The road beyond the turnout was filled with shallow dips and in the hollow of each a heat mirage lay in wait for him. For each one that he passed through, causing it to disappear, another would take its place, somewhere ahead of him. For a while he counted them, marking miles with them, until the road at last straightened out and there was only one mirage, thin, shimmering, touched with a crystalline bluish light. This last mirage lay at the base of a distant purple range, for Rex, the hills of home, and it was toward them that he pressed, driving faster now than he had in several days. Because for the first time since the theft of the Mystery of the Mojave, he was a man with a plan. It wasn't a complete plan yet. But it was forming—a palpable sensation and he felt at the edge of something—some vast coalescing of elements, the movement of momentous tides, as if soon he was to be right there, a witness to creation. Or something like it.


Rex drove hard. Memories of Dina trailed him like the residue of a bad dream and the sunlight, entering the cab now from the rear window, tore at the back of his head with the persistence of termites at rotting wood. A lone bat swung suddenly from an outcropping of rust-colored stone as he made the slow turn that would carry him home. Above him, bare and white before the dull brown hillside, the Terry rested on its blocks. Halfway up the grade he could see there was something stuck to his door. When he got there he found that it was a note—a large scrap of brown paper folded in thirds and stuck to his door with a piece of duct tape.

The note turned out to be from Tom Shoats, a resident of the junction. *Come see me,* the note said. *It's about Floyd.* Rex stood in the heat in front of the trailer and held the note in his hands. In spots the paper had gotten wet and the ink had run from the letters to form pale ripples and gaseous-like patterns of great intricacy. Rain, Rex thought, or the tears of angels.

On the way back down the hill Rex stopped at the ragged cluster of mailboxes which served the community. The boxes were perched atop a series of uneven wooden posts and steel poles and reminded Rex of something he had once seen in a movie. They reminded him of the heads of dead men. He discovered two pieces of junk mail in his box. One was an advertisement for pornographic material, the second was a brown envelope upon which a message had been stamped in red ink. The message read:

> The customer named below
> has been singled out for a rare
> opportunity . . .
> quite possibly, unlike anything
> ever seen or heard about before.

Harlan had seen the six-fingered hand three times: once in an African slum, once from a freeway in East Los Angeles, and once in Sarge Hummer's Desert Museum. He still found the idea that the three objects were in some way connected fascinating.

So far there was not much more to go on but this: Sarge Hummer had once advertised the possibility that the Mystery of the Mojave was in fact the body of an alien being. The Sons of Elijah appeared to be an outfit interested in such things. A medallion bearing what might be their symbol had been found in Sarge Hummer's workroom.

It was what Harlan thought about as he sat on the shoulder of the interstate and looked down on the junction below him. He had a clear view of the Desert Museum and the Chevron station. The rest of it trailed away from him like so much litter cast among the rocks. The place was filled with sour memories but it was the only starting point he knew.

It had taken longer than expected to make it back, but the delay had proven financially agreeable. It had turned out that one of the brothers in the Vegas area was the owner of a car-rental business. It was one of those outfits where you can save money by renting a wreck. In Harlan's case the wreck had come free of charge, courtesy of the brother for as long as he needed it. The car was a 1950 Studebaker, a lemon-yellow Starlight coupe. The thing had recently been painted, dents and all, and there was still yellow paint on the tires and along the edges of the glass. The son of the man who had loaned Harlan the car said it reminded him of a flying saucer. It was an observation Harlan found both accurate and appropriate—in ways the boy would never guess. He felt slightly ridiculous behind the wheel of the thing but the price was right and it had gotten him back to the Desert Museum. The only problem with that was, now that he was back he had to do something about it. He'd already been on the shoulder of the road for the better part of an hour, watching the Chevron and the museum for signs of life, and he was beginning to feel like the detective in a dime-store novel.

At last he started the car. He made a U-turn on the highway, drove back toward the road which would take him to the museum, and started down it. His shirt stuck to his back. Gravel pinged in the wheel wells and he was aware of the dull beat of his pulse against the plastic steering wheel beneath his hands. It was not altogether clear to him whom he expected to find or what he expected to say. He supposed his best bet would be to locate the owner. But then the owner of the museum was related to the owner of the Chevron. A variety of unpleasant scenarios presented themselves for inspection. Harlan drove on. To learn more of what the Wheeler boy had stolen was to learn more of a next move. And there was either a next move or there was the drive back to Los Angeles.

The rains had fixed it so that Harlan's car raised no dust. He parked before a supine telephone pole and a wooden sign which said: WELCOME TO SARGE HUMMER'S DESERT MUSEUM, HOME OF THE THING, THE MYSTERY OF THE MOJAVE. Harlan stopped the car and got out. It was just past midday. There was a slight amount of humidity in the air. To the east the sky was clear, but to the west there were clouds. Back of them the sky was the color of brushed aluminum. The clouds themselves were broken into huge, turbulent clusters which had been tugged at by the wind until they too had the look of something metallic and appeared to hang there before the aluminum sky like some vast invading armada whose threat was immeasurable. Harlan got out of the car and walked across the dirt to the steps of the museum. Nothing moved.

He found the building open, as he had left it the morning he had gone to look after Neil's car. He knocked anyway, on the wall. When there was no answer he went inside. He went directly to the workroom. The medallion still hung from the rafter in front of the plastic moldings. He looked at the medallion. He studied the moldings in some detail. He opened and closed a number of drawers filled with tools. Beneath a workbench he found a pair of wooden Coca-Cola crates partially covered by a piece of canvas. The crates appeared to contain paperwork of some kind. When he had pulled one out and lifted the canvas he saw the paperwork was, in fact, a collection of old magazines.

The cover of the magazine Harlan found himself looking at contained the colored drawing of a fantastic creature—something like a two-headed lizard from whose back sprouted half a dozen pairs of delicate, batlike wings. The heads were mostly mouths and eyes. The mouths were filled with dripping fangs, the eyes with lust. The object of the monster's desire was a scantily clad blond woman with very large breasts. She was trying to run but was caught already by what appeared to be the monster's tail. She screamed in terror.

There were more magazines. More monsters and more women. Two of the crates were filled with such nonsense. The magazines bore titles like *Fantastic Tales* and *Weird Creations.* In another crate, however, Harlan found something more to his liking. He found what had the look of being the entire canon of *UFO Alert!*

The light in the workroom was bad and Harlan decided to take the crate out to the porch. Not only would he have more light, he could keep an eye on the road as well. There was something quite exhilarating about this find, Harlan thought, and he was surprised by the amount of enthusiasm with which he set about dragging the thing out into the light—as though he were really on to something.

He eventually discovered two items of interest in the crate. He found the article the brother from New York had mentioned on the phone. It was entitled "Whose Mind Is It? Magnetism and Mind Control," by Leonard Maxwell. For the most part, Harlan found the article unreadable. He scanned it for several minutes, wading through such magnetic definitions as "Magnetic Hysteresis—occurs when a ferromagnetic substance is subjected to a varying magnetic field and causes the magnetic induction to lag behind the changes in magnetizing force."

That evil was in fact a magnetic phenomenon appeared to be an idea which had sprung from Maxwell's contemplation of the work of a man by the name of Mesmer in the field of animal gravitation, or animal magnetism—the magnetic tides of attraction Mesmer had found to be moving in and around all living things. It was the ability to influence and alter such tidal flows which provided the Controllers with their power. The Controllers went unnamed in the article, but Harlan took them to be the Ancients of current Sons cosmology.

The other two items of interest were found together. One was a pamphlet, one the page to which the magazine containing the pamphlet fell open when Harlan picked it up. What Harlan saw on the page was a photograph of Ceton Verity, the editor of *UFO Alert!,* the benefactor of Leonard Maxwell.

The man in the photograph had a big, well-fed look about him. Facially, there was a vague resemblance to W. C. Fields. The expression with which he stared into the camera suggested a certain blend of arrogance and determination. He looked, Harlan thought, like a man who knew what he was about. He wore a safari jacket and wire-rimmed glasses. At his back a landscape much like the one now before Harlan spread itself across the page. Beneath the photograph was a caption: "The Author at the site of his proposed Electro-Magnetron in the Mojave Desert."

The pamphlet which marked the photograph was of immediate interest since its cover bore the symbol Harlan now associated with the Sons of Elijah. The tract was folded up like a small accordion and when Harlan spread it open he found that it produced a puzzle. It was one of those puzzles that link certain images which, when added up properly, generally reproduced some common saying. At least that was how Harlan had seen similar puzzles used in the past. There were several questions accompanying the puzzle, however, and the questions suggested that the meaning of the puzzle Harlan now held lay in knowing what the symbols stood for and how they related to one another. If you knew that, you would presumably know what they added up to, for the symbols were linked by plus signs, followed by an equals sign and a question mark. The questions were as follows:

Can you identify these symbols?

Do you know what Magnetic Secrets were covered by Nazi mining operations?

Do you know why the United States government closed mining operations in the Mojave Desert in 1942?

What does it mean that the President of the United States has recently reversed that decision?

How does the puzzle affect your future?

The symbols themselves were these:

A swastika, a bar (Harlan thought that possibly it was a gold bar, or a magnet. There were little rays coming out of each end), a pentagram, a wagon filled with rocks, a shape (Harlan took it to be a shape from a map—the outline of a country or a state, perhaps), the head of a man (Harlan's guess was that the man was the President). Above the President's head there was a small, six-fingered hand.

For the exact solution to the puzzle, readers were encouraged to send money. There was apparently a book. There was an address to which the donations were to be sent—a post offic box in Inglewood, California.

Harlan was never sure in such cases if he should be angered or saddened by the fact that people would indeed send money, that the Leonard Maxwells of the world could, in fact, command their fleets of bulletproof limos. He thought about this for a moment and then began looking through the box at his side to see if perhaps Sarge Hummer had sent any money himself. It was what he was doing when it became apparent to him that he was no longer alone in the lot. The sense of being watched descended upon him like an unwelcome draft. When he looked up he saw that there were in fact three men standing not twenty feet from the porch upon which he sat.

It was impossible for him to say just how or when they had arrived. His first impulse was toward fear, his second, toward anger at having become so engrossed in Maxwell's ration of horseshit that he had missed something important.

He took the men to be men of the town. They had the look of the desert about them. They wore boots and khaki trousers. One wore a trucker's hat. One looked like an Indian. One, a huge, sloppy-looking man with a graying crewcut, held a shotgun in the crook of his arm.

It was the man with the gun who spoke. "Maybe you would like to tell us just what the fuck you're doing here," the man said.

Harlan was wrong about the men. They weren't from the town. The man with the gun claimed to be from the sheriff's department in Ridgecrest but he offered no ID, nothing except the double-barreled gun. The gun was enough. Harlan told the men what he was up to. It was an abridged version, but essentially the truth. He thought for a moment about telling them something else but then passed on it. He had come this far. Maybe he would learn something from them.

He was wrong about that, too. When he was finished talking, the man with the gun looked at the Indian and grinned. "These are popular people," he said.

"You're looking for them too?" Harlan asked.

The Indian looked at Harlan, looked him up and down and then, apparently having satisfied himself about something, looked toward the hills at the north end of town.

"These people are criminals," the man with the gun said. "It's a matter for the law." He looked straight at Harlan. "Your best bet would be to take a hike. That way." For Harlan's benefit he pointed with the gun in the direction of Los Angeles.

"Back with all the other creeps and weirdos," the third man said. It was the first time he had spoken. He was a tall, skinny man with such angular, bony shoulders, it looked to Harlan as if a clothes hanger had managed somehow to remain stuck in his shirt.

"That's right," the man with the gun said. "You people kill me. You come out here trying to tell folks what to do and you dump shit on the place." It occurred to Harlan that the man with the gun was rather weird-looking too. The guy looked like he had been put together with tires. His head looked a bit too small and the crewcut had the look of something that had been put in place with a hammer. Pink flesh shone in the sunlight between the well-oiled shafts of silver hair. But Harlan didn't argue with the man. They had dumped shit here. The shit was what Harlan was trying to clean up. "I won't argue with you," Harlan said. "I was hoping to help set it right."

The Indian, who had been looking toward the town, laughed. The Indian's legs were much too short for his torso—which was thick and heavily muscled. He wore dun-colored boots with red tips on them. A thin golden earring sparkled in the lobe of one ear.

The man with the gun said nothing. He raised his eyebrows and pointed toward L.A. with his gun.

Harlan crossed the dirt and got into his car. The man with the gun followed him. When Harlan had closed the door the man placed the barrel of the gun into the open window so that it was pointed at Harlan's face. Harlan had begun to lean forward, toward the ignition, when he noticed he was still holding the pamphlet. The first idea which came to him was that the man was going to accuse him of stealing something.

"You wouldn't," the man asked him, "happen to know anything about a red car with two niggers and an Indian in it?"

Harlan slipped the folded pamphlet into the ashtray so that it was held by a corner, flat against the dash. "Not a thing," he said.

*   *   *

Harlan was an hour out of the junction before he came to a gas station. The station was located in a place called Four Corners. It was an ugly little spot. There was a gas station and a crummy-looking restaurant on each corner. There were some concessions set up along the highway, which sold the kinds of things you would expect from a Mexican border town. Cheap articles of gold and silver, together with a garish display of crockery, decorative mirrors, and Indian rugs hung about in a lifeless fashion beneath a mean-tempered sun.

There were roads going in four directions out of Four Corners. One could go east toward Vegas, west toward Bakersfield, south toward San Bernardino and Los Angeles, or north, toward nothing at all. Harlan stood in the shade of the metal roof which sheltered the pumps and looked toward a train yard off to the west. What he was thinking about was that picture of Ceton Verity and the desert landscape before which he had stood.

"Let me ask you something," Harlan said. He was addressing himself to the man who had come around to collect money for the gas. "Have you ever heard of something called the Electro-Magnetron?"

The man laughed. He was a thin man with dark hair and when he laughed a gold tooth lit up in the sun. "Sure," he said, "I've heard of it. What do you want to know about it?"

"Do you know where it is?"

The man took his cap off and ran a hand back over his hair. "Oh, not exactly," he said, "it's up around Table Mountain and Trona and all that shit somewhere."

"Table Mountain?"

"That way," the man said. He pointed north. "Take you maybe another three hours to the turnoff. I don't know about after that."

"You know what else is up there?"

"What else? Well, there's a lot of stuff. I mean it's a lot of nothing. There's some old mining towns. There's Trona. You can get to Death Valley that way, if you want to see that. They tell me there's some people up there in a couple of those towns now. Hippies or some damn thing. Got themselves one of those communes I guess. I don't get up that way much myself." The man put Harlan's money into the front pocket of his shirt.

Harlan looked north. The horizon in that direction appeared to be built up in bands of blues and grays. The bands undulated beneath the sun. "Three hours you say?"

The attendant had begun to turn away. Harlan's car was already pointed north. The man waved his arm. "Just keep going like you're going," he said. "You'll see the signs."

Harlan sat for a moment in the car after the man had gone back inside. He looked into the bands of whitened colors. There were a number of things on his mind. There was what the man with the gun had told him. There was also the prospect of driving back to Los Angeles. When he thought of L.A. he envisioned the scene in which he would begin to explain how he had come to arrive in the rental car from Las Vegas. He envisioned this so clearly that he abandoned it almost at once. He abandoned it for a number of reasons. He abandoned it for what the station attendant had said about hippies and communes. Obadiah and the girl he had gone off with were about the right age for that sort of thing. And there was something about finding the pamphlet in the magazine as he had, as if the two things had something to do with each other. And finally there was what the man with the gun had asked him. The guy had not said the black men were looking for something in the museum, but this was the impression with which Harlan had been left. Perhaps it was the impression with which he had wanted to be left, feeding as it did a particular theory of his. And when he thought of the theory he thought of the little puzzle contained in the pamphlet. Perhaps, he thought, he should begin a puzzle of his own, and he began to think of the things he could put in it: Leonard Maxwell, Ceton Verity, Sarge Hummer, Sarge Hummer's girl, two black men and an Indian in a red car. Maxwell's puzzle supposedly added up to something. Harlan didn't know if his did or not. And yet he was within three hours of a possible answer. The idea was difficult to leave alone. He looked at his watch. He considered the time of day, the choices which ringed him, visibly in Four Corners, like the points of a compass. In the end he went with the puzzle. He went for three hours and fifteen minutes. He went believing there would be enough daylight left for a look around and he was right about half of it. There was light, enough so that even before leaving the highway for the turnoff the station attendant had told him about, he could see that something was wrong.

What Harlan saw first, rising above the tops of the creosote bushes which lined the highway, were the roofs of the cars. The roofs were green—the color of State cars. After making the turnoff, he could see that the cars had been parked in such a way as to block any further progress in the direction Harlan was headed.

He drove slowly for the last few yards and then coasted to a stop as two Rangers walked toward him. The men wore tan uniforms with Smokey the Bear hats and gold-rimmed aviator shades. One of the men leaned forward, taking a look around Harlan's car as he spoke, "Afraid this road is closed," the man said. "You have business in Table Mountain?"

"Just sightseeing. What's the problem?"

The officer didn't say anything right away. He continued to look around the car. "May I see your driver's license?" he asked. The other man, Harlan noticed, had by now taken up a position at the opposite window where he, too, stood looking into the car. Harlan pulled his wallet from his hip pocket, flipped it open and passed it to the man. "Registration," the man asked.

Harlan took some papers down from the visor above his head. "It's rented," he said. "I've been doing business in Las Vegas."

The man looked at the paperwork. He looked at Harlan. "You get that eye in Vegas?"

The question caught Harlan flat-footed and he was a moment in replying. At last he smiled. "Had a little accident," he said.

The man leaning toward the window did not return the smile, "Traffic accident?"

"No." Harlan hesitated once more, thinking how ridiculous this was. "I slipped," he said. "Found some wet concrete during those rains."

The man looked once more at the papers Harlan had given him. The man on the other side of the car was now looking into the backseat, trying to see if anything was on the floor. Harlan rubbed at his cheek, feeling his right eye twitch. It was very quiet and

Harlan could hear the boots of the officer on the passenger side of his car as they twisted the gravel beneath them. The air was warm and dry and the rays of sunlight had begun to lengthen across the spines of the ridges, giving the sky an orange, dusty look. To Harlan's left the mountain peaks had snow on them and in the canyons the shadows were blue and purple in the dusty light.

"I'll be a minute," the man with Harlan's papers said. He went with them back to one of the cars. The other man was in the back now, looking down on the trunk, and Harlan could see the sunlight glinting off the gold-rimmed shades. The soldiers in Liberia had worn gold-rimmed aviator shades too—some of them, courtesy, Harlan had learned later, of the U.S. Air Force. Harlan rested his hands on top of the wheel. He moved his head from side to side in an effort to loosen the muscles in his neck. Whenever the brothers in Liberia were stopped by soldiers they were asked for party cards. Everyone was supposed to carry such a card—proving loyalty to one of the political parties active in the country. The Friends, of course, refused to do this. Their refusal was considered an act of sedition.

Harlan looked toward the canyons, the rugged snow-capped peaks. At last the man returned with his license and vehicle registration. "You can turn around here," he said. "The dirt's hard enough on the shoulders."

"Is there any access to Table Mountain?" Harlan asked.

"Not tonight," the man told him.

Harlan started the car. It took him a couple of passes to get the thing turned around. "Don't make 'em like this anymore," one of the men said. Harlan agreed that they did not.

"Try Death Valley," the man who'd taken Harlan's papers said. "Sightseeing's better there anyway."

Harlan nodded. As he made the turnaround he thought of his little puzzle. He tried to decide what this did for it. If it did anything at all. He had hoped for more. It seemed all he was able to manage was a three-and-a-half-hour drive bookended by men with guns who wanted to tell him what to do. Maybe he should put them in the puzzle too. It was something to think about. The rest of what there was to think about, backtracking now, toward a reddening sky, were the varieties of unpleasant shit which must have come down out there somewhere in the desert, come down hard enough to bring out the Rangers and close the roads, and to wonder—if his hunch was anywhere close to being right—if his boy had been there when it had.

* * *

As it turned out, Harlan did not have to wonder about the shit for long. He found that out in the first town he came to—a dismal-looking place by the name of Trona. He'd noticed the name when he'd passed it on the way up—a sign saying TRONA. Death Valley. There was an inn he'd heard of in the valley and he had decided that he would head in that direction—get a shower, a decent meal, a decent night's sleep, then think about what to do next. Lately a lot of people had been telling him what to do next. He found that what he wanted was some time to think about it for himself. He also found that talking to the Rangers had given him a thirst and he stopped in Trona for a beer.

He planned to drink the beer in the car, and stopped at the first place he saw, a market at the edge of the highway, and that was how he discovered what had closed the roads. It was all right there on the front page of the *Trona Star Eagle*. BODIES FOUND NEAR DOCTOR'S DOME was how someone had chosen to put it. Harlan found the paper lying on a bench near some vending machines.

There were two photographs accompanying the story. One was a picture of one of the people who had been killed. The photograph was of poor quality and the name that went with it meant nothing to Harlan. The second photograph contained a peculiar-looking building identified as the late Ceton Verity's Electro-Magnetron. The bodies, Harlan read, had been found near the site of the building. There were three bodies altogether and as yet two remained unidentified. The bodies had been mutilated, apparently in some ritualistic way: certain organs—the article was not specific—were still missing.

By the time Harlan had finished with the newspaper the last of the light had drained from the sky and a handful of stars lay scattered above him. As he walked back toward his car a cool wind whipped the cuffs of his slacks about his ankles. He sat heavily in the front seat and squeezed the back of his neck with his right hand. At his side the two bottles of beer squeaked against one another in the brown paper bag, which had begun to go wet beneath his hand. It suddenly occurred to him that he'd been here, in the desert, for one week. It felt like a very long time. It felt like a long way from home and he found it remarkable to think that if he wanted to he could be back in Los Angeles before the sun came up. He started the car and drove east, into the heart of the desert.

By the time he reached the summit of the range which formed

the western wall of Death Valley a full yellow moon had risen to face him from the crest of the valley's opposing wall and what looked to be the entire valley lay spread before him in a kind of snowy splendor—a lunar landscape of pans and flats and jagged ridges. To the north a sea of sand dunes glistened in the pale light. It was a spectacular vista and he realized he had timed his arrival at the summit perfectly—meeting the moon like this, the valley between them. It had happened purely by chance, of course. One of life's little gifts. Harlan polished off the last beer and began his descent.

He was bone-tired, the moon high and white, by the time he maneuvered the coupe into a sparsely populated parking lot before a large opulent-looking building of Spanish design. An oasis of cottonwood and palm had grown up around the building and when Harlan killed the engine he could hear the sound of water tumbling over rocks somewhere in the darkness. There were some lights up on a hillside back of the building and a few brilliant patches of white stone were illuminated before the blackness of the night sky.

Harlan sat for several minutes, listening to the water, observing the Milky Way as it curved overhead. It seemed to him an impossible number of stars filled the sky here—nothing at all like the sky over Los Angeles. Harlan put the empty beer bottles back in the brown paper bag and stuck it behind his seat. He got out and stretched his legs, took his suitcase from the trunk. He'd driven to Table Mountain on a hunch. He hoped now the hunch had been wrong. Walking toward the building, he began to think once more of his puzzle but pushed it from his mind. A swimming pool would be nice, he thought. A couple of martinis. A steak. A Jacuzzi. Christ, there was no end to it. He walked toward the lights and the sound of water.

The Blue Heaven Motel had a pool. It was a small kidney-shaped affair which, had there been water to fill it, might, Delandra guessed, have been good for about three strokes. As things stood now it wasn't good for much of anything. The motel consisted of about a dozen identical rooms which had been built in one long row set at a right angle to the road. At the end of the motel closest to the road there was a gravel lot and a tattered neon sign. At the other end was the pool. There were two wooden dressing rooms near the pool. His and Hers. They were painted blue but the paint was weathered and peeling. It was white beneath the blue and green beneath that. There was a concrete slab around the pool and half a dozen rusted metal deck chairs—survivors of a more prosperous time. Or perhaps, Delandra thought, only a more optimistic time. It was hard to imagine there had ever been anything like prosperous for the Blue Heaven.

Delandra was seated in one of the chairs. She was smoking a joint, her last, and staring into the bleached interior of the empty pool. She was wearing the rose-colored glasses with which the late Mr. Ott had provided her but they did little to brighten the view.

If she looked to the right she could see her car, or at least the front end of it, sticking out from behind the dressing rooms. It was not a pretty sight. All four tires had been slashed—a kind of going-away present from Jack and Lyle. If she looked to the left she was treated to the sight of Obadiah Wheeler. He was with Bill, of course. The two of them were standing near the crest of a small ridge at the far end of the pool—looking for time nodes, no doubt. Delandra shook her head and looked away. She looked at her car and took a drag on the joint, held the smoke down as long as possible. It would have been bad enough just being stuck here, no tires, no money, no Thing. Still, they could have done something. They could have sold the car for junk, pawned the guitar, started out on foot for Christ's sake. Not her favorite mode of travel, but what the hell. They could be history in this dump right now, if not for Bill Richards and Judy Verity. She coughed and adjusted her shades. The big If. Like some grim specter it darkened her morning. Nor was she a stranger to its shadow.

Bill and Judy had arrived the morning after, which was how Delandra chose to think about the day following the visit of Jack and Lyle. Obadiah had gone out to check the car and Delandra had been left alone to answer the knock on the door.

She had taken an almost immediate dislike to the couple she had found there, even before she knew who they were or what they wanted. There was just something about them. Judy was small and blond. Her hair was short and tucked behind her ears. She wore silver wire-rimmed glasses. She was not unattractive. She reminded Delandra of someone you might find on a college campus taking a degree in English literature. Bill Richards was much larger. He had the look of a good-natured real estate salesman who had played football in college. They introduced themselves as Bill Richards and Judy Verity.

"As in Ceton Verity?" Delandra had asked. "His daughter," Bill had replied. And Delandra had looked, not without some sense of wonder, into the pale blue eyes of someone who might after all be somehow like herself.

"The guy who built the Electro-Magnetron?" Delandra had asked, just to be sure.

Judy Verity nodded, solemnly.

"Oh, daddy's way out there," Delandra had suggested, looking for some trace of sisterhood in that frail face. She had drawn a blank and it was all downhill from there.

Delandra was disturbed in the midst of these recollections by the sound of loose rock tumbling into the empty pool. She looked up as Bill and Obadiah made their way down the side of the ridge. She was by now trying to hang on to her joint with a bobby pin. She sucked at it once more and burned her lip, then let the roach fall to the concrete beneath her. Too little too late. She eyed the remains with contempt. "I didn't know your organ would be so small," she said. "I didn't know I would be playing in a cathedral," he said. It was a joke. She didn't know why she thought of it now. She didn't even like jokes. Maybe that was it. Maybe it was something to remind her of how little she liked what had become of her and Obadiah's trip.

The bad part was that Delandra could, at least to some extent, see herself as the architect of her own demise. It was apparently all those stupid phone calls she'd made trying to get through to someone in Verity's group that put Bill and Judy onto their trail. There was still some confusion in her mind as to how, exactly, they had been led to the Blue Heaven, though by now the how seemed beside the point. The fact was, they were here. They had moved in next door and, while unwilling to loan Delandra enough to put new tires on the Dart, were, the cheap sons of bitches, apparently quite ready to subsidize some sort of expedition into the Mojave in search of a gateway to another dimension, or some damn thing it made Delandra angry even to think about, should Obadiah and Delandra care to join them. It was, from whichever side you cared to examine it, a peculiarly fucked situation.

She listened to the sound of footsteps upon the deck. She hoped Bill and Obadiah would not see that she had been crying and for the moment was grateful for the shades.

"Find any time warts?" she asked when the two men were within striking distance. It was better she thought to go first.

"Time nodes," Bill said good-naturedly, correcting her. Bill, it seemed, was always correcting her. Obadiah stood silently behind him, the position of the sun making his expression impossible to read.

"Maybe I was thinking of time warps," Delandra continued. "Any of those?"

"None of those, either," Bill said. He was still smiling but the smile had something pinched about it. "And it's like I told you the other night. First you have to locate the block. Then come the nodes. And, of course, none of it works without the crystal."

"Of course," Delandra said. "The crystal." It seemed one of the things Bill and Judy had been up to when they heard about Delandra's efforts to contact the group was checking out some piece of automatic writing they had picked up from a contactee in New Mexico. The writing had directed them into the Mojave, where they hoped to find some sort of crystal which, according to the note, might be of use in locating and then opening some sort of time block also mentioned in the note. For there were, Bill Richards had explained, certain areas of particular magnetic sensitivity —magnetic blowouts, which, with the crystal as a key, might be used as gateways into other dimensional planes. And once through the gate, it should, at least theoretically, be possible to negotiate the various nodes. Delandra actually remembered all of this. She couldn't help herself. But she liked to pretend that she did not.

"I thought nodes were those little things in your neck."

"You're thinking of lymph nodes," Bill told her. "And anyway, you know all of this is just theory, something we're checking out." It was a line Bill and Judy fell back upon when they caught themselves sounding too weird. After all, they had not come up with the writing. They were simply trying to verify certain aspects of it, and the suggestion of doorways to other dimensions did seem to connect in some way Delandra was not completely clear about with what had brought Bill Richards into the Mojave in the first place— an investigation into the history of a particular indigenous tribe— and Bill, when not scouring the countryside for time warts and magnetic blow-jobs, could indeed be found poring over a thick, important-looking volume entitled *Mojave Ethnopsychiatry and Suicide: The Psychiatric Knowledge and Psychic Disturbances of an Indian Tribe*. Delandra, unfortunately, was able to remember this title as well. It was that she either had recently been cursed with total recall or had simply found something too grotesque in Bill and Judy to ignore, she could not decide.

She had at last managed to pry from Bill that his college education consisted of a degree in business management from UCLA. Though, of course, he had started out in physics. "But after I had done enough of that I began to see . . ." he had explained, pausing here to look thoughtfully out a window, allowing Judy time to admire the pose, "that, well . . ." It was, of course, a difficult thing to explain to laymen. "What I was learning was really all along the conventional laws of science. What I wanted was to completely reevaluate those laws." Enough said, he had stopped to stare at the floor, a rather satisfied expression on his broad face. And so here he was, reexamining the laws of physics and chasing down time nodes, all the while, Delandra imagined, judging by how the two of them seemed to live, ringing up quite a bill Judy Verity was apparently willing to foot—her father, unlike Sarge in at least that respect, having left in his estate a good deal more than one home-made monster, so that there were times when Delandra guessed Richards was not quite as dumb as he looked and was perhaps doing something more with his business degree than met the eye.

Delandra was suddenly aware that Bill had stopped talking and began at once to search for some new way to goad him, a pastime she had unfortunately discovered she was capable of pursuing for hours at a time. She was saved from this, however, by the arrival of J (Delandra had recently taken to referring to Bill and Judy as B&J, or simply BJ, as in blow-job). "My, these motel walls are thin,"

Delandra said by way of greeting. She was aware of Bill smiling at her out of the sun.

J, as in Job, was not smiling, however, and seemed in fact to be more agitated than usual. She went hurriedly past Delandra, waving a newspaper which she handed to Bill. "You had better take a look at this," she said. Something in her tone made Delandra sit still, waiting to see what would come of it.

Bill read for a moment in silence, then passed the paper to Obadiah. "Isn't this one of the people you were telling me about?" he asked.

Delandra was the last to get the paper. She got it from Obadiah and when he stepped over to hand it to her he moved out of the sun and she could see his face for the first time since he'd come down from the rocks. He did not look good.

The paper was the Saturday evening edition of the *Trona Star Eagle,* and what Delandra saw in it, Sunday morning, was a photograph of Lyle Blackledge. There was also a photograph of the Electro-Magnetron. She read through the accompanying article, aware as she did so of the three faces peering down on her from the sky. She guessed they were waiting for some response. She looked back over the pictures, trying to assess what it was she felt. Really, the only thing that came immediately to mind was that somehow, when all was said and done, she believed she would have preferred the company of Jack and Lyle to the company of B&J. "It must be true," she said at last, passing the paper back to Judy, "only the good die young."

I t had begun for Obadiah—the grim revelation of plot —with the date he'd scribbled into a secondhand copy of the first volume of The Books of Bueltar. He had tried several times to make it go away. He had alternately believed and dismissed it—suspected it to be nothing more than a paranoid delusion worthy of Bug House himself. But like some recurring nightmare, the thing was not easily put aside.

He sat now in a cluttered room amid the debris of his research. Upon the coffee table the first volume of The Books of Bueltar lay facedown upon the pink Formica. On the dresser was Bill Richards's copy of *Mojave Ethnopsychiatry and Suicide: The Psychiatric Knowledge and Psychic Disturbances of an Indian Tribe.* A Bible lay open upon the bed. And then, of course, there was the *Trona Star Eagle,* the one with Lyle's picture in it.

Obadiah picked up the paper and stared one more time into the grainy black-and-white photographs on the front page. He had repeated this gesture many times since Judy had shown up with the paper that morning. He was particularly drawn to the photograph of Lyle for it seemed to him a transformation barely short of miraculous had been worked on it—as if the narrow hick face had in the end managed some degree of dignity Obadiah would not have thought possible, as if the vacant, cramped eyes had taken on the light of something only to be wrested from a profound suffering. This combined with the fascination to be had from the knowledge that somewhere, someone had taken him out—no small task that, no boy's errand. It was something to chew on. Beyond a narrow rectangular window the beginnings of a sunset stirred the sky. Obadiah had been alone in the room since noon. He had reached a kind of conclusion. He folded the photographs until they were small enough to fit into the breast pocket of his shirt and went outside to look for Delandra.

He found her in the Dart. She was in the back, where the seat used to be, ass on the floorboards, legs crossed at the ankles and swung up to rest on the back of the front seat so that all you could see from the outside were her boots pointed toward the sky. She had the red-faced guitar in her lap and a tall can of malt liquor at her side. There were a couple of empty cans on the floor and Obadiah stepped on one getting inside. It gave beneath him with an empty aluminum crunch. "Obondigas Wheeler," Delandra said by way of greeting, "you old Bible thumper."

Obadiah squeezed himself past the front seat from which Delandra seemed unwilling to move her ankles and sat down beside her. He drew his own legs up and rested his forearms on his knees, admiring for a moment the blaze of glory with which the day was giving up its light. The iron-colored ridge had taken on a violet hue with the sky a deep orange behind it. The orange ran to a misty yellow, a bright turquoise, and then, abruptly, to an inky blue. To his left the walls of the Blue Heaven Motel had achieved a certain opalescent brilliance which was really quite remarkable—ice to the evening's fire.

Delandra let a hand fall across the strings of the Hummingbird and a slightly muted chord clattered about the back of the car. "So Obondigas," she said. "What's the lowdown, Brown?"

Obadiah picked up the can which now sat between them and tested it for weight. It was half full. He poured some down his throat and waited for it to hit bottom. The lowdown was what he had come to give. "You know," he began after some moments of silence, "some of this is starting to make sense."

Delandra put her head back against a piece of metal. "I was afraid it might," she said.

Obadiah rubbed his neck. It still hurt from the crack Lyle had given it and there were times when he imagined it was affecting his vision. At the moment, for instance, Delandra appeared to have receded so completely into a shadowed corner that he was barely able to make her out. This scared him. He drank more of the malt liquor and looked outside, toward the walls of the motel. When the illusion had passed he began. "I want to tell you something," he said. But he felt himself growing short of breath and stopped long enough to finish the malt liquor. He was aware of Delandra watching him and he hoped that his voice would not betray him. What was needed, he felt, was a certain brand of level-headed seriousness—a tone he might once have achieved in explaining to some befuddled householder that the concept of an immortal soul was not of Judaic origin but had grown rather from the early church's brush with Hellenistic thought.

"It began," he said, "with Sarge's note. The wind, the flash of light, the crystals. It seemed to me at the time there was some biblical connection there—something about crystals having been found at a site where fire was once said to have come down from heaven. Well, I found the incident. It was Elijah's contest with the Baal worshipers at Mount Carmel. The contest was about whose god was the strongest. Elijah won. When he spoke the Word, fire came out of heaven and consumed the offering. It not only consumed the offering, it consumed the altar, the rocks around it, the whole shot. The crystals were found much later and were, at least according to what I read, an indication there had once been some kind of extreme heat in that area—just like in Sarge's note. At any rate, I kept thinking about these crystals. As you know, crystals are mentioned in Richards's note too. I started using the concordance, looking for other references. And it put me on to something—a pattern, if you will." He quoted for her from the tenth chapter of the book of Daniel, the part about the man in white, his body like chrysolite. "Now it just so happens," he told her, "that chrysolite is a crystal. This is only one reference out of maybe two dozen, but you can probably guess the pattern—the association of a particular crystal with the appearance of supernatural beings." Watching her he could not tell if she had guessed anything or not. He cleared his throat and went on. "It fits Bill's note too," he said. "And it fits with something the Indian who gave it to him had to say. The Indian claims to be in contact with beings he calls the Others. He doesn't know where they are from. He claims, however, that one of the things which makes their appearance possible is the possession of a certain crystal. Now this in turn connects with something Richards has been interested in for some time. You've seen his book. Well, the book is about a particular group of Mojave Indians—the Table Mountain People. They were Mojaves but they were different from the Indians around them. They were incredibly more advanced, in a number of ways, one of them being their artwork. Then, six, seven hundred years ago, they vanished. Some think their disappearance has something to do with the god they worshiped. The god's name was Mastamho. Mastamho was supposed to have gone insane. It was something he passed on to his followers and it drove them to suicide."

Delandra had not spoken in some time. Her face was turned toward the windshield but her eyes were closed, her mouth open, and for a moment Obadiah was afraid she had gone to sleep. When he stopped talking, however, she opened her eyes and looked at him. "Don't tell me," she said. "Let me guess. Bill Richards has another idea."

He was somewhat annoyed that after all of that she was still one step ahead of him. But he knew where he was going. He knew there was a trump card that eventually he would play. "Always the smartass," he said. "Bill Richards has another idea. One of Mastamho's powers was the ability to alter his form. He could vanish as one thing and reappear as another. Richards has the idea that maybe the Table Mountain People didn't commit suicide. Maybe they achieved transference. Maybe that's how advanced they were."

"Transference?" Delandra asked.

"They moved on. They adopted new forms." He stopped here.

A cool wind had begun to sweep the flats. The sky was black and the light which found its way into the car came from the spots attached to the rear of the motel. "One more thing," he said. He had begun a search of the car's floor, hoping that he had missed some of the malt liquor, that perhaps a stray can had rolled beneath a seat. "The Indians did these drawings—various bizarre creatures in circles—a lot of the artwork was done on large bowls or dishes, the creatures all linked in some way, then a break in the link, as if there were one creature missing, or, and this is Richards's idea, as if the creatures around the edge were really all the same creature undergoing various transformations, at last disappearing altogether. At the center of these transformation drawings there is always a rounded object in the middle of the circle, what appears to be a stone. On some drawings the stone has been given a reddish color—as if to indicate it was glowing or reflecting light, acting, in other words, like a 'crystal.' "

Obadiah gave up looking for a stray can. When he raised his eyes he found that Delandra was looking at him in a way which made him uncomfortable. "So now we come to the Electro-Magnetron." He was approaching the end. "There seems to be some confusion as to just what, exactly, it was supposed to be used for. I've heard one thing from the old woman in the bookstore and read another in Verity's book. Even Bill and Judy don't know for sure."

"I don't get it," Delandra said. "Didn't the old man know what it was for? He built it, for Christ's sake."

"The catch there was, he was building it under orders. He wouldn't know what it did until everything was assembled. And, as you know . . ."

"There was a part missing."

Obadiah nodded. "And it's beginning to look to me like the part may have been the crystal."

"It's that hard to find the stuff?"

"Well, that's just it. What stuff? There are all kinds of crystal around. And none of the references I've been citing are very specific. Even the biblical texts—they don't say the stuff is chrysolite, there are just all of these references to something being like chrysolite. But that gets back to Sarge's note. He says he found the crystals near the spot where he found the Thing. Which, if it were true, would mean that the stuff he found was probably the right stuff."

"If it were true," Delandra said.

"But that's just it. Don't you see? Sarge says that when he found the Thing he found the crystals. Now he could have made it up. But there are at least two strikes against that. One is the Thing itself. The other is this pattern. I mean it fits. And there's one more thing. If you believe Sarge's note it would support the idea that the deaths of Verity and Sarge were not accidental. Remember what

Sarge said? He said he'd asked someone about the crystals. Now suppose this: Verity was looking for this stuff. He was also by that time attracting some pretty marginal types. What if some of these people knew what he was looking for and word got back to them somehow—Sarge doesn't say who he talked to—that Sarge had some. They might have killed him for it. Then maybe Verity found out, and they killed him too. I'm not saying it happened that way, but it could be something like that. It might explain why the two men died so close together."

"But if somebody," Delandra said, "killed Sarge for the chryslerama, why didn't they start up the Electro-Magnetron? Why is the part still missing?"

"Because they didn't get it. They killed him but they couldn't find the crystal. And that could explain why Jack was out there that night, in the desert. They had been watching the museum, waiting for something to break. When we drove off with the Thing they knew something was up."

"They waited for two years?"

"I don't know. It's possible. You've got to admit it would explain why Jack was following us."

Delandra stared into the seatback in front of her. She lifted the guitar from her lap and slid it over the seat so it rested behind the wheel—a six-eared chauffeur taking them nowhere. "If it was Jack at the burger stand."

Obadiah shook his head. "I don't believe you," he said. "Something is going down out here. I'm not going to tell you I know what, exactly, but something."

Delandra put her fingers to her temples. "I can't stand it," she said. "I've got to move. You've got to move. This is bullshit."

Obadiah just looked at her. "Don't give me that. Your father may have been killed. You're not interested?"

Delandra continued to rub her head, making little circles with the tips of her fingers. "Can't you see what you're doing?" she asked. "You're making all of this up. This theory of yours all depends on believing Sarge when he says he asked somebody about the crystals. I mean crystals? Come on. The man was a bullshit artist. He could have picked up an idea like that anywhere. And I've seen plenty of notes where he claimed to have shown something to someone. Strictly bullshit. Can you imagine any reputable person driving to the desert to examine the Mystery of the Mojave? And if the stuff about the crystals is bullshit, then where are you? Sarge was sick, Obo. There were no marks on his body.

You've seen the Thing and now you're trying to build this big elaborate theory around it."

Obadiah had been staring into the empty pool where a sliver of white light curved across the concrete bowl. He could not pretend to be unaffected by Delandra's words. It was the kind of thing he had been wrestling with himself throughout the afternoon. One minute it would all appear to fit—like the bits of colored glass in a kaleidoscope, arranging themselves in an intricate pattern only to be dissolved with the next flick of the wrist, so that he would be left reminding himself of certain tragic fools from his recent past: the crazed, lonely people he had met on more porches than he cared to remember, alone with some weird theory they had hatched all by themselves—strange paranoid systems built from the detritus of years of unenlightened research on any number of marginal subjects until eventually everything they heard or saw could be made to fit the pattern—intrigues and conspiracies multiplying around them like cancerous cells. And he had wondered if it would end that way for him too—one more ragged pilgrim on the road toward some bankrupt enlightenment, endlessly sorting information while the truth rolled on, untouched, beneath his very nose. But then Bill Richards had knocked on his door. He had come bearing gifts and what Bill Richards had shown him, Obadiah was now about to show Delandra. He wished, however, to preface the revelation with one more gem of wisdom. "I know one thing," he said at last. "You can take just about anything and make it sound ridiculous. You can also make it sound credible. I've lived with that sort of thing. I mean I grew up in a group most people will dismiss out of hand as being half-baked. And yet there are some very smart people there. And when you hear them talk about it you see there are ideas at the core that are not half-baked at all. And nine out of the ten people who are putting it all down are people who really don't know anything about it. They're just parroting what others have said, or repeating ideas they assume to be hip."

"And you think that's what I've been doing with Bill and Judy?"

"What if there was a way," Obadiah asked her, "to check out some of this stuff?" When Delandra didn't say anything he went on. "Because there is something else. Something new."

It seemed to Delandra that with this statement a peculiar expression had attached itself to Obadiah's face. The expression was something between a smirk and a sheepish grin. He looked like a man who had just taken all her checkers and her first impulse upon seeing this smile was to punch him in it.

Obadiah dug a hand into the pocket of his jeans. "Richards and

Judy went back to the rest stop," he said. "I told them about Sarge's note. They went over the place with a fine-tooth comb." Obadiah opened his hand. In his palm lay an irregularly shaped piece of crystal. Delandra groaned. "They found some of these in the towel dispenser."

Delandra stared at the rock with a kind of horror. For it seemed to her that with the arrival of the stone, another presence had entered the car—something anonymous and malignant, an icy blackness to which she was no stranger.

"They said from the looks of the dispenser, no one had touched it for years. There's a very good chance this is it, Delandra. And there's a way to find out."

So it was true, Delandra thought, there was something, what till now she had been content to call the Hummer Curse, and it had taken those who should have meant the most—all the men in her life. For she had seen them recede, drawn away into fantasy or madness, into some private hall of mirrors where no one else was allowed. Like some well-worn deck of flash cards, a handful of stratagems spread themselves in her mind. They were, however, by now quite familiar and of doubtful value. She had always believed in moments of sensitivity—moments in which a simple touch might wound or heal. It was a belief which had thus far done little more than fuel a nagging sense of guilt. And where now to place Obadiah Wheeler in this spectrum? Was there time yet to snatch him back from the void? Might she fuck him just desperately enough to save him? And yet even as she turned toward him he was going on about something else. "It's like there are all of these elements," he told her. "And there are these relationships between them. This, for instance, is the area in which the Table Mountain People lived. It's where Verity was sent to build his dome. Archaeologists found these unusual crystals at Mount Carmel. Now these people Bill knows of have found more crystals in the Table Mountain range, at a site which may have been used by the Table Mountain People, and those crystals may be like the ones Sarge found on the flat. And Trona itself? Do you know what that means? It's a crystal. And then there's all this secret government stuff out here—as if someone was on to something, but not telling anyone. And all these mining sites? . . ." Delandra might have bolted but the hour was late. The wind had begun to toss bits of loose rock into the bowl of the empty pool and somewhere at the back of the motel a shutter had begun to bang against a blue stucco wall. And though she continued to make the appropriate responses at the appropriate times, it was all on automatic pilot now, and that was something she was good at. The late Mr. Ott had owned an airplane for Christ's sake. A Beechcraft Bonanza with room for four.

There were in fact several Jacuzzis at the Death Valley Inn, plus two bars, a couple of good-looking restaurants, and three heated pools. Harlan made no use of any of it Saturday night. He showered, lay down on the bed to rest his eyes before dinner, and when he woke up it was twelve o'clock noon, Sunday. At which point he'd taken a second shower, eaten a huge ranch-style breakfast, and returned to his room to use the phone. He wanted to get hold of the brother he'd spoken to earlier in New York but was told Brother Mitchell had gone to the farm and would not be back before Monday.

Harlan had sat for some minutes on the edge of his bed, thinking this over. He had wanted to talk to Mitchell again before moving on, though he could not say he found the prospect of a second night at the inn unattractive. He'd looked from his window, past the shading fronds of a well-kept palm toward a distant yellow ridge. At certain points along the ridge brilliant outcroppings of chalk-white stone rose abruptly like teeth before a turquoise sky. And he had thought, too, that until he managed to get hold of the brother in New York, no one would know where he was. There would be no phone calls, and none of the guests would address him as Brother Low.

Later he'd gone to a gift shop and bought several articles of clothing. He'd bought a pair of sandals, a pair of swimming trunks, a loose-fitting Hawaiian-style shirt, and a straw hat. The hat had a brown band and a red feather in it and was engineered along the lines of those made famous by Frank Sinatra. That evening he'd treated himself to double martinis in an uncrowded lounge near a huge stone fireplace and then taken himself into the Lotus Room for salad and prime rib, coffee, and a little something in the brandy snifter, and on the way back to his room, watching a sunset at the west end of the valley, had congratulated himself on only inter-rupting his meal once to think about the bodies with the missing parts and Obadiah Wheeler. In his room he had napped. On the second night, however, he awoke in time for the moonlight swim he had promised himself the night before.

He woke to a full moon, a mild dry wind. He stood for a moment on his balcony, his eyes closed, his body turned to the wind, before returning to look for the trunks he had purchased that afternoon.

There had only been one pair which fit him. They were dark brown with large green and pink flowers on them, and looking at himself now in the room's full-length mirror, he was beginning to have second thoughts about wearing them in public. The trunks were dark. His chest, belly, and thighs were embarrassingly white. He looked like a lousy refrigerator on its way to Florida, a refriger-ator with a black eye, and bruised ribs, nothing at all like what he had felt, naked on the balcony, in the wind. At last he swung a towel around his neck and went outside, his new rubber sandals flapping loudly against the bottoms of his feet.

The water in the pools was warm with a light mist rising from glassy turquoise depths. There were flagstone planters built up around the pools and there were palms in the planters. Their fronds rustled gently in the breeze. Harlan had one of the pools to himself. Perhaps fifty yards away a pair of couples sat with drinks in a Jacuzzi—bodies blurred in the mist, their voices reaching him across the stone.

He swam leisurely laps in the warm water, moving with surpris-ing grace for a man of his size, letting the tension seep from his neck and shoulders, letting his mind drift. At some point it oc-curred to him just how long it had been since he had done any-thing like this. When he left Africa it was supposedly to rest, but really it had only been to step into another position of responsibil-ity and there never had been much of anything resembling a real vacation. And that, in a backassward sort of way, was, he could see now, at least part of what he'd been after with this trip into unas-signed territory. Backassward because of course he was still the man in charge, still the guy who had to tell everyone else what to do and when to do it. And maybe that was what lay back of his fight with the mechanic—just too much stress, for too long. And yet perhaps this was all he had needed. Just this. He could not believe, sliding now through the water which was as soft and warm as summer air, that he had really gone looking for a fight. It seemed like a bad dream, or the dumb move of some other moron he had only heard about.

He cruised to a stop at the shallow end of the pool and hooked his elbows up over the sides, left his body and legs to float out in front of him, occasionally breaking the surface with his toes. He had been doing this for several seconds when he became aware of someone watching him and looked back along one arm to see the cocktail waitress who had served him in the Lotus Room seated now on a plastic deck chair. He wondered how long she had been watching him. "Come on in"—Harlan heard his own voice booming in his ears, somewhat surprised by his own good humor—"water's great."

The girl laughed. She was perhaps twenty-five. She had dark hair and wore one of those little butt-twitcher uniforms common to her trade. Her legs were long and shapely, made to look even longer by the short dress and high-heeled shoes.

"I'm still working," she told Harlan. "I'm on a break."

He could see now the red tip of a cigarette glowing near her knee.

"Too bad," Harlan said, the crazy part being that he meant it.

"I could maybe bring you another drink," the girl offered. "Grand Marnier, wasn't it?"

"Why not?"

"It's on the house," she told him when she returned.

Harlan thanked her. He was seated now on the deck, his legs still in the pool. He sipped the drink while the girl sat back down in the plastic chair and crossed her legs.

"Traveling by yourself?" she asked him.

Harlan said that he was, that he was out from Los Angeles on business. He thought for a moment that she was going to ask him something about his business, or that she would say something about the bruises on his face. But she didn't. Instead, she asked him about where he was from. He told her that he was from the Midwest originally, but that just recently he had returned from Africa. She seemed to think it was quite interesting that he had been there, though she did not ask much about that either. She began instead to talk about herself. She told him she was from Arizona and had never been much of anywhere. She was divorced and had one kid, a girl. She asked Harlan if he had any children and he said no. She did not, he noticed, ask if he had a wife but went rather into a fairly extended rap about the difficulties of

meeting men. Harlan went along with her. He said he didn't see
how she could possibly have any problems in that regard. She
pretended to be flattered. "You know what I mean," she said.
There were, of course, a lot of men around, but too many were of
the young, fuck-up sort, a breed with which she'd had her fill.
Older, more mature men were evidently where it was at, at which
point Harlan began to believe that, strange as it seemed, she was
indeed coming on to him. He felt the warm water lapping the
insides of his knees, the brandy warming his chest and face. What,
he asked himself, would it take to make this evening complete?

"I get off in a couple of hours," the girl, who had by now identified herself as Deborah, told him as she stood up. "I have to go back
to work but the bar will be open till two. Come by if you feel like it.
You can tell me some more about Africa."

Harlan said it was very kind of her to offer. He sat at the edge of
the pool and watched her walk back toward the glass and stone of
the building. He wondered if she was a hooker, or if the part about
the fuck-ups and the older men was the real thing. It flattered him
to believe the latter and so he went with that. He dried himself
with the towel and padded off to his room in his bare feet. He
showered and then sat naked on the edge of his bed. He sat there
for a long time. He watched the clock on the dresser strike twelve.
He thought of Deborah, alone in the Lotus Room. He thought of
stone fireplaces and moonlight upon the leaves of palms. In the
end he supposed that one mistake per trip was enough. He killed
the lights and stretched out on his back in the darkness. But he lay
there for a long time without sleeping, a lonesome traveler on a
peculiar road which seemed to run from euphoria to dread and
back again, from something which might have been contentment
to what he knew was plain, stone-cold remorse.

Harlan was up early enough on the following morning to catch Brother Mitchell before the meeting for field service in Brooklyn.

"You're up early," Mitchell told him. He seemed surprised that Harlan was still in the desert. Harlan told him something of what had gone down. He told him about the bodies. This was followed by a moment of silence. "You think this brother may be involved?" Mitchell asked.

"I don't know," Harlan said, "but I would like to find out. You know the boy's presiding overseer had asked me to have a talk with him before this whole thing began."

There was a soft clicking sound on the line. "I don't think chasing him all over the Mojave first was part of the deal, was it?"

"Not part of the deal," Harlan said. He was able to imagine Mitchell seated at the edge of his desk. He imagined the expression on the brother's face. It would be not dissimilar to that worn by the man with the gray crewcut at Sarge Hummer's Desert Museum when he had pointed toward Los Angeles with his gun.

"So what can I do for you?" Mitchell asked.

"I don't know, really," Harlan said. He felt suddenly a bit foolish about what he was up to, as if his reasons for staying in the desert were a poor excuse for not getting back to the city. But he said nothing to Mitchell about the rest of it. Mitchell would hear about that soon enough. For the moment Harlan went with what he had started. He asked for the rest of what Mitchell had on the Sons of Elijah.

Mitchell cleared his throat. "We've got a book here," he said.

It seemed someone had written a book about Leonard Maxwell and his group. There was also stuff in the book about Verity—the two men having once been partners. Before Harlan hung up he learned what the stuff was.

Mitchell had been wrong about Maxwell claiming contact. Maxwell had received a book.

*"The Book of Stones?"* Harlan asked.

It was *The Book of Stones.* Verity was the one who had claimed contact. He claimed to have met an alien on the East Coast who sent him west with plans for a building. The author of the book believed that at one time the two men had planned to form a group together, but that Maxwell had queered the deal by trying to market one of his devices. He believed that most of what Verity had written was a rip-off of Maxwell's ideas and that Maxwell had invented the racial stuff to get back at Verity.

"I take it the author of this book is not a believer."

"I wouldn't say so," Mitchell said. "So you've got Verity and you've got Maxwell. Now there is one other group the book deals with, something called New Light. And that's something that Verity's daughter has begun just in the last few years. The principal texts are her father's. But the old man is out in your neck of the woods fooling around with hippies. The author thinks he's out there trying to get even with the daughter for forcing him out of his own publishing business. It seems the daughter's got this boyfriend whose father was one of the prime movers in a big West Coast cult group of the thirties. Ever hear of the Mighty I Am?"

Harlan had not.

"Nazis," Mitchell said.

Harlan looked from his window toward some reddish outcroppings of stone. The stone was just now beginning to color beneath the sun. "Sounds like a lot of people trying to get even with each other," he said.

Mitchell laughed. "A regular soap opera. If you believe the book." He paused. "Is it going to do anything for you?" he asked. "There's more if it is."

Harlan scratched his ear with the receiver. He visualized his puzzle. UFO cults with axes to grind? Something the boy had walked into, maybe? Or nothing at all? But then it did seem to feed rather well into what he had begun on the steps of Sarge's museum. "Anything in the book about a guy named Sarge Hummer?"

"No," Mitchell said, "I don't think I would have forgotten the name."

When Harlan had hung up he stood looking into the gathering colors of morning. Soon the colors would be gone, lost in the oven of the coming day. Mitchell had left him with a final thought: Verity, taking a break from his business during the war, had served for a time as part of an intelligence outfit based in England. Maxwell had spent time in England as well, recovering from wounds received in Europe. This was from the book. The book was interested in the hows and whys of these groups. A variety of theories was presented to account for what the groups were *really* up to. The theories were very conspiratorial in nature. One in particular was built around the rumor that at one point, shortly after the war, there had been talk in certain circles about using some of the high-level intelligence machinery generated during the war to fake some kind of outside threat—UFO phenomena, say—in an effort to maintain peace.

"What you're trying to tell me," Harlan had said, "is that Verity and Maxwell may have begun with good intentions."

"I thought you would like it," Mitchell said.

Harlan thought about that now as he stood looking at the rocks. Beyond the balcony at his window it had grown warm enough so that a water mirage had formed at the base of the yellow ridge. It was a perfectly detailed illusion, complete with the reflected images of the white outcroppings jutting into a blue sky, and he found himself wondering how long it would take to walk there. Distances were hard to judge in the desert. People had died here, or so he had been told, believing they could reach some point they'd picked out in the cool of the morning only to wind up trapped by the heat of the day, the point they had started for no closer than when they had begun. And, of course, there had been no fancy inns to welcome the first visitors, no pools or Jacuzzis. Just the land. Pieces of ground you could fry an egg on. Tricks done with mirrors. There, Harlan thought, was a conspiracy for you.


When Harlan had dressed he went outside. He wore his new flowered shirt and the Frank Sinatra hat. He went into the Lotus Room and drank two bloody marys. He looked for Deborah but she was not around. The girl who worked in her place was short and thin. She had red hair and pale skin and Harlan was moved by a sudden impulse to ask after Deborah. He let it slide. He went next door for breakfast and then back to his room to pack. He had in mind a return trip to Trona—one more crack at learning something new there. If he drew a blank he would return to the city.

It was still early when he had finished with the room. He locked his suitcase in the car, slipped on his dark glasses, and walked back to the highway. He had noticed a desert museum—hopefully of a more legitimate variety than the one he had visited last—at the entrance to Furnace Creek. It was a pleasant morning and he wanted a little exercise before hitting the road.

* * *

The museum was a single-story building made of concrete blocks. It was just opening for the day when Harlan reached it and there were perhaps a dozen middle-aged couples standing around out in front. Some had cameras dangling about their necks. A couple of the men wore flowered shirts much like Harlan's. Harlan stood by himself at the edge of a small patch of grass and waited for the others to go inside. When he could no longer see anyone near the door, he removed his dark glasses, folded the stems so that they might fit into the front pocket of his shirt, and entered the building.

The museum consisted of two long rectangular rooms. The rooms were well lit, filled with low glass cases, maps, and charts. The charts provided information about things like the average amount of rainfall one could expect annually in Death Valley. Harlan strolled slowly among the exhibits, his hands clasped behind his back, his hat pushed well back on his head. He wanted to allow enough time for the others to stay ahead of him. This was easier said than done. A number of the glass cases contained miniatures of various kinds—the twenty-mule teams once used to haul borax out of the valley, the mining works at Trona, and so on. Items which two of the men seemed intent on taking photographs of from all possible angles. And then there was one of the wives who insisted on reading all printed information out loud in a nasal, singsong voice for the benefit of the others. All in all, it was a slow-moving crew, forcing Harlan to take more time than he would have liked. He had in fact gotten stuck above the miniature of Trona, feigning an elaborate interest in what was mined there when something the woman said caught his attention. "The Mystery of the Mojave," the woman read, and then mumbled something Harlan could not catch before picking it up again. "Creators of this remarkable art remain one of the great unsolved mysteries of the American West. They lived along the northwestern edge of the Mojave Desert from roughly A.D. 100 to about 1150, at which time the culture seems to have simply vanished. Scholars today do not even know what this relatively small band called themselves but refer to them as the Table Mountain People—the name being taken from the Table Mountain range where much of their remarkable art has been found. According to legend passed down among surrounding tribes, the group may have committed suicide, though nothing is known for certain and some believe their demise may have simply been the result of the curve of rising population crossing the arc of falling natural resources. Basis for the belief in the suicide legend among neighboring clans resides in the Table Mountain People's worship of the god Mastamho. According to Mojave mythology, Mastamho is said to have become insane. To this day many of the indigenous people believe that the appearance of Mastamho, even in a dream, will lead the dreamer toward insanity and a suicidal death."

Harlan stood above the miniature town of Trona listening to the woman. Her voice issued from the farthest of the two rooms and when at last she had finished and the couples had filed back out into Harlan's room once more, he went to see about the Mystery of the Mojave for himself.

He found that the entire second room had been given over to a display of the Table Mountain People's art. The work itself consisted of dozens of ceramic pots on which either geometric designs or figures had been painted. Some of the figures were recognizable as people or animals. Others were of a more imaginative variety—bizarre combinations of birds, animals, insects, and people, so that Harlan was in fact reminded of another group of fantastic creatures he had recently seen in the other desert museum.

He stood for some time before the glass cases, quite taken in by the graceful lines of the work, the strange creatures which stared back at him from the hollows of the bowls. Eventually he found one piece in particular to which his attention kept returning. He found the piece referred to in the catalog as the Decapitation Bowl. At the center of the Decapitation Bowl there were two figures. One, dressed in a type of ritual garb, squatted on his haunches above the supine figure of the second. The squatting man held a weapon in one hand, the head of his opponent in the other. The longer Harlan looked at the bowl, the more he noticed. He noticed, for instance, that the body of the fallen man was black but his head was white. He noticed that the dead man had two right hands, each with six fingers. The printed information which accompanied the exhibit indicated that scenes on many of the bowls were believed to have derived from certain explicit scenes and characters from various Indian myths. The Decapitation Bowl, it was thought, depicted the victory of one of the Little War Twins over a witch at the time of the Emergence.

Scattered among the bowls was a variety of poster-size pieces of mat board upon which information regarding the Table Mountain People had been printed. From these Harlan learned that the Little War Twins were the ones responsible for leading men out of the cave womb in which they had been created. The cave womb, it seemed, was not much of a place. One poster described it thus: "The Underworld was a place of moral and social disintegration as well as physical morass. Everywhere were unfinished creatures, crawling like reptiles over one another in filth and black darkness."

The last thing Harlan noticed about the bowl was the eyes. He had missed them for some time. The bowl was ringed in a kind of pattern—what Harlan had first taken for an optical pattern in which it becomes impossible to distinguish object from ground. Finally, however, he saw that the pattern was in fact composed of two separate but concentric rings—one which appeared, the more he looked at it, to move to the right, the other, to the left. A wheel within a wheel and the wheels were full of eyes all around.

A t the intersection of the road which led from the inn and the interstate, there was a gas station and a market. Harlan filled the coupe there. He also purchased two quarts of beer. The day was heating up. He drank one of the beers in the shade of a lone cottonwood behind the store. The other now sat between his legs as he drove the narrow asphalt road which would lead him back to Trona. The sun was straight overhead, the desert spread flat beneath her light—hostile and yet beautiful. He drove toward distant, pale blue ridges and sand drifts the color of sunburned flesh.

As he did he tried to put his finger on just what it was he found so irksome about the bowl he had just left in the museum. He was working on this little package, that was it. There was a hand in the package and what he wanted to believe about that hand was that it was the child of Leonard Maxwell. Now the stuff in the bowl seemed to hint at something else. It created one more loose end which, together with the already existing loose end, the African hand, seemed to point to another, quite different point of origin. And there, he thought, was the question. Was there a point of origin out there somewhere, in the real world, or was what he had stumbled onto nothing more than a coincidental grouping of common images? There had, after all, only been two of these things exactly alike and those were the ones on the temple and in the pamphlet, the ones directly traceable to Leonard Maxwell. As for the rest of them—no two were alike. They were similar, combining certain common elements—the eyes, the extra finger, the wheel within a wheel—just enough alike to be variations on a theme, and yet just different enough not to be connected in any way at all. It probably didn't make much difference. It didn't affect what had happened here. What had happened was that Harlan Low had disgraced himself in a stupid fight and that the Special Service boy Obadiah Wheeler had run off with a woman and taken something that did not belong to him. That was what mattered. It mattered that Harlan might have a chance to set things right. The rest of it, the back story which might or might not link Sarge Hummer to Leonard Maxwell and Ceton Verity, the point of common origin which might or might not exist for a variety of peculiar-looking hands, was of interest but probably not important, perhaps nothing more than a game with which one might kill time along the lonesome stretches of blacktop it was necessary to follow for hours to get anywhere in this part of the country—a puzzle, the likes of which he had found in Maxwell's pamphlet.

Harlan uncapped his second beer and stared across his pointed yellow hood at an arrow-straight road which eventually lost itself somewhere miles ahead in the shimmering illusion of water. He took a long pull on the bottle. Harlan's problem was that if he did not work on something like the puzzle—Maxwell's, or his own, in which Maxwell's had come to have a place—he was inclined to reflect on other things: the fight with Floyd, the return to Los Angeles, the image of Deborah seated at the edge of a shimmering turquoise pool. He elected to play.

He went back to it by way of trying to remember if anyone had ever told him exactly what the African hand was supposed to have meant. About all he could do now was to connect it in some way to the underworld. He recalled an old African sister once explaining some of her tribal beliefs. She had held her hand out flat before him. The world of the living, she had said, was what was on top. The bottom side belonged to the shades. The world itself was constructed along the lines of a pancake. On top everything was as you saw it. But on the bottom, everything was reversed. Mountains pointed down instead of up, as did trees, houses, etc. Some diviners, she had gone on to say, saw things upside down all the time, which was why they walked around with their heads cocked over to one side—it was a sign they were in more or less constant communication with the shades. Other diviners saw things upside down only when they were receiving visions. But then the shades, Harlan seemed to recall, had nothing to do with the hand. What had it been? The hand he had seen in Monrovia had been black. Shades were white, which meant they could be seen at night, and were not necessarily malevolent. But there was something else in the underworld—there was an African name the woman had said, but it was difficult and she did not care to pronounce it. For Harlan she had only spoken of this thing as the Others. The Others were not white like the shades. They could change themselves. They could be black and hence invisible at night and were therefore much to be feared. They were connected to all manner of evil and it was with the dark Others that Harlan was certain the hand had been associated.

Add to that now the fact that he had found a similar hand in the Mojave Desert, one associated with a suicidal tribe and an insane god—the similarity was enough to give one pause. And then there was this black-white element running through the thing as well. In the African story. In the Indian bowl. It led him eventually to speculate upon how all of this might fit Maxwell's upside-down universe of malevolent gods and heroic nephilim. The task was not without its rewards. The Indian creation account, for instance. There was a fallen beginning for you, made you stop and think about where the creators of the cave womb had their heads. It had taken the Little War Twins, a pair of supernatural beings, to lead the people at the time of the Emergence. Interesting that there were only two of them. One thought of Elijah and Melchizedek. And the Emergence stories were linked in time to the Indian Deluge stories. Something perhaps like the end of the Elder World. And yet the people had been left to wander, searching for the lost middle. One could read—lost powers. And then there were those mythic beings, the monsters of the bowls, with which the Little War Twins had done battle. Zedroes, maybe, the Ancients' crippled tools. At which point he caught himself at it and made himself stop. He smirked into the yellow glare of his hood, a liquid sky. He was trying to make sense of gibberish, for Christ's sake. At his feet a pair of empty quart bottles clinked against one another and rolled beneath his seat. He glanced into his rearview mirror and shrugged at his own reflection. "Must be whiskey talkin', Lord," he said—the lines to a dimly remembered country song. "I swear it wasn't me."

\*   \*   \*

The Studebaker was running hot by the time Harlan reached the summit of the range which formed the west wall of the valley. There was a turnout there and a small, shaded rest area with some wooden picnic tables and a pair of stone buildings.

The rest area was deserted and Harlan parked the coupe in the shade. He raised the hood and then went into the rest room to relieve himself and wash his face. Back outside he stretched out on top of one of the tables. It was a good deal cooler on the summit than in the valley below and without intending to, Harlan slipped into a light sleep.

The sun woke him. It had moved in the sky and he had lost his shade. He woke with a dull headache, his shirt wet with perspiration. When he went to the rest room for more water, however, he discovered that a maintenance man had arrived while he slept and turned the water off. The guy was doing something to some pipes beneath one of the sinks.

More than a little disgruntled, thirsty, desperate for a beer, Harlan Low returned to the Starlight coupe and headed out of the mountains. The temperature climbed as he descended. Soon he hit level ground and the car began to run hot once more. The plastic wheel grew hot beneath his hands and his shirt clung to his back. Miles of barren ground stretched away on all sides of him—chalk-white, tan, or gray, the edges blurred beneath layers of heated air. There was something hypnotic in the miles of desert road, the rush of hot wind through the open windows, and Harlan was groggy, fighting sleep, when he was jolted by the sight of what appeared to be a hitchhiker emerging from a shimmering mirage at the edge of the road some distance ahead of him.

Eventually it became clear the hitchhiker was a woman, and something of a trollop it appeared from the way she was dressed—red-and-yellow boots, tight jeans, a black-and-white leopardskin halter top—certainly not someone he would have stopped for under normal circumstances. But then these were hardly normal circumstances and Harlan Low began to ride his brakes. She stood at the intersection of the main highway and a small dirt road and once, downshifting into second, Harlan glanced in his rearview mirror—just to make sure there were no other possible rides following somewhere in the distance. The mirror was empty. The girl wore white-rimmed shades and she seemed to be smiling at him as the car came to a stop. A black guitar case rested on the pavement back of one leg and a dark leather purse swung from

one tanned shoulder. He would take her, Harlan promised himself, no farther than the town of Trona. She had the look of someone it might be hard to get rid of and it was not until she began
walking toward an open passenger-side window that he noticed
the sticker on the guitar case which she had left in the road behind
her. Black squiggly letters on a bright yellow field. The words had
been hidden by her leg. He could, however, read them quite
clearly now. The words said: I SAW THE THING!

R ex Hummer sat at his uncle's bedside on the second floor of the Kleco Community Hospital. Beyond a rectangular window, sunlight danced on an
asphalt parking lot, across the colored roofs of the cars. Rex looked
often at the cars. He had not eaten in many hours and in the
direction of town a huge yellow and black Denny's sign reminded
him of his hunger. Staring in its direction, however, was preferable
to staring at Floyd. It was not a pretty sight and what Rex kept
thinking was, it might have been me. He did not take much pleasure in this recognition, but there it was. It might, after all, for
Christ's sake, have been him: minus one spleen, jaws wired shut,
eyes reduced to angry purple slits. Rex looked toward the cars
once more, the Denny's restaurant. The room was warm and still.
Floyd had drifted into a light sleep but now seemed to be stirring.
At last he whispered Rex's name.

"Yes," Rex said, "I'm here, Floyd."

Floyd, before he had drifted off for the first time, had been
trying to tell Rex what it was like, how the men had come back,
how the big guy had begun to cause trouble, how three of the local
boys had gone after him—so much grist for the mill, but it was
difficult for Floyd to speak. He tried often and had to rest. For a
moment Rex thought his uncle was going to doze again, then it was
clear he meant to continue. Rex slid forward on the edge of his
chair and leaned against the bed.

"I musta got knocked out," Floyd said. "Because the next thing I

know, I'm outside. On my back and it's hard to breathe." He
stopped and looked pitifully at Rex. Rex held his breath. There
were tears in the corners of his uncle's eyes—of rage or pain, Rex
could not say. Somewhere down the hallway an old woman began
to moan. Floyd hefted a beefy, bruised hand and clutched suddenly at Rex's shirt. Rex felt himself drawn forward, lifted from his
chair so that he had to rest both forearms on Floyd's bed. His
uncle's misshapen face rose before him like a full desert moon. A
peculiar medicinal stench enveloped him. Floyd's voice was weak
and strained. Something gurgled in his throat and even from this
distance Rex had to strain to hear what he said. "Those niggers
ain't human, man. They burned down my goddamn truck and you
want to know how?"

Rex said nothing. He looked into his uncle's face.

"The big guy did it. And don't ask me how, you little shit. He just
looked at it." There were tears running away from Floyd's eyes
now, squeezing out from the corners and running in tiny streams
to dampen the pillow on either side of his head. His flattop was
shining with grease and the sides, where it was long, were fanned
out on the pillow like some greasy black halo and for the first time
in his life Rex felt sorry for Floyd Hummer. "You hear what I'm
telling you," Floyd went on. "He didn't do anything. He just
looked at it. A funny kind of light came out of his head, I think, and
he smoked the son of a bitch. What do you think of that shit?"

Rex maintained silence. Down the hallway the old woman was
still moaning.

"Well, say something, God damn it."

Rex blinked. "I'm sorry," he said.

"Jesus Christ." Floyd released his grip on Rex's shirt, allowing
Rex to sink back into the chair. "You believe me? You think I'm
fuckin' crazy? I wanted to tell the cops. How do you tell somebody
shit like that, man? I know what I saw, but how do you say it?" He
looked away, back toward the ceiling. He rolled his head from side
to side. "It's a goddamn nightmare," he said, and slipped once
more into a troubled sleep. Rex rose from his chair and walked to
the window.

Daylight had begun to ebb by the time Floyd came around
again and before he could say anything a nurse came in to tell Rex
he had only another five minutes. Rex went once more to his
uncle's bedside. There was still the inevitable question, for which
Rex had tried to prepare himself on the road from the junction.

Floyd now prefaced the question with a brief tirade aimed at Rex Hummer's half sister. "The scummy cunt," Floyd croaked from between wired jaws. "She thought that son of a bitchin' Thing was worth something and she stole it," he said. "If I thought you had anything to do with that I'd throw your ass out that fuckin' window right now. And don't think I couldn't do it, either." Rex would not have bet against him. He listened as Floyd raged on, his volume cut down but somehow suddenly more like the Floyd of old. "What in the hell did your old man have out there?" Floyd asked at last, arriving where Rex had known he would.

"I don't know," Rex said. There was orange light entering the room now, breaking through the blinds, splashing patterns upon the pale green walls.

"Yeah, yeah, you don't know. But you knew it was something. Didn't you? You little shit. You knew it was something. You've known it all along, known it and left it lying out there for anyone to find. Not some goddamn piece of scrap like the rest of them. You knew it was something."

Rex nodded in the darkening light. "I knew it was something," he agreed.

Floyd moved his head on the pillow while more tears squeezed out of his eyes. "And you kept your mouth shut and now who the hell knows where it is." Floyd stopped and then went on. "Well, I'll tell you one thing." By this time the nurse, a hefty middle-aged black woman, had come back into the room. "I hope those niggers catch up to your whore of a sister and that Bible-thumping twat licker she ran off with. Serve 'em both right. And I'll tell you what else." Floyd had by now worked himself into a severely agitated state, attempting to raise himself on his elbows so that the nurse felt called upon to place a hand in the middle of his chest. "Now, now, Mr. Hummer," she said. "Why don't we just lie back down and try to relax. I'll have something for you in just a minute."

"If those fuckin' niggers from outer space don't fix them, I will," Floyd croaked as loudly as he was able while the nurse pushed on his chest.

"I'm afraid you'll have to go now," the nurse said to Rex over her shoulder. "I'm going to give him something to make him sleep."

Rex Hummer backed from the room and into a dank, foul-smelling hallway at the far end of which the sun was like a dull red flame in a distant window. He could hear the nurse talking once more as he walked away. "Really now, Mr. Hummer, where did you say these brothers were from?"

* * *

Where, indeed. The sun was dying quickly by the time Rex reached his truck. It lay gut-shot and bleeding upon the western horizon, losing mass even as Rex watched it until there was nothing left but a blood-red stain upon the evening sky.

The Denny's sign was lit now, casting a yellowish glow, and past that Rex could make out a pair of golden arches and the Spanish-style facade of a Taco Bell. Rex stood watching, letting the hunger work on him. He felt slightly light-headed after his talk with Floyd. The pavement hummed gently beneath his feet. At last he climbed into the pickup and drove east, putting the neon at his back and opting instead for a small bag of Planters peanuts and a pint of Jim Beam purchased at a liquor store on the edge of town.

He drove into a gathering darkness, thinking of how it would be with Floyd. He could see him now, back of the bar, explaining to anyone who would listen how the Negroes who had kicked his ass and burned his truck had only appeared to be Negroes. He would spill his guts to one incredulous listener after another, but looking them in the eye, his flattop and boxcars shining mean and black, daring them to call it bullshit. And who would there be to call bullshit on Floyd Hummer? And so the story would take its place in the canon of the other desert tales, stories of Indian ghosts, UFOs, wrinkles in time, one more in a long line of tricks played upon the mind by a hostile land, something to be marveled at over a campfire and a pint. Rex Hummer was at the moment missing the campfire but in possession of the pint.

The bottle was empty by the time he reached the public library in the city of Victorville. It was dark. The building was a large concrete box of a building with windows running up and down in tiny narrow slits and there were yellow lights back of the narrow black pieces of glass. Rex Hummer got out of his truck and went into the building. It was almost closing time and except for two lady librarians and one black janitor, the building was empty.

Rex went to a desk and stood before it. The woman behind it wore a gray suit and glasses with mother-of-pearl above the lenses, flaring out into little wings. "Yes?" the woman asked.

Rex took a piece of yellow paper out of a small box on her desk. On it he wrote the word *psionic*. "I want to know what this means," he said.

The woman looked at her watch, then she looked in a dictionary. The word wasn't there. She looked in a couple more books.

"Psionic," she said aloud. Eventually she told Rex that she was unable to help him.

He walked from the desk, swaying slightly as he went. The whiskey made it feel like his feet were not properly connected. As he neared the door he was taken by the arm by the janitor he had passed on his way in. He was an older man. His hair was flecked with gray and the whites of his eyes were the color of egg yolks. He smelled of disinfectant and cheap wine. The hand with which he gripped Rex's arm was unusually strong. "Psionic device," the janitor said, "is a device which derives its power from the mind of its operator."

Between Victorville and the junction Rex pulled in part of a talk show on the radio. It sounded as if the program was coming from a great distance. You often, Rex had found, got things like that out on the desert at night—programs so laced with static it was difficult to hear, just bits and pieces of music, or faint, metallic voices which sounded as if they had wafted across the blackened plains all the way from Texas, or someplace beyond it. "Psionics," explained the narrator, "means psychic electronics." After that, the program faded from the air.

When Rex reached his trailer and went up the steps the first thing he found inside was the piece of mail he had taken from his box just before Tom Shoats had given him the news concerning his uncle. He looked one more time at the message stamped in red on the manila envelope:

> The customer named below
> has been singled out for a rare
> opportunity . . .
> quite possibly, unlike anything
> ever seen or heard about before.

Rex's name was indeed on the envelope. When he opened it, however, he found nothing more inside than someone trying to sell him something. It became clear to him that the message on the front and what was inside had nothing to do with each other. His mail had been tampered with.

Before dawn a vision had manifested itself to him. It had come with the muted chorus of a song and in it he had seen everything—each aspect of his life in relation to every other aspect in complete clarity—a web of dazzling intricacy.

\*    \*    \*

By midmorning the sunlight clung once more to the land like honey, and Rex Hummer was once more behind the wheel of his truck. The entire Hum-A-Phone lay disassembled, packed into the bed beneath the camper shell behind him. The gun rack behind his head held Sarge Hummer's twelve-gauge shotgun. Rex himself was dressed in the white buckskins he'd purchased from a thrift store in Goldfield, Nevada, with the reopening of the Desert Museum on his mind. He had a window down and the wind whipped the leather fringe about his sleeve. The sunlight sparkled in the rubies of cut glass arranged to decorate his cuff. He had seen Tom Shoats once more on his way out of town and he had heard about a man in a yellow car nosing around the museum in his absence. He was a big man, Tom had said, big as the Sarge. A sign, no doubt. A man as big as the Sarge. Rex sought to interpret the sign. Would the man oppose him or aid him? In the end the sign went unread. It was best, Rex decided, to concentrate on the vision. There was a certain fragility about the thing—as about a pressed butterfly, and it was Rex's fear that exposure to sunlight would damage it in some way. Already the yellow-eyed janitor, the voice out of the radio, and the vision itself had become slightly blurred, as if the lines of demarcation between the three had begun to bleed into one another like the colors of a sunset. And so Rex thought no more about the man. He rested in the knowledge that to every thing there is a season: "A time to be born, and a time to die; a time to plant, and a time to pluck up that which is planted . . ." It seemed to him that Roseann Duboise, the Buffalo Woman herself, had in fact brought this text to his attention: "A time to mourn, and a time to dance. A time to cast away stones, and a time to gather stones together . . ."

When Obadiah was a boy, there was a girl in the congregation who developed a curvature of the spine. Her parents had elected to try to cure the girl with chiropractic treatments, as opposed to the more conventional surgical technique. They apparently found a chiropractor willing to tell them this could be done. He was wrong; the girl wound up a hunchback.

You couldn't exactly blame this error in judgment by the girl's parents on the organization. They had not, as far as Obadiah knew, been advised against the more conventional treatment. And yet it had seemed to Obadiah later that a willingness to go against the conventional wisdom was one of the side effects of looking at the world in a particular light.

It began when you realized the churches had been lying to you about the contents of the Bible. If clergymen were willing to send their flocks to war, educators, to whitewash history, politicians, to break promises, and so on, it followed there were not many you could trust—a kind of vision in which the world took on the look of one huge used-car lot, a place where phony deals shimmered in the lights and men with polyester sport coats and forked tongues waited in smoke-filled closing rooms. If the cynicism was understandable, however—and to Obadiah it was—what had always perplexed him was the innocence which seemed to accompany it, the willingness to pay attention to nearly anything which started out by saying the conventional wisdom was wrongheaded. It was something which led down a peculiar road along which one might pause to dabble in everything from colonic irrigations to brain breathing.

Now Obadiah had often, even when among the faithful, sneered at the girl's parents. It was a sneer born of disbelief at the willingness to take such a risk in the face of such odds, to proceed without better information. And yet it seemed to him now, bouncing on his tailbone in the back of Bill Richards's Land-Rover as it bucked across a steep stretch of bad chalk-white road, that there was a lesson somewhere in that which he seemed to have missed, that searching for gateways to other dimensions in the Mojave Desert was not what grown men did with their time.

When he tried to imagine what it was that grown men did do, he was inclined to think of men like Harlan Low, or even of his own father. Grown men were hardworking. They were serious. They would tell you right off that looking for time portals in the desert was a fool's errand. On the other hand, the grown men Obadiah had looked up to in his life were Christians and lest he feel too guilty he was inclined to remind himself of the words of Paul: "If in this life only we have hoped in Christ we are of all men most to be pitied." In which case someone like Harlan Low, courageous as he may have proven himself to be, was really just one more in a long line of saps. The trick, of course, was in figuring out who was right and who was wrong. At times he wondered where you even began. There was, for instance, this business of information theory: "The surprising conclusion of information theory," he had once copied from a textbook,

> . . . is that experiments done within a system can never increase total knowledge of that system at the most fundamental level. All knowledge is counterfeit. Acquisition of knowledge about one part of the world requires equal sacrifice about other parts. Ignorance can at most be shifted around.

He would cop to not knowing exactly where that left you. You might decide that since the big questions appeared unanswerable it was a waste of time to ask them—a position seemingly taken by a certain Delandra Hummer, though he doubted her conclusions were in any way the results of considering the philosophic implications of particle physics. But then, what did Obadiah Wheeler know of particle physics? The stuff about information theory was just something he had copied out of a book. And where, he wondered, was his field of expertise—something he might at least rummage around in for some serviceable set of metaphors with which to frame his questions? He supposed he knew more about the Bible than the man on the street but even that advantage—if in fact one could think of it as such—seemed of late to have soured on him as well, until at last here he was, slightly nauseous from the effects of doughnuts and coffee on an empty stomach shaken by miles of washboard roads, bound eventually for the sight of Ceton Verity's Electro-Magnetron because just possibly the key to its secret meaning had turned up in the bathroom of a run-down rest stop on the side of I-15.

And yet even that was not the worst part. The worst part was that he had undertaken the mission at the risk of great personal loss, because it did not appear that Delandra Hummer would be waiting for him in the Blue Heaven Motel. He had made his pitch. He had shown her the crystal. She had called his bluff. He, of course, had called her bluff as well. He'd walked out the door leaving her seated on the dresser, the guitar case at her feet, the early morning light streaking her hair, and her lashes, beneath which her eyes had acquired a certain haunted quality he did not believe he had seen there before. It was a look, was all. But it had sufficed to weaken the backs of his knees as he made his way toward Bill Richards's Land-Rover. And it was what he rode with.

"Do you know what Lyle said?" Obadiah asked. He was looking for diversion. Beyond the window the desert was white and dusty; alone with the monotony he was inclined to feed his depression.

"No, what?" Judy asked. She feigned boredom but Jack and Lyle were a sore spot with her and Obadiah could generally get a rise out of her by mentioning them. He didn't know what was so great about getting a rise out of Judy Verity. It was admittedly a pathetic pastime. He felt that he did it now in honor of Delandra Hummer, and this in fact only fueled his depression after all. Still, he had started.

"He told me your father was Jesus Christ."

Judy turned a palm toward the sunlight which filled the windshield. She spoke to Richards rather than Obadiah. "What did I tell you?" she said.

"He wasn't Jesus Christ?" Obadiah asked.

"He was a scientist," Judy replied. "His ideas were not conventional, so of course he was never accepted by the academic community. But he certainly never claimed to be Jesus Christ."

"He believed," Richards said, "that evil was the direct result of electromagnetic manipulation. He believed that without this interference man might soon achieve a godlike state. But he also believed that even with the interference people could better themselves. He developed a series of mental and physical disciplines aimed at freeing the thought processes. Eventually he believed that people would find a way to put an end to the manipulators themselves."

Obadiah had seen mention of the manipulators in the introduction to the *The God Within*. But that was as far as he had gotten and he was still a bit unclear as to just who they were supposed to be—apparently some ancient race of gods determined to fuck with people's heads, something like the demons of a more conventional Christian theology.

Richards, however, had resented the reference to traditional Christian anything. "I'm afraid he hadn't much use for Christianity per se," Bill said. "Which of course is why the suggestion that he was Christ is so absurd."

"He wasn't very big on the pie-in-the-sky approach," Judy added. "He believed that if man was going to be saved, he would have to do it himself."

"Through exercise?"

"I don't know that I like his tone," Judy said. She addressed herself to Bill once again, speaking of Obadiah in the third person. "I thought you said he was interested in learning something."

"He is," Bill replied, "he's here."

Obadiah was about to say something else but found that the finality of Richards's statement had cast a shadow upon his enthusiasm. He was, after all, here. He settled back into his seat and looked in an easterly direction from the rear window of the Land-Rover. He looked toward a dusty sky, a white and merciless sun. It was indeed, he thought, a cramped and narrow road.

The road continued to climb. It felt like a long time. Eventually the thing jackknifed hard to the east, rose steeply, and then left them at the crest of a ridge. Bill Richards killed the engine and they sat, for the first time since leaving the motel, in complete silence while the dust settled about them.

Facing them from across the valley was another ridge, and at its base Obadiah could see the town of Table Mountain, a single row of buildings set like bad teeth in barren soil.

They were perhaps a mile away. The town looked bone-dry and deserted in the heat. "Empty," Obadiah observed.

Judy made a short snorting noise and looked away, out the window of the Land-Rover.

"Yes, yes," Richards said. He sounded pleased with himself. "The dipshits have definitely blown it in a large way."

Obadiah had, while needling Judy on the road from Trona, learned a number of interesting things about Ceton Verity and the Table Mountain People. It seems that Verity's work in the desert had indeed attracted some marginal types. The hippies, as Judy liked to call them, had taken up residence in the ghost town of Table Mountain, where, upon Verity's death, they had taken to mixing his ideas with a lot of drug-induced idiocy of their own. They had also taken to doing odd things with animals. They were even, according to Judy, responsible for her father's death.

This last bit had perked Obadiah's interest considerably. Pressing her further, however, he found her theory less dramatic than his own—probably more believable as well, so that he was able to imagine Delandra Hummer nodding her head, smirking at him as Judy spoke.

Apparently the old man had had a bad heart and was supposed to take it easy. The Table Mountain People, however, had encouraged what Judy would only refer to as "certain excesses." "It was all," she told him, "part of a lowlife plot." At which point he had learned that shortly before his death, Ceton Verity had done a very silly thing. He had signed over all of the land he owned in the Mojave to the Table Mountain People. The Electro-Magnetron. The landing strip. The museum. Ceton had made to the hippies a love offering of the whole righteous mess. The reasons for this rash act were still unclear to the rest of Verity's followers but ran the gamut from electromagnetic manipulation, through disintergant energy flows in the ion flows along the neurons and connecting tissues and visualization screens in the mind, to simply too much pussy. It seems that the Table Mountain People were a loose-living lot—though this last bit of information was passed on by Bill Richards while Judy was off taking a leak behind some rocks. It was, however, Obadiah guessed, what she had meant by the aforementioned excesses.

And finally, he had learned that since the deaths of Jack and Lyle and the woman, all of the Table Mountain People had been rounded up for questioning, leaving both the town and the site of the Electro-Magnetron empty, and closed to public access, and Bill Richards was still grinning about it.

"I believe," he said, "that our friends have at last managed to fuck themselves in their collective asshole."

"Must we put it so crudely?" Judy asked.

Richards looked at Obadiah in the rearview mirror and winked. "You might get away with cutting the tits off a few cows," he said, "you start separating men from their *cojones* and you start putting folks up real tight."

Obadiah looked once more at the town. "But Jack and Lyle were with them, or so I thought. You really think the Table Mountain People would kill three of their own?"

Judy snorted. "You're talking as if these were rational human beings," she said. "These people are animals."

Bill, in his present good humor, seemed to find this amusing as well. "Come on," he said, looking back over his shoulder at Obadiah, "let's get up on top of those rocks and have a better look." Having said that, he reached around behind his seat and pulled a cardboard box off the floor. Inside the box there was what looked to Obadiah to be an aluminum pith helmet, except that the metal had a slightly bluish tint to it. Bill Richards set the cap on his head and got out of the Land-Rover.

Obadiah climbed out of the back and started with him toward the rocks. "Unusual-looking helmet," Obadiah observed.

"Isn't it," Richards said.

"Aluminum?"

"No. It's a special material that Judy's father invented. It's . . . well, I won't go into how it's made. The deal is, it can protect you from electromagnetic radiation."

Obadiah looked at the hat once more. "Electromagnetic radiation?"

They had by now reached the rocks and had begun to climb toward the top. It was an easy climb, and Richards answered as they moved. "You should read the book you bought," he said. "But, to put it as simply as possible, electromagnetic radiation may be a tool of the manipulators. Military intelligence, both in this country and in Russia, were doing research on the subject as early as 1945— the effects of electromagnetic radiation on humans, what we also call extremely low frequency, or simple ELF. Verity believed it was possible that ELF might be used to induce hallucinations, possibly paralysis; in other words, something connected with mind control. He believed the Germans had a device by the end of the war that made use of ELF in this way. The Russians may have a similar device now. The United States may too. It's hard to say."

"But I thought you said it was a tool of the manipulators. What do the United States and Russia have to do with the manipulators?"

They were by now on top of the rocks and looking down on the town once more. It didn't appear to Obadiah that they could see much more from here than from the car. The place still looked empty. Richards was shaking his head, apparently at the naiveté of Obadiah's questions. "Read the book," he said.

"And you think there is some danger of the ELF out here?" It was the first time he had noticed Richards wearing the hat.

"Take a look around you," Richards said. "That's all owned by the military, brother. Try and find out what they do with it some-time." Richards paused to chuckle. "And down there"—he waved toward the town—"an outpost of full-on manipulator drones. All in all, I would say yes, we are in a high-risk area."

"What do you think they do down there?" Obadiah asked. He was speaking of the weaponry ranges to the south.

Richards looked at him for a moment and smiled. "If I told you," he said, "you wouldn't believe me." He clapped Obadiah on the shoulder with the palm of his hand. "Now let's get back to the car and get out of here."

Obadiah followed Richards out of the rocks. He thought about ELF and a military in the hands of the manipulators. He supposed it was something like believing the world was in the power of the Wicked One. After all, how could Satan have tempted Christ with the kingdoms of the earth if they were not his to give? Ahead of him Bill Richards's metal helmet bobbed up and down, a silver light among the red rocks.

Once again in the Land-Rover, they set out for the dig Richards had spoken of. At the dig they would compare the crystals found in the dispenser with those found at the site and they would begin to see about getting back into the Electro-Magnetron. Right now the place was off-limits to everyone. But Richards had heard rumors of some kind of underground access route that not many knew of, and he was eager to find something out. There was also the possi-bility that Judy, as an immediate family member, might be able to gain legal access. At any rate, once inside they could begin the experiments with the crystals.

It sounded bizarre enough when you said it. And yet, Obadiah thought, he had seen the Thing. And now a fragile network of possibilities had been erected in its honor—like some rickety sus-pension bridge, they spanned the void beneath them and one could only wonder about where the whole thing might lead. Into the past? Across another dimension? Or would a man go halfway only to find the whole silly thing breaking apart beneath him and a tiny voice singing somewhere in the back of his mind: "Welcome to the funhouse, fool"?

But then what, he wondered, was a poor boy to do? It was a counterfeit world men had made for themselves and one could hardly get very interested in it. The Thing, on the other hand, at least had the look of something genuine. And so an opportunity like this came along and you went with it or you stayed home. You could risk playing the fool in this life or you could take your place among the countless bovine householders he had faced across the countless porches of his youth. He had made a decision and he would have liked to stop second-guessing himself. But he couldn't. He had begun the moment it became clear Delandra was really not going to accompany him. Did he want it that badly? He tried to console himself with clichés. Nothing ventured, nothing gained. He might have felt better about it right now had he not gotten a look at Bill Richards's hat. The foolish thing lay on the seat beside him, the metallic spark he had followed off the ridge. He looked once more from a dust-streaked window into the light of the Mojave. "Happy," he said to himself, "is the man conscious of his spiritual need, for the Kingdom of the heavens belongs to him."

B y late afternoon they had reached the site. Half a dozen run-down house trailers and one shiny new Winnebago sat grouped at the base of a large rocky hill. The hill had paths cut into the sides of it, winding round it like seams in a baseball. Near some of the paths Obadiah could see a few holes and ditches. Some of the holes had sticks of wood coming out of them and bits of canvas awning stretched between the sticks to provide shade for the holes.

The road which led to the dig had, for the last two hundred yards, been covered with loose gravel and looking back now in the direction from which they had come, Obadiah could see the gray dust raised by their tires still hanging in the air. The rocks in the area were of a uniform color, a kind of dirty copper which ran to a deep reddish brown or black—as if everything had been baked in some tremendous kiln, or tossed out in a volcanic upheaval— which, he supposed, was a good possibility. There was very little vegetation—just a few bits of sage here and there, struggling for life among the volcanic stones, and the only available shade was provided by the awnings erected between the trailers. The whole encampment had a kind of naked arbitrary look about it and

Obadiah was reminded—as he had been in the town of Trona—of some encampment on an alien planet.

In this case all Obadiah could see of the landing party itself were two women and a man who were just now emerging from the clearing between the trailers. The women wore work boots, cutoff jeans, and blue cotton chambray work shirts with the sleeves rolled up on their forearms. The man wore jeans and a T-shirt. He held a beer out in front of his stomach.

"You must be exhausted," one of the women said. She was a large woman, with mousy blond hair pulled back beneath a red and white bandanna. She had heavy breasts and a slightly pock-marked face.

"We are," Judy said. She stood in front of the Land-Rover wiping her forehead with the back of her hand.

The man said there was more beer on ice and Bill and Obadiah went with him back toward the awning. Bill, Obadiah noticed, had left his hat in the car. Apparently the site was not in the high-risk zone. Judy went into one of the trailers with the two women. Later, one of the women—a short, athletic-looking woman with brown hair whom Obadiah guessed to be in her early thirties, came back out and joined them in the shade. "It will be cooling off soon now," she said to no one in particular. Obadiah pressed the sweating aluminum can the man had given him to the side of his face. He seated himself Indian style at a corner of the shade.

"Not out of gas, are we?" Richards asked. He had been in a cheerful mood ever since their view of an empty Table Mountain. "Come on," he said. "I want to show you what we're up to here."

Reluctantly Obadiah hauled his ass off the ground and followed Richards toward one of the paths leading up into the side of the rocky hill.


The sun had slipped low into the western sky but the heat upon their backs as they climbed was still quite intense. The path was narrow and steep. The man who had given them the beers stayed below but the woman had come with them. They moved single file —Richards out front, then Obadiah, with the woman in the rear.

Richards talked as he went. "We have reason to hope," he said, "that this may prove to have been an encampment of the first Table Mountain People—there have been some bits and pieces of pottery, nothing conclusive as yet, however."

"The ground here is difficult," the woman said. "Very alkaline. It eats things up."

They stopped at the edge of a long, narrow ditch and the woman showed Obadiah a number of stones which had recently been exposed. The woman told him they were tools but they looked more like simple rocks to Obadiah. He said nothing, however, and tried to look interested. The woman bent to replace the stones, rattling off some dates as she did so. As she leaned forward, her breasts, loose beneath the faded cotton shirt, were exposed to the nipples. Obadiah felt the beginnings of an erection pressing against the hot fabric of his jeans. He looked away, into the barren acres of volcanic rock which lay beneath them. He felt tired and gritty and somewhat disgusted with himself. He didn't even feel like asking the woman about the methods used to arrive at her dates. That once he would no doubt have done so with great zeal served now only to fuel the disgust.

He wondered how many more uninteresting holes it would be necessary to peer into before starting back. Richards was already out of the ditch, moving ahead of them, farther up the mountain. Obadiah wiped his brow with the back of his hand. The woman was still with him in the ditch. They had been introduced but Obadiah had forgotten her name. They were both standing now and he noticed that the woman was smiling at him. "Pretty boring stuff," she said.

Obadiah returned her smile. "Where did you find the crystals?" he asked. He was hoping that topic might prove more interesting than the stuff about the tools. The woman stopped smiling. Her eyes were clear and green.

"What crystals are those?" she asked.

Delandra had been watching the car for a long time. At first it had appeared as a tiny yellow flame above the red asphalt of the road, not really discernible as a car at all—though, of course, there was really nothing else it could have been. Later, she could see what was clearly the rounded metal of a roof. The car was still a long way off and the rest of it was lost in a mirage so that it looked as if the thing were driving across the bottom of a lake to reach her. She straddled her guitar case and waited, continuing the imaginary conversation she had begun some time ago with a missing Obadiah. She had begun the conversation because she wanted him to know a few things. She wanted him to know that he had been right, back there in Trona, in front of the theater; she had planned to walk on that trail. But he had been wrong about a lot of it too. She had really not thought of selling the Thing until those men had shown up offering Rex money for it. That was when she had thought of Verity and his conventions, and put it together with her new friend's recently proposed trip to Canada. Too bad the boy had come down with a terminal case of Mystery of the Mojave on the brain. Too bad about B&J, which in fact was the point of the conversation; she wanted him to see just how bad it really was. And just when she thought she had him scared with the bailbondsman story.

She couldn't decide now if she wanted him to know the truth about that or not. On the one hand, she felt that the whole running-scared business had managed, in Obadiah's eyes, to make her look an even bigger flake than he seemed to have begun to take her for already. On the other, there was something about the story that amused her. She supposed the amusing part lay in the difference between what she had invented, and what she knew to be true. There were, after all, three Indian brothers in Victorville, and one was a bailbondsman. One was a lawyer. The other was a crooked mechanic who used to do things to cars for Fred Ott, which was how she knew about them in the first place—a trio of useless lard buckets, perhaps as dangerous as the Three Stooges, unless you happened to have the mechanic do something to your car. Now, that was dangerous. It was also true that when she had first glimpsed the Indian at the junction she had taken him for the bondsman, though a closer look had told her this was not the case. In fact, she didn't know who the men at the junction were. She supposed they were what they appeared to be, some trio of hipsters looking for diversion along the Vegas trail. She didn't really want to think much about the men at the junction. Thinking of them made her think of her brother and that, really, was not what she needed, not just now, with Obadiah to talk to. The fact was, taking the Thing had not set as well with her as she had hoped it would. It was not that it was only half hers. It was that Rex was goofy over it. What she had told herself at the time was that getting the Thing away from him would probably do him good. What she feared now was that it would only make him goofier. Someday she would make it up to him. It was just one more item she had to talk about as she stood stewing in heat and remorse at the side of an empty highway, which was where the first ride of the day—a pair of drunken rednecks in a jeep—had dumped her when she made it plain she did not care to accompany them to Darwin, a mining town some distance off the main road. It had been an ugly little scene, uglier even than what had gone down before it at the Blue Heaven Motel, and by the time the yellow car

appeared on the horizon, she had begun conducting her imaginary conversations out loud, something she took for a bad sign.

It seemed to take a very long time for the car to reach her, and
with the heated air distorting things so, the machine did not appear quite real until it was nearly on top of her, its engine hissing
softly in the stillness, spraying the tortured asphalt with steaming
water.

The car was piloted by a large, broad-faced man wearing a
flowered shirt, sunglasses, and a straw hat. The guy looked like
such a caricature of a tourist that it was almost a joke and she
decided he must be something else. Like maybe he was a Fed. Or
some runner who had broken from the mob and was hightailing it,
incognito, Vegas to L.A. on the back roads. Probably a horse's ass
but the day was warming up. Talking to herself was getting to be a
drag and she was still a bit worried about the morons in the jeep.
The jeep was yellow and black and when she had first caught sight
of the car she had for a moment believed it to be the jeep, circling
back for round two. The idea was not a pleasant one. She didn't
really care where she wound up, Furnace Creek, where she might
find work at the ranch, or Vegas, or even back the other way,
toward Los Angeles; anywhere, in other words, than where she
was.

She crossed the asphalt to discover the driver's destination, and
to have a closer look at him. When the word *Trona* fell from his
lips, her heart sank.

"Jesus," she said. "Somebody cut me some slack. Trona? That's
it?"

The man looked at her for a moment. He was leaning slightly
toward her, one arm braced atop the seatback next to him. She
could see now that the dark glasses covered most of what must
have been a badly blackened eye. "To be honest with you," he
said, "I don't know if that's it or not." He paused. "You see, I'm
looking for this friend of mine."

Delandra sighed. The man was obviously some sort of yo-yo. It
was also possible that the bruised face fed into her mob theory. She
looked across the yellow roof of his car and lo, a flash of metal
caught her eye—what looked, before vanishing in a dip in the
road, to be a truck moving in her direction. It might have been a
band of angels. She was about to tell this *turista* what he could do
with his destination when a certain name issued from the interior

of the car. "You wouldn't," the man asked her, "happen to know a guy by the name of Obadiah Wheeler?"

"What?" Delandra said. It was the best she could do on the spur of the moment. In the distance the truck had crawled out of the dip—a white sixteen-wheeler. And it was coming her way.

"Obadiah Wheeler," the man repeated.

As a rule Delandra believed in copping to nothing. She hesitated, however, and it cost her the diesel. It rumbled past them, clattering like an empty freight. Was it fate, or what? "Suppose I do?" Delandra asked.

An hour later they were back in Delandra's room at the Blue Heaven Motel. The man had taken off his hat and was seated on the floor, his back against the bed, his legs out in front of him, crossed at the ankles. It was where Obadiah Wheeler had sat after Lyle hit him. He held a tall can of Colt 45 malt liquor in one hand and a copy of Bill Richards's book in the other. So far all the man had told her was his name and that he was a friend of Obadiah's, but Delandra had pretty much figured out the connection.

The room was dark and stuffy and Delandra drew a curtain to let in some light. She felt tired and somewhat foolish. It was only about six hours since she'd stood here watching Obadiah dress to go off into the desert with Bill and Judy, trying to come to terms with the incredible notion that she was losing out to the Mystery of the Mojave one more time. The sad part was she had threatened not to wait and he had gone anyway. The little fucker. Nothing could have pissed her off more and she could not deny that she had come back just now half expecting to find he'd gotten hip to what he'd walked out on and walked back, out of the desert to her, just the way someone might in a lousy movie.

The Blue Heaven, however, seemed to be fresh out of Hollywood endings and she could not shake the feeling that she had been had. So it was true, what they said. Everybody plays the fool. But the situation was growing just a little desperate. She was flat out of money, out of a set of wheels, out a friend and somewhere out there in the heat there was one demented mother-in-law and a trio of fat Indians thirsting for blood. Hers.

She walked from the window and seated herself by the door. She could actually hear the heated air boiling on the flats behind her. The warm odorous winds on Trona licked at the nape of her neck like fetid tongues of flame. Harlan Low was still on the floor. He was shuffling papers and drinking malt liquor. As she watched him, he popped the top on a fresh one and killed what looked to be about a third of the thing with one pull. She wondered if the guy ever got drunk but somehow she doubted it. It was funny, but the guy reminded her of the Sarge. Sarge drank like that. He could drink all day long and never get drunk. Maybe it had something to do with size. The man had discovered Bill Richards's book. He was looking at the cover with a quizzical sort of expression on his big red face. She wondered if his face was red from the heat or if he was one of those people whose faces were always red. She bet it was the latter. The man opened the book and began to scan the table of contents.

"You're him, aren't you?" Delandra asked. The silence was beginning to annoy her. It was beginning to annoy her that the guy would not just come right out and tell her why he was looking for Obadiah.

The man turned his face toward her and she could see a scar light up along his temple and cheek. "Him?" he asked.

"You're the Elder, right?"

Harlan admitted that he was. Under the circumstances he'd not been planning to advertise it.

"You're the hotshot from New York."

Harlan studied the girl in the chair. She was slouched way down with her legs stuck out in front of her, her hands folded on her stomach, the light from the parking lot shining in her hair.

"I suppose I would like to be thought of as something besides a hotshot," he said. He had not felt anything like a hotshot for several days now.

"Come on. Obo says you're a regular celebrity. I believe you're a hero of his or something."

Harlan just looked at her. He shook his head. "The boy's somewhat confused." He was pleased to see the girl had sense enough to laugh. She got out of her chair and went again to the door. It seemed difficult for her to remain long in one place. It was also clear she had not yet told him what she knew. On the ride into Trona she had only said that maybe Obadiah would be there when they got back, and that maybe he wouldn't.

He wasn't. And now Delandra, for her part, was wondering just how much of the sorry tale it was wise to lay on this guy with the flowered shirt and the straw hat. And to complicate matters further there was a pair of mutually exclusive options butting at one another inside her head like a pair of deranged billy goats.

She might, on the one hand, tell the guy any story she wanted to. She might tell him that Obadiah was in Tonopah, or Vegas, or San

Berdoo, hoping of course that he would take her, at which point she could say good-bye and fade into the crowd.

On the other hand, there was the possibility that if she threw in with the guy she might just see Obadiah one more time. They might find him. There might be another chance. One plan had the look of something smart about it. The other appeared to be the plan of a fool. It was what she thought about, staring into the heat, and the smell, and the white shimmering flats. God knows this landscape made her feel old. She'd been staring into it all her life and it was still just the same. "I don't expect him to be back," she said at last. "He went to look for time warts with a couple of goons calling themselves Bill Richards and Judy Verity."

"Verity, you say?"

Delandra nodded. "The name mean something to you?"

"It does," Harlan said, "if her father happens to be the Verity who built the Electro-Magnetron."

Delandra pushed a hand through her hair and sighed once more. "That's our girl," she said, and she told him the rest of it.

The room seemed curiously silent when the girl had finished and Harlan allowed himself a moment or two of drifting in it. "Then that's what all this is about," he said. He raised a hand to wave at what he had been looking at, the detritus of Obadiah's research. He had found that for some reason the sight of the stuff made him angry.

"That's what it's about," Delandra said, "a regular backyard scholar. I sometimes wonder what I see in him."

Harlan was silent once more. He was watching the girl. He was beginning to believe she had a better head on her shoulders than one might imagine at first glance. She was seated just now on the bed, leaning back on her elbows, her eyes fixed on the light fixture above them. He watched the soft curve of her shoulders, the graceful line of her throat. "What did you see in him?" he asked. He couldn't help himself.

The girl laughed. She got up again and went to stand by the door. She put a shoulder against the door jamb and her back to the room. Beyond the hand-tooled leather of her boots Harlan watched the heat beneath a thin rectangle of turquoise sky.

Delandra stared at the highway. It was more or less what she had been asking herself, off and on, throughout the day and the truth was, answering it was more difficult than one might imagine. He was not bad to look at. And she liked fucking him—he was so sincere about it. But there was more mixed up in it than that. "What I see in him," Delandra said at last, "are possibilities."

She was grateful when the man did not respond. She continued to examine the landscape. The possibilities would have been hard to pin down. They had nothing to do with the straight life but rather with whatever it was which had driven him from her door. The Hummer Curse. The fact was, the boy had it written all over him and when she ran up against it there was nothing to do but lock horns with it all over again—what she supposed would have to pass for her own strain of the disease, that she should compete for the attention of men with Noah's Great Rainbow. It had something to do with her penchant for continuing to come up short in the struggle. Which somehow fed back into the question about why she was here. Did she in fact love him—like everyone said you should? Or did she just flat hate to lose? The landscape offered no answers. But then it never had been much of a companion and it was stupid to expect anything of it now. The whole thing lay silently before her. The illusion of water. The undulating air. The dry wind. *This is your life.* She believed for a moment that the words had been spoken, delivered with all the sincerity of a television game show host with sculpted hair. The words were followed by a smattering of canned applause—as if the machine were on the blink. And she recalled that Obadiah Wheeler had found the balls to ask her about Fred Ott. Obadiah's problem was that he didn't understand what it meant to start with nothing. He didn't know anything about these pitiful little attempted beginnings, each seemingly more grotesque than what had preceded it. Delandra knew of such things. Her memory was well stocked with false starts: the community college in San Bernardino. Night classes on speed. Instructors on the make. Living out of a car in the parking lot. Doing the Burger Man's dirty work for him by day. Beauty college in Victorville. Now that was starting with nothing. What did Obadiah know of that?

She supposed, however, that the question of the moment was what difference, in the long run, might Obadiah make? Was he like the rocks in her collection, the ones that only looked like something, or was there really something new and different on the inside? She had on occasion asked herself the same thing about Sarge. Never having cracked him, however, she had never answered it. "You know all I ever really wanted," she said aloud (she was speaking more or less to Harlan Low but she didn't look to see if he was paying attention). She was watching a small-time twister blow its wad upon the salted plain. "Was just a little something I couldn't get at home."

The fact was, Harlan had not been paying attention for some time. To his great annoyance he found that he had just solved Leonard Maxwell's stupid puzzle. It had been like asking Delandra about Obadiah—he flat couldn't help himself. The key lay in his lap, marked in translucent yellow ink in the pages of Bill Richards's book:

> In the following account the noncapitalized pronouns "he" and "they" refer to the shamans or to the laity, as the case may be, while the capitalized pronouns "He" and "They" refer to the "Ancient Ones," from whom Harav He:ya derived his shamanistic powers. Unfortunately, the exact identity of these "Ancient Ones" is one of the unsolved problems of Mojave ethnology. All we know is that shamans whose power comes from the "Ancient Ones" are said to be more powerful than those whose power comes from the gods and that they use the right, rather than the left, hand in treating their patients. The most likely hypothesis concerning the identity of these "Ancient Ones" is that they are the culture hero Mastamho and his contemporaries.

He stared into the poorly antiqued dresser before him. Three days ago he had asked himself if the hand he had seen in Africa could possibly be connected to the two he had seen since returning to the States. Then he had found out something about the Sons of Elijah and decided that they could not. Several hours ago he had discovered the Table Mountain People, an image in a bowl, and a slice of myth one might compare to what he had found in Africa—both of which, if one were imaginative enough, might be seen to have a place in Maxwell's implausible cosmology. It was an unlikely pill to swallow and a number of things argued against it. The variety of combinations, for instance. Maxwell's were still the only two alike. Unless, and this was the key, unless the rest of them were right hands. A test for this hypothesis suggested itself. He pulled himself abruptly from the floor and walked outside. He went to the car and took Maxwell's puzzle from the dashboard. The images floated upon the page before him. A left hand on the cover, a right in the circle. He folded the accordion. The puzzle continued to float, an afterimage before the sky. A swastika, a pentagram, a magnet, a load of ore, a shape from a map, the head of a man. The right six-fingered hand. It was clearly Maxwell's contention that Nazis had used phony mining operations as a cover for some task performed in the service of the ancients, some combination of Magnetic Secrets and Occult Mysteries (the questions were of use here). The task had been taken up in the deserts of the American West as well. Someone had gotten wind of this as early as 1942 and imposed a ban. But now the ban had been lifted. The President was a Drone. A Great Society indeed.

Harlan stood in the heat of the lot. Of course this could have no real meaning. In the real world. On the one hand, he felt like a man on the brink of solving a difficult chess problem. On the other, he felt much the way he always imagined those single missionary boys at the home must have felt waking from a wet dream.

When he looked toward the motel he found that Delandra Hummer had come outside to lean against the wall.

"You want to know something?" he asked her.

"It all depends," Delandra said.

"This guy, Richards. Did you know his father was a Nazi?"

"I would have guessed that he was an asshole, at least."

"He was connected with a big Nazi cult in the thirties. Now you say his boy has an interest in some mines around here?"

Delandra shook her head. "The boy knows some people who work an archaeological dig around here. They found crystals at the dig. They found crystals in the bathroom. Remember?"

Harlan had forgotten about the crystals. "But the boy's father was a Nazi. Do you know what that means?"

"It means," Delandra said, "that we're going to go after them."

The desert, at noon, was filled with afterimages, a variety of auras. When Harlan looked at the wall against which Delandra stood he found her image repeated, the colors reversed. He wanted to say that was exactly what it meant but he refused the indulgence. Because if you were going out there, he thought, you had to be very clear about the reason. The reason Harlan had come this far was to do something about the mess. There wasn't anything else. If he thought, for instance, that there were mines in

West Africa, in the Bomi Hills, that the mines were within thirty minutes of the port of Monrovia, or that he seemed to recall someone telling him the first to get interested in those mines were the Germans, prior to the war, if he thought all of that was going to add up to something here, in the heart of the Mojave, then he really was a fool, in a land where fools got swallowed whole— gaping wide-eyed at mirages while the desert ate them alive. So some other meathead would have to cop to the soiled sheets. No wet dreams for Harlan Low. The remains of Obadiah's were what cluttered the room and he knew now what had angered him at the sight. Without really thinking about how it might look to her, Harlan went past Delandra and into the room. He held Maxwell's pamphlet in his hand and there was a minor ritual on his mind. He took it directly to the bathroom where, eyeball to eyeball with a single pink flamingo in a sea of turquoise tile, he struck a match from the Lotus Room and disposed of Maxwell's bit of rubbish in the sink. When he finished he found the girl watching him once more. There was an odd expression on her face and he felt that some explanation was expected. "For both the Jews ask for signs," he told her, "and the Greeks for wisdom, but we preach Christ impaled."

Delandra stood for a moment at the doorway, the scent of burning paper in her face. "We'll go," she said. "But you've got to promise me something. You've got to promise not to preach to me. I've had just about all of that I can stand."

Harlan's large red face widened in a grin above the sink. "You have my word," he said.

"There's an extra box of shells in my car," Delandra said, "I'll get them."

"Shells?"

She pulled the handle of Sarge's gun high enough out of her purse for Harlan to see what it was. Then she went outside. She left Harlan at the sink, his hands still wet from rinsing down the ash, doing his best to keep it straight, to pretend that he had not in fact begun to imagine that the emptiness beyond the shower curtain and the tile was really not emptiness at all but the vast, incomprehensible shape of something impossible to name—but whose presence he had felt once before.

Delandra crossed the lot. She looked both ways up and down an empty highway and she thought about what they were up to. It was why she wanted the shells. She might have invented an ax handle for her bondsman, but she hadn't invented the bodies in the desert. Those had made the papers and whatever Obadiah had been wrong about, he had been right about one thing. Something was going on out there. People had been divided into parts and, as near as she could tell, she and Elder Low were about to drive off into the middle of it. It struck her as just the kind of thing she might do. It seemed, however, to evidence a remarkable lack of good judgment on the part of a straight arrow like the Elder. As if the alcohol did have some effect on him after all. Or maybe those African boys had hit him on the head harder than anyone knew. Maybe he was no longer the ace he was cracked up to be. It was something to think about. She sat with it in the unpleasant wind while the man finished his business in the bathroom.

That the undertaking was not half-baked was attested to, Harlan felt, by the fact there had been preparations. Delandra had gone for bottled water; Harlan had purchased some antileak stuff for the freeze plug. They had consulted a map. Side by side in the front seat of Harlan's rented coupe they had traced the line of a dirt road from the northern tip of Trona until it disappeared into the emptiness of the Table Mountain range. "Couldn't be more than two or three hours," Delandra had said. Harlan had looked into the map. Nothing but white space where that road ended. Washed clean in the blood of the lamb.

It was toward the white space they now drove and Harlan was still trying to tell himself it was all right. The road had been level for some time but as it entered the Table Mountains it began to rise. The range itself looked pretty much like the other ranges Harlan had been looking at for the past few days, barren rocky ground, bands of colored rock—mostly oxidized reds and dirty yellows; here and there, though, the chemistry was more lively and one could see a bright patch of blue or green, a bright orange, a chrome yellow.

Delandra's theory was that the road would flatten out soon, following the crest of the ridge in a westerly direction. This was based on information she had gotten from Obadiah, who had gotten his from Bill Richards, who supposedly knew what he was talking about. "The thing is . . ." Delandra said. She was sitting forward in the seat, one arm on the dashboard, a hand braced on the seat at her back, "we can't get too lost. We've got the mines to zero in on."

This was true. Or at least Harlan liked to think that it was true. He was encouraged in this belief by the fact that the dirt road had been clearly marked back at the highway by a small wooden sign which read, TABLE MOUNTAIN MINES: 12 MILES. The uncertainty would come after they had found the mining site, at which point it would be necessary to more or less guess about the direction of the dig. From what Delandra had gotten from Obadiah, however, the dig was not a great distance from the mines. Nor did it, according to the map, look as if they could get too lost. To the south there was a weaponry range, to the north, mountains. The dig had to lie west of the mines and Richards had said there was road all the way.

So there was room for optimism. The problem was, the grade wasn't doing the car any favors. The freeze plug had begun to leak again, making it necessary for Harlan to stop at regular intervals and add water, and the last time he looked, the water pump had begun to leak as well. Around each bend another piece of road continued the climb. Loose rock banged against the undercarriage of the car and white dust floated behind them, marking their ascent.

Delandra found that the dust made her nervous. Behind each rock she imagined killers. The sunlight burned her arm against the dash. Harlan drove hunkered forward, looking too big for the wheel, as if one good turn would wrench it from the rest of the car. She saw them in a kind of Laurel and Hardy escapade, pieces of the car dropping behind them, Harlan looking at the wheel with an expression of consternation on his big face, then throwing it out the window. Another fine mess . . . they would arrive with their arms around each other, nothing but wheels separating them from the ground.

"This may have been a mistake," Harlan said. He had begun to think that it would be best to turn back, maybe put some new tires on Delandra's car, try it again, with an earlier start. "We're running out of daylight. The car's hot."

There was, in fact, steam rising from the hood now. Delandra drummed at the dash with her fingertips. "It can't be much farther." She wondered why she persisted. Something in her character, she supposed. The Hummer Curse. It would surely do her wrong.

To their left a huge outcropping of stone loomed, a sheer rock face streaked with red. Before it were the first signs they had found the mines: a pair of shacks. A hole in the rock. The grade eased, turned downward into a shallow valley. Harlan slipped the car into neutral, allowing them to coast. As he did so, he was struck with an almost overwhelming sense of déjà vu. It had, in fact, plagued him for some time, a shadow at his shoulder. It took him head-on now. It was the face of the cliff. The red rock, the blue sky. It was the Bomi Hills. Except that Harlan had never taken that particular drive. Perhaps he had seen pictures. Perhaps someone else had gone—his wife? He groped for an answer. "We're here," he said. He coasted off what there was of the road, missing a hairpin. The car bounced over rocks larger than those to which it had grown accustomed and flattened a rotting wooden post.

"Jesus," Delandra said.

Harlan apologized. He put the car in gear, swung back on the road, and parked. They were in the V of the valley. Its sides were covered with a variety of skeletal structures, shacks, and holes. The outcropping of red stone cut into the brightness of the sun on the left-hand side of the car.

"We're not anywhere yet," Delandra said. "These are the mines. He's at the dig, remember?"

"But this guy's father has something to do with the mines. He owns one. Used to own one."

Delandra sat looking at Harlan's profile. There was sweat on the back of his neck, running down into the flowered shirt. His hands sat atop the wheel like a pair of hambones. She didn't like it in the valley. "What are we talking about?" she asked. The man was beginning to worry her.

Harlan looked at the girl. Her eyes were as black as the barrels of guns. Why did he think this was it? The mines? He shook his head. It was the heat, he told her.

"Listen," he said, "we can't keep climbing." The road rose again; they could see it exiting the valley, a curving chalk-yellow snake crawling among the rocks. "Let's rest it, let it cool down. We'll hike to the crest and see if we can follow the road, see what it does. Maybe we can see the dig." He looked at Delandra. She looked across the hood and raised a hand. The crest was not far.

Harlan killed the engine and got out of the car. The silence was like something you stepped into—like the direct heat of the sun.

He began to walk toward the ridge. The girl was somewhere behind him. The fact was, he was embarrassed about saying This is it. Where was his frigging head? Heat, my ass. He had Maxwell's puzzle on the brain. The frigging thing was making him see things. He knew, of course, there was a dig. The sight of the mines had excited him. As if this was where he meant to find something.

Ahead of him the ground rose sharply, bending toward the ridge, taking him by surprise with its angle of ascent. He looked up, bending himself backward toward that spot where the red stone met the sky. He kicked a rock with his shoe and started a miniature landslide. He heard the girl say something behind him. It crossed his mind to say something witty. Timber—or bombs away. Something really witty, like that. The ascent was making him short of breath, however, and he didn't say anything. He turned his head a bit to see where she was. He saw a shaft. Turning his head pulled him slightly off course. He stumbled over some pieces of wood set close to the ground. There was more wood directly in front of him. He started toward it. He was thinking about the red rock and the hole in the cliff. The girl said something. He looked at the sky. He was looking for that line of rock, the collision of red and blue. He walked onto the wood and he stood there, looking toward the west. He didn't stand there for long. The wood beneath him was old and gray, bleached until it was the color of oatmeal. One fool had used it to cover a shaft. It had taken another to find it. The thought was a fleeting one. Face still turned skyward, Harlan Low sank like a stone, the wood beneath him coming apart as if it had no more to it than the fragile balsa wood wings he'd built for his gliders as a boy. The red rock vanished, taking the sun.

**D**elandra saw him disappear. She saw a rainbow-colored streak that marked the disappearance of his flowered shirt followed by the black slash of his glasses. The straw hat seemed almost to hang suspended for a moment above the ground as if this were some kind of cartoon where the guy falls and his hat remains hanging in the air for comic effect. It was something like that only it was far from comic and Delandra found that she had begun to scream as she ran toward the spot on the hillside where Harlan Low had vanished.

Harlan heard the screaming. For a moment he believed that he had screamed himself, then saw that this was not so. It was dark and he couldn't see much. The feeling was gone from his right arm and hand but there was a hard shooting pain moving out of his shoulder, around his collarbone, and up into his neck. It was clear to him that something was broken but it was hard to say exactly what it was. He seemed to have come to rest on some kind of platform because when he tried to move, whatever he was on moved as well and he could hear bits and pieces of something falling and hitting something else much farther down. The things that fell, fell for a very long time.

There was a patch of sky at the end of the hole above his head. The way in which the boards had broken made the sky look jagged around the edges. Eventually the head of Delandra Hummer appeared in the patch of ragged sky and Harlan was somewhat relieved to see that he had not fallen as far as he had at first believed. He guessed the distance at somewhere between ten and fifteen feet.

"I'm okay," he said right away, but then found it necessary to amend the statement. "I've broken something," he heard himself say. And there was something about hearing himself say it out loud which scared him—as if his fears had in some way been confirmed: he was indeed a clumsy ox. He might well die here. It was the second time in just over a week that such thoughts had flooded his mind and it occurred to him that a man could only push his luck so far. It was clear the girl would never get him out by herself and for a moment he thought he was going to puke. The sky seemed to go dark and light several times above him. The feeling lasted for several seconds and then passed. "I'm hurt pretty badly," he said. "You're going to have to get help."

With the sun off to the side, behind the ridge, there was no light going into the hole, and looking into it, Delandra could see nothing at all. The effect was disturbing. "I can't just leave you here," she said.

"You'll have to. You'll never get me out by yourself."

"Maybe I can find some rope."

Harlan shook his head, though no one could see him. "It's no good. I'm too heavy, and my arm's shot."

Delandra dragged a hand through her hair. She suspected he was right but figured she might at least take a look around. If there was a rope she could tie one end to the car, drag him out that way. "I'm going to look for something up here," she said. "I'll be right back."

Harlan ground his teeth against the pain. He tried to calm himself, to think it through. The girl's head was gone and the sky was empty above him. Jesus, he thought, what if she falls into something too? There was an idea for you. He was wearing a watch, but when he tried to move himself in such a way as to see its face, the thing he was on made a kind of grinding noise and terrible pains moved through his shoulder and up into his head. He lay still and watched the sky.

After some indeterminate length of time the girl came back. "There's nothing up here but wood."

"Listen to me," Harlan said. "I'm not on the ground. I'm on some kind of platform and it doesn't feel that sturdy. We're going to need a winch and some line. You're going to have to go find someone. There's a Ranger station not far from the beginning of the dirt road out there. I passed it on my way out of the valley. They would know what to do. And it's mostly downhill getting out of here. You should be able to make better time."

Delandra thought about the drive back. It had taken them hours to get this far. Still, it was clear she had to do something. It would be dark soon. "You think you will be all right?" she said. It struck her as a fairly ridiculous thing to say.

"I'll be all right," Harlan replied.

Delandra was a moment in replying. "Okay," she said at last. "Just hang on. I'll go as fast as I can."

Harlan looked at the vacant sky. He heard the girl moving away from the hole. He wondered if he would be able to hear the car. He listened for some time. There was nothing to hear. A musty draft moved along the edges of the hole and something brushed his face. Harlan lifted a hand. He believed himself to be completely alone now and began to talk out loud to himself. He was interrupted, however, by the voice of Delandra Hummer—whose face now appeared above him once more. "I hate to say this," Delandra said, "but I think you've got the keys."

Harlan Low looked skyward. His first impulse was to laugh. His second was to scream. He squeezed at the pocket in his slacks with his good hand. The keys were there. He experienced a moment of amazement at the stupidity of it all. "Yes," he said. "I have the keys." He dug them out, wondering if he was going to be able to throw them high enough to reach her.

He didn't think about it for long and his next move was inspired by equal parts rage and panic. Bringing as much of his arm as possible into play he tossed the things upward. The platform groaned beneath him and seemed to tilt several inches to the right. The keys kicked off a piece of wooden shoring and fell back toward him. They landed on his leg. Somewhere in the middle of it all he was aware of Delandra shouting at him.

"For God's sake!" Delandra yelled. "Hang on to the bastards!"

Harlan clutched at the keys. His heart had begun to pound. All he could think of was throwing them again.

"Will you listen to me?" the girl called. "There's all kinds of sticks and boards up here, and nails. I'll rig something and lower it down. You can hook the keys onto it."

Harlan looked stupidly toward the light. It certainly made more sense than trying to throw them out. "Of course," he said. And he put his head back against the floor of the platform and tried to work some moisture back into his throat. Of course. That was how it was done. Use your head, man. He squeezed the keys, allowing the cold hard shapes to dig into his flesh. He squeezed them until the metal began to feel hot in his grasp. He looked into the ragged blotch of orange sky above him and he waited. And at some point —he could not even guess how long it had been—it occurred to him that he had been waiting too long.

Obadiah didn't ask any more questions about the crystals. When they had seen the hill, they returned to the trailers. The sun had by now come to rest upon the mountains which lay to the west, creating the impression that the entire range had begun to erupt. Soon it would pass from sight altogether and the air would begin to cool, as the woman had predicated.

He sat on the ground beneath one of the canvas awnings, his back against the side of a thirty-foot fifth-wheeler. He was watching the fat guy someone had called Jim turning chicken legs on a beat-up-looking grill. The smells of burning fat and barbecue drifted toward him across the hard-packed dirt. Bill Richards, still wearing his safari tans—shorts and a short-sleeved shirt with epaulets on the shoulders—was standing at the far corner of the compound talking to a couple of guys who had shown up while Obadiah was on the hill. They had come in a jeep. It seemed to Obadiah that he had seen three men from the hill. Perhaps he had been mistaken. Perhaps the third man had been from the camp. The jeep the men had come in was parked alongside Bill Richards's Land-Rover. There was a pair of bumper stickers on the back. One was a Confederate flag, the other something about Billy Graham.

One of the men was tall and thin. He had on jeans and work boots, a shirt like Richards's. He had red hair and a beard and he was wearing one of those Australian cowboy hats—the kind with the brim turned up on one side. The hat had a camouflage pattern on it. The other man was shorter, and thicker. He was without a shirt, but he had a vest, a leather one with fringe on the back. He wore jeans and a pair of high-topped moccasins which rose to just below his knees. The shorter man wore one of those Greek fisherman caps pulled down tight on his head. The hair which stuck out from beneath it was bright black in what was left of the light.

Obadiah got off the ground and walked in a leisurely fashion toward the jeep and the Land-Rover. He wanted to appear nonchalant about it. He had this idea he was being watched. He pretended to look for something in the back of the Land-Rover. He saw Bill Richards's silver hat on the floor. Through a dust-streaked window he took a closer look at the jeep. There was a two-way radio in it and a rifle between the seats. On the rear bumper, between the stickers, there was a beat-up license plate frame upon which the name Victorville was visible through the dust.

Obadiah got out of the Land-Rover. The sun was back of the ridge now, leaving the camp in shadow. Jim stood before the orange flame of his grill. He had been joined by the men from the jeep. Richards was alone by a storage trailer, drinking a beer. When he saw Obadiah he chucked the can into a trash barrel and crossed the yard.

There was something about the way he did this which struck Obadiah as odd. In a moment he realized the guy was half in the bag. This struck him as odd as well. They had not been long off the ridge. The trip had already begun to turn a little funky at the edges and the sudden image of Bill Richards as a bad drunk didn't do much for it. The man soon stood leering at him in a way which seemed to suggest he was privy to some joke of which Obadiah was the butt.

"Begun to miss the little lady?" he asked.

Obadiah shrugged.

"Take 'er or leave 'er, huh? A regular Lance Romance."

Beyond Richards's shoulder Obadiah could see Jim putting chicken onto plates. He had intended to ask Richards about the crystal. It struck him that now was not the time. The man, it appeared, had something on his mind.

"Yeah, well," he said, "you know these cunt are all alike. I imagine she'll be there when you get back."

"I don't know," Obadiah said, "I'm not so sure."

"What's that supposed to mean?" There was something distinctly belligerent in Richards's tone, as if he found in the suggestion cause for offense.

"It means she may not be there. She didn't think a lot of this particular expedition."

"That dirt bag?" Richards said. He was clearly bothered. About something.

Obadiah nodded. He had to admit that he rather enjoyed seeing Bill Richards bothered. "She thinks maybe you guys were bullshitting me about those crystals. When I asked the woman on the hill about the ones you found here she didn't seem to know what I was talking about."

Richards made a kind of snorting sound. The light was getting poor now. It did things to Richards's face. "Uh huh," Bill said, "well, she should know. About bullshit artists, that is."

Obadiah assumed he was talking about Delandra.

"Listen, if you're not doing anything real important there, why don't you come over here for a minute. I've got something I want you to look at."

Richards didn't wait for Obadiah to say anything. He turned and walked off across the camp. Obadiah stood there for a moment. He looked around. There didn't seem to be much point in not going. It was like the song said: Nowhere to run. Nowhere to hide.


Richards was waiting for him on the step of a storage trailer. The trailer had no windows, just one pair of sliding glass doors which had been left open. There was a light on inside.

Obadiah went up the step. The trailer was one long rectangular room maybe thirty feet in length. There was some electronic gadgetry and camping equipment piled around one end. The other end was empty save for a wooden box the size of a coffin.

Richards waited for Obadiah to go into the trailer, then stepped in behind him. He stood at Obadiah's shoulder and waved toward the box. "Take a look," he said. "I think maybe you two are old friends."

Obadiah went to the box and looked inside. He did so with a combination of anticipation and dread. Neither, it turned out, were called for.

The head was not bad. There were large cavernous sockets with something that looked like shriveled egg yolks in them and beneath that a yellow set of sharp, canine teeth. There was a kind of thin, mummified skin stretched taut across a bony skull, but even the face was not perfect. If you looked closely enough at the neck where it attached to the skull, just behind the jaw, you could see a small patch of raised chicken wire. The body was not as good as the head. There was what looked to be rabbit fur on the chest and a lot of feathers along the arms, but the whole arrangement had something hollow and lifeless about it. A corner of newsprint was plainly visible at one wrist.

"Well," Richards asked him, "what do you think? Alien being? Missing link? You're the judge now, Buford."

"My guess would be early Hummer." He was only going by what Delandra had told him. "Maybe 1955 or thereabouts."

Richards did not seem to think this was funny. "You trying to be funny?" he asked.

Obadiah looked away from the case. "You asked," he said.

"What you're trying to tell me"—Richards spoke slowly, as if he was concerned about being understood—"is that this is not what all the fuss was about?"

Obadiah laughed. He couldn't help himself. "The fuss," he said, "was about something else."

"Something else like this?"

"No," Obadiah said, "the fuss was about the Mystery of the Mojave." He found that he took some pride in saying it, as if he were the veteran of something. He found himself recalling with a certain fondness the expression on the face of Lyle Blackledge when he had first seen the Thing. He owed his life to that one, whatever it was, to the Thing itself for having crossed the line or to Sarge Hummer, for having gotten good enough at what he did to put the fear of God into one deranged hick. It all depended upon what you were willing to believe. It was the same old shit. What he knew for certain was that the one in front of him had no part in the debate.

"This is all you wanted me to see?"

Richards was still at his side, staring into the case. When he looked up, Obadiah's first impulse was to duck because he had the feeling the man was going to swing on him. He stayed where he was. Richards stared at him, then looked past him and Obadiah realized they were no longer alone. Turning, he saw that the man in the vest had come to the trailer door. Obadiah could not say how long he had been there. The light from the trailer shone on the bill of the man's cap and on the leather which covered his shoulders. He had a big hard-looking stomach which stuck out through the open vest. The light shone on his stomach as well. There was a long pink scar running across one side of it, down into his jeans. He was leaning against the edge of the slider with one foot in the trailer.

"So okay," Richards said. "Why don't you go eat while there's something left." He was addressing himself to Obadiah. There was something strained about his voice, however, and Obadiah got the feeling the man in the doorway was making him nervous. Obadiah turned to go. He was on his way out when he noticed something which had been propped near the slider at which the man stood. A shortened, double-barreled shotgun.

Obadiah looked at it as he approached the man. The man was taking up most of the doorway and he moved just enough to give Obadiah room to squeeze through. Obadiah stopped short. He suspected it might cost him—which would make it stupid, but he found himself enjoying Bill Richards's discomfort. "So tell me," he said, "where did this one come from?"

Richards was a moment in replying. "It came from the stars," he said. He said it without smiling.

Obadiah went past the man and into the evening. He found the conversation in the trailer had not done a lot for his appetite. He drifted across the compound and seated himself at the edge of the clearing. He was staring into the dwindling fire when the girl who had accompanied him and Bill to the hill approached him with a plate of food. "Hungry?" she asked.

Obadiah looked at the girl. "I'm sorry," he said. "I don't remember your name."

"Rachel." She extended the plate.

Obadiah took it. He set it on the ground beside his leg.

"Not hungry?" Rachel asked. "Thirsty maybe? A beer?"

Obadiah agreed to the beer. When the girl returned she sat down next to him. She had come with two beers. Obadiah listened to the soft hiss of air as she lifted the aluminum rings. "Found your crystals yet?" she asked. The crystals seemed to amuse her.

Obadiah drank some of the beer. "Tell me," he said. "Are you part of Bill Richards's group?"

"I thought it was Judy's group."

Obadiah shrugged.

The girl smiled. "No," she said. "I'm not part of anybody's group. Bill Richards is an old friend of the woman who runs this place." She looked into the fire and drank some of her beer. "The fact is, the woman who started this had a grant. Now the grant has run out and she's having a hard time getting the work financed."

"Why is that?"

"Oh, it's a long story. Basically, what it comes down to is that not everyone is so sure we're really on to something here."

"You mean the Table Mountain People?"

Rachel smiled once more. "No," she said. "The Table Mountain People are what Bill is interested in. We think the dig may date to a much earlier period, which in fact is what a lot of the controversy has been about. That's what I was trying to tell you about on the hill. We think the dates of some of these rocks go way back." She paused to look into the fire. "Unfortunately not everyone agrees. If we don't get some more funding soon, we may have to shut down."

"And this woman, she's probably hoping that Bill and Judy will come up with some."

"Probably."

"Particularly if they think this place has something to do with the Table Mountain People."

"Bill and Judy have some funny ideas," Rachel said.

"And money."

"And money."

Obadiah finished his beer. As he did so he noticed for the first time that the jeep which had arrived while he was on the hill was gone. And then he noticed a couple of other things as well. He noticed the skinny redhead with the hat. The man was coiled in the shadow of a trailer, gnawing at a bone. His companion, the man with the vest, had come with Bill Richards out of the trailer. The two men were now standing with Jim, watching as he scraped one of the grills into the fire. "Those men," he asked. "You know anything about them?"

"I know they're friends of Bill Richards's."

"Anything else?"

"I don't know that I would want to know anything else." She said this as she was standing up. "It has been my experience that Bill Richards's friends are about like his ideas."

"That Land-Rover," Obadiah said. The woman had started away from him. When he spoke she stopped and looked back. "Is that the only vehicle in camp?"

"I'm afraid so, for this evening at any rate." The shadows made it difficult to tell, but it seemed to Obadiah that she was smiling at him. "Why, Mister Wheeler," she said. "You're not thinking of leaving us? Without your crystals?"

With the woman gone Obadiah felt suddenly quite alone. The sky was black now. Arching above him, the Milky Way had the look of something that had been spilled there, the work of vandals. He found that his mouth had gotten dry and there was a peculiar burning sensation at the center of his chest. It runs in threes. Someone had told him that once, speaking of bad luck. And it seemed to him just now, seated alone before dying embers in a camp whose founders may or may not have been on to something, that he was in fact acutely aware of exactly three things. He had seen a third man from the hillside. Wherever the bogus Thing in

the storage trailer had come from, it wasn't from the stars. And the
last time he had seen a gun like the one in the doorway, he had
gotten hit with it.

W hat, eventually, Obadiah decided he wanted
was another look at the gun. He had this idea
that if it really was the one which hit him he
would recognize it. There would be a name, a mark. There would
be vibrations. There would be something.

It was necessary of course to wait. He made a camp for himself
not far from the Land-Rover and lay down to watch. He watched
Bill Richards go into one of the trailers. He watched the man in the
leather vest walk into the desert. He watched until everyone, one
by one, had turned in somewhere for the night. And then he
waited some more. The camp grew quiet. The embers lost their
glow. The passage of time seemed to him something he could feel,
along the skin of his arms, the back of his neck.

Eventually he pulled himself out of the sleeping bag and stood
up. It wasn't that he thought he had waited long enough so much
as it was a fear that if he didn't move soon he would never move at
all. Already his legs had grown stiff and uncooperative beneath
him, making it necessary for him to coax them forward. Small
steps. Over the rocks and into the center of the camp. He went
right up through the middle of it—past the blackened fire ring, the
trash can which had held the beer. He figured it was best to look
like he knew what he was doing.

The glass slider was still open, just as he had left it. The bogus
Thing was still in its box, and the gun was still propped against the
wall. He lifted it, held it on his palms, waist-high, as if it were an
offering. There were no perceptible vibrations. There was, however, something. He found it changing positions, letting one hand
move along the smooth wood of the stock until it found the mark—
a rough spot beneath his thumb.

He took the gun to the step and turned it toward the moon. It seemed that someone had carved a small hand there. It was poorly done. There was even an extra finger. Now who, he asked, among his most recent acquaintances, might do such a thing? Certainly not a smooth operator like Bill Richards. One could, however, with a minimal amount of work, imagine the narrow bony face of a certain Lyle Blackledge contorted in some weird attitude of concentration, intent upon just such a task.

He stood by the door and stared out upon the failing dig, the black sweep of desert as it rolled away from him, down toward the great weaponry ranges, the salt flats of Trona. And it was like he had said to Delandra at the Blue Heaven Motel. There were these elements. He thought now they were not dissimilar to the pieces of the Erector sets he had played with as a boy. You could make things out of them. And he began to consider just what it was he was making out of them now. It was a devilish sort of thing. That much seemed certain—all gears and hooks, a regular death trap. The centerpiece was the gun with the hand on it—exhibit A. And Richards did have motive. He had Judy's land. You wouldn't, at first, suppose it was the kind of thing people killed for. But then the land did have something on it. It had Ceton Verity's Electro-Magnetron. And Bill Richards was the owner of a silver hat. It was hard, Obadiah thought, to know what to make of the motives of a man with a hat like that one. Would he take someone out to impress a girlfriend? Or did he just like that sort of thing? Perhaps he was a man of faith. What it came down to for Obadiah was that he had been had. He was not sure how, exactly, only that he was supposed to be here. And so was Delandra. Why else had Richards asked him about her? It did make one wonder about that third man and the missing jeep. Because if the missing crystals were B, the gun A, then the jeep from Victorville was C, Victorville, after all, being the home of the man with the ax handle. So that what Obadiah was left with were the vague outlines of some monstrous agreement. A deal. Something between Richards and the Indian. The Table Mountain People for Delandra? The Electro-Magnetron for the Thing?

Having discerned the outlines, he tried to step back far enough to see whether it made sense or not—at least enough sense to send him packing, down fifteen miles of bad road in the dead of night. The trouble was he was having a hard time seeing anything but those fifteen miles of bad road. The urge to bolt was nearly overpowering. He was reminded, in the middle of it all, of a particular exploit on the part of Bug House. It was shelved under "Bug House Meets the Hit Men South of the Border." It was a simple story. Bug

House had planned to visit Cabo San Lucas by train. Halfway there two men in dark suits had boarded. Bug House, unable to shake the conviction they had come for him, turned around and came home. Obadiah had found the story amusing in its own bleak way when he first heard it. Now he wondered: the crystals. The gun. The jeep. He was certain the pieces could be put together in other, less sinister ways. And yet he had come to feel much the way he imagined Bug House must have felt waiting it out down there in some chicken coop of a station. South of the border. Way south. Harder in fact to get any farther south. Checking out the schedules and the time of day, the glint in the eye of the old woman back of what passed for a counter, wondering if he could trust the water supply to wash down the Thorazine, or if perhaps some lowlife just one step ahead of him had gotten to it first . . .

He was interrupted in the midst of this by the sound of voices in the camp. They exploded suddenly upon the stillness and continued, at odd intervals—sentries firing in the night. He stepped away from the glass and down into the full shadow of the storage room. He was too far away to hear what was being said. Once, however, when the man spoke, he heard the word *money*. The other voice belonged to a woman. The voices rose once more, both people talking at once, only to be cut short by a sharp, cracking sound—skin on skin. The slap was followed by several more, and then a kind of thumping sound. The woman, by now, had begun to sob. He knew that it was Judy Verity. Nothing else in the camp stirred. The sound had an odd effect on him. It was like watching something die.

He was about to break cover when the door of one of the trailers swung open, emitting the stumbling figure of a man—too big to be anybody but Richards. Even from a distance Obadiah could see the guy was drunk on his ass. He still wore the shorts and hiking boots. The safari shirt had been replaced by a white T-shirt. The T-shirt seemed almost to glow in the moonlight and there was something dark swung across one shoulder. Halfway to the Land-Rover he stopped and shouted back toward the trailer. "It gets it done," he said. "You don't like it, find yourself another boy." In answer, the trailer door swung shut with a hollow pop. Richards responded by pausing long enough to urinate on the rocky soil. After that he was into the Land-Rover and headed up the grade, in Obadiah's direction.

Obadiah moved along the front of the trailer. He rounded one end and crouched there in the shadows. He could hear Richards dragging things around inside the storage room. Finally he heard him load something into the Land-Rover and drive away. He hadn't seen a thing but he had a pretty good idea of what had happened. Richards had picked up his bogus Creature and split.

With Richards gone the only sound in the camp was the sound Judy Verity was making in the trailer. The sound was hard on the nerves and there really wasn't, he supposed, much point in hanging around. For whatever had gone down here, or was going down, or whatever he had come to believe about his critical faculties, there were a couple of items he was sure of. He didn't much like being had. And he knew the end when he saw it. The quest for the next dimension had gone the way of countless other such quests before it. It was out of gas. But it wasn't just the egg on his face. It was those fifteen fucking miles of bad road, in the dead of the night. It was the missing jeep. It wasn't just that B&J were assholes. It was that just maybe they were something worse. No city of gold, Bud, just more swamp. He felt that he should hitch up his pants, but he didn't. He hadn't the heart. He pointed himself toward fifteen miles of the most lonesome road he could imagine and he started down it. He went out past the rocks that Bill Richards had pissed on. They shone softly in the moonlight. The woman continued to cry—a weak, plaintive sob muted by aluminum walls; it was what followed him into the night.

The night welcomed him. Her embrace, however, was that of the strange woman whose feet are descending into Sheol. His first impulse was to blame it on Judy Verity. Her crying had set his nerves on edge. There had been a lot on his mind. The upshot was, he lost the road. One minute it was right there—an irregular strip of earth slightly less cluttered with rock than what was around it, and the next it was flat gone, swallowed by the ground which now looked the same in all directions. He actually went down on all fours, groping after the thing like a blind man after his cane.

He'd been counting on the mining site for his landmark, knowing at that point just how much farther he had to go to reach the highway, knowing, too, that from there the road would be easier to follow. As things stood now, however, he might not even be able to find the mining site. And without the mining site . . . the thought slipped away from him. There was a lump in his throat the size of a baseball. It occurred to him that there may have been beer left in the trash barrel at camp. There may have even been bottled water. He had, of course, not thought to look. There came a time—he knew it—when a man had to learn to think, lest the world make short work of him. Perhaps, he thought, his had already come and gone.

In the end he decided his best bet would be to get to the top of the ridge in whose shadow he rested. If he could see nothing in the moonlight he would sit on the thing until the sun came up. Perhaps with the first light he could see more, could find the road.

He had guessed the summit to be reasonably close but it seemed to take him forever to reach it. Rocks slipped and rolled away beneath him. At times things got steep and he went down on all fours. The air burned in his lungs. He yearned for the beers he had forgotten to bring, for the water he'd forgotten to look for. He thought about this book he'd seen in a desert bookstore called *The Victims of Death Valley.* It was a collection of stories about people who had fucked up in a large way. There was one in it about a couple of guys who'd gone off hiking in the middle of summer clad only in tennis shoes and shorts. They'd hiked for four hours to get wherever it was they were going. It was by then high noon, time to turn around and hike back. The trouble was, their water was gone and the ground temperature was up to around a hundred and fifty degrees. One guy made it, the other guy died. He remembered thinking about how stupid that was as he'd stood in the store. He wondered now what he would think about it tomorrow, if he couldn't find the road.

When at last he reached a kind of rock cap that formed the crest of the ridge, he was amazed to find the entire Table Mountain mining site spread out almost directly beneath him—its spidery, skeletal towers and ruptured sheet metal shacks all silvery and black in the light of a high, white moon.

He was so amazed by the discovery, and then so elated, that he nearly cried out loud. He wanted to do something, to jump, to wave his arms. What he did instead was twist the holy shit out of his ankle.

It happened getting off the ridge. He wanted to get off the crest as quickly as possible and it had felt good, after the climb, to suddenly be making what seemed like decent time, to feel the wind generated by his own speed in his face and for a moment he'd actually gone fairly hopping down the grade, sliding here and there, using the large outcroppings of rock to break his speed. But he'd felt in control. He'd felt in control right up to the moment in which his ankle twisted beneath him with an audible pop and he landed hard on his hip, sliding another fifteen yards in loose rock.

When he stopped sliding, he sat looking down on his ankle, one hand wrapped around his shin, the other pressed against the ground beneath him. He was almost sure the miserable thing was broken. It hurt like hell. He tried moving it. Then he tried moving his toes. Both things worked, so he guessed maybe it wasn't broken after all. When he tried to put weight on it, however, bright flashes of pain exploded in the darkness around him. It was almost something he could see.

He actually wound up working his way back to more level ground on his hands and knees. When he was on something that looked like the road he had lost he tried walking once more.

The ankle hurt but he found that he could move on his feet. It was slow going. He was down among the shacks now and the night smelled of dirt and rust and he had begun to look for something he might make a crutch out of when he saw the car.

He went down flat on his stomach in the road and inched his way over to the nearest bit of shelter—a scrap heap of rusted sheet metal and old wood. He lay there looking back toward the car. It was an odd-looking car, light-colored, with circular bits of chrome that shone in the moonlight. The hood was open, as was the trunk and one of the doors. There was just no telling what someone might be up to out here. The night was filled with phantoms and what Obadiah thought about, his chest pressed to the ground, were the photographs on the front page of the *Trona Star Eagle*. He thought about the discoveries one might make in the empty shacks around him—the debris left by a few psychos just doing their own thing out here by the light of a dispassionate moon.

He lay there for a long time, looking at the car, listening for noises. Nothing happened. No one came or went. He heard nothing. At last he got to his hands and knees. Maybe there was something in the car, he thought. Maybe there was something there he wouldn't want to see. Or maybe there would be keys. Or maybe there would be some regular citizen around who would take him back to the Blue Heaven Motel and Delandra Hummer. Not likely. But what the hell. Dozens of possibilities crossed his mind, some worse than others. The blood banged in his ears. He reached the car without incident and used it to pull himself up. There was nothing in the trunk. He worked his way around to the passenger-side door, where he saw there was something in the backseat. When it showed no signs of life he pulled the seatback forward for a better look. The black shape was a guitar case. The side facing him was blank. He reached for the handle and stood the thing up on its edge. He was not without hope. A light-colored sticker with black letters was plainly visible by the light of the moon and when he saw that he went down hard on his ass, on the running board of the car. He put his face in his hands and he began to weep.

W hen Rex Hummer was turned back at the Ridgecrest turnoff by the California Highway Patrol, his disappointment was temporary. He started back in the direction from which he had come and upon reflection understood that this was as it should be.

Everything had its purpose, its given function in the economy of the universe. The rantings of Dina Vagina, for instance. In the time Rex had spent with her she had done a lot of talking, much of it gibberish, much of it hateful. And yet in the end the oyster had given up its pearl. It had come in the form of what Dina knew about the Frenchman's tunnel.

Rex had heard of the Frenchman's tunnel. He'd known it was somewhere in the vicinity of Table Mountain. What he hadn't known was that the thing was no longer a dead end.

The Frenchman had once lived in the town of Table Mountain. Rex knew little more of him than that. For some reason all his own the man had spent the last fifteen years of his life digging a tunnel into the side of the Table Mountain range. He had apparently hoped to reach the Table Mountain valley on the other side. In terms of any practical necessity, the project was totally useless. For the Frenchman it was something to do. The desert was filled with things just like it. The Frenchman dug for fifteen years and died. He left the project unfinished. One man Rex knew of who had seen it had called it the Frenchman's hole. A tunnel, he had explained, was something that opened out at either end. This was a goddamn hole.

For a time after the Frenchman's death, his wife had attempted to turn the hole into a tourist attraction. She'd built a concession stand in front and something like an altar at the dead end. The altar contained a rack of small candles and a portrait of the Frenchman. The concession stand sold souvenirs and saltwater taffy. The attraction failed. The town went bust. Twenty years later few people remembered. Even locals like Rex, while having perhaps heard of it, would have been hard pressed to find it.

Ceton Verity, however, had found it. He had found as well, in the course of his explorations with the Table Mountain People, that the tunnel was set up in almost a direct line from the town to the Electro-Magnetron which had been built closer to Trona, on the valley floor. He conceived immediately of a secret access route into his dome. He had in fact discovered the purpose behind the Frenchman's seemingly arbitrary act. He would later point out to his followers that the Frenchman had been "directed" in his work.

It was left to Verity and his group to complete what the Frenchman had begun and when they were finished there was indeed an underground route virtually no one but themselves knew anything about. And now, thanks to the motormouth of Dina Vagina, it was known to Rex Hummer as well. And Rex was able to see not only why the Frenchman had dug his hole but why Verity had chosen to extend it. He saw why Dina had spoken of it and why there were Highway Patrolmen at the Ridgecrest turnoff. It was beautiful, really. He marveled that there were people in the world who believed in the existence of chance. At one point, so secure was he in this belief, that he decided on a little test. Passing through the town of Trona he stopped at the first store he saw—it happened to be a bookstore—and walked inside. He went to the rear of the store and took a book from the shelf. While looking at the fluorescent tube above his head he allowed it to fall open, at random. He looked down. A passage had been clearly marked in red ink:

> The steps a man takes from the day of his birth until that of his death trace in time an inconceivable figure. The Divine Mind intuitively grasps that form immediately, as men do a triangle.

Satisfied, he left the store. Stepping back onto the sidewalk he found that there was an enormously fat Indian peering into the bed of his truck. When the man saw Rex coming he turned and walked away. Rex could see him for some time, however, waddling along in the sunlight. The man wore high-topped moccasins with silver ornamentation. He wore tan pants and a black vest. The silver on the man's moccasins flashed in the sunlight, as did his hair, which was thick and black and long enough to reach his shoulders.

Rex turned to his truck. He wanted to be sure that there were no signs of tampering. This done, he looked back into the street. The Indian was gone. He supposed the man could have gone into one of the three or four buildings which lined one side of the street in that direction. He supposed that if he looked into those buildings he would see the man again. His truck was fine, however, and he saw no real point in taking the time. He crossed the street and went into the market which faced the bookstore. He purchased two half-pint bottles of an inexpensive bourbon—he liked the way the half pints fit the hip pocket of his jeans—beef jerky, and Planters peanuts. He resumed his drive.

The sunlight leaped before him. The earth glowed in the light of her fire. Rex broke the seal on the bottle of bourbon. There was something about the heat of the whiskey in the heat of the day. He settled in behind it. But he continued to think about the Indian. The hair like that of a woman. The silver. One could not pretend that these were without meaning and for the first time since leaving the junction Rex had the feeling that he was being followed.

By the time he reached the ruined entrance of the eastern road the sun was low in the west. He pulled off the highway and killed his engine. It was where he had once fought with Dina Vagina. This time he would not worry about the condition of the road. There had been a lot of sunlight between now and then. Between then and now he understood that the road had been made right for him. The Indian continued to bother him, however, and when he walked back to the turnout to get another look down the highway, it seemed to him that there was something—not a car. A motorcycle? He listened. There was no sound, only the soft hiss of a gentle breeze against his ears. A horse, perhaps? The road was filled with curves, gentle hills, and dips as it snaked its way among the outcroppings of rock and sandy washes which marked the beginnings of the Table Mountains and it seemed to him that when at first he had put his boot upon the asphalt and looked to the southwest he had, in fact, seen something—a dark shape cutting quickly off the highway, vanishing among the rocks. But then the light was becoming tricky—the road filled with lengthening shadows—and as Rex returned to his truck the sound of his boots, first upon asphalt, then gravel, was all that he heard.

* * *

The first stars had already appeared when Rex found the yellow outcropping of rocks the girl had told him to look for. And past the rocks, up a wash, then a shallow gorge, so that it was well hidden from the road, he found the entrance to the Frenchman's tunnel.

The Table Mountain People had used what was left of a concession stand to build a gate for the tunnel entrance. Above the gate they had hung a circular piece of wood. The wood looked to have had something painted on it at one time but it appeared to Rex, moving his light across it, that someone had been using the thing for target practice, so that there was not much left of the original surface—just a lot of scarred wood, streaked here and there with shiny bits of paint.

He made a dinner out of the beef jerky and Planters peanuts. He sat on the rocks above the tunnel. He could see his truck from there, and some of the road. The water had left some boulders at the mouth of the gorge and to get past them he was going to have to move the Hum-A-Phone piece by piece. Once inside, he hoped to tie the instrument to a sled he had brought and drag it behind him. He would also have to do something about the gate, but he had come prepared. There were tools in the truck and the gate was not what was bothering him. Nor was it the moving of the Hum-A-Phone.

He cracked the seal on a fresh half pint while the moon rose up yellow and nearly full, spilling light across the eastern ridges of the valley. The light spilled all down beneath him, breaking into the gorge, splashing right up to the tunnel entrance and the foot of the ridge upon which he sat. He watched the desert for a long time. He felt his eye grow keen and quick in the dark, fired by the bourbon. At last, satisfied that he was alone, he came down off his perch and he began to work.

He worked for some time, moving slowly back and forth between the truck and the tunnel. In places the soil was loose and sandy. In other places it was firm, and yet with a certain sponginess about it, as if it were not really ground at all, but something made that way on purpose. Occasionally he would have to fight the belief that he was being watched. He would stand until his breathing had become soft and regular. He would strain to hear something more than the dull throbbing of his own blood. And then he would go on.

He was at the back of the truck, pulling out one of the last pieces of his instrument when he heard the engine. There was no question about it this time. He put down the piece he was holding and turned to look back down the road—trying to make some guess as to how far away it was. He didn't have to guess for long. He was still at the back of the truck, ass against the tailgate, when the lights hit him and he felt himself freeze like a rabbit on the highway.

For a while the lights were in his face and he couldn't see what kind of vehicle it was, or how many people were in it. Table Mountain People, or cops. He guessed it would be one or the other. Somehow he did not think this had anything to do with what had scared him on the road. At last a man got out of the vehicle and came walking toward him out of the light. He was a big man. When he got close enough, Rex could see he wore a metal helmet, that there was a handgun in a holster at his waist. There was, however, something unsteady about the man's step and Rex could see quite early on—perhaps it was something he sensed, even before the man had begun to speak—that the man was drunk. "What are you doing here?" the man asked him. His voice had that thick, swollen sound to it that Rex often associated with strong drink.

Rex might have asked the man the same, but he didn't. The man, being drunk, made him both wary and relieved at the same time. "I'm camping," Rex said.

"This is a restricted area," the man said. "You'll have to find another spot." He was close enough now so that Rex could smell the whiskey on him.

"I've already put out some of my gear," Rex said.

The man stepped to one side and looked into the back of Rex's truck.

"You call this camping equipment?" He was looking with some curiosity at the last few pieces of the Hum-A-Phone.

Rex said nothing.

"You have any ID?" the man asked.

"You a cop?"

The man had both his hands at his waist now, his thumbs hooked on the belt which held the holster. He was a good eight or nine inches taller than Rex. Rex had still, in the available light, not been able to get a good enough look at the man's vehicle to determine its color. It had struck him, however, that this was the man Tom Shoats had warned him of—the big man who had come to the Desert Museum. Tom Shoats had not known what the man was after. Perhaps, Rex thought, this man did have something to do with what he had seen on the road after all. The thought gave him courage. This man was drunk. His fly was open. "I'll see your ID," the man said.

Rex shrugged. "My wallet's with my gear." He pointed back into the darkness of the gorge.

The man looked in that direction as well. He looked to Rex as if he was trying to figure out if there was anyone else back there. "Why don't you get it," he said. "And start on your stuff while you're at it. Like I said, this area is closed to all use."

For a moment Rex could not tell if the man was going to accompany him or if he was going to wait. In the end he waited and it was, Rex thought, the man's second mistake. The gun was at the mouth of the gorge and from the rocks Rex would have a clear shot. It was not something he had counted on and yet as he walked back along the wash he began to understand that for which the desert's white-hot light had tempered him, like fine steel, in a high heat.

The man had begun by nosing around. Now he was trying to interfere. He should have known better, Rex thought. He should have laid off the booze and kept his fly zipped. Because there were some things you "just knew." They were like natural laws or something. A man should just know, for instance, that it was unwise to pass between a lion and her cub, a bear and its prey. And God knows it was a mistake to fuck with a man of destiny when his time was at hand.

Harlan waited for a long time for the girl to return. Even after it had become clear to him that she would not, that something terrible had happened. Once he thought he heard the sound of an engine. On another occasion he thought there were distant flat popping sounds that might have come from a gun. Without her, of course, he would die. He tried to get used to the idea. It was necessary to get used to several ideas at once. That it was his fault, that he had allowed the two of them, ill-equipped as they were, to come after Obadiah, that he had been stupid enough to fall into a hole, that he had taken the keys with him. It went on and on.

At times he slept—or something like it. There was a dream. The dream seemed to repeat itself at regular intervals. In it, Harlan was carrying water. He carried it the way he had carried it in Africa, in a large wooden bucket on his head. It was the way they made him carry it. Only it wasn't Africa in the dream. It wasn't anywhere, as near as he could tell. There was no yellow-green blades of grass, and no mud, and no riverbank and no biting flies. It wasn't the desert, either, exactly. Only there was red asphalt and a yellow sky. Mainly there was just all this weight squeezing the top of his head flat and compressing the vertebrae in his neck until he felt that his eyes would explode in their sockets and sometimes there was water in his face and he would try to lick it away from his lips, knowing that it was dirty, that it would make him sick. On occasion he was aware of a sound he took for laughter.

At other times, when he was more or less awake, he imagined what it was he would have said to Obadiah Wheeler had he been able to catch up with him. He imagined a little sermon built around the text he had quoted in the motel room: Paul's words to the Corinthians, "For both the Jews ask for signs and the Greeks look for wisdom; but we preach Christ impaled." But then he changed his mind and thought perhaps he would use the fifth chapter of Hebrews instead. There was a nice series of verses there, beginning with the eleventh: "Concerning Christ we have much to say and hard to be explained, since you have become dull in your hearing." And he would end with the fourteenth verse, which spoke of the ability to distinguish both right and wrong. For it seemed to him the Wheeler boy had indeed become dull in his hearing, that he had lost sight of something fundamental and Harlan meant to remind him. He seemed to have forgotten that without Christ impaled the world was without hope. And extra dimensions, and time tunnels, and alien beings—if in fact any of these things actually existed—were not going to change it. In the Father's house there might be many mansions but on planet Earth, Jesus Christ was still what it was all about.

There was that. And then there was the other part, the part about not screwing up. The way Harlan had screwed up when he fought the mechanic, the way the Wheeler boy had screwed up when he stole something that was not his. It was the part about God's word being a mirror, the part about keeping honest. The

Word was what called people to decision and it was what changed their lives. It flat kept them from killing each other. It kept their miserable asses in line and without it, it was like the man said, it was all vanity, and a striving after the wind.

Harlan imagined himself saying all of these things to Obadiah Wheeler. He imagined the boy sitting rather dejectedly before him, the prodigal son with tears on his cheeks, nodding his befuddled head at the beauty of Harlan's wisdom.

He'd heard, of course, that there were no atheists in foxholes, not with death staring down on you like some black shining spider with a grinning skull for a face and a silvery web strung clear back to the beginning of time, and yet Harlan Low, who had never been an atheist in life, found it difficult to pray. He tried but found the whining tone of his voice unbearable and went back to alternately lecturing Obadiah Wheeler on the fundamentals and carrying the water. In time he saw that these activities had their purpose. Without them he was inclined to tamper with his puzzle. And that, in the blackness of the hole, in his present condition, was bad news. There was something about the hole. The conventional logic did not seem to apply. It was as if the edges of the hole were doing something to it, bending it back upon itself, forcing it into bizarre and unnatural shapes. The thing was, certain things were possible in the hole which should not have been possible at all. He was largely at fault, much of it was stuff which should have been left alone. He could see that now. And he supposed he would have, had it not been for an instant in time: Harlan's African Experiences. It had, he thought, a certain ring.

It was not that he couldn't make sense out of that experience well enough within the framework of his own system. He could do that. It was just that there was something about the Thing, as if It— whatever that was—did not want to be contained so easily, leaving him compelled to seek out other explanations. It was like picking at a wound, looking for something you hoped wasn't there. And yet now, here, either as the result of his picking or because it really existed, he had found something—an unlikely combination of myth, superstition, and pulp science fiction which seemed, horrific as it was to contemplate, to add up to something—another explanation at least as good as his own. And there, he thought, was the terror in the night, the shape at the door. And without the water to carry, or the boy to lecture, it was what he was left with, until at last he found himself mumbling a kind of prayer after all. He asked for the water, or for the boy. He asked deliverance from the twisted shape of his own thought, from the half-things toiling somewhere below him, in the cave womb of the world. He asked that when his time came he might not go whining into the night. And when he first detected what appeared to be the sounds of someone sobbing—the sound was faint and seemed to come from a great distance—it was as if he had been granted some glimpse of the infinite mercy of his God, and he vowed to preach as he had not preached before: The Act of Love. The Word as a call to decision. The Word that would be as a fire in his bones. And his would be the voice, crying out in the wilderness, setting straight the way of his Lord. Making it plain, in other words—the parable of the talents and the minas, the ten virgins, the prodigal son. He had the boy in his sights now and he meant to run it all down, had in fact begun, when something interrupted him and in a moment of illumination he perceived that the boy was not simply an aspect of his dream, but that there was, in fact, a shape at the edge of his hole, a voice independent from his own. At first he suspected a trick. His vision had been bent back upon itself, as had his logic. It was the power of the hole. But this was not the case. He could see. There were stars. There was a shape. There was a voice. The voice spoke his name.

Harlan stared into the night sky. "Obadiah Wheeler?"

"Obadiah," the voice repeated. "Harlan, is that you?"

Harlan was sweating now, freely, as if he had broken a fever. "You simple asshole," he heard himself say, "thank someone I'm not your old man." It was a moment of particular lucidity. When it passed he commenced to bear witness.

T he first thing that came into Obadiah's mind when he realized it was Harlan Low in the hole—before he thought to question how Harlan and Delandra had come to be together in the first place, or to wonder what they were doing on the road to the mines—was that they had crossed paths with the wrong people, possibly Richards himself, that Harlan had been thrown into a mine shaft while terrible things were done to Delandra. Eventually he understood that this was not the case, that Harlan had fallen into the hole by himself, that Delandra's fate was unknown.

It took some time to get this far. The man in the hole was in bad shape. There were periods of delirium. At one point Obadiah believed the man had referred to him as a simple asshole. This was followed by a kind of sermon. The sermon appeared to take the form of a snake swallowing its own tail. It was during those relatively brief periods of lucidity that Obadiah learned about the fall, the keys, the distant popping sounds which might have been gunfire.

He limped about in the blackness, circling the hole. He called to Delandra. There was no response. When he had done that he began to look for a stick himself. What he found were a couple of pieces of nylon cord. He knotted them together and returned to the hole. Looking down the thing was like looking into an inkwell. He half expected to see his own reflection. There was a certain uncanniness about hearing a voice come out of it that was difficult to accept. He put the makeshift line into the shaft and waited for Harlan to attach the keys. It had been agreed that he would try for the Ranger station Harlan had seen going into Death Valley.

Obadiah knelt among the shards of wood while Harlan fumbled with his end of the line. Eventually it was done and Obadiah hauled the keys to ground level. He took them down the grade and slid in, behind the wheel. He fumbled with them until he found the one which fit the ignition. He turned it and hit the gas. The car made a kind of chugging sound and then stopped. Afterward there was only a sharp electrical clicking.

He wound up making several trips back and forth between the hole and the car while Harlan tried to figure out what was wrong with it. He had Obadiah doing various experiments with the lights and the battery. The trouble was that neither of them knew much about cars, Harlan only slightly more than Obadiah, and in the end they gave it up.

Obadiah closed the doors and went back to the hole. He started out trying to walk but his ankle was feeling like it might explode and he wound up crawling back on all fours. As he crawled he thought that Neil Davis would probably have been able to figure out what was wrong with the car. It was, he thought, a stupid thing to think about but there it was and he thought about it anyway. When he reached the hole he sat down in the dirt. His throat was raw from thirst. He had been thankful for the car. Useless as the fucker had proven to be, it had kept his mind occupied. At the

edge of the hole he thought about Delandra. He thought about
how righteously fucked up it all really was. Delandra was gone.
Harlan was in a hole. Jack and Lyle and their ladyfriend had been
divided into parts. Sarge Hummer was dead. Ceton Verity was
dead. And it was damned hard to say why. Because there was a
part missing on the Electro-Magnetron. Because Bill Richards was
afraid the thing might work. Because Judy Verity wanted her
daddy's land back. You could more or less take your pick. Possibilities had been made manifest. What was clear was that the car
wouldn't start and that Obadiah himself had led them here—an
architect of dumb death. "It's useless," he said. He had till now not
had the heart to put it into words.

At rest upon his platform Harlan heard the news about the car.
A single piece of shoring near the edge of the hole was lit now by
the moonlight. The rest of it was wrapped in blackness, so that the
hole he was in might have been without sides, might not have
been a hole at all—the illusion was such that at times he felt
himself to be adrift in space. He focused upon the bit of shining
wood. It was not clear to him why Obadiah had left the camp. Or
why he could not go back now, for help.

Obadiah told him about finding the gun.

"And the gun belonged to one of these people who were killed."
Harlan wanted to keep it straight. His mind seemed to be working
against him. He was alternately cold and hot. At times his teeth
chattered against one another with such force, it was necessary to
stop talking, to massage the hinges of his jaw with his good hand.

"I think so," Obadiah said. In fact he had begun to question his
conclusions once again. What if he was wrong? The camp was a
good deal closer than the highway. Could he find it again? Throw
himself on the mercy of Bill Richards? But then what if he had
been right? He tried to envision that scene—he and Richards
driving back out here, alone.

"So it hangs," Harlan said, "on whether or not that gun is the
one you think it is." It occurred to him there was a lot riding on the
gun.

Obadiah rested his head in his hands. "It was the same kind of
gun," he said, "and the thing had this lousy little hand carved on it.
All I could think of was, who would do something like that, and the
only guy I could imagine doing it was Lyle. And that seemed to fit
with the rest of it—Richards thinking how great it was that the
Table Mountain People had been busted, Judy wanting that land
. . ." He let it trail away. The question now was, did it fit well

enough? It was coming down to a hard choice. Harlan's next question was not, however, the one he anticipated.

"What did this hand look like?" Harlan asked.

Obadiah had his legs out in front of him, his elbows on his thighs and his chin in his hands. In part he was hunkered so in protection from the cold. In part he felt he had been bent into this position by the weight of choice. Harlan's question surprised him. "It was small," he said. "It was poorly done, carved with a penknife or something. It had six fingers."

The silence in the hole lasted a long time—so that for a moment Obadiah believed the man had lost consciousness. At last, however, Harlan said something. He said, "Forget the camp, brother. You'll have to try for the road."

Obadiah wanted to be certain he had heard correctly. The voice was not without authority. It was as if the choice was being removed. "I don't understand," he said.

"Listen to me," Harlan said. He wanted to say several things at once and was not sure where to begin. The moonlight was gone. He drifted. The darkness changed colors before his eyes—a kind of aurora borealis, a magnetic disturbance. "What you don't understand," Harlan said, "is that the road to these mines was built by Nazis." And he began to talk about the hand.

Obadiah tried to follow it. It seemed there was a road. Somewhere. Which led to some mines. Which had been built by Nazis. Harlan seemed to think he was on it. Later he remembered the road was in Africa and corrected himself. Richards's father, however, was a Nazi. There was a golden medallion in the Desert Museum. Perhaps Obadiah had seen it. There was a sign at the side of the freeway in Los Angeles. The Temple of the Sons of Elijah. And there was a tricky little thing there with that text. One verse added. One omitted. If you believed Leonard Maxwell. And yet Harlan had found certain evidence . . .

Obadiah followed it as far as he could, until it had become clear to him the man had begun to rave, that the discourse on hands had gone the way of the sermon which had earlier preceded it. And yet there was something different about the two as well. The discourse had a dark side which had been missing from the sermon. It had something to do with the fact that whatever it was Harlan was talking about, it was something which frightened him.

It was this hand. What Harlan seemed to believe was that there was something out there of which this hand was the symbol. It had something to do with Nazis, mines, Indians, the Table Mountain People, Africa, and, quite possibly, the Thing itself. Whatever it was, it was worth being scared of, however, and without knowing anything more about it than that, Obadiah found that he was.

And then he knew why. It was because he knew more about it than he thought he did. He knew, for instance, about the Indian—the one who had been interested in the Thing from the very beginning, the third man at the camp. And when he understood that, he understood what was wrong with his original assumption—that there had been a deal between Richards and the Indian. What was wrong with that was the Indian himself. If he was all that Delandra had said he was, what would he need with Bill Richards? But if they were both part of the same thing . . . Then it would work. The Indian would have known what was going down all along—he'd just let Richards lure them into the desert was all, except that Richards was having some trouble with his end. He'd only gotten one of them into the desert. And somehow he had wound up with the wrong Thing—enough, Obadiah supposed, to make any man sweat, the way he had seen Richards sweat in the trailer, particularly when your partner favored ax handles and swift justice. And now the jeep was gone and the blackhearted bastard was out there somewhere. Maybe he was even what was behind the deaths of Sarge and Verity. Maybe he had orchestrated everything, from the beginning—if anyone could do that. And yet if the Indian was a part of this thing that Harlan was afraid of . . . It was a hell of a conclusion to arrive at, alone, in the middle of the desert, in the middle of the night. Nor was that the end of it. There was the part about the Indian having pulled out, Delandra having turned up missing. The part about the noise that might have been gunfire. And what would the man do if he had her? Would he circle back? To find the car? Would he find the hole with Harlan in it?

Obadiah began to look for a weapon. He set out on all fours. The night was alive with the black shapes of things. His heart beat against his ribs like a caged animal. The moon slunk like a beaten stray along the black spine of the ridge. He found a stick with a pair of good-sized nails sticking out of one end and he returned with it to guard the hole. He would meet this Indian in the valley of shadow. He stared hard into the night—until his eyes burned as badly as his throat. He gripped the foolish thing until his arms ached. The camp was out of the question. The road was too far. And there was no way he would leave Harlan alone. The man was here because of him. A man like Harlan gone down for a simple asshole like himself. The least he could do was guard the hole. And then he remembered something he had seen in the car and it struck him that there was something else he could do, after all. He leaned toward the inky blackness of the hole and called Harlan's name. The man had been silent for some time now and Obadiah had no idea if he was conscious or not. But he wanted him to know. "Listen to me," he said. He pushed his voice down into the shaft. "I have an idea," he said. "I'm going to try something."

Harlan was conscious. Something had happened to him during the course of his discourse. It had begun with a sense of elation at his newfound ability to, under the circumstances, articulate complex issues so clearly. This elation, however, was soon followed by the discovery that he could not stop talking. He kept thinking of things to say. One sentence followed another. He spoke faster. He became panicky. The sweats came once more. And at the same time that his voice speeded up, his mind did something else. It became clear to him, in a terrible moment of lucidity, that he was making no sense, that this in fact was the "little talk" for which he had pursued his young charge across the Mojave Desert. The insight was a crushing one, eventually it snuffed out the discourse altogether, leaving him with only a bone-deep weariness against which he now fought in an effort to come up with at least one or two meaningful sentences. His mind felt like a bowl of hot mush. He became aware that the boy was saying something to him.

"What?" he said. He was stalling for time.

"I'm going to send up a flare."

"What kind of flare?" asked Harlan. It was the best he could do.


Obadiah found the matches in the car. He used his shirt for the wick—got some gas on it out of the carburetor, then stuffed the thing into the tank. He lit it and ran for the hole. He was carrying Delandra's guitar. The blast knocked him to his stomach and filled the sky with light.

Harlan felt the blast. It began with a deep rumbling which seemed to issue out of the darkness beneath him. The sky went yellow and then orange and for a moment the light reached into the hole so that he saw it for the first time—the dirt walls, the wooden shoring, the wooden ladder with only a few rungs gone near the top, nearly within arm's reach. The fireball passed. The light above him shifted toward red. The walls disappeared once more. The rumbling continued, however, deep, distant. It might, he thought, have been the first stirrings of ancient stone hearts, locked for millennia in the secret places of the earth—that, or some rash act on the part of his boy. Suspended in the twilight of Obadiah's flare, he groped for the ladder as the platform shuddered beneath him.

# V

---

*take a vacation, move out to the farm*
*in the long run, we're gonna have fun*
R.F.F.
*Ground Hog Day on Mars*

Looking for a stick at the Table Mountain Mines, Delandra ran into the same two rednecks whose ride she had refused on the road out of Trona. Her first thought was to distance herself from the hole, to hope that she had seen them before they saw her, and she had made for the nearest standing shack. But it was no use. She could hear the men whooping as the jeep came bucking down on her across the rocky ground.

Her second thought had been to start shooting. But then she remembered the scatter-gun she'd seen between the seats when she'd argued with the men over the ride. She also knew that her chances of actually hitting anything at any kind of range with Sarge's cannon were next to none. The thing swung like an anchor at the bottom of her purse. She felt it bang against her hip as she ran. In the end, winded, scared, pissed beyond belief, she had appealed to the men's sense of fair play. "Listen to me," she said. She spoke before either of them could say anything to her. She was standing in the still settling dust of their arrival at the edge of the shack. "I don't have time for games. A friend of mine is trapped in a shaft. I need help."

One of the men, a white-faced guy with yellowish hair and eyes which seemed to rest on the sides of his face, had shaken his head. "That's too bad," he said.

"But it's a good story," the second man said. The second man wore a small leather cap and mirrored shades.

Delandra could see herself in the shades. She looked like someone who had gone looking for mercy and come up short. When the man with the leather cap started out of the jeep she tried for the shack. The driver cut her off and the guy with the mirrors got her by the arm. His strength took her by surprise. She felt herself twisted and fairly flipped into the space back of the seats. The driver then took them over the ridge and down to another group of shacks. The ride was much too rough and fast for her to do anything except hang on. She was on her back with her legs up in the air, her boots against the roll bar in an effort to steady herself. The men seemed to find this amusing. There was more whooping. Her head banged against the metal floor. Her boots kept slipping from the bar. At last she managed to hook an ankle between the bar and one of the braces which supported it. She could feel the ankle twisting against the grain in her boot in a kind of slow sprain. But it steadied her long enough to get a hand into her purse. What she had going for her at the time was that neither man had been smart enough to search her—that, together with the fact that the ride was too rough for either of them to keep a good eye on her. They were too busy hanging on themselves, looking for rocks in what was left of the light, and whooping like assholes in heat. By the time the driver brodied to a stop in front of the shacks she had a little something for them. She had Sarge's forty-one in both hands, her finger on the trigger and her thumbs on the hammer.

She kept them in the front seat. She'd been on her knees by then, in the back, waving the gun back and forth between them. She'd come close to wasting them both. She could have. Point-blank range in the base of the skull to the guy on the passenger side, at which point the driver would have turned and she could have blown his face off. She'd decided instead to try to get them into the shack. For a minute she had believed it was going to work. The gun was big enough to make someone who knew anything about it nervous and she could see that they were, that they didn't like the way that big barrel kept swinging around between them or the crazy-woman eyes behind it.

She'd gotten them out of the jeep, one at a time, very slowly, and had moved them around to the front. She was about to back them into the shack when the guy with the mirrored shades did something funny. Later, it was difficult to remember exactly what he had done. Whatever it was, he had preceded the action with a kind of smile. Maybe it was just the smile that had done it. Or maybe he really had made a move. The fact was, she shot the bastard. He'd put a hand out and she had shot him through it. Only the bullet had done some very weird things. It appeared to have removed about half of his hand, gone up his arm somehow, and torn a piece of his ear off. After that it had put a hole in the door of the shack.

The man went down on his knees, the other man standing over him. She almost felt sorry for the beggar. It did, however, make getting them into the shack easier. The driver wasn't about to make any moves and the other guy was fresh out. He'd lost his mirrored shades in the process of being shot and without them his eyes had a kind of milky helplessness about them. The driver's eyes were the ones that had gone glassy, like a wounded animal's.

They tried to tell her she couldn't leave them there, making it necessary for her to point out to them that they were wrong. She not only left them, she took their jeep. She supposed that if the wounded man was lucky she would get help back to him before he bled to death, or died of shock, or did whatever it was that people did when they'd lost something. Once, driving away from the shack, in the very last of the day's light, she thought she noticed a finger on the hood of the jeep. Graciously, the light failed quickly, and she could not be sure if that was what she had seen or not.

But then the finger, if in fact there was a finger, was the least of her worries. She had Harlan Low to think about and the sunlight was gone. The jeep had no winch and no rope, nothing except that scatter-gun between the front seats. There wasn't even any drinking water and in the end she had decided to try for the highway. It seemed to make the most sense. There were now two casualties to report. This, however, like everything that had preceded it, turned out to be harder than it looked. It took her a while to get her bearings in the dark and at about the same time that she hit the interstate, she ran out of gas. She wound up walking into Trona. It was a long walk. Her ankle felt mushy and swollen in her boot. Her back hurt and her head ached from banging against the metal floor. By the time she got to Trona it was very late indeed. She woke up some guy who lived behind the market and asked for a phone. The man stood around in a pair of boxer shorts and bedroom slippers, watching her while she made the call. When she was finished he told her they had themselves a little chopper in Ridgecrest. He offered to take her to the mines, just to make sure everyone got found.

"Thanks," Delandra said, "but no."

The man shrugged. He shuffled off into his kitchen and began running water. Delandra went back outside, into the cool air that had the first taste of morning on it. If she wasn't sure about the man, she was at least sure about the cops. If she went anywhere near them there would be a lot of unpleasant questions and as soon

as they'd had time to run a make on her she would be on her way
to Victorville in the back of a truck.

What she had on her mind was another ride. She went to the
front of the market and waited. She actually put out her thumb
once. A station wagon came rolling out of the west and slowed
down. The thing was filled with a family but she put out her thumb
anyway. The people looked at her like she was from Mars—everybody except the husband. He pretended not to notice. She could
see him in there, hunched over the wheel, peering into the market
like that was all there was. The little scene made her so tired, she
went back to sit on a pair of wooden soft drink crates someone had
stacked near the Coke machine and when the next car came by—a
truck with a single man in it—she didn't even bother to get up.

She sat on the crates for a long time. Sometimes she closed her
eyes and sometimes she looked into the yellow light which had
begun to blossom in the east until at some point she noticed that
the flats had lost the look of dirty snow which was their true color,
which you only saw at dusk and at dawn, that they had begun to
shine.

She was still on the crates when the man who had let her use his
phone came outside. He was still wearing the bedroom slippers
but he'd put on a flannel shirt and some jeans. He had a cup of
coffee for her. "I imagine they'll take your friend back to Ridgecrest," he said. "There's a hospital there. I can drive you if you
want me to."

Delandra had looked one more time into the flats. The sunlight
was upon them now and they seemed to be made of something
impossibly pure and bright and for a moment it seemed to her as if
all the choices had already been made. "Why not," she said.


The man took her directly to the hospital. He loaned her a
twenty-dollar bill and let her out in the parking lot at the emer-
gency exit. But there were some cops standing around near the
reception desk and she was afraid to ask about Harlan Low lest she
be identified as the person who had made the call.

Across the hall from the nurse's desk there was a small waiting
room. The room held a pair of orange Naugahyde couches. There
was a television set mounted on the wall. Delandra went to the
vacant couch and sat down. On the other couch there was a
woman with a little boy. There were some ice skaters on the
television. The woman was trying to get the boy to watch the
skaters, but the boy was more interested in climbing on the furni-

ture. When Delandra sat down he came straight to her and leaned against her knee. He was holding some kind of disgusting candy on a stick with one hand and the stuff was all over his face. Delandra took a cigarette from her purse. When she lit it the woman came and got the boy.

Later a man in work clothes came in and sat with the woman and the boy. The two cops who had been outside left but a third cop showed up. He entered the waiting room and sat next to Delandra. The cop made her nervous. She had the idea he was looking at her. She got up and went into the hall.

She was thinking about leaving and coming back later when a pair of double gray doors swung open to emit an orderly with a gurney and she caught sight of something at the end of the room. What she saw was a straw hat on the back of a chair.

She put her cigarette out on the floor and went through the doors. She went for the hat and found Harlan in a bed not far from it. There wasn't a lot of time. They were getting ready to put a pin in his arm.

"He's here," Harlan told her, "somewhere." And while the nurse went to see about X rays Delandra heard about how it had gone down. She heard about how Obadiah had left the camp, and how he had set off a flare. She heard about the stick with nails on it. Harlan was a bit dopey from what they had given him and this detail seemed to please him. It took her a moment to get the picture. In the end, what she gathered was that Obadiah had been guarding the hole from an Indian. At some point she realized it was her Indian. There had apparently been a big argument when the time came for them to get into the chopper. Obadiah didn't want to put down his stick. It was the part Harlan seemed to enjoy the most. "We were pretty tired by then," he told her. "It had been a long night."

Once outside, it occurred to her that she had not slept in a long time. She crossed the street and found that she was about half a block from the Ridgecrest police station. She walked past the station. She passed a couple of bars and a number of those chapels that perform speedy wedding ceremonies. She went into the lobby of the first hotel she found. The hotel was called the Rose Hotel and the carpet had once been covered with roses. She could see this by looking at the borders. The nap with which the roses were made was raised so that the patterns of leaves and blossoms and long, curving stems had once covered the floor in swirling, art deco patterns. At the center of the floor, however, the roses had long since been worn down to nothing. In the center everything was slick and black with dirt and in some spots there was nothing but threads with the floor shining through underneath. The single rooms were seven dollars a night. She registered under an assumed name with a tough-looking Mexican. He gave her a key and she went upstairs. There was a bed, a dresser, one chair, and a bathroom. There were curtains at an open window. The curtains looked to have been from the time of the carpet. The window was open and the sounds from the street below drifted into the room.

Delandra took the last cigarette from her purse and went to the window. She put the cigarette, still unlit, between her lips and leaned against the sill, the heels of her hands pressing down upon the wood which had grown hot in the direct light of the sun. Her trial date was nearly upon her now. Soon, she thought, she would indeed be a wanted woman. A warm breeze slipped past the curtains and brushed her cheek. It smelled faintly of garbage and sunlight. She had no idea of what she expected to happen next. At first the image of Obadiah's long vigil in the face of her invented Indian had only depressed her. But there was perhaps a change in the wind. She could feel it, staring into the harsh light, the brassy sky. She had this idea that maybe she would come around. She even had this idea that in time the incident might achieve a certain radiance. Looked at long and hard enough, in fact, the thing might even shine. A beacon in the darkest of nights. But then she was tired. Her head did ache. And it was like Harlan had said, it had been a long night.

When she had finished the cigarette she went in to use the bathroom before getting into bed and found that a list of the house rules had been posted on the door for her edification. No alcoholic beverages. Of any kind. No loud music. No loud guests. No cigarettes in bed. No dancing. Perhaps, she thought, she had inadvertently joined an order. The thought made her dizzy. On her way to bed she found herself wondering if these rules were strictly enforced. There was a wastebasket at the foot of the bed, however, and in it an empty Gordon's gin bottle. The sight relaxed her mind. The Rose Hotel was just like everything else. It was a fucking sham.

Obadiah had no place to stay. And since he was wanted for some questioning the police captain offered him a cell. They ran a file on him. They took three sets of fingerprints and took away his belt so he couldn't hang himself. The captain told him the file would be stamped "sleeper" to show he had not been arrested. Obadiah said he didn't plan to hang himself over any of this but they took his belt anyway. An officer led him down a dimly lit hallway and put him in a cell by himself. Obadiah had never been in a jail cell. It was long and narrow with a toilet at one end and a small rectangular window with a heavy screen high on the wall at the other. In between there was a narrow bunk with two blankets and a pillow on it. The bunk was hard. He sat on the edge of it as the guard closed the door. When it slammed shut he could hear the tumblers drop. Without the light from the hallway it got dark fast. The quality of the stuff took him by surprise. "It's dark," he said. Nor was the finality of the tumbling locks something he had counted on. He was set upon by a wave of claustrophobia as thick and as strong as the blackness.

The guard, apparently having heard what Obadiah said, spoke to him through the metal door. "What did you want to do, Sport, sleep or play pinochle?"

Obadiah, humiliated, said nothing. He thought of Harlan Low in the hole. The thought comforted him. He was very tired but it was hard to unwind. He'd spent most of the day around the hospital and the police station, answering questions. His ankle was not broken. Just badly sprained. The doctor told him he was lucky. He wanted to believe he was.

There had not been much that he or Harlan could do to keep Delandra's name out of it. Even before either of them talked to anyone what was left of Harlan's car had been identified. It had also been recognized as a car which had tried to enter Table Mountain from another direction the day before. And then there was Delandra's guitar case with the Thing sticker and her name, so that by the time someone got around to asking questions they already knew about Delandra Hummer and the Desert Museum. They knew about Harlan's fight with Floyd and about the missing Thing. They had done their homework. There wasn't much left to do but play it straight and answer questions. The trick lay in answering the questions while still hanging on to some shred of one's dignity. This became increasingly difficult and for Obadiah the feeling of losing it came while trying to explain for about the fifteenth time just exactly what he had hoped to find in the desert with Bill Richards and Judy Verity. After that he just gave up and answered questions. He didn't worry about dignity, but he felt himself growing steadily less substantial, collapsing inward by sections. He believed that ultimately he would disappear. It was what he had to look forward to when the sun rose.

It seems some dickhead at the station, an old-car buff, had passed the word that the Starlight coupe Obadiah had destroyed was already something of a collector's item. In the wake of this, Obadiah had become known as the guy who blew up the car. Harlan was the guy who had fallen in the hole. Unless you were talking to the men who had brought them in, in which case Obadiah was the guy with the stick. The funny thing was, all things considered, he really didn't mind the car. He had come to hold the position that the car meant something. It marked the spot. It was like the Table Mountain Mines. No one would do anything with it. It would sit there for hundreds of years. He imagined that someday he and Delandra Hummer would visit it together. They would bring the kids. "See," someone would say, "this is where it went down."

He slept fitfully. The feeling of claustrophobia came and went. At some point during the night they put someone in a cell, or in the drunk tank, and the guy wouldn't be quiet. Obadiah heard him alternately howling and cackling for the rest of the night. It was hard on the nerves. He kept imagining that he was in fact a prisoner here, that the sleeper business had been a ruse. They would never let him go. He could look forward to spending the rest of his life in places like this. He had seen something he shouldn't have. He had fallen into the hands of the manipulators. Or possibly they had done something to his mind. He couldn't seem to stop imagining things. Once, before leaving the hospital he had even imagined that he had seen Delandra Hummer pass an open doorway at the end of a hall. Once more, later, from a window in the police building, he had imagined that he had seen her go into a cheap hotel. He knew he hadn't. She was too smart for any of that. He had lost her. And when he wasn't battling waves of panic generated by the closeness of the walls he was chewing on remorse. At some point, however, he did manage to sleep because when the guard came in the morning he had to wake him. But he didn't feel like he had been sleeping. He felt like he had been digging ditches. The guard took him to a room where there was coffee and a box of doughnuts. After that they went to another room to answer more questions. He had expected to have to answer questions alone but the captain had decided it was time to question both him and Harlan together and Harlan was already in the room, waiting for him. For some reason Obadiah found the sight reassuring. It must, he thought, have been the way those African brothers felt, the Liberian flag fluttering above them in the dawn's early light.

H arlan was looking at his cast. He could hardly help it, what with the way the thing was, sticking out in front of him, supported by a stick, which in turn was fastened to a belt he wore around his waist. It was a ridiculous arrangement. Looking at it made him think of things he no longer wanted to think about.

He found that the authorities had done a thorough job of checking him out. There had even been a phone call to New York, which in turn had generated a return call from Jim Mitchell. Mitchell had wanted to know if Harlan was in need of legal help. Harlan had said no, that he didn't think so. He wasn't being charged with anything. They just wanted to ask him questions. It was embarrassing, was all. Mitchell had advised him to "hang in there." And so he was. He was hoping today would be the end of it.

He looked up when Obadiah and the captain came through the door. He had not seen the boy since leaving the hospital. The boy was on crutches, his ankle wrapped up in a thick Ace bandage with a silver clip on it. He watched as Obadiah hobbled over to a metal folding chair near his own and sat down. Beyond the narrow rectangular windows which sat high along one wall Harlan could see patches of blue sky. The windowsills were colored by a golden morning light.

A third man came into the room before they could begin. Harlan had not seen him before. He was a tall, thin man, with a receding hairline. He was dressed rather nattily, in a pale gray suit, a white shirt, and dark red tie. He took a seat near the windows. He did not speak to anyone and the captain did not introduce him. Harlan looked at the man now and then as they talked. He seemed to spend a good deal of time looking at the ceiling. Every now and then he would take a small blue notepad from his breast pocket and jot something down.

They went over it all again. They started at the beginning, the captain asking questions, sometimes of one of them, sometimes of both. He didn't seem to be in any hurry. One of the points he wanted to be sure about was that Obadiah had acted independently when he and Delandra took the Thing. He seemed rather hung up on the idea that if the Table Mountain People, Bill and Judy, perhaps the Sons of Elijah, were all so interested in the Thing, then why not Harlan and his people as well.

It was ground Harlan had already been over numerous times. He went over it again, trying to present in some coherent fashion what it was his people did believe, that their interest in alien beings was slight at best. Part of the problem, however, was that Harlan and Obadiah had not done themselves any favors in this regard early on. There had even been a point, getting from the chopper to the hospital, at which Harlan had actually begun to talk about the hand. It had seemed so plain at the bottom of the hole. Outside the hole it had sounded so ridiculous that he had simply stopped talking. But the damage had been done—between the stuff about the hand and Obadiah's scene over the stick.

The captain listened to Harlan's explanation one more time. He nodded in appropriate places. He was a big man with a long, horsey face. The face was tanned and creased with the creases running vertically at the sides of his nose and mouth, and then horizontally across his forehead. He had a way of nodding his head when you told him something which made it appear he was listening to the explanation of some rash act on the part of a small child.

"Your only interest," the captain said, "was in going after this young man."

Harlan said that this was right.

The man looked at Obadiah as if this concept—given the young man in question—was particularly offensive, or difficult to comprehend.

"We wanted to talk to him," Harlan said. "We had reason to believe he might have been in some danger."

"Ah yes, from Bill Richards and Judy Verity. Something about a Nazi cult, wasn't it?" He had by now heard everyone's story several times. He behaved, however, as though he found repeating any of it quite painful. "And Mr. Wheeler was worried about the Indian." When Obadiah had first mentioned the bondsman from Victorville the captain had nodded, saying that yes, he knew Sam Corasco. He had left it at that. For Obadiah it had been enough. When the captain spoke again he was looking for the first time that morning at the man in the gray suit. "Lots of dangerous people out there," he said. The man gave him a little smile. The captain went on to enumerate those dangers he considered real as opposed to imaginary. It was not the first time he had done so. He seemed fond, however, of repeating it. He liked to count—using his thumb, checking off against the other fingers: lack of proper clothing, lack of water, no equipment, failure to notify Rangers, etc., etc. It was a lengthy list.

Harlan listened with growing impatience. The man had a point but he was not being altogether fair about it. There were, in fact, some dangerous people out there and the man knew it as well as Harlan. If there weren't, the captain's co-workers would not be out there just now, still hunting down body parts. Nor would, he suspected, this stranger with the expensive suit and high, pale brow, be here listening to them, writing things down in his little pad.

He thought of saying something to this effect. What he said instead, however, was something else. "Our only intention," he said, "in coming here in the first place, was to talk to people about matters that concern us, that we believe should concern all people." He felt called upon to say something like this, though his heart was not really in it. His shoulder hurt. So did his head. Still, old habits were hard to break and he did not enjoy being made a fool of, even when he had acted like one.

The captain nodded once more. "Only this time you did a little more than talk. You beat up a mechanic. You nearly got yourselves killed, and four people have turned up dead since your boy and his girlfriend began trying to sell her daddy's monster."

Obadiah was aware of an acute sinking sensation. To the best of his knowledge there had been three deaths. "Who was the fourth?" he asked.

The captain looked at him for a moment. Then he looked at Harlan Low. "The fourth," he said, "was Bill Richards. A pair of locals whose jeep your girlfriend stole found his head on the side of a road out there near the Table Mountain Mines." He paused a minute, looking at each of them once more, then went on. "We have a pretty good idea about who did it," he said. "It was a messy job. There was blood. A lot of prints."

When no one said anything the captain got up and crossed the room. He stood next to the wall, looking up toward one of the thin patches of blue. He was carrying a manila folder with him and he tapped his thigh with it. The tapping was the only sound in the room. "And neither of you know anything concerning the whereabouts of Delandra Hummer."

Neither of them knew.

The captain tapped once more at his leg. "You know," he said, "that Miss Hummer has a trial date pending on a possession charge. She is currently free on bail. A stipulation of that bail was that she remain in San Bernardino County. We are not in San Bernardino County. If she was here I would have to put her under arrest." He waited for a moment then stepped away from the window. He shook his head. "You know," he said. "I remember her old man. I stopped at that damn place of his once, the Desert Museum. Had my boy with me. We were on our way back from Victorville with this new trailer I'd bought down there. The kid wanted to see the Mystery of the Mojave. We stopped and looked at the stupid thing and by the time we got back outside some idiot had pasted a pair of bumper stickers to the rear of that new trailer. I didn't see the bastards till we got home. When I did, I damn near turned around and went back."

He looked at the man in the suit for the second time that morning. The man in the suit produced a replica of the smile he had shown earlier. He had his pen and pad both back in his pocket now. He had his legs crossed, the fingers of his hands interlaced about one of his knees. "Tell me," he said. He was speaking to the captain. His voice was soft and evenly modulated. "Which one of them blew up the car?"


The golden light at the windows was gone by the time the captain said it was over. It had been replaced by something which bespoke the heat of midday.

"If we get a trial out of this, one or both of you may be called to testify." The captain was addressing himself to Obadiah and Harlan. He was standing before them, looking at the material in his folder. "You," he said, nodding at Harlan, "are free to go." Closing the folder he turned to Obadiah. "And you," he said, "can come with me. I've got something I want you to look at."

Obadiah watched Harlan walk slowly from the room. He had been right. They weren't going to let him go. He took his crutches from the floor and got to his feet. He felt light-headed and a bit dizzy. As he followed the captain from the room he had this terrible idea that what they were going to make him look at was Bill Richards's head.

The man in the suit went with them. What they made him look at instead was the bogus version of the Thing they had found in the back of Bill Richards's Land-Rover. It looked like it had looked at the campsite, except that now there were these dark splotches on parts of its fur. They wanted to know if this was what all the fuss had been over. He told them it was over something else and after that they let him go. He went down a long tiled corridor and stepped into a pool of black asphalt and brilliant sunlight.

Still, he had this idea that they were not done with him. He could imagine one cop saying to another: "Put a tail on him." The way you might see it in a movie.

He used diversionary tactics. He went around the block. He cut through a bar and went down an alley. His breath was coming hard and the crutches hurt his armpits. He looked for a tail but he couldn't find it. He went to the hotel where he thought he had seen Delandra.

There was a tough-looking Mexican at the door. When Obadiah started past him the guy got in his way. "You staying here?" the man asked.

"I'm looking for someone," Obadiah told him.

"Three dollars," the man said.

Obadiah was not sure he had heard correctly. "Three dollars?"

"You pay me three dollars, I let you inside."

For a moment he thought of laughing, but then the guy at the door didn't look like he thought it was a joke. He looked like a man who wanted three dollars. Obadiah had two dollars and eighty-three cents. He put it into the man's palm, which was thick and dark and scarred in a way that reminded Obadiah of a well-worn cutting block. The man looked at the money. He looked at Obadiah. His fingers closed around the coin. His thumb came up pointed in the direction of the lobby. Obadiah lurched inside. He almost thanked the man. He went to a counter and asked another tough-looking Mexican if there was a woman registered by the name of Delandra Hummer. The man looked in a book. "No," he said.

Obadiah could feel his shirt, wet with sweat, clinging to the skin of his back. He could feel the blood in his cheeks. He was aware of the man at the door. The man was watching him. The man behind the counter was pretending to look for something in a drawer. Obadiah began to describe Delandra Hummer. He did his best to keep his voice from shaking. What he had begun to appreciate was that this was only the first in an endless series of just such scenes. It was the kind of scene from which the rest of his life would be constructed.

The man continued to look into the drawer as Obadiah spoke. Once he exchanged glances with the man by the door. Finally he looked at Obadiah. Obadiah had finished talking. He clung to the soiled wood of the counter as if it might save him. The man looked at him for what seemed an unusually long time. At last he re-opened the book. "There is someone like that," he said. He paused, as if examining a lengthy list, or as if he was still trying to make up his mind. He pointed at a signature on a yellowed page. "Lucy Silverfish," he said. "Third floor. End of the hall."

W hen Rex had not returned from the mouth of the gorge the man had come looking for him. Rex had a clear shot at him but he hadn't taken it. His nerve failed. He did not trust himself with the gun. His eyesight was poor and he had not fired one in years. He lifted a rack of horns belonging to the Hum-A-Phone and started with it across the soft dirt of the gorge. The man met him halfway and Rex could see the moonlight on the gun in his hand.

The man had followed Rex back to the truck, holding the gun on him as he loaded the horns into the bed. "This isn't camping equipment," the man said. "I want to know what the fuck is going on."

"This is a musical instrument," Rex said. "It plays the music of the spheres." As Rex was laying the horns in the bed he saw beside the wheel well the short-handled shovel his father had used in defeating the Mystery of the Mojave.

"How much more of this thing is there?" the man wanted to know.

"A lot," Rex replied.

"Shit." The man leaned into the bed to examine the horns. "The music of the spheres, huh?" He laughed. He was still laughing at the horns when Rex hit him with the shovel.

It seemed to happen in two ways at once, both slowly and quickly. Reaching for the shovel took a long time. It was as if Rex had to push his hand through something a good deal thicker than air to get it done. Reaching it, however, was like flipping a switch. He could remember the reaching part in minute detail. Afterward, the details began to swirl around one another with increasing speed—sand in a whirlwind.

The man had pitched forward, his helmet clattering against the bed of the truck. The handgun had gone off. Rex had pretended to simply be shifting things in the bed, but had drawn the shovel up quickly, gotten both hands on the handle, and hit the guy with the squared-off piece of steel which provided a grip at one end. He'd caught the man just beneath the ear and just back of the jaw. He had hoped to knock him out. The man, however, did not go quietly. The first bullet had made of the window separating the bed from the cab a web of fractured glass. Rex was momentarily stunned by the explosion. He had seen, however, that the man was twisting himself up on the tailgate, trying to position himself for another shot; he had been forced to hit him again. It was not something he took pleasure in. He'd gotten both hands up near the grip this time and he had swung the shovel like an ax. More shots pierced the night. One grazed Rex's ear. Another took a chunk from his arm up high, near his shoulder. At some point he must have hit a major artery with the shovel because suddenly there was a lot of blood. It hit the roof of the shell with enough force to make a noise. It was not a noise Rex Hummer would soon forget.

The man scissored him with his legs, all the time spraying blood like a ruptured hose. Rex, trying to free himself, backing up, dragged the man from the truck bed then fell himself beneath t' weight of the man's legs, which were still locked around him, and for a moment they had rolled there in the moonlight, on ground gone slick and dark with blood, until Rex had managed to free himself—he had used the shovel as a lever. Once on his feet he had held the shovel out in front of him like something you would use to dig postholes with and he had come down with it hard. He'd come down hard and he hadn't stopped until it was done, until the big body had ceased to buck and heave and thrash with its legs and the only sounds were the after-sounds—stuff letting go, like a blown engine which has begun to cool, its fluids loosed upon thirsty soil.

When it was over there were a lot of things to do he hadn't thought of before. He had to hide the body. He had to hide the truck. He had to get the last of the Hum-A-Phone to the mouth of the tunnel. It all seemed to take a very long time and it was only after he had driven the Land-Rover back to the northern side of the dirt road upon which he had entered and dug a shallow grave in the loose sandy ground between some creosote bushes, that he noticed he had lost the man's head; that it must have fallen out of the truck somewhere between the gorge and the grave site.

He was still looking for it when he discovered that the sense of being watched had returned. He noticed also that the struggle had done something to his sight. It was as if his field of vision was now ringed with a pulsing silver light. The intensity of the light rose and fell. At its dimmest, it was a vague, foglike halo. At its brightest it was a glowing ring, filled with tiny dancing sparks—brilliant enough to all but obliterate the landscape.

The phenomenon both terrified and fascinated him. When it all but went away he halfway wanted it back, just to examine it again. When it came on strong he was afraid it would shut out the night completely. He would lose the tunnel. He would wander blindly in the night, tracked by whatever it was that watched him from the rocks, whatever it was, he knew now, that had come to stop him.

This sensing of a malign presence—suddenly the night was alive with it—was what at last drove him from his search. He fled the scene of the struggle like some scavenger bird driven from its find by a larger predator. He ran blindly back across the spongy soil of the gorge, the last piece of the Hum-A-Phone, a lamp pole with metal shade, like the stake of the Savior, slung over one humped shoulder. He ran between the walls of the wash and whatever it was that watched him ran too. There was loose rock tumbling now —tiny landslides of dirt and gravel, one per footfall. It followed him to the wooden gate, the ruined wooden wheel. He stumbled inside and he swung the gate closed behind him. Once he thought he saw something out there, back in the gorge, looking at him through the wooden bars of the gate. What he thought he saw was the fat Indian from town holding the head of his opponent like a lantern before the night. Sparks flew before the vision and when the sparks were gone so was the Indian.

He took some rope from the Hum-A-Phone, and his belt. He tied the gate closed, pulling the knots as tightly as he could. His arm was throbbing now—it was the first time since being shot that he was actually aware of the pain.

Only after securing the gate did he realize he was without his light. The darkness which lay before him was absolute. Behind him, however, there was nothing but blood and destruction. There was whatever it was that had watched him.

The Hum-A-Phone was still disassembled but the pieces had been stacked upon a wooden sled and tied down. He put the length of rope that was attached to the front like a wagon tongue over one shoulder and he started into the blackness. It swallowed him whole. He could see neither his hands nor the rope they clung to, though both were within inches of his face. He stumbled head-long into the cool heart of the tunnel. She welcomed him with a musty breath, with webs and dust. He kept his head down. He kept his legs pumping. He made a picture of an engine, pistons sliding in their shafts. He held it in his mind. If he was moving toward something he was moving away from something as well and at last he heard it—a kind of distant scraping sound, what could only have been the wooden gate at the tunnel entrance. The sound was like the light, it came and went, starting when he started, stopping when he stopped, and then he saw what it was. He was being fucked with, that was what. He was inside and it was rattling his cage.

Harlan was sitting on a bench which faced the street in front of the courthouse when Obadiah came out of the hotel. Obadiah crossed the street and sat down next to him. There was no wind and the sun was bright on the asphalt and cars.

"You been in there all this time?" Harlan asked. He gestured with his head in the direction of the jail.

"No. That didn't take long. They found Richards's Land-Rover with the old Thing in it. They wanted to know if it was what we were trying to sell."

"What did you tell them?"

"I told them we were trying to sell something else."

Harlan looked into the street. He had learned about the bailbondsman from Victorville during all the talk. He felt the man's existence suggested an explanation of things which could only add to his embarrassment. "You should have told me the Indian was a bailbondsman," he said.

Obadiah shrugged. "He was interested in the Thing, whoever he was."

"Business," Harlan said, "strictly business."

There was something in the man's voice, Obadiah thought, anger, disappointment, possibly disgust. A red, white, and blue school bus with religious slogans on it rumbled along the street in front of the courthouse.

Obadiah watched the bus. He was able to share with the man at his side a moment of contempt. "Okay," he said, "business. But whose business?"

Harlan shook his head. "I'm afraid you and I are talking about two different men. I'm talking about the man in the red car."

The man in the red car was the man they knew about. The third man belonged to Obadiah. The jeep, after all, could have been taken away by someone else. The gun might not have been Lyle's. It was an impressive list. The frustrating part was what no one but himself seemed to appreciate—the fact that the real Thing was still out there somewhere, that someone had it. "You know," he said, "I thought of something back there I hadn't thought of before." He looked at Harlan. "You interested?"

Harlan made a gesture with his free hand. Obadiah took it as one both of resignation and an offer to continue.

"Delandra once told me that years ago Verity tried to buy one of Sarge Hummer's Things. I think he did buy it. And I think that's it, in there." Obadiah nodded in the direction of the jail.

A fly landed on Harlan's cast and started to rub its front legs together. It looked as if it was praying. Harlan watched it. He said nothing. He was waiting for the boy to go on.

"It's one of two things," Obadiah said.

"It always is."

Obadiah noticed the man was looking at him out of the side of his face. It was what Delandra called giving someone the fisheye.

"Or maybe three. What it comes down to is, Who has the Thing? I've been thinking lately about Ceton Verity. Did you know no one ever found his body? They say he was transferred."

"They would."

"But suppose he didn't die. Suppose he faked it." The idea seemed to open up a whole new range of possibilities.

Harlan nodded, pretending to give it some thought. In truth, it was not that he was totally uninterested. It was just that he had done what he could. It was out of his hands. "So let me ask you something," he said. "About this Thing. Are you sure that one back there isn't the one you took? Think about it. That must have been quite a moment for you, when you decided to help the girl. Maybe you saw what you wanted to see. It wouldn't be the first time, you know."

Obadiah laughed out loud. He hadn't meant to. This big stupid guffaw had just broken from his throat like a bird from a cage.

"I say something funny?"

Obadiah sat shaking his head. He was fighting the urge to laugh once more. The thing was, he had suddenly seen why no one but himself was very excited about the missing Thing. It was because they didn't believe in it. They thought they had it. It made perfect sense, of course. The boy had run off half-cocked. He'd gotten excited. They thought he was saying the one in the jailhouse was the wrong one because to admit otherwise would be too humiliating to bear. Perhaps they thought he was deluded. The funny part was, he couldn't blame them. He would have thought so himself. Anyone would. It seemed to make going on about it rather pointless. Still, the man had tried to give him a way out, and now he was waiting.

Obadiah shrugged. "I can see your point," he said. "But yes, I'm sure that the one back there isn't the one we took. My point was that if you knew who had it now. Verity. The bondsman. Maybe even . . ."

Obadiah's voice trailed away. It was swallowed by a pause pregnant with meaning. Harlan shifted his weight on the bench. He was deeply embarrassed about what had happened here. He had gone into the desert when he shouldn't have. He had behaved foolishly. He had fallen into a hole. He had said some things. He knew that what Obadiah had just stopped short of doing was making reference to that something of which the hand was perhaps the symbol. The suggestion made him want to grind his teeth. He hadn't forgotten what he had put together. Nor had he forgotten that moment which had spawned it. Still, this stuff which had transpired since his fight with the mechanic—the driving, the puzzles—it was coming for him, more and more now, to have about it the quality of those water mirages with which he had lived for the past several days—a trick done with mirrors, an eccentricity of the land itself. He thought he saw how it worked. Obadiah had come with a cast of conspirators, Harlan, with his Cult of the Hand. In a kind of magic moment at the edge of the hole the stories had merged, each lending weight to the other. But the moment had passed. The stuff about the bailbondsman had helped. "I suggest you forget the 'maybe even' part," Harlan said. "As for your detective work, you're talking to the wrong guy." He pointed over his shoulder with his usable thumb. "It's the Man's problem, now."

After that they sat for several moments in the shade, without speaking. At their feet the sunlight swam in the street. The buildings baked in it. The day, Harlan thought, had that slow, hot feel about it. You wanted to stay in one spot. He was working on his. He had his bailbondsman. The boy could keep the Thing.

"You know," Obadiah said at length, "you're right about the detective work." He was looking for a way to get past something. It was what he and Harlan still had between them and it seemed to him that something ought to be said about it. "It's his problem but it's hard to stop thinking about it. I mean, thinking about what happened is like thinking about the Thing." He stopped for a moment and then went on. "When we were out there . . ." He nodded toward that end of town which ran into the desert. "I had this idea that everything that had happened had been orches-

trated in some way. You see, I still think Delandra and I saw Jack
the night we stole the Thing. And when you started talking about
this hand I thought maybe I was beginning to see who it might be.
Delandra's position was always that no one was orchestrating anything, that it was all just a bunch of random events. The deaths of
Sarge and Verity, for instance—if Verity is really dead. A guy that
just looked like Jack following us that first night. Jack and Lyle
carved up by the Table Mountain People, just like the Man says.
Nothing too intricate, in other words. About the time I decided I
would never know for sure it came to me that it was going to be
that way with a lot of things."

"I take it you're not going to go hunting, then."

"No."

Harlan nodded. He removed his hat and wiped his brow. He had
an idea of where the boy was headed. He had an idea as well that
this in fact was the "little talk" for which they had come, that he
had been given a second chance. He ran a thumb along the rough
crease of the hat and set the thing back on his head. "No one ever
promised us it wouldn't get complicated," he said. "What you
want to understand is that a man can't use the complications in
pretending he doesn't know right from wrong." He was thinking
of the words of James 4:17: "Therefore if one knows how to do what
is right and yet does not do it, it is a sin for him."

Obadiah listened to what Harlan had to say. The words were not
without effect. They suggested accountability and he guessed
maybe that was something else he couldn't stop believing in. He
felt accountable. To whom, exactly, it was harder to say. Because
no matter how Harlan's words affected him, they were, at least in
context, part of something bigger. It was the something bigger
that had failed him—if not him, exactly, then life itself perhaps—
the very thing it had sought to contain. It seemed to him there
ought to be some way of saying this. "Do you know anything about
information theory?" he asked.

" 'I publicly praise you, Father,' " Harlan said. He was in the
tenth chapter of Matthew, the twenty-fifth verse. " 'Because you
have hidden these things from the wise and intellectual ones and
have revealed them to babes.' "

"Or what about that movie," Obadiah said. He was looking for
another tack. *Sunset Boulevard?* I was thinking of something
Norma Desmond says to William Holden: 'I *am* big. It's the *pictures* that got small.' "

It was not, Harlan thought, that he was without affection for the
boy. It was just that rarely had he felt himself in the presence of

someone whose every other word or deed so begged for an ass kicking. "I'm afraid I don't follow you," he said.

Obadiah turned from the street to find Harlan staring at him. The man's face was bruised and sunburned and looked about as wide as one of the brick buildings at their backs. "It stopped making sense," he said.

"Maybe you worried it to death."

"That happens?"

"I think so. You wind up forgetting what Paul said about it. Remember?"

Obadiah could not say that he did.

"For at present we see in a hazy outline by means of a metal mirror."

Obadiah nodded at the street. The fact was, he was not, after all, up for this; he found that Harlan's words had produced in him a particular weariness he had not counted on. It was an awkward moment. On the one hand, he believed the man at his side to be at some very fundamental level, dead wrong. On the other hand, he believed that what the world wanted was more of him. Nor did he wish to appear ungrateful. In the end, he supposed it was the reference to Paul which made for him a way out. Or made, at least, for a common ground and a way for him to say what else he had come to say. "I believe," he said, "that you quoted Paul in the desert."

Harlan wiggled the fingers at the end of his cast. "I was hoping," he said, studying the fingers, "that the desert had been laid to rest."

"It was something from Paul. For both the Jews ask for signs and the Greeks for wisdom. But we preach Christ impaled."

Harlan said nothing.

"The act of love," Obadiah said. It seemed quite plain to him, really; suggested in part by Harlan's sermon it had become so somewhere between the edge of the hole and the lobby of the Rose Hotel. It was how one kept one's finger on the pulse, the something with which a man might go armed into the night.

Harlan massaged his jaw with his free hand. It was a habit he had picked up in the hole. He could not recall having spoken of the act of love. Perhaps it had gotten weirder out there than he had imagined. He was willing however to let the brother finish.

"The thing is," Obadiah said, "I've asked Delandra to marry me. She's here, in town. A friend of mine is driving out from Pomona with some money, then he's going to stick around and be best man. After that he's going to drive us back. He can drive you back, too, if you're interested."

Harlan was struck somewhat dumb. "To Pomona?"

"I'll have to square things with my family."

"You can do that?"

"I can let them know what's going on. We'll have to come back to San Bernardino in time for the trial."

Harlan adjusted the shades on the bridge of his nose. "You're going to be married today?"

Obadiah gestured across the street toward a red-brick building. The bricks seemed to have acquired a slick, shimmering surface in the afternoon light. At the side of a doorway there was a window with lacy white curtains in it and between the curtains a pair of pink neon hearts and some red neon letters which read: THE CHAPEL OF ETERNAL LOVE. In one corner of the window there was a green-and-brown-neon palm tree and a small white sign which said: TROPICAL SETTINGS AVAILABLE.

"I don't know what to say," Harlan said. And in fact, for the moment, he didn't. It occurred to him that these little talks of his had been taking odd turns of late—something like a car on an icy road. The boy's instincts for absurd decisions appeared unfailing.

"The thing," Obadiah was saying, "is that my friend is bringing some money for the ceremony. But I would sort of like to give her a ring. You know? And there are all these pawnshops around here. And I was wondering if you could maybe front me enough money to pick one out. I could let you have it back real soon."

Harlan shook his head. He massaged his jaw. His first impulse was to laugh out loud and it seemed to him that massaging his jaw might help. It occurred to him that he never had gotten around to quoting James 4:17. Seated now, however, before the afternoon's pale fire what he found himself thinking of instead was the four-teenth verse of the same chapter: "For what is life?" the Apostle asked. "It is even a mist, that appeareth for a little time, and then vanisheth away." In the end he kept both verses to himself. He suppressed his laughter. He stared instead into the shining brick building which faced them from across the street. The Chapel of Eternal Love. For some reason—perhaps it was only the time of day, the dusty light—the thing looked to him as if it were on fire. "How much money?" he asked.

Rex Hummer had, in the course of his life, successfully engineered the deaths of only two living things. Both events were very much alike. This bothered him. Neither had been a clean job. Both had included a messy decapitation. Perhaps it was the only thing he knew. Of the two living things, one was a chicken. The other, a man.

Sarge kept chickens once. Delandra said she would cook one if Rex killed it. Rex tried to chop the chicken's head off with a small hatchet. Only the chicken was hard to hold and it moved at the last minute and Rex only chopped its head halfway off. At which point the chicken had gotten away from him and run and flopped and sprayed the back of the Desert Museum with blood before Rex could run it down and finish the job. Delandra had screamed and hooted. Sarge had put his head out of the museum and looked around. He had looked at the hatchet in Rex's hand, at the headless chicken, the blood-spattered ground. He'd looked directly at Rex Hummer and said, "For the love of Christ," then he had gone back inside.

It was what Rex thought of as he inched his way through the blackness of the tunnel. He remembered the look of disgust on Sarge Hummer's face as he stood at the back of his workroom and surveyed the carnage. Sarge, Rex knew, had killed men in the war, but it was not something he talked about.

Now Rex had killed a man but it was not something he wanted to think about. He didn't want to think about how the big body had bucked and heaved beneath him, or about the weird sucking noises it had made, or how the blood had sounded as it hit the glass in the truck. But he did.

He thought of other things, too. He thought about how when Sarge had made his first Thing he had been scared by it—he was still too young to be embarrassed. He'd had this recurring dream, for something like six months, in which the Thing climbed from its coffin and chased him into the desert. He would wake screaming. Sarge would come trudging into the room he had built for Rex at the side of the trailer wearing a white sleeveless T-shirt, baggy khaki pants. He would sit down by his son's bed and he would talk to him—it was just about the only time they did talk—when Rex woke up scared. Sarge, it seemed to Rex then, was always up himself, sitting on the deck with a bottle or a six-pack, alone in a straight-backed wooden chair. When he came into Rex's room he would sit by the bed. He would preface whatever he was going to say by saying, "Now look, boy." He rarely used Rex's name. It was always "boy." Once he even took Rex out to his workshed in the dead of night and took one of the Things apart so that Rex could see how it had been put together. "See, boy," Sarge had said, "it's just junk." It had always seemed to Rex, looking back on it, however, that saying it had not given the man pleasure.

He tried to imagine the Sarge with him now, in the darkness of the tunnel. "Now look, boy," the old man would say, "that noise back there is all in your head. Do you understand that?"

Rex was not sure if he understood it or not. Nor was he sure why he shouldn't be afraid of something because it was simply in his head. If it was in his head, it was somewhere. He put the question to Sarge.

Sarge looked at him the way he had looked at him the day he cut the head off the chicken. "If it's in your head," he said, "make it go away."

Rex tried to make the rattling of the wooden gate go away. It didn't work. It followed him yard after invisible yard, all the way to the end of the Frenchman's tunnel, which he located with his head. He had been moving at an angle, bent forward in his struggle with gravity, when suddenly the blackness hardened into a wall of rock and smacked him in the face. The collision sent a shower of sparks into the darkness and a pain down one arm. It was the arm from which the bullet had taken its bite. He dropped the rope and leaned back against the wall. There were matches in the pocket of his jeans. With both hands needed for the sled, however, they had been of little use to him until now.

With the match, he saw the inside of the tunnel for the first time. It was higher than what he had imagined. Tasting a bit of night air, he saw that there was an air shaft in the ceiling above him. He saw the steel ring near his feet which marked the trapdoor Dina Vagina had spoken of. And he saw what was left of the altar built by the Frenchman's wife. The thing was drooping across the wall of a small alcove which had been dug out just to the side of the wall Rex had found with his face. The candles he'd heard of were gone. In their place was a row of beer cans. Above the beer cans was the

painting of the Frenchman. Rex caught a glimpse of it before the
flame of his match reached his fingers, then exhausted two more
matches looking at it.

The man's skin was dark, like a Negro's. His features, however,
were more like those of a white man—straight nose, thin lips. His
hair was thick and black, reminding Rex of the Indian he'd seen in
Trona. His eyes were the color of the sky. The expression with
which the man stared into the blackness he had created reminded
Rex of the expressions he'd seen on the portraits of certain Indian
chiefs. The man had his arms folded across his chest. One hand was
tucked beneath an arm, out of sight. The other hand rested on a
bicep. The hand, however, had been tampered with. Somebody
had painted out all but the middle finger, so that what the Frenchman had been left doing was giving the bird to his life's work.

When the third match was gone Rex went down on all fours and
began to grope for the ring. Finding it, he raised the door. At once
a faint, greenish light seeped up and into the tunnel. The light
revealed the rungs of a wooden ladder descending into a circular
passageway lined with brick.

Rex returned to his sled. It was while he was untying the first
piece that he realized he had not heard the scraping sounds in
some time. In a moment, however, he realized the sound had been
replaced by something else. His own breathing had become more
regular since resting from his labors. What he realized was that
between his breaths, he could hear the breathing of something
else, a shallow panting in the blackness. He quickly retied the
rope. There would be no time to carry the stuff down piece by
piece. He dragged the sled to the entrance of the passageway. He
raised one end and pointed it down. Fortunately the hole was
large enough to accommodate it. He couldn't hold it that way for
long, however, nor could he say how far the drop was, being
unable to see clearly the floor of Verity's extension in the weak
light. At last, unable to lower it any farther without dropping it, he
let it go. The ladder groaned beneath its weight. He heard the
sound of splintering wood. The sound was followed by a metallic
banging, a waterfall of random notes, and then silence. Even the
breathing he had heard was gone for the moment. Rex moved
toward the hole and lowered himself into it. Reaching for the
handle on the bottom of the trapdoor he found that there was a
mechanism there with which the thing could be locked from the
inside—a dead bolt, a ring, and a padlock. Pulling the door down
over him he shoved the bolt into the hole prepared for it in the
brick wall. He flipped it around so that the brace came down over

the ring and he took the padlock in his hand. It occurred to him that without a key, without knowledge of what other exits might or might not exist, he might in fact be locking himself in, just as he was locking out what was perhaps a figment of his imagination. He seemed to hear the voice of the Sarge somewhere behind him— "Now look, boy." He reopened the door. He strained to hear something through the crack he'd made between the door and the floor of the tunnel. What he heard was the sound of breath sucked into heaving lungs. It was like the rasp of a plane moving across rough wood. With trembling fingers he reset the lock. He passed the arm of the padlock through the ring and he snapped it shut.

Harlan had remained on the bench for some time after Obadiah limped off into the light on his silver crutches. He could remember very little of what had passed between them at the Table Mountain Mines. He wanted to believe that this was not his fault.

He stayed on the bench until the sun had gotten below the rooftops opposite him and the shade he had sought earlier was no longer doing him any good. It wasn't like there was nothing to do. There was still the matter of the Studebaker left at the mines, which was going to necessitate a phone call to the brother in Las Vegas. There would also have to be a phone call to his wife in Los Angeles, and a suitcase of his belongings was still at the hospital. He supposed that he would take Obadiah up on his offer of a ride back to Pomona. He couldn't drive himself and it seemed preferable to any of the alternatives he could imagine. It would be the ride in which the fewest explanations would be demanded of him. Before doing any of it, however, he needed a drink.

He wound up in a tall western-style building calling itself the Silver Boot Saloon, where he drank a pair of double Jack Daniel's, with beer chasers, and listened to a fat bartender in a red and black flannel shirt make dumb jokes about his arm. After that he went back to the hospital for his things.

*       *       *

On the ground floor of the hospital there was a pharmacy and a small gift shop. Harlan had a prescription for some pain pills and while he was waiting for it to be filled, he browsed through the gift shop. It was filled with the usual junk one found in such places—an array of trinkets and cards and small stuffed things. Harlan bought a pack of gum and went to the counter to pay for it.

The counter was glass on three sides. There were turquoise rings and watches and fake Indian jewelry on black velvet beneath the glass. On top of the glass, near the cash register, there was a tall golden rack which sported a thick collection of chintzy-looking medallions on gold-colored chains. Harlan was standing very near the rack, fishing in his pockets for enough change to pay for his gum, when it occurred to him that the medallions in question were all of a kind. They were six-fingered hands in slender golden circles. Upon closer inspection he found that there were both right and left hands within the circles, that some of the circles were smooth, while others had little marks on them—what might, he supposed, pass for eyes.

"Will you be taking one of those too?" the woman behind the counter asked him.

Harlan looked up. She was a middle-aged woman with too much makeup on her face and a stiff-looking red wig perched upon her head. She reminded him of the woman he had seen at the junction after the fight, the one wearing the black wig. "What are these?" he asked. He was pointing at the rack.

"They're hands."

"Yes," Harlan replied, "I was wondering about the fingers and the eyes."

"The fingers and the eyes?"

"The hands have six fingers."

The woman leaned toward the rack and looked at the medallions. "So they do," she said. "Probably seconds. That's why they're on sale."

Harlan paid for his gum and went back outside, into what was left of the afternoon. He kept thinking about the cheap medallions that might or might not have been seconds, about how easily Sarge Hummer might have picked up such a thing. One could, of course, wonder why Sarge Hummer would have picked up such a thing. Harlan declined the gambit. He then found that he was troubled by the fact that the woman in the red wig had reminded him of the woman in the black wig he had seen through the window of a car after the fight at the junction. But then he declined that gambit as well. They were only marginally tempting, anyway. Perhaps it was the heat, or the alcohol. He understood there would be others. Even when he had their number. But he knew what he would say. He would say it was the desert.

He was thinking about one more Jack Daniel's just to clear the slate, as it were, when he glanced at his watch and realized that the wedding of Obadiah Wheeler was about to commence. The act of love indeed. Maybe it was his fault. The blind leading the blind in classic fashion. He would, he promised himself, be more careful in the future, would try to remember what he had begun to tell the boy with that business from Paul—though he'd been cut short by the wedding announcement—that it was, in the end, one's self one had the chance of seeing most clearly—he who peers into the perfect law of freedom and all of that—a little self-knowledge. That was about what one could hope for; the chance to make of oneself someone one could live with. He allowed himself a moment in which to marvel at how easily this might be forgotten. It didn't take much. A change of climate, an atmospheric disturbance. He was still on the sidewalk in front of the entrance to the hospital where there was a lot of glass, and he found that he could indeed see himself just now, reflected among the glossy tinted panes. He noticed that he looked like a fool. He noticed as well that he was grinning. "Well, what the hell," he said to the fellow in the glass. "I paid for the lousy ring; I may as well watch it."

I n the tunnel at the foot of the wooden stairs there were messages in Day-Glo paint sprayed on the wooden shoring which lined the walls. One of the messages informed Rex that he had entered the tunnel of space and time. Other messages were less distinct, or appeared to have been written in another language. "Though I speak in the tongues of angels . . ." one began, but it trailed off into the nothingness of a wall of earth. In other places there were spray-painted figures.

The figures were more or less humanoid with insectlike bodies and large heads which were all eyes.

Beneath one of the drawings, a skeletal creature with bat wings and the horns of a cow, there was a rather lengthy inscription which read:

> And I saw a star that had fallen from heaven to the earth, and the key of the pit of the abyss was given him. And he opened the pit of the abyss and smoke ascended out of the pit and out of the smoke locusts came forth upon the earth. And the likeness of the locusts resembled horses prepared for battle; and their faces were as men's faces, but they had hair as women's hair. And the sound of their wings was as the sound of chariots of many horses running into battle.

Beneath the words there was an old mattress and a lot of litter—beer cans, filter tips, plastic pill bottles together with half a dozen empty aerosol paint cans.

Rex sat down on the mattress beneath the red devilish figure and the words about the pit. The thought which occurred to him was that he himself was that star. He thought once more about certain things the girl had told him, the stuff about the Indian gods, the part about how the Old Ones had entered through a secret tunnel which led upward from the center of the earth.

At last he got to his feet and began to inspect his sled. He found that the thing had been broken in half, but that the instrument was still tied to it. The Hum-A-Phone was what held it together now; but it was still workable. He pulled the rope up and over one shoulder—the position in which he had moved thus far. He didn't start out just yet, however, but stood listening for sounds above him. Once he thought he heard a scraping at the top of the ladder—something like the way an animal will scratch at a door. Then the sound went away and he heard nothing. He started down the second tunnel. The greenish light grew brighter. There was more trash, and more of the Day-Glo writing, more strange creatures peering out at him from the sides of the mountain.

Verity's tunnel was a good deal shorter than the one dug by the Frenchman. The light seemed to help. Soon he had reached an oval doorway which opened out into a large circular room wherein the walls were lined with something that looked like aluminum foil.

The light came from the circular room. It emanated from what looked to be a plastic box about one foot square. The box was attached to the floor in the same way a light fixture might ordinarily be attached to a ceiling. Above him, there was a mass of gridwork. The gridwork had been built to support what looked to be at least two additional floors. The floors, like the dirt floor upon which Rex stood, were circular. The first was like a doughnut, with a hole in the center. The second was smaller and solid. It looked, in fact, to be about the same size as the hole in the first, as if the two floors could be fitted together. High above the gridwork, the catwalks, and the floors, there was darkness and tiny pinpoints of light so that for a moment Rex imagined what he saw was the sky, that the structure he had entered was without a roof. Then it occurred to him that there was something wrong with this observation. At first he thought it was only that there were not enough stars. But as he looked longer and harder he began to be able to discern a curve in the space above him and he understood that he had in fact entered the Electro-Magnetron, that what rose high above him was the domed room which had been painted black and upon whose interior stars had been painted as well. Or perhaps the stars were tiny light fixtures. He was too far from them to tell. It also occurred to him at this point that the stars were arranged in a more orderly fashion than those one actually saw at night. These were a perfectly delineated series of constellations following one another across the black arc of painted sky and he remembered what the girl had said to him about the stars being right. He got the idea that the stars had always been right inside the Electro-Magnetron.

He stood for some time contemplating what had been done here. It was not, he thought, unlike something he might have done himself. The foil extended to eye level. After that, there was a ring of stonework, and above that a ring of bare earth. The bare earth ended at what he took to be ground level—some thirty feet perhaps from where he stood. After the earth came the gridwork and the domed roof, which probably rose another thirty feet so that all in all he was perhaps sixty feet from the stars. At the base of the structure, at the edges of the floor upon which he stood, a number of smooth round stones had been placed in a circle, following the edge of the floor as it curved beneath the foil. He counted the stones. There were twelve in all. Farther up, set in what appeared to be a narrow ring of metal above the ring of brick, there were twelve electrodes. The stones had been positioned so that each had an electrode above it. The stones were like the sacred stones he had seen in the trailer of the Buffalo Woman.

There was more writing in the room. Some of it had been done upon a large oval piece of wood or metal—it was hard to say which. The letters, neatly stenciled across the softly shining surface, had been done in a style he associated with knights in armor and biblical texts. The inscription read:

> Of such great powers of beings there may be conceivably a survival; of a hugely remote period when consciousness was manifested, perhaps, in shapes and forms long since withdrawn before the tide of advancing humanity, forms of which poetry and legend alone have caught a flying memory and called them gods, monsters, mythical beings of all sorts and kinds.

Beneath the plaque there was more writing, but of an inferior quality. One phrase in particular caught his attention. It was a single line of Day-Glo pink which began at the bottom of the wood and dribbled down across the brick until it reached the foil. The message in pink said: Fuck Me Harder.

There was more writing, at various heights above the foil-covered portion of the wall, but Rex was done with it. There wasn't time. He could no longer use his sled, not for moving the Hum-A-Phone up into the gridwork, and yet that was where he intended to take it, as far as he could, up into the rarified heights of Verity's dome.

O badiah met his best man at the entrance to the court building. Bug House was late, of course, but this was to be expected and he was only off by an hour. Still, Obadiah had been pacing the stone steps when at last he'd seen the green Plymouth approaching the parking lot and had swung off on his crutches to meet it, lest the man miss him and make once more for the highway, believing it had all been some sort of plot.

Obadiah shouted and waved a crutch. He saw Bug House nod at him and then maneuver the large four-door car into a parking space behind the building. "Almost didn't make it," Bug House said as he climbed from the car. And he went on to enumerate a list of catastrophes and near catastrophes which had plagued him since leaving Pomona. Someone had removed water from his radiator, causing the car to overheat near Fontana. Richard Nixon had chased him for several miles on the freeway but Bug House had managed to lose him in Riverside. A tire had fallen off his car in San Bernardino and the cops had tried to bust him.

"Tried?" Obadiah asked.

Bug House grinned in a sly way, as if to imply that strings too complex for Obadiah to ever understand had been pulled on his behalf, or as if to imply that Bug House himself knew none of it was true but knew as well that some sort of outlandish story would be expected of him. It was always hard to tell. The man worried constantly about his image. On the eastern edge of San Bernardino, Bug House said, he had picked up a young girl who told him to stay out of the desert because the world was about to end.

"If the whole world is going to end, what difference will it make if you are in the desert or not?" Obadiah asked. They were by now on their way to the Rose Hotel to meet Delandra Hummer. Bug House produced the sly smile once more; it was a difficult thing to look at. "She give you a date?" Obadiah asked.

"Soon," Bug House said. "Real soon."


Bug House had arrived in Ridgecrest for Obadiah's wedding dressed as Doc Potty. It was one of his more conservative costumes, consisting of black jeans, a black T-shirt, a black cowboy hat, and a white doctor's jacket upon which someone had stenciled DOC POTTY in large black letters across the back, except that the DOC came out looking more like DOG, so that the jacket actually read DOG POTTY, which was what Delandra started calling him right away.

She was waiting for them in the lobby of the hotel. There was no furniture in the lobby, so she sat on one of the steps. She wanted to be someplace where she could see the street. No sense making them pay three dollars apiece to get past the Mexican at the door. When she saw them she got up and went outside. She took Bug House by the shoulders and turned him this way and that to get a good look at him. "Funny," she said, "he doesn't look like a best man."

They went to a coffee shop for hamburgers and then to the Chapel of Eternal Love to await the appointed time. The sun was low in the west and the sky was filled with the makings of one more desert sunset. Obadiah looked into the gathering orange light. He sucked down the fresh, dry air and leaned upon a lamppost. He looked both ways, up and down the street. He was looking for Harlan Low. The man had loaned him the money but had been unclear as to whether or not he would attend the ceremony. Obadiah hoped that he would. He believed Harlan's presence might bring a note of dignity to the affair. And it was, all things considered, an affair which could use all the dignity that could be managed. He knew this, but he was doing it anyway, and standing at the edge of the street he was by turns embarrassed, proud, sad, and happy. At his back he could hear Delandra chatting with Doc Potty. She didn't seem able to leave him alone.

"You need black boots to go with that outfit," she said. Bug House was wearing what looked like a pair of red bedroom slippers.

"You're right," he said. "I had a pair."

"What happened?"

"Can't say," Bug House told her. Soon he began to talk to her about the girl he had picked up in San Bernardino and the end of the world. "You see there's this secret cult," he told her. "They worship ancient gods from the center of the earth. Actually the gods have been trapped in another dimension or something."

"The other dimension is in the center of the earth?"

"Oh, I think so. I was a little confused about all of that." He paused to scratch an armpit. "What happens, though, or what is going to happen, is that the cult is going to bring these gods back to life and that's when the world ends. She left this book in my car." Bug House produced a battered blue paperback from his pocket and began to thumb through it. When he had found an appropriate passage he began to read. He read something about a huge shapeless thing which had come from the stars. There were a lot of words like *nameless, horrible, foul, monstrous,* and so on. Between adjectives Bug House would pause to make sure Delandra was paying attention.

"You had to listen to this from San Bernardino to Victorville?" she asked.

Bug House began to cackle, as though some clever remark were on the tip of his tongue. Then he began to cough. His face turned bright red and he stomped both feet on the ground. Delandra began to pound him on the back. "This guy," Bug House managed, "this girl says he tells it like it is."

"No."

Bug House nodded. He was seized by another spasm of coughing, however, and was unable to continue.

Obadiah turned away. He turned toward the eastern end of the street just in time to see Harlan Low walking out of a bar. The man was dressed in the clothes Obadiah had seen on him the morning they left for the desert—the dark slacks and gold sharkskin sport coat. Except that the coat was not really being worn. It was just hung upon one shoulder and covered just one side of his torso, the other side being free to accommodate the large plaster cast. Above all of that he wore a pair of black-rimmed wraparound shades and the silly-looking straw hat which had somehow emerged with him from the hole in the desert and Obadiah was aware of whatever note of dignity he had hoped for dissipating in the cooling air.


Bug House was still coughing when Harlan Low reached them. Delandra kissed him on the cheek and Bug House rose to shake his good hand, though there were still tears running down his cheeks and he was unable to speak.

"Weddings always make him cry," Delandra said. "Isn't it sweet?"

"It's the end of the world," Bug House spluttered. "A girl told me."

"Well, the last days, at least," Harlan said. He winked at Obadiah and seemed, Obadiah thought, for some reason to be in excellent spirits. Perhaps it had something to do with the scent of whiskey on the man's breath, though he did not appear intoxicated.

"Mr. Wheeler. Miss Hummer?" someone said. Obadiah turned to find that a silver-haired man in a dark suit had come to the doorway of the building. "Would you care to step into our waiting room?"

Delandra entered first. Obadiah was about to enter but Bug House had him by the arm and was tugging on it. There was a mischievous twinkle in his red-rimmed eyes. "I still haven't told you the good part," he said. "This chick, man, the one who told me the world was going to end, she had her twat dyed red, white, and blue. I got me a look at that item, bro." Bug House extended his lower jaw and the scar tissue along the right side of his face glistened in the neon light which had begun to flutter above the doorway which led to the Chapel of Eternal Love. Obadiah smiled weakly at Harlan and moved forward to shake the hand of the man with the silver hair and then on to the red velvet, the white lace, and marbled mirrors of the waiting room. Behind him he could hear Harlan coming through the door. "You must be the father of the bride," he heard the silver-haired man say. "Yes," Harlan Low said, "I am."

I t might have been hours, possibly days. Perhaps the dome had been built in order to alter time. So that perhaps an entire age had gone the way of sand in an hourglass as Rex Hummer climbed toward the stars. He had long ago shattered the crystal of his watch and so knew nothing of the day or the hour.

For a while the Sarge had spoken to him. As near as Rex could tell, the man had been trying to "talk sense" to him. At one point, somewhere near the first floor, Rex had relived the day his sister put his eye out with a pellet gun. He had remembered the Sarge scooping him up in arms as big and hard as clay pipes, running him to the truck while Delandra ran behind. He remembered her voice and the color of the sky. He remembered the long ride into town, Sarge driving the truck as hard as it would go. He remembered his head in Delandra's lap and the towel pressed hard against his wound. He remembered her hair blown back in the wind above him and her tears, like a warm rain blown all about the cab on a summer storm and how for that one piece of time—he'd thought then it was the first, and later, he'd thought it was the last —he'd known what it was like to be a part of something, the three of them, bound together in the pain that was rightfully his.

Somewhere, though, along about the third floor, the voice of Sarge had begun to fail along with the greenish light. The sounds of pursuit were gone there, too, though once, peeking through what he discovered were the Electro-Magnetron's windows—tiny rectangular slits it was necessary to actually press one's face against to see out of—he thought he saw something outside. It was daylight out there. And what he saw was a man in a uniform, a gun on his hip, being pulled by a dog on a string across a yellow patch of stone. The scene did not appear quite real to him, and, pulling back from it, he took it to be like the sounds which had thus far plagued him. A test was all. Tests were not that uncommon in these situations—he thought for instance of Christ in the wilderness. His glory was that He had met the challenge. A single spray-painted message waited for him at the third level, the words in a luminous Day-Glo green streaked across the metal floor at his feet: "In the world you are having tribulation, but take courage! I have conquered the world."

Delandra had chosen a tropical setting because it matched Obadiah's shirt. She thought now that he looked quite nice in it, flanked by two delicately potted palms and the twin heads of Tiki gods which appeared to have been carved from the trunks of older, larger palms. Dog Potty stood to Obadiah's left, his damp brow shining in the phony torchlight which issued from the heads of the gods. Harlan Low was somewhere behind them but when the minister asked if someone would give away the bride Harlan said that he would and when Delandra looked back over her shoulder to find him she was startled once again by his resemblance to her own father and she was moved in a way she had not expected.

Obadiah felt her hand tighten on his arm as Harlan Low's voice issued from the back of the room and it did, he thought, lend a certain dignity to the affair after all. At his side Bug House was standing in such a way that Obadiah could see the blue cover of the paperback sticking out of the side pocket of his jacket. He assumed the book was a collection. The name, H. P. Lovecraft, was printed in bold orange letters across the top. There was a list of titles: "The Dunwich Horror," "The Whisperer in the Darkness," "The Shadow over Innsmouth." The titles disappeared beneath the material of Bug House's coat. The only one which meant anything to him was "The Call of Cthulhu." It seemed to him that at some point in his youth—that time in which he had been devouring almost anything resembling sci-fi in the Pomona Public

Library—it was one of the things he had read. Cthulhu, he seemed to recall, was some sort of ancient god banished long ago to something like another dimension, where he had remained through the ages but from which he occasionally emerged—usually because some unwitting mortals had fooled with something they should have left alone. In the story in question he seemed to remember something about a group of sailors. And now this girl claimed to be part of a secret cult and she had said the author of the dime store collection had told it like it was. Well, why not? Mastamho for Cthulhu. A girl with her twat dyed to match the Electro-Magnetron. A cult of the hand—just as Harlan had imagined. For a moment he could almost imagine it adding up to something after all. It was a little like believing the Table Mountain People had achieved transference. But there you were. Maybe they had. Or maybe they had just gone crazy and killed themselves. And maybe toward the end there they had worn funny hats and gone dancing on the edge, out where there was no such thing as random noise, but where the dancers danced alone, in ever-widening orbits, until a kind of heat death had set in and, with no one checking it out, the pulse had been lost altogether, the lamp gone like an evening's mist in the desert's hard white light. And it did tend to get a little funky in the darkness—what with the pilgrims cutting off one another's balls and such.

Still, he did try, for a moment anyway, call it for old time's sake, to imagine it—the transference of the Table Mountain People, the return of Mastamho. You had to wonder, though, just what there was left for the old boy to do anyway—if suicide and insanity were his stock in trade? The dude had after all been a long time gone. What if, upon getting one good look at what had come down in his absence—his own shadow as it were, the son of a bitch should lose his nerve, turn right around and beat it, straight back to the safety of eternal night. A big disappointment, no doubt, for all concerned. At Obadiah's side, Bug House, having squared his shoulders, had begun to grin. The thing was aimed at the minister—the fixed eyes, the ridged jaw, the small eyes twinkling in that mask of shining flesh. The minister, Obadiah noted, was having no part of it. He was looking at the book.

When the silver-haired gentleman at last looked up it was to ask Obadiah if there was a ring. There was. After a moment of fumbling, Bug House produced it. Obadiah placed it upon Delandra's finger. Or maybe, he thought, Mastamho had leaked out ahead of time and Sarge Hummer had brained him with a shovel—the Thing, after all, being what the fuss was all about. Another big

letdown. But then they did say time had a way of making fools—
even of the great ones. One thought of Joe Louis in wrestler's garb.
Maybe even gods had dues to pay. The maybes multiplied. A
parlor game for pilgrims with time to kill. Or what it was all about.

"You may kiss the bride," the man told him.


Outside a chunk of moon had risen in a purple sky and a cooling
breeze stirred in an empty street. Doc Potty wanted to kiss the
bride. Harlan Low stood alone at the edge of the curb, looking
back toward the lights of town. He had his dark glasses in his
pocket and his straw hat pushed back on his head so that he
reminded Obadiah of the beleaguered newspaperman in an old
movie. With his arm stuck out in front of him it looked as if he were
trying to find a ride.

"It was nice of him to do that," Delandra said.

"Yes, it was."

"Now that Dog Potty is another story."

"Yes," Obadiah replied, "he is."

"He told me he was in the war."

Obadiah shook his head. "He tells people that."

"He wasn't?"

"He was in the service. He was in a war. No one is sure just
which one it was. The closest he got to Vietnam was Hawaii."

"He went crazy in Hawaii?"

Obadiah nodded slowly. "He set fire to a kitchen and something
blew up. The Veterans Administration's had him off and on ever
since. As you can see, they've done wonders for him."

A white pickup truck went by in the street and some guy in a
cowboy hat stuck his head out the window and whistled at Delandra. Obadiah shivered in the thin cotton shirt. His ankle had begun
to throb from standing too long and he circled Delandra's shoulders with his arm for support. He watched the luminous rose-
colored tint Harlan Low's cast had acquired beneath the neon
lights of the Chapel of Eternal Love. "You know the Doc called me
one night from the VA hospital," he said.

"Doc Potty?"

"The same. We grew up together. I met him in the first grade,
the first day of class. He was wearing this Superman T-shirt and
some kid from the third grade bet him he couldn't fly. The Doc
seemed to think he could. He jumped from the top of a jungle gym
and broke the hell out of his leg, hooked it between a couple of

bars on the way down." He paused for a moment envisioning the scene; it had been with him for a long time. "At any rate," he said, getting back to what he had started, "the lad called me one night from Long Beach. They had him down there in the veterans hospital and they were doing a lot of fucking around with him. We'd heard he was back but no one had talked to him yet. Anyway, I got this call, collect, and it was Richard. He said he just wanted to tell me something. He wanted to tell me there's a happy man in every crowd."

"That was it?"

Obadiah nodded. Delandra put her arm around his waist. They had begun to walk away from the chapel, back along the street. They were following Bug House and Harlan Low.

"So what do you think?" Delandra asked him. "Is there?"

Obadiah watched the two men walking ahead of him. They appeared to be having some sort of conversation and he found in the mere suggestion of this cause for an absurd amount of pleasure. Their two hats bobbed in and out of the shadows and Harlan's cast flashed suddenly pure and white in the lights of a passing car. "You know," Obadiah said, "I believe there is."

Rex Hummer was alone upon the circular floor and he had the sensation of floating. The painted constellations arched above him through the black emptiness of space. From somewhere far below him a pale greenish light rose upward. It passed the electrodes and the sacred stones, dissipating as it reached the black arc of the dome. Even the pain, he found, had left him. So that he really was alone. And yet he felt nothing like loneliness. He was in fact the still point of the turning world and he imagined for a moment it was the way God Himself must have felt just prior to the moment of creation when all was formless and waste and yet everything that would ever be had been born already, in the mind of the Creator, all eternity existing in one pulsating instant, waiting only for him to say it: Let there be light. Rex Hummer shifted his ass upon the tractor seat and gazed down into the machinery before him, his arms raised, the bloodstained buckskins already stiffening about them, his hands poised above the charred keys of a child's xylophone as he prepared to strike the first notes.